Author Abraham Cady first became aware of the concentration camp at Jadwiga when he learnt that it was the place where his family had been exterminated. This discovery gave impetus to his decision to write a great book that would stir the conscience of the human race. And with the publication of *The Holocaust* his goal was accomplished.

Eminent surgeon Adam Kelno—knighted by the Crown for his contributions to medicine—has been mentioned in *The Holocaust* as one of Jadwiga's most sadistic inmate-doctors, working directly under an SS Colonel. Kelno denies this—and plans to stand and fight to prove once and for all that Cady is a liar.

Leon Uris

QB VII

CORGI BOOKS

QB VII
A CORGI BOOK 0 552 08866 8

Originally published in Great Britain
by William Kimber & Co. Ltd.

PRINTING HISTORY
William Kimber edition published 1971
Corgi edition published 1971
Corgi edition reprinted 1972 (twice)
Corgi edition reprinted 1974
Corgi edition reprinted 1975 (twice)
Corgi edition reprinted 1976 (twice)
Corgi edition reprinted 1977
Corgi edition reprinted 1978
Corgi edition reprinted 1979
Corgi edition reprinted 1980
Corgi edition reprinted 1981
Corgi edition reprinted 1982
Corgi edition reprinted 1984
Corgi edition reprinted 1985

This book is set in Times 10/11 pt.

Corgi Books are published by Transworld Publishers
Ltd., Century House, 61–63 Uxbridge Road, Ealing,
London W5 5SA, in Australia by Transworld Publishers
(Aust.) Pty. Ltd., 26 Harley Crescent, Condell Park,
NSW 2200, and in New Zealand by Transworld Publishers
(N.Z.) Ltd., Cnr. Moselle and Waipareira Avenues,
Henderson, Auckland.

Printed and bound in Great Britain by
Cox & Wyman Ltd., Reading, Berks.

I dedicate this book to my darling wife
JILL
On her twenty-third birthday
And to
CHARLIE GOLDBERG
Aspen, Colorado
April 16 , 1970

AUTHOR'S NOTE

The English legal profession adheres to an extremely formal protocol and a rigid etiquette. I have not attempted to bind myself to all these customs but have used a reasonable literary licence so long as the novel remains within a framework of credibility.

The characters contained herein are purely fictitious.

LEON URIS

ONE

THE PLAINTIFF

ONE

November 1945—Monza, Italy

The corporal cadet stepped out of the guard hut and squinted out over the field. A shadowy figure ran through the knee-high grass toward him. The guard lifted a pair of binoculars. The man, half stumbling, carried a single battered suitcase. He waved and gasped a greeting in Polish.

It was a familiar sight these days. In the backwash of the war, all of Europe had become a tangled river of refugees, east going west, west going east, and burgeoning refugee camps all but collapsed under the swell. Hundreds of thousands of liberated Polish slaves roamed about desperately seeking contact with their countrymen. Many wound up here in Monza at the Fifteenth Free Polish Fighter Wing of the Royal Air Force.

'Hello! Hello!' the man shouted as he crossed out of the field and over a dusty road. His run had slowed to a limp.

The corporal cadet stepped up to him. The man was tall and slender with a high-boned face capped with a head of solid white hair.

'Polish, Free Polish?'

'Yes,' the guard answered, 'let me take your suitcase.'

The man leaned against the guard to stave off fainting.

'Easy, father, easy. Come, sit down inside my hut. I will call for an ambulance.'

The guard took him by the arm and led him. The man stopped suddenly and stared at the flag of Poland which flew from its staff just inside the gate and tears came to his

11

eyes. He sat on a wooden bench and held his face in his hands.

The corporal cadet set the suitcase down and circled the handle of the field phone. 'Post number four, send an ambulance. Yes, a refugee.'

As the man was driven into the confines of the camp, the guard shook his head. Ten a day? A hundred some days. What could be done but put a few hot meals into their shrunken bellies, scrub them, give them shots against the raging diseases, a set of ragged clothing, and then dispatch them to a refugee centre girding for a terrible winter. Europe would be one large house of death when the snows came.

The bulletin board in the officers' club carried a daily list of refugee arrivals. These Free Polish sought the miracle of contact with a relative or even an old friend. On some rare occasions there would be an emotional reunion of old schoolmates. Almost never was there a meeting of loved ones.

Major Zenon Myslenski entered the club, still dressed in flight jacket and fur-lined boots. He was warmly greeted, for Myslenski, with twenty-two kills of German aircraft, was one of the few quadruple aces of the Free Poles and a legend in a time of legends. He stopped automatically at the bulletin board and glanced at the new orders, the list of social events. There was a chess tournament he must enter. He was about to turn away when he was drawn to that frustrating catalogue, the new refugee list. Only four arrivals today. It was so futile.

'Hey, Zenon,' someone called from the bar. 'You're late.'

Major Myslenski froze, eyes fixed on a name on the refugee list. Arrived, November 5—Adam Kelno.

Zenon knocked once, then burst the door open. Adam Kelno was half asleep on the cot. At first Zenon did not recognize his cousin. God, he had aged. At the outbreak of the war he didn't have a grey hair in his head. He was so bony and drawn. Through a haze, Adam Kelno felt the presence of someone. He groggily propped on an elbow and

12

blinked his eyes.

'Zenon?'

'Cousin——'

Colonel C. Gajnow, Commander of the Fifteenth Fighter Wing, poured himself a stiff shot of vodka and lifted the pages of a preliminary interrogation of Dr. Adam Kelno, who had petitioned to be allowed to join the Free Polish Forces.

ADAM KELO, M.D.—Born near the village of Pzetzeba, 1905. Educated—University of Warsaw, Medical College. Entered practice as a physician/surgeon in 1934.

There was testimony by his cousin, Major Zenon Myslenski, that Kelno was always identified with Polish Nationalist movements even as a student. At the beginning of the Second World War, with Poland occupied by the Germans, Kelno and his wife, Stella, immediately went into the Nationalist underground.

After several months their activities were discovered by the Gestapo. Stella Kelno was shot to death by a firing squad.

By a miracle Adam Kelno was spared and sent to the infamous Jadwiga Concentration Camp located midway between Krakow and Tornow in the southern region of Poland. It was an enormous manufacturing complex to feed the German war machine and manned by hundreds of thousands of slaves.

The report continued on that Kelno became a leading figure among the prisoner/doctors and did much to lift the primitive medical facilities. Kelno personally was a selfless and dedicated physician.

Later in the war when extermination facilities were introduced into Jadwiga, Kelno was responsible for saving thousands of lives from the gas chambers by falsifying reports and death certificates, through the underground, and by his medical skill.

He became so prominent that toward the end of the war the chief German medical officer, SS Dr. Colonel Adolph Voss, took Kelno, against his will, to help him run an ex-

13

clusive private clinic in East Prussia.

At the end of the war, Kelno returned to Warsaw, where he ran into a shattering experience. The Polish Communists had betrayed that country to the Soviet Union. During his stay in Jadwiga, as a member of the Nationalist underground, he was constantly in a life and death struggle with the Communist underground. Now, many Communist doctors, most of them Jews, had rigged a conspiracy against Kelno with statements that he had collaborated with the Nazis. With a warrant out for his arrest, Adam Kelno fled immediately and made his way across Europe to Italy, where he made contact with the Free Polish.

Colonel Gajnow set the report down and called for his secretary. 'On the Kelno matter,' he said, 'I am declaring a commission of inquiry to be composed of five officers with myself as chairman. We shall inquire immediately to all Free Polish Forces and organizations which may have knowledge of Kelno and we shall convene for consideration in three months.'

When Poland fell in the Second World War and was divided between Germany and the Soviet Union by pact, many thousands of soldiers were able to escape. A government-in-exile was formed in London and fighting units put into the field and in the skies under British command.

During the war many thousands of other Polish officers fled to the Soviet Union, where they were interned and later massacred in the Katyn Forest. The Soviets had designs to take over Poland and naturally a Nationalist officer Corps stood as a threat to this ambition. At the end of the war, the Soviet Army stood at the gates of Warsaw and did not budge to assist the Nationalist underground in an uprising but allowed the Germans to destroy them.

The Free Poles were to remain in England, rightfully bitter, tightly knit, and forever fanning the dream of a return to their homeland. When the call went out on the matter of Adam Kelno it quickly reached the entire Polish Community.

On the face of it, things seemed clear enough, Dr. Adam Kelno was a Polish Nationalist and when he returned to

Warsaw he was to be eliminated by the Communists just as the officer corps had been in the Katyn Massacre.

Within days of the launching of the inquiry, sworn statements began to come back to Monza along with offers of personal testimony.

I HAVE KNOWN DR. ADAM KELNO FROM 1942, WHEN I WAS SENT TO JADWIGA CONCENTRATION CAMP. I BECAME ILL AND TOO WEAK TO WORK. HE HID ME AND SAVED ME FROM THE GERMANS. HE SAVED MY LIFE.

DR. ADAM KELNO OPERATED ON ME AND NURSED ME BACK TO HEALTH WITH GREAT CARE.

DR. KELNO HELPED ARRANGE MY ESCAPE FROM JADWIGA.

DR. KELNO OPERATED ON ME AT FOUR O'CLOCK IN THE MORNING WHEN HE WAS SO TIRED HE COULD HARDLY STAND UP. I DON'T THINK HE EVER SLEPT FOR MORE THAN A FEW HOURS AT A TIME.

HE SAVED MY LIFE.

On the day of the commission, the camp was visited by Leopold Zalinski, a legendary figure of the Polish Nationalist underground during the occupation. His code name, Kon, was known by every Pole. Kon's testimony erased any doubts. He swore Adam Kelno to be a hero of the Nationalist underground before his imprisonment and during his years as a prisoner/doctor at Jadwiga. With letters and testimonies from two dozen others without conflict, the commission cleared him.

In a moving ceremony at Monza attended by many Polish colonels of the Free Forces, Dr. Adam Kelno was sworn in as a captain and his pips were pinned on him by his cousin.

Poland had been taken from these men but they continued to remember and dream.

TWO

The Sixth Polish Hospital,
Foxfield Cross Camp,
Tunbridge Wells, England—March 1946

Major Adam Kelno walked slowly from the surgery tugging at his rubber gloves. Sister Angela untied his surgical mask and dabbed the perspiration from his head.

'Where is she?' Adam asked.

'In the visitors' lounge. Adam?'

'Yes.'

'Will you come to my flat?'

'Yes, all right.'

'I'll wait.'

As he walked the long dim corridor, it was obvious Angela Brown's admiration was more than professional. It had been but a few short months that they had worked together in surgery. From the onset she was impressed by his skill and a kind of dedicated zeal in which he performed half as many operations again as most of his colleagues. His hands were magnificent.

It all happened rather plainly. Angela Brown, a commonplace sort in her mid-thirties, had been a capable nurse for a decade. A first short marriage ended in divorce. The great love of her life, a Polish flyer in the RAF, was shot down over the Channel.

Adam Kelno was nothing like her fighter pilot so it became a new kind of love. A rather magic spot in time the instant he peered over his mask and caught her eye as she placed instruments in his hands, his quick decisive hands, and the closeness of spirit as they worked together as a team to save a human life. The exhilaration of a successful operation. The exhaustion of a failure after a difficult battle.

They were so lonely, both of them, and so it happened in

a very undramatic but lovely manner.

Adam entered the visitors' lounge. It was very late. The operation had lasted more than three hours. There was a look of stunned anticipation on Madame Baczewski's face. Afraid to ask. Adam took her hand, bowed slightly and kissed it, then sat beside her.

'Jerzy has left us. It was very peaceful.'

She nodded, but dared not speak.

'Is there anyone I should call, Madame Baczewski?'

'No. There was only us. We are the only survivors.'

'I think we had better put you in a room here.'

She tried to speak but her mouth went into a trembling spasm and tiny little grunts of agony emerged. 'He said ... get me to Dr. Kelno ... he kept me alive in the concentration camp ... get me to Dr. Kelno.'

Angela arrived and took charge. Adam whispered to have her put under.

'When I first met Jerzy Baczewski he was so strong like a bull. He was a great Pole, one of our foremost dramatists. We knew the Germans were out to destroy the intelligentsia and we had to keep him alive at any price. This surgery was not that difficult. A healthy man would have gotten through this, but he had no stamina left after two years in that putrid hell hole.'

'Darling, it was you that told me a good surgeon has to be impersonal. You did everything. . . .'

'Sometimes I don't believe my own words. Jerzy died a betrayed man. Lonely, his country taken from him, and a memory of unbelievable terror.'

'Adam, you've been in surgery half the night. Here, darling, take your tea.'

'I want a drink.'

He poured a stiff one, tossed it down, and poured another. 'All Jerzy wanted was a child. What kind of a damned tragedy are we? What kind of curse is on us? Why can't we live?'

The bottle was empty. He chewed at his knuckles.

Angela ran her fingers through that thicket of white hair.

Then she sat on the footstool before him and laid her head in his lap. 'Dr. Novak called me aside today,' she said. 'He told me to get you out of the hospital for a little rest or you're going to break down.'

'What the hell does August Novak know. Get me another drink.'

'My God, turn it off.'

As he began to arise she grabbed his hands and held him, then looked pleading and kissed his fingers, each one.

'Don't cry, Angela, please don't cry.'

'My auntie has a lovely little cottage at Folkestone. I'm going to stay with her next week and I'm sure there'd be a welcome for you too.'

'Perhaps I am a little tired,' he said.

The days at Folkestone all went so quickly. He was renewed by long quiet walks along the leas on the cliffs overlooking the sea. France was across the Channel in shadowy outline. Hand in hand in silent communication they walked wind-blown along the shrub-lined rosemary path to the harbour and in the distance the sounds of the band concert at the Marine Gardens. The narrow little streets had been bombed out but the statue of William Harvey, the discoverer of the circulation of the blood, remained. The steamer to Calais left daily again and soon there would be vacationers for the short summer season.

The evening chill was dulled by a crackling fire that threw odd shadows over the old low-beamed ceiling of the cottage. The last lovely day had ended and tomorrow they would return to the hospital.

A sudden moroseness came over Adam. He drank rather heavily. 'I'm sorry it's over,' he mumbled. 'I don't remember such a beautiful week.'

'It need not end,' she said.

'Everything for me must end. I can have nothing that is not taken from me. Everyone I have ever loved has been taken from me. My wife, my mother, my brothers. Any who have survived are in virtual slavery in Poland. I can make no commitments, never again.'

'I've never asked for one,' she said.

'Angela, I want to love you, but you see, if I do, I'll lose you too.'

'What's the difference, Adam? We'll end up losing each other without even giving it a chance.'

'There's more to it, you know that. I am afraid for myself as a man. I have this deadly fear of impotence and it's not the drinking that does it. It's ... so many things that happened in that place.'

'I'll keep you strong, Adam,' she said.

He reached out and touched her cheek and she kissed his hands. 'Your hands. Your beautiful hands.'

'Angela, would you give me a child right away?'

'Yes, my darling darling.'

Angela became pregnant a few months after their marriage.

Dr. August Novak, executive surgeon of the Sixth Polish Hospital, returned to private practice and, in a surprise move, Adam Kelno was moved over a number of seniors to be named head of the hospital.

Administrative work was not what Adam desired but the enormous responsibilities at the Jadwiga Concentration Camp had trained him for it. Along with budgets and politics, he managed to keep his sure hand in as a surgeon.

It was so good to come home these days. The Kelno cottage in Groombridge Village was a few miles from the hospital at Tunbridge Wells. Angela's belly was filling beautifully with their child and in the evenings they would walk, as always, hand in hand in communicative silence up the wooded path to Toad Rock and take their tea at the quaint little café. Adam drank much less these days.

On an evening in July he signed out at the hospital and his orderly put in the groceries in the rear seat of the car. He drove to the centre of town and in the Pantiles Colonnade he bought a bouquet of roses and made for Groombridge.

Angela did not answer to his ring. This always gave him

a start. The fear of losing her hovered behind every tree of the forest. Adam juggled the grocery sack and fished for his key. Wait! The door was not locked. He opened it.

'Angela!'

His wife sat on the edge of a chair in the living room, ashen-faced. Adam's eyes went to the two men hovering over her.

'Dr. Kelno?'

'Yes.'

'Inspector Ewbank, Scotland Yard.'

'Inspector Henderson,' the second man said, holding out his identification.

'What do you want? What are you doing here?'

'I have a warrant for your arrest, sir.'

'My arrest?'

'Yes, sir.'

'What is this all about? What kind of joke is this?'

Their sullen expressions denoted it was no joke.

'My arrest . . . for what?'

'You are to be detained at Brixton Prison pending extradition to Poland to stand charges as a war criminal.'

THREE

The setting was London but the room seemed something out of Warsaw. Angela sat in the anteroom of the Society of Free Poles where walls were adorned with enormous sterile paintings of Pilsudski, Smigly-Rydz, Paderewski, and a gallery of Polish heroes. It was in this place and others like it around London that the hundred thousand Poles fortunate enough to escape perpetuated the dream of Poland.

Angela's pregnancy now showed heavily. Zenon Myslenski comforted her as she wrung and knotted a handkerchief nervously. A tall door opened from an inner office and a secretary approached them.

Angela adjusted her dress and waddled in on Zenon's arm where Count Anatol Czerny came from behind his desk. He greeted Zenon as an old friend, kissed Angela's hand, and bade them be seated.

'I am afraid,' the dapper little aristocrat said, 'valuable time has been wasted by contacting the government-in-exile. England no longer recognizes them, and we were unable to get any information from the British Home Office.'

'What in the name of God is it all about? Someone has to tell us something,' Angela emoted.

'All we know is that about a fortnight ago a certain Nathan Goldmark arrived from Warsaw. He is a Jewish Communist and a special investigator for the Polish Secret Police. He has a number of sworn statements from ex-inmates of Jadwiga, all Polish Communists, making various allegations against your husband.'

'What kind of allegations?'

'I have not seen them and the Home Office is most secretive. The British position is this. If a foreign government with whom they have a mutual pact requests extradition and establishes a prima facie case, they treat the matter as routine.'

'But what possible charges could there be against Adam. You've read the testimony from the investigation in Monza. I was there myself,' Zenon said.

'Well, we both really know what is happening, don't we,' the count answered.

'No, I don't understand it at all,' Angela said.

'The Communists feel it necessary to keep up a constant parade of propaganda to justify their seizure of Poland. Dr. Kelno is intended as a sacrificial lamb. What better way than to prove a Nationalist was a war criminal.'

'What in the name of God can we do?'

'We will fight this thing, of course. We are not without

21

resources. It will take a few weeks for the Home Office to review the matter. Our first tactic is to get a delay. Madame Kelno, I want the liberty of engaging a firm of solicitors who have been most helpful to us in these matters.'

'Yes, of course,' she whispered.

'Hobbins, Newton, and Smiddy.'

'Oh, my poor darling Adam. . . . Oh, dear God.'

'Angela, please.'

'Are you all right, Madame Kelno?'

'Yes. . . . I'm sorry.' She pressed her white folded knuckles to her lips and drew deep sighs.

'Come now,' Count Czerny said. 'We are in England. We are dealing with a decent, civilized people.'

The Austin taxi stopped in the centre of Pall Mall, found an opening in the opposite flow of traffic, and did a swift U-turn in a circle no larger than a halfpenny, stopping before the Reform Club.

Richard Smiddy jammed his bowler on tightly, tucked his umbrella under an arm, opened a tattered change purse and carefully doled out the exact fare.

'And a sixpence for you,' he said.

'Thank you, governor,' the cabbie said, putting on his FOR HIRE light and pulling away from the kerb. He shook his head as he pocketed the frail tip. Not that he wanted the war, mind you, but he wished the Yanks were back.

Richard Smiddy, son of George Smiddy and grandson of Harold Smiddy of that fine old law firm marched up the stairs to the entrance of the Reform Club. He was rather pleased about getting an appointment with Robert Highsmith in less than a week. As protocol required. Smiddy's clerk wrote a hand-delivered note to Highsmith's clerk at Parliament and arranged the meeting. Smiddy did have his man denote that the matter had some urgency. For a passing moment Richard Smiddy had contemplated bypassing tradition and picking up the telephone but only the Americans did business that way.

He deposited his umbrella and bowler with the hall

22

porter and made the usual remark about the foul weather.

'Mr. Highsmith is expecting you, sir.'

Smiddy trotted up the stairs to that place where Phileas Fogg began and ended his trip around the world in eighty days, then into the lounge off to the right. Robert Highsmith, a heavily set fellow indifferently tailored, moved his largeness from a deep leather chair that was cracked with age. Highsmith was somewhat of a colourful character having bolted a family of landed gentry to be called to the bar. He was a dazzling barrister of extraordinary skill and, at the age of thirty-five, recently elected to the House of Commons. A zealous crusader by nature, Highsmith always seemed to have his finger in some pudding of injustice. As such he headed the British office of Sanctuary International, an organization devoted to the defence of political prisoners.

'Hello there, Smiddy, sit down, sit down.'

'Good of you to see me so soon.'

'Not soon enough. I had to put a lot of pressure on the Home Office to hold things off. You should have phoned me for an appointment with time so short.'

'Well yes, that did occur to me.'

Highsmith ordered a whisky neat and Richard Smiddy ordered tea and cakes.

'Well, I've got the gist of the charges.' Highsmith said. 'They want him for just about everything in the book.' He balanced his specs on the end of his nose, brushed back his dishevelled hair, and read from a single sheet of paper. 'Giving fatal shots of phenol to prisoners, collaboration with the Nazis, selecting prisoners for the gas chambers, participating in experimental surgery, taking an oath as an honorary German. And so forth, and so forth. Sounds like a bloody monster. What kind of a chap is he?'

'Decent enough sort. A bit blunt. Polish, you know.'

'What's your office got to say about all this?'

'We've gone over the matter very carefully, Mr. Highsmith, and I'd wager my last quid that he's innocent.'

'Bastards. Well, we're not going to let them get away with it.'

23

Sanctuary International
Raymond Buildings
Gray's Inn
London WC 1

The Under-Secretary of State
Home Office
Aliens Department
10 Old Bailey
London EC 4

Dear Mr. Clayton-Hill,

I had advised you earlier of the interest of Sanctuary International in the matter of Dr. Adam Kelno, now being detained in H.M. Prison at Brixton. As a matter of procedure, our organization looks with suspicion on any demands for political prisoners being extradited to Communist states. Dr. Kelno is clearly a political victim.

On further scrutiny it is our belief that the charges against Dr. Kelno appear to be totally without foundation. The affidavits against him are either from Polish Communists or Communist-oriented persons.

In no event has anyone claimed to have personally witnessed any wrong-doing by Dr. Kelno. These affidavits are based on the loosest kind of hearsay that would be inadmissible evidence in any court of law in the Western world. Furthermore, the Polish government has been unable to produce a single victim of Dr. Kelno's alleged cruelty.

In our opinion Poland has absolutely failed to establish a prima facie case. Those persons who are able to testify to Dr. Kelno's magnificent behaviour in Jadwiga cannot go to Poland and under no circumstances will the man be given a fair trial. If this extradition is permitted it would be tantamount to a political murder.

In the name of British fair play, Sanctuary International pleads for the unconditional release of this blameless man.

Yours faithfully,
Robert Highsmith

Hobbins, Newton, & Smiddy
Solicitors
32B Chancery Lane
London WC2

The Under-Secretary of State
Home Office
Aliens Department
10 Old Bailey
London EC4

Re: Dr. Adam Kelno

Dear Mr. Clayton-Hill,

Further to the matter of Dr. Adam Kelno. I have the pleasure of enclosing twenty more statements from former inmates of the Jadwiga Concentration Camp on behalf of our client.

We are appreciative of your granting a delay which has allowed us to bring forth over a hundred affidavits. However, Dr. Kelno has been in prison for nearly six months without a prima facie case against him.

We shall be obliged if you will inform us whether you are now satisfied on the evidence we have produced and can arrange to release Dr. Kelno or if we are to go to further expense and labour.

May I call your attention to an honorary tribunal consisting of representatives of all the Free Polish organizations which has not only exonerated him but cites him as a hero.

Faithfully yours,
Hobbins, Newton & Smiddy

In the House of Commons, Robert Highsmith gained support from his fellow-members and exerted growing pressure for the release of Kelno. A rash of opinion was growing against the obvious injustice.

Yet, equally insistent was a feeling of anger from Poland that a beastly war criminal was at large and being protected by the British. From their point of view it was a Polish matter and England was bound by treaty to return him for trial.

Just as it seemed that Sanctuary International was turning the corner, Nathan Goldmark, the Polish investigator who was in England pressing for the extradition, found an unexpected witness.

FOUR

The skyline of Oxford was punctured by a hundred spires and towers. Nathan Goldmark of the Polish Secret Police nibbled on his knuckles and pressed close to the train window as fellow-passengers pulled their luggage down from the overhead rack.

Oxford, he had read on the ride up from London, dated back to the twelfth century and had grown to its present conglomerate of thirty-one colleges with assorted churches, hospitals, institutions, all joggled about in winding ways, a terribly romantic stream, Gothic richness, fluted ceilings, ancient quadrangles, and the chancellors, and masters, and readers, and students, and choirs. Colleges such as the Magdalens and Pembrokes and All Souls counted their history and their heroes in hundreds of years. The Nuffields and St. Catherines in mere decades. All of it was filled with the roll call of immortals that was the greatness of England itself.

Nathan Goldmark found the taxi stand and handed the driver a slip of paper that read, Radcliffe Medical Centre. He lowered his window despite the chill drizzle as they drove toward a flood of bicycles and jaunty students. On an ancient wall in paint in red letters were the words, JESUS WAS A FAIRY.

In the sterile sanctuary of the medical centre he was taken down a long corridor, past a dozen laboratories to the tiny, dishevelled office of Dr. Mark Tesslar, who had been expecting him.

'We will go to my place,' Tesslar said. 'It is better to speak there.'

Tesslar's apartment was a few miles from the centre of Oxford in the countryside, in a converted monastery at Wytham Abbey. It took only a moment or so for Dr. Mark Tesslar and Nathan Goldmark to size each other up, for they were both members of the same unique club, the few and far between Polish Jews to survive Hitler's holocaust. Tesslar had matriculated through the Warsaw Ghetto, Majdanek and Jadwiga Concentration Camps. Goldmark was a graduate of Dachau and Auschwitz. The rivulets of deep furrows and sunken eyes betrayed the past of one to the other.

'How did you find me, Goldmark?' Tesslar asked.

'Through Dr. Maria Viskova. She told me you were in Oxford working on special research.'

The mention of Maria brought a smile to an otherwise rigid, bony face. 'Maria ... when did you see her last?'

'A week ago.'

'How is she?'

27

'Well, in a favourable position but, like all of us, trying to find out where life is again. Trying to understand what happened.'

'I begged her, when we were liberated and returned to Warsaw, to leave Poland. It is no place for a Jew. It's a graveyard. A vast, hollow place filled with the smell of death.'

'But you are still a Polish citizen, Dr. Tesslar.'

'No. I have no intentions of going back. Never.'

'It will be a great loss for the Jewish community.'

'What Jewish community? A smattering of ghosts sifting through the ashes.'

'It will be different now.'

'Will it, Goldmark? Then why do they have a separate branch of the Communist Party for Jews. I'll tell you. Because the Poles won't admit to their guilt and they have to keep what is left of the Jews locked in Poland. See! We have Jews here. They like it here. We are good Poles. And people like you do their dirty work. You have to keep a Jewish community in Poland to justify your own existence. You're being used. But in the end you'll find out the Communists are no better for us than the Nationalists before the war. Inside that country we are pigs.'

'And Maria Viskova ... a lifelong Communist?'

'She will be disenchanted too, before it's over.'

Goldmark wished to disengage the conversation. His face pinched nervously as he sucked at one cigarette after the other. As Tesslar made his attack, Goldmark became more restless.

Mark Tesslar limped slightly as he took the tray of tea from his housekeeper. He prepared it and poured.

'The reason of my visit to Oxford,' Goldmark said, 'concerns Adam Kelno.'

The mention of Kelno's name brought an instant visible reaction. 'What about Kelno?'

Goldmark smirked a little, chomping with the sudden importance of his revelation. 'You've known him a long time?'

'Since we were students in 1930.'

28

'When was the last you saw of him?'

'Leaving the Jadwiga Concentration Camp. I heard he came to Warsaw after the war, then fled.'

'What would you say if I told you he was in England?'

'Free?'

'Not exactly. He is being detained at Brixton Prison. We are trying to get him extradited to Poland. You ought to know the situation here in England with the Polish fascists. They have made a cause célèbre out of him. They've managed to attract enough attention in high places to make the British do a fence-sitting act. You knew him intimately in Jadwiga?'

'Yes,' Tesslar whispered.

'Then you must be aware of the charges against him.'

'I know he committed experimental surgery on our people.'

'How do you know this?'

'I saw it with my own eyes.'

The Under-Secretary of State
The Home Office
Aliens Department
10 Old Bailey
London EC 4

Hobbins, Newton & Smiddy
Solicitors
32B Chancery Lane
London WC 2

Re: Dr. Adam Kelno

Gentlemen:

I am directed by the Secretary of State to inform you that he has carefully considered all the circumstances including information furnished by the Polish government. With the recent sworn statement of Dr. Mark Tesslar the

Secretary of State considers that a prima facie case has been established. It is not within our jurisdiction to comment on the right or wrong of Polish law but to comply with treaties in effect with that government.

Therefore, the Secretary of State has decided to enforce the deportation order by sending Dr. Kelno to Poland.

> I am, gentlemen
> Your obedient servant,
> John Clayton-Hill

FIVE

The guard led Adam Kelno into the glassed consultation room where he was seated opposite Robert Highsmith and Richard Smiddy.

'I'm going to come right to the point, Kelno,' Highsmith said, 'we are in a nasty bind. Nathan Goldmark has obtained a very damaging affidavit against you. What does the name Mark Tesslar mean to you?'

Fear was evident in him.

'Well?'

'He is in England?'

'Yes.'

'It is all very clear. Once the Polish government could not establish a case against me, they sent one of them after me.'

'One of whom?'

'The Communists. The Jews.'

'What about Tesslar?'

'He swore to get me years ago.' Kelno hung his head. 'Oh

God, what's the use.'

'See here, man, you pull yourself together. There is no time for sinking spells. We have to keep our wits.'

'What do you want to know?'

'When did you first meet Tesslar?'

'Around 1930 at the university when we were students together. He concluded his medical training in Europe, Switzerland, I think.'

'Did you see him when he returned to Warsaw to practise before the war?'

'No, but he was known to carry out abortions. As a Roman Catholic it was difficult for me to recommend abortions, but a few times I felt it best for the life of the patient, and once a close relative was in trouble. Tesslar never knew I sent people to him. It was always done through a blind party.'

'Go on.'

'By some insane quirk of fate I met him again in Jadwiga. Late in 1942 the Germans took him from the Warsaw Ghetto and removed him to Majdanek Concentration Camp outside the city of Lublin. Here he was charged by the SS doctors to keep the camp prostitutes free of disease and to perform abortions when necessary.'

Smiddy, who had been writing notes quickly, looked up. 'How do you know this?'

'Word of this sort spreads quickly even from one camp to another. The doctors were in a very small community and a few transfers here and there would give us all the news. Also, as a member of the Nationalist underground I had access to this kind of information. We all knew about Tesslar when he arrived in Jadwiga in 1943.'

'You were the chief medical officer, so you must have had close contact with him?'

'No. It was not the case. You see, there were twenty-six barracks in the medical complex but Barracks One to Five were where the SS doctors conducted secret experiments. Tesslar lived down there. It is he who should be standing trial, not me. I warned him he would have to answer for his crimes, but he was under the protection of the Germans.

31

When the war was over, Tesslar became a Communist and joined the secret police as a medical officer in order to save himself. That is when he swore those lies against me.'

'I want you to answer this very carefully, Dr. Kelno,' Highsmith accentuated. 'Did you ever perform any amputations of testicles and ovaries?'

Kelno shrugged. 'Of course. I performed ten thousand, fifteen thousand operations. Large ones, small ones. A man's testicles or a woman's ovary can become diseased like any other part of the body. When I operated, I did it to save a patient's life. I recall cancers and tumours of the sexual glands. But you see how such things can become distorted. I never operated on a healthy man.'

'Who accused you of that?'

'I know all of Tesslar's accusations. Do you want to hear them? They are stamped on my brain.'

'Very well,' Highsmith said. 'We were able to get a short delay in order to give you time to answer Tesslar's statement. You must go about it coldly, dispassionately, and honestly and don't inject your personal animosity against him. You must answer every charge, point by point. Here, study this statement tonight with great care. We will be back tomorrow with a shorthand writer to take your answer.'

'I categorically deny that I boasted to Dr. Tesslar the performing of fifteen thousand experiments in surgery without anaesthetic. Too many people have testified to my good behaviour to make this anything but the wildest sort of slander.'

'I categorically deny I ever performed surgery on a healthy man or woman. I deny I was ever inhumane to my patients. I deny ever taking part in any experimental surgery of any sort.'

'It is a pure fabrication that Dr. Tesslar ever saw me perform surgery. He was never, at any time, in any theatre where I operated.'

32

'Too many of my patients are alive and have testified on my behalf to give validity to the charge that my operations were badly performed.'

'It is my sincere conviction that Dr. Tesslar made these charges to take the onus of guilt off himself. I believe he was sent to England as a part of a conspiracy to destroy all remaining traces of Polish nationalism. The fact that he has asked for asylum in England is merely a Communist trick, and is not to be trusted.'

As the time of decision drew close, Adam Kelno went into a deep depression. Even the visits from Angela failed to lift his spirits.

She handed him a set of photographs of their son, Stephan. Adam set them down on the table without looking. 'I can't,' he said.

'Adam, let me bring the child so you can see him.'

'No, not in a prison.'

'He's only an infant. He won't remember.'

'See him ... so I can carry the tortured remembrance of him through a mock trial in Warsaw. Is that what you are trying to tell me?'

'We are fighting just as hard as ever. Only ... I can't see you like this. We've always drawn strength from each other. How easy do you think this has been on me? I work all day, try to raise a child by myself, come to see you. Adam ... oh, Adam ...'

'Don't touch me, Angela. It is becoming too painful.'

The special basket of food she brought to Brixton four times a week had been inspected and passed. Adam was disinterested.

'I have been here almost two years,' he mumbled, 'watched over like a condemned man in solitary confinement. They watch me at meal times, at the toilet. No buttons, belts, razors. Even my pencils are taken away at night. I have nothing to do but read and pray. They're right ... I have wanted to commit suicide. Only the thought of

33

living to see my son as a free man has kept me alive but now ... even that hope is gone.'

John Clayton-Hill, the Under-Secretary, sat down at the table across from the Secretary of State, Sir Percy Maltwood, with that damnable deportation order between them.

Maltwood had called Thomas Bannister, King's Counsel, into the Kelno affair on behalf of the Home Office to see if his opinion differed from Highsmith's.

Thomas Bannister in his early forties was a barrister of stature equal to Highsmith's. A man of average build, prematurely greyed, and ruddy in complexion. All that seemed extraordinarily placid leaped into exquisite and brilliant action within the walls of a courtroom.

'What will your report say, Tom?' Maltwood asked.

'It will say that there is a reasonable doubt as to either Kelno's guilt or innocence and therefore the Polish government is obliged to produce more evidence. I don't think they have established a prima facie case because what it all boils down to is Tesslar's word against Kelno's.'

Bannister gracefully moved into a seat and looked through the now heavy records. 'Most of the affidavits supplied by the Polish government are based on pure hearsay. We have come to know, have we not, that Tesslar is either lying to save himself or Kelno is lying to save himself. Both of them obviously dislike each other. What happened in Jadwiga happened in total secrecy so we don't really know if we would be hanging a political victim or freeing a war criminal.'

'What do you think we ought to do, Tom?'

'Continue to hold him in Brixton until one side or the other comes up with concrete evidence.'

'Off the record,' Maltwood said, 'what is your opinion?'

Bannister looked from one to the other and smiled. 'Come on, Sir Percy, you know I won't answer that.'

'We are going strictly on your recommendation, Tom, not your hunches.'

'I think Kelno is guilty. I'm not sure of what, but he's guilty of something,' Tom Bannister said.

The Polish Embassy
47 Portland Place
London, W 1
January 15, 1949

The Secretary of State

Sir:

The Polish ambassador presents his compliments to His Majesty's Principal Secretary of State for Foreign Affairs and has the honour to inform him of the Polish government's attitude on the subject of Dr. Adam Kelno. The Polish government holds the view that:

It has established beyond doubt that Dr. Adam Kelno, now under custody in Great Britain in Brixton Prison, was a surgeon in Jadwiga Concentration Camp and is suspect of having perpetrated war crimes.

Dr. Kelno is listed as a suspect war criminal by the United Nations' War Crimes Commission and the governments of Czechoslovakia and the Netherlands as well as Poland.

The Polish government has supplied all required evidence to His Majesty's government sufficient for a prima facie case.

Further evidence should be preserved for the proper Polish courts.

The government of the United Kingdom must now comply with requests for the extradition of war criminals under existing treaty.

Furthermore, public opinion in Poland is outraged by this undue delay.

Therefore, for finalizing once and forever the fact that Dr. Adam Kelno should be deported to Poland, we shall produce a victim of Dr. Kelno's brutality and will, in accordance to British jurisprudence, bring forth a man who was castrated by Dr. Kelno in a brutal manner as a part of a medical experiment.

I am, sir,

Most faithfully,
Zygmont Zybowski,
Ambassador

SIX

Opposite glorious old Covent Garden stood that grim grey stone Palladian edifice, the Bow Street Magistrates' Court, most noted among London's fourteen police courts. A line of chauffeured limousines parked before the station testified to the importance of the occasion taking place behind the closed doors of a large, draughty, shabby conference room.

Robert Highsmith was there, hiding his tension behind a relaxed posture. The proper Richard Smiddy was there, nibbling at his lower lip. The magistrate, Mr. Griffin, was there. Nathan Goldmark, the dogged hunter, was there. John Clayton-Hill of the Home Office was there, and so were officers of Scotland Yard and a shorthand writer.

Someone else was there. Thomas Bannister, K.C. Doubting Thomas, one might say.

'Shall we proceed, gentlemen,' the magistrate said. Everyone nodded. 'Officer. Bring in Dr. Fletcher.'

Dr. Fletcher, a nondescript man, was ushered in and

asked to take a seat opposite the magistrate at the end of the table. He gave his name and address to the shorthand writer. Magistrate Griffin proceeded.

'This hearing is rather informal so we shan't bind ourselves with too many rules unless counsel become argumentative. For the record, Mr. Goldmark and Mr. Clayton-Hill may ask questions. Now, Dr. Fletcher, are you a registered medical practitioner?'

'I am, sir.'

'Where do you practise?'

'I am the senior medical officer at His Majesty's Prison at Wormwood Scrubs and I am senior medical adviser to the Home Office.'

'Have you examined a man named Eli Janos?'

'I have, yesterday afternoon.'

The magistrate turned to the reporter. 'For the sake of identification, Eli Janos is a Hungarian of Jewish ancestry now living in Denmark. At the instigation of the government of Poland, Mr. Janos volunteered to come to England. Now, Dr. Fletcher, would you be so kind as to inform us as to the findings of your examination in particular regard to Mr. Janos's testicles.'

'Poor devil is a eunuch,' Dr. Fletcher said.

'I should like that stricken,' Robert Highsmith said, unfolding himself quickly. 'I don't think it's proper to inject such personal observation and editorial comment as "poor devil".'

'He's damned well a poor devil, isn't he, Highsmith?' Bannister said.

'I should like the Learned Magistrate to inform my learned friend here . . .'

'All of this is rather unnecessary, gentlemen,' the magistrate said with a sudden show of the authority of British justice. 'Mr. Highsmith, Mr. Bannister, will you stop this immediately?'

'Yes, sir.'

'Sorry, sir.'

'Please continue, Dr. Fletcher.'

'There is no trace of testicles in the scrotal sac or the

inguinal canal.'

'Are there scars of an operation?'

'Yes. On both sides, just a bit over the inguinal canal, which I would deem orthodox scars for the removal of testicles.'

'Can you tell the Learned Magistrate,' Bannister said, 'if you have an opinion as to whether or not the operation on Janos's testicles was performed in a normal, skilful way?'

'Yes, it appears to be proper surgery.'

'And,' Highsmith snapped, 'there is nothing to show abuse, bad surgery, complications, that sort of thing?'

'No ... I would say I saw nothing to indicate that.'

Highsmith, Bannister, and the magistrate asked a number of technical questions about the manner of the operation after which Dr. Fletcher was properly thanked and dismissed.

'Bring in Eli Janos,' the magistrate ordered.

Eli Janos had many of the manifestations of a eunuch. He was fat. When he spoke, his high pitched voice was broken. Magistrate Griffin personally escorted Janos to his seat. There was a beat of awkward silence.

'It is quite all right if you wish to smoke, gentlemen.'

There was fishing through pockets for the relief of tobacco. Pipe, cigar, and cigarette smoke bellowed out, then drifted to the high ceiling.

Magistrate Griffin glanced through Janos's statement. 'Mr. Janos, I take it you speak sufficient English so you will not need an interpreter.'

'I can pass.'

'If there is anything you don't understand, do ask us to repeat the question. Also, I realize that this is an ordeal for you. If, at any time, you become upset, please let me know.'

'I have no more tears left for myself,' he answered.

'Yes, thank you. I should first like to review some of the facts in your affidavit. You are Hungarian by birth in the year of 1920. The Gestapo found you in hiding in Budapest and transported you to the Jadwiga Concentration Camp. Before the war you were a furrier and at the concentration

38

camp you worked in a factory making German uniforms.'

'Yes, that is correct.'

'In the spring of 1943 you were caught smuggling and taken before an SS tribunal. They found you guilty and sentenced you to have your testicles removed. You were then removed to the medical compound and interned in a place known as Barrack III. Four days later the operation was performed in Barrack V. You were forced at gun point to undress and were prepared by prisoner/orderlies and thence castrated by a Polish prisoner/doctor whom you accuse of being Dr. Adam Kelno.'

'Yes.'

'Gentlemen, you may question Mr. Janos.'

'Mr. Janos,' Thomas Bannister said, 'I should like to establish a little more background. This charge of smuggling. What was this about?'

'We were always in company with the three angels of Jadwiga, death, hunger, and disease. You have read what has been written of these places. I do not have to elaborate. Smuggling was a normal way of life ... normal as the fog of London. We smuggled to stay alive. Although the SS runs the camp we are guarded by Kapos. Kapos are also prisoners who earn their favour with the Germans by collaboration. The Kapos can be as brutal as the SS. It was a simple matter. I did not pay off certain Kapos so they turned me in.'

'I should like to know if any of the Kapos were Jewish?' Bannister asked.

'Only a few from every hundred.'

'But most of the labour was Jewish?'

'Seventy-five per cent Jews. Twenty per cent Poles and other Slavs and the rest criminals or political prisoners.'

'And you were first taken to Barrack III.'

'Yes. I learned that in this barrack the Germans kept the raw material for medical experiments ... and then I was taken to Barrack V.'

'And forced to undress and shower?'

'Yes, then I was shaved by an orderly and made to sit naked in the anteroom.' Janos fished for a cigarette and his

39

story slowed and his voice varied now with the pain of memory. 'They came in, the doctor with an SS colonel. Voss, Adolph Voss.'

'How do you know it was Voss?' Highsmith asked.

'He told me, and he told me that as a Jew my testicles would do no good because he was going to sterilize all the Jews so I would be serving the cause of science.'

'In what language did he speak to you?'

'German.'

'Are you fluent in German?'

'In a concentration camp, you learn enough German.'

'And you claim,' Highsmith continued, 'that the doctor with him was Kelno.'

'Yes.'

'How did you know that?'

'In Barrack III it is known and said Dr. Kelno was the head of prisoner medicine and often performed surgery for Voss in Barrack V. I heard of no other doctor's name.'

'Dr. Tesslar. Did you ever hear of him?'

'At the end of my recovery a new doctor came to Barrack III. It may have been Tesslar. The name sounds familiar, but I never met him.'

'Then what happened?'

'I became panicked. Three of four orderlies held me down and another gave me an injection in the spine. Soon my lower body became dead. I was strapped to a trolley and taken into the operation room.'

'Who was there?'

'The SS colonel Dr. Voss and the Polish doctor and one or two assistants. Voss said he was going to time the operation and wanted the eggs removed quickly. I begged in Polish for Kelno to leave one testicle. He only shrugged and when I screamed he slapped me and then ... he took them out.'

'So,' Bannister said, 'you had ample time to see this man without a surgical mask.'

'He wore no mask. He did not even wash his hands. For a month after, I almost died from infection.'

'To be absolutely clear,' Bannister said, 'you were a

normal healthy man when you were taken to Barrack V.'

'Weak from the concentration camp life but normal sexually.'

'You had no prior treatment of X-ray or anything else that could have damaged your testicles?'

'No. They only wanted to see how fast it could be done.'

'And would you describe your treatment on the operating table as less than gentle.'

'They were brutal to me.'

'Did you ever see the Polish doctor after the operation?'

'No.'

'But you are absolutely certain you can identify the man who operated on you.'

'I was conscious the entire time. I will never forget the face.'

'I have no further questions,' Bannister said.

'No questions,' Highsmith said.

'Is the inspection line-up ready?' Magistrate Griffin asked.

'Yes, sir.'

'Now, Mr. Janos. You understand what a police identification parade is?'

'Yes, it has been explained.'

'There will be a dozen men behind a glassed-in room, dressed in simulated prison clothing. They are unable to see into the room where we shall be observing. One of the men is Dr. Kelno.'

'I understand.'

They filed from the conference room, down rickety stairs. Each man was still full of Janos's tale of horror. Highsmith and Smiddy, who had fought so bitterly for Adam Kelno, felt an unavoidable twinge of apprehension. Had Adam Kelno lied to them? The door of Barrack V had been opened for the first time giving a glimpse of its horrible secrets.

Nathan Goldmark's chest nearly burst. The moment was at hand for vengeance for the death of his family, for justification to his government. The orgasm of victory. From here, there could be no further delays. The fascist

41

would be brought to heel.

Thomas Bannister took all of this with the apparent dispassionate calm that stamped his personality and career as a human refrigerator.

To the man who had suffered the most, it mattered the least. Eli Janos would still be a eunuch when it was over and it did not matter one way or the other.

They were seated and the room darkened. Before them was a glass-panelled room with a height marker on the rear wall. The men in prison uniform were marched in. They blinked from the sudden shower of light. A police officer directed them to face the dark room beyond the glass.

Adam Kelno stood second from the right in a mixture of tall and short and fat and thin people. Eli Janos leaned forward and squinted. Immediate identification eluded him so he started at the left side of the line-up.

'Do take your time,' Magistrate Griffin said.

All that broke the silence was the deep wheezing of Nathan Goldmark and it was all he could do to restrain himself from jumping up and pointing at Kelno.

Janos's eyes stopped for a long search of each of them, probing for recognition of that terrible day in Barrack V.

Down the line. One, then the other. He came to Adam Kelno and hunched forward. The officer inside ordered everyone to turn left profile, then right profile. Then they were marched out and the light turned on.

'Well?' Magistrate Griffin asked.

Eli Janos drew a deep breath and shook his head. 'I do not recognize any of them.'

'Have the officer bring in Dr. Kelno,' Robert Highsmith said in a sudden, unexpected flare.

'It's not required,' the magistrate said.

'This bloody business has been going on for two years. A blameless man has been in prison. I want to make completely certain of this.'

Adam Kelno was marched in and made to stand before Eli Janos and they stared at each other.

'Dr. Kelno,' Highsmith said, 'would you speak to this

man in German or Polish.'

'I want my freedom,' Adam said in German. 'It's in your hands,' he concluded in Polish.

'Does the voice mean anything?' Highsmith said.

'He is not the man who castrated me,' Eli Janos said.

Adam Kelno sighed deeply and bowed his head as the officer led him out.

'Are you willing to swear a statement?' Highsmith asked.

'Of course,' Janos answered.

There was a formal letter that His Majesty's government regretted any inconvenience to Adam Kelno for his two year detention in Brixton Prison.

As the prison gate closed behind him, the patient and loving Angela rushed to his arms. Behind her, in the alleyway that led to the entrance, his cousin Zenon Myslenski with Count Anatol Czerny, Highsmith, and Smiddy. There was someone else. A little boy who wavered cautiously under the prodding of 'Uncle' Zenon. Then he toddled forward and said . . . 'Daddy.'

Adam lifted the child. 'My son,' he cried, 'my son.' And soon they passed down the long high brick wall into a rare day of sunlight in London.

The conspiracy had been beaten, but Adam Kelno was filled with an even greater fear without the protection of prison walls. He was on the outside now and the enemy was relentless and dangerous. He took his wife and son and fled. He fled to the remotest corner of the world.

SEVEN

'Adam! Adam!' Angela shrieked.

He tore over the veranda and flung the screen door open at the same instant Abun, the houseboy, arrived. Angela had flung herself over Stephan to shield the child from the cobra coiled near the bed, tongue flicking, head bobbing in a death dance.

Abun motioned Adam Kelno into stillness, slowly unsheathed his parang. His bare feet slipped noiselessly over the rat mat.

Hisssss! A flashing arc of steel. The snake was decapitated. Its head bounced off and the body crumpled after a short violent tremor.

'Don't touch! Don't touch! Still full poison!'

Angela allowed herself the luxury of screaming, then sobbed hysterically. Young Stephan clung to his mother and cried as Adam sat on the edge of the bed and tried to calm them. Adam looked away from his son guiltily. The boy's legs were still full of welts from leeches.

Yes, Sarawak in the northern corner of Borneo was about as far away as a man could run and deep as a man could hide.

A few days after his release from Brixton Prison and in a state of overwhelming fear the Kelno family booked secret passage for Singapore and from there a rotting tramp steamer took them over the South China Sea to the end of the earth ... Sarawak.

Fort Bobang, a classic pesthole, stood on a delta formed by the Batang Lampur River. The outpost held a hundred thatched huts on hardwood stilts that nestled on the river's edge. A bit inland, the town consisted of two muddy streets of Chinese-owned shops, warehouses for the rubber and sago exports, and a dock large enough to accommodate the

44

ferry that shuttled to the capital at Kuching and the long boats that travelled the endless rivers.

The British compound was a smattering of peeled, faded white-washed buildings scalded by the sun and beaten by the rain. In the compound was an area commissioner, a police station, a few banished civil servants, a clinic, and a one-room schoolhouse.

A few months prior to the incident with the cobra, Adam Kelno had been interviewed by Dr. MacAlister, the Chief Medical Officer of Sarawak. Kelno's credentials were in order. He was a qualified physician and surgeon and men who desired to come to this place were not asked too many questions about their past.

MacAlister accompanied the Kelnos to Fort Bobang. Two male nurse assistants, a Malayan and a Chinese, greeted the new doctor without particular enthusiasm and showed him through the shoddy clinic.

'Not exactly the West End of London,' MacAlister understated.

'I've worked in worse places,' Adam answered tersely.

Adam's trained eye photographed the meagre inventory for drugs and equipment. 'What happened to the last man?'

'Suicide. We get quite a few of them out here, you know.'

'Well, don't have any thoughts like that about me. I've had the opportunity. I'm not the type.'

After the inspection, Adam curtly ordered a thorough scrubbing and cleaning of the building, then retreated to his quarters on the opposite side of the compound.

Angela was disappointed but did not complain. 'A little touching up here and there and everything will be just lovely,' she said, convincing herself least of all.

The view from the screened-in veranda was to the river and the docks below them back up to the hills that rose behind the town. It was all in low palm and an incredibly deep luscious green. As their drinks arrived, the sounds and smells of dusk invaded and a blessed blade of coolness cut through the wet suffocating heat of the day. As Adam stared out, the first drops of rain sprinkled down in prelude of the daily torrent to follow. The usual power failure of the compound's generator flicked the lights off and on, off and on. And then the rain came for fair, gushing and hopping off the ground as it hit with trip hammer impact.

'Cheers,' said MacAlister. His time-wizened eyes studied the new man. Old Mac had seen them come and go, so many of them. The drunks and the dregs, and those filled with the fale hope of bettering mankind. He had long forgotten his own missionary zeal, which was squashed by his mediocracy, the crown's bureaucracy, and finally wrung out by the hot wet jungle and those savages down the river.

'The two boys you have with you are quite good. They'll help you learn your way about. Now that Sarawak has become a crown colony, we're going to have a bit more to spend on medicine. Spruce things up, here and there.'

Adam stared at his own hands and flexed them and wondered. It had been so long since they had held the surgeon's tools. 'I'll let you know what I'll need and what changes I plan to make,' he said abruptly.

Rather a cheeky sort, MacAlister thought. Well, he'll get all that beaten out of him. He had watched them withdraw and grow cruel and cynical by the month, once they realized the unthinkable situation.

'A bit of advice from an old Borneo hand. Don't try to change things here. The people down the river will thwart you on every turn. They're only just a generation or two removed from being head-hunters and cannibals. Life is hard enough here, so take it easy on yourself. Enjoy our meagre comforts. After all, you've brought a woman and child to this place.'

'Thank you,' Adam said, not really thanking the man at all.

Stinking Sarawak. Hidden from humanity in a corner of Borneo. It was peopled by a conglomerate of Malayans who were the Moslems and there were Kayans and the tribes of Land Dayaks and the Ibans, who were the Sea Dayaks, and, of course, the omnipresent Chinese, the shopkeepers of the Orient.

Its modern history came about a bit over a century ago

when trade over the China Sea between the British colony of Singapore and the Sultanate of Brunei on Borneo increased to such an extent that it became a prime target of pirates.

The Sultan of Brunei was not only raided by the pirates but constantly plagued by uprisings within his own kingdom. Law and order arrived in the person of James Brooke, a swashbuckling English soldier of fortune. Brooke stamped out the rebellions and sent the pirates packing. As a reward, the grateful Sultan ceded to him the province of Sarawak and James Brooke became the first of the fabled 'white rajahs'.

Brooke ruled his domain as a benevolent autocrat. It was a steamy little state, with but a few miles of dirt roads. Its highways were the rivers which poured down from the hilly thick forests into the deltas of the South China Sea. It was a land blanketed in tropical foliage, inundated by two hundred inches of rain a year, and co-inhabited by crocodiles, rats, snakes, bats, and wild pigs. Its natives were beleaguered and decimated by leprosy, elephantiasis, worms, cholera, smallpox, dropsy

Oppression was their lot. With pitiful little farmland, their meagre crops were under constant attack by pirates and neighbours or taken by taxation.

They made war on each other and went into battle resplendent in feathered dress, and the head of the vanquished hung in the home of the victor. Those who were not murdered were sold into the slave markets.

Over a period of time, James Brooke and his nephew, who succeeded him as rajah, established some form of order so that one merely had to concern himself with the task of survival against the land.

The third and final white rajah, Sir Charles Vyner Brooke, ended the hundred-and-five-year reign of his family after the Second World War. During the war the Japanese occupied Sarawak for its oilfields at Miri and when the war ended, Brooke ceded the state to the British crown and Sarawak along with Brunei and North Borneo became crown colonies.

Sir Edgar Bates, the first governor of Sarawak, was to take over a state that had grown to fifty thousand square miles and held a half million people. Most of these were the Ibans or Sea Dayaks, the former head-hunters of uncertain origin. Some say they were seagoing Mongols.

Sir Edgar, from the upper middle civil servants, did his best toward education and eventual self-rule. But all of those things passed over in the time of the white rajahs had taken their toll. The new Sarawak-Orient Company explored for oil and minerals and attempted to exploit the unending forest. Yet, progress was measured as the snail crosses the land and bogged in a quagmire of ancient pagan taboos.

When Adam Kelno arrived in 1949, he became the thirtieth doctor in Sarawak. There were five hospitals. This was the facility for a half million persons.

He was assigned to Fort Bobang in the Second Division of Sarawak, in the land of the Ibans, the tattooed head-hunters of Borneo.

EIGHT

Adam Kelno's boatmen deftly manoeuvred the thirty foot thatched roof dugout over the bubbling rapids where the Lemanak tributary rushed into the Lampur River. It was not difficult to tell the doctor's boat for it had the largest outboard motor of any that pushed up the Lemanak. It smoothed and they glided past a brace of sleeping crocodiles. The sound of the motor sent them slithering down the sandbank into the water. A tribe of monkeys shrieked at them leaping along the treetops.

For ten miles up the Lemanak tributary there were a

series of long houses of the Ulu tribe of Sea Dayaks. Each of the houses was a communal village unto itself built on hardwood poles and housing from twenty to fifty families. The long houses running up to lengths of over two hundred feet hugged the river front. A pull-up ladder, once a defensive measure against attacking neighbours, served as a stairs to the common veranda. Facing the river were a long uncovered drying platform and communal kitchen and work area. In the rear of each house there were small private rooms for each family. It was all roofed in palm leaf and shingles and beneath it pigs and chickens ran wild amid human faeces and mangy curs struggled for existence.

Fifteen such long houses formed a tribal unit of the Ulus under the rule of a chieftain named Bintang, after the stars.

The arrival of Dr. Kelno's boat was greeted by the clap of gongs, the usual welcome for any visitor. During the day, as Dr. Kelno held clinic, the Turahs, the heads of the other long houses of the tribe, arrived for the council meeting that Bintang had promised the doctor.

By evening they had all assembled, bedecked in woven jackets of blazing colours, cone-shaped hats topped with feathers, and assorted arm and leg bracelets. They were olive-skinned men of five feet in height, with semi-negroid features mixed with that of Oriental. Their shiny black hair was pulled back to buns behind their necks and their shoulders, legs, and hands bore heavy tattoo markings. Some of the older Turahs sported such tattoos awarded to a warrior for his kills as a head-hunter in days not so long past. From rafter beams, all about the long house, hung dozens of heads, all scraped clean as the inside of pumpkins. As the Turahs gathered Bintang offered them hot rice beer and they drank and chewed betel nuts and puffed cheroots in a corner of the common veranda.

Beyond them on the drying deck, the women went about their business of cooking, weaving rattan mats and bright cloth, making jewellery, and curing the sago, a starchy food from tree trunks. Beneath their bare breasts they wore corsets made of many brass rings encircling the entire body and these adornments were decorated with coins and chain jewellery, and their ear lobes were deformed by heavily weighted earrings.

The mood of the Turahs, which had been lively, changed to sombre as the dour Dr. Kelno and his translator joined them. Feelings about him were definitely mixed. Bintang bade them to place their highly coloured and ornamented seat mats on the rattan floor. Dr. Kelno and his translator, Mudich, sat opposite them all. Bintang and his chief magician Pirak, the Manang of the tribe, sat off to a side. Pirak was one of the hereditary fakirs called by the spirits to administer health and the wisdom of the gods. There were numerous categories and ranks of the Manangs. Pirak, a wrinkled old specimen, was of a special breed known as Manang Bali, a male in female's dress and behaviour. He was a seducer of young males but bisexual as well. Pirak received exorbitant fees of gifts and food for performance of his mystic hokum. Too old to inherit chiefdom from Binang, Pirak was determined to hold his exalted position and felt that Dr. Adam Kelno presented a threat.

Meaningless amenities flowed and then the translator began the business, as the half-starved dogs snapped up the remains of the plates of delicacies.

'Dr. Adam say,' Mudich began, 'that monsoon season is almost upon us and river will swell. Dr. Adam not come back for long time. Last year during monsoon, cholera very bad. This year Dr. Adam wants no such. He ask to give medicine through needle to save from cholera. Only twenty families in all of the long houses agree. Why is this so, say Dr. Kelno.'

'Because Wind Spirit, Sea Spirit, Forest Spirit, and Fire Spirit are chosen by the Chief Spirit, Patra, to rule over sickness. We have prepared birds to sacrifice and will beat gongs four nights after first monsoon. Tell Dr. Adam, we have many way to fight sickness.'

'Many, many way,' Pirak the magician added, pointing to his bag of omens, healing stones, and herbs.

A murmur of agreement arose among the Turahs.

Adam drew a deep breath, controlled himself, and leaned

over to his translator. 'I want you to ask Bintang the following. I will give my medicine to the families that want it. If, after the monsoon season is over, the families I have treated are all well but many others who were not given my medicine are dead from fever will that prove that the gods favour my medicine?'

Mudich pretended not to understand. Adam repeated it slowly. The translator squirmed, then shook his head. 'I cannot ask such question of Bintang.'

'Why not?'

'It will embarrass chief before his Turahs if you prove to be right.'

'Well, isn't he responsible for the health and well-being of his people?'

'Bintang also responsible to keep the legends. Sickness come, sickness go. Legend remain.'

All right, Adam thought to himself, I'll get at this another way. He once again explained carefully to Mudich the question he was posing.

'Dr. Adam say to Bintang, why is burial ground so close to river? Dr. Adam say it must be moved because it make water unclean and bad water cause sickness.'

'No true,' Bintang answered. 'Spirit cause sickness.'

Again the Turahs all nodded in agreement.

Adam saw the anger in Pirak's eyes. The Manang Bali was responsible for the disposal of the dead and burial was a source of much of his income and riches. 'Legend say, must bury on hill rising from river. Burial ground in right place now. Must not be moved.'

'Dr. Adam say burial unclean. People not buried deep enough and many without a box to put them in. This Dr. Adam say spoil water when it runs next to burial ground. Pigs and dogs no fenced so they come to burial ground and eat dead. When we eat pigs and drink water it cause sickness.'

'If woman die bleeding when giving child, she cannot have coffin,' the Manang Bali answered. 'If warrior die he must be buried close to water to ease his journey to Sebayan.'

'But when you bury him with all that food in the ground, the animals dig it up!'

'How can he travel to Sebayan without food? Besides, Dr. Adam, in Sebayan he no longer has trouble so is better to get there,' Bintang said.

'If chief die,' Pirak added, 'he must be burned and given to Fire Spirit. Dr. Adam no understand we must bury depending on how someone die.'

Moving the cemetery site now became another utterly useless pursuit. Kelno was being swamped under the weight of mysticism and taboos. He persisted.

'Dr. Adam say, last time he come he brought seeds and vines of okra to plant in field near sago tree forest. Bintang promise to plant okra because is good for us to eat and make us strong.'

'We learn,' Pirak said, 'in omen from birds that fields by sago forest are cursed.'

'Just how did you come to that?'

'Very difficult to read bird omens,' Pirak said, 'take many years learning. Way bird fly, way bird sing, way bird cry, way two birds fly together. Birds give such bad omen we slaughter pig in ceremony and read markings on pig's liver. Everything say fields are cursed.'

'Dr. Adam say we have only half the farm land we need. We must make use of all of it. Okra will drive out evil spirits from the fields. Okra is sacred food,' Mudich translated, as Kelno tried to use their own taboos to gain his end. But the frustration wore on.

'Dr. Adam buy four water buffalo from Chinese. Why you no go to town of Sarebas and bring back?'

'Buffalo sacred omen, like moth and blue bird.'

'But you not bring them to eat but only to work with in field.'

'Curse to make sacred omen labour.'

After another hour of it, Adam was exhausted. He begged to be excused from the feast and the cockfight and tersely bid them farewell. Pirak, the Manang Bali, was now filled with kindness, having won all his arguments. Dr. Adam would not return till after monsoon. As he climbed into his boat and curtly ordered the boatmen to cast off, the Ulus on shore waved a half-hearted farewell. When the boat turned the bend, Bintang looked to Mudich and asked, 'Why does Dr. Adam come here if he hates us so much?'

NINE

The closeness of the British compound at Fort Bobang imposed friendships on persons who would have spent a lifetime avoiding each other. Angela was particularly adaptable to the narrow social circle. Adam was not.

He had a particular dislike for L. Clifton-Meek, the Commissioner of Agriculture for the Second Division. Clifton-Meek's office adjoined his clinic and their homes were only separated by that of the commissioner, Jack Lambert.

The Empire was a haven that saved the mediocre from obscurity. Lionel Clifton-Meek was a prime example of the shoe clerk, the railroad ticket seller, the humbled assistant tailor who had wiggled his way into a niche in His Majesty's far-flung interests. It was a small hole to crawl into indeed, but once staked out it was his and his alone. Clifton-Meek carefully guarded against either taking on responsibility, or making decisions, or outside intrusions. He clothed himself in a blanket of paper work to expand a belief in his own importance. In this safe place he could wait it out and end up with a nice pension for loyal service to the crown.

If L. Clifton-Meek personified a low echelon of civil servants, his drab, turkey-necked wife, Mercy, even more vividly portrayed what was hated by the black and yellow people they ruled.

In England, the Clifton-Meeks would have lived a grey life in a brick-row house in a grey town or in London in a walk-up cold-water flat, where her only qualification to augment her husband's insufficient income would be to hire herself out as a maid.

But the Empire did much for the lowly of England. In Sarawak they had stature. In the Second Division there was no other agricultural commissioner. Clifton-Meek had much to say about the rice fields, and the rubber plantations, and spent much of his time frustrating the Sarawak-Orient Company by the endless chain of command. A bone in the throat of progress.

Mercy Meek had at her beck and call two Malayan houseboys, who slept on the veranda and chased after her with an umbrella to shade her milky freckled skin from the sun. And she had a pure Chinese cook. The artificial snobbery of their low ancestry caused them to hyphenate their name as a further gesture of self-importance. And to top it all, Mercy attempted to bring the God of the Episcopalians to these heathens. On Sunday, the compound vibrated with her playing of the organ and pounding the fear of Jesus into them to a response of listlessly mumbled prayers.

Commissioner Lambert was another sort. Like Adam's superior, MacAlister, Lambert was an old hand in these parts, a good administrator who calmly listened to the complaints of the native chiefs, did little about them, and saw that everyone was well supplied with British flags and portraits of the King for their long houses. Basically, Lambert and Kelno left each other alone.

But that time had to come when L. Clifton-Meek had been buggered about once too often by that certain foreign medical officer and filed an indignant report.

Before Lambert let the report go into channels, he thought a meeting ought to take place between parties. It commenced in the commissioner's boiling peeling office under a tired overhead fan, which did little to bring comfort. L. Clifton-Meek's pinched white face quivered as he clung to the books of governing regulations while Lambert thumbed through the thick report.

Lambert mopped his wet jaw. It was a strange place for a man to perspire from, Adam thought. 'It appears, Dr. Kelno, that we have a misunderstanding of sorts. I rather it not go beyond this desk if we can all reach an agreement.'

Clifton-Meek arched his back as Adam glared at him with contempt.

'Have you familiarized yourself with Clifton-Meek's complaint?'

'I read it this morning.'

'Not really a serious matter.'

'I consider it quite serious,' Clifton-Meek said in a voice that trembled with fear.

'What I mean,' Lambert soothed, 'is that there is nothing here that we chaps can't bandy about a bit and simply overcome.'

'That depends on Dr. Kelno.'

'Let's take a look here,' Lambert said. 'First, there's the matter of the okra fields proposed for the Ulus on the lower Lemanak.'

'What about the okra fields?' Adam asked.

'According to this, it seems you recommended the planting of okra fields at the fifteen long houses under Chief Bintang, and you brought seeds and pods to them for that purpose.'

'Guilty as charged,' Adam said.

L. Clifton-Meek smirked and rattled his skinny fingers on Lambert's desk. 'Okra is a malvaceous shrub, a planted crop that falls quite clearly under the agricultural commissioner. It has nothing to do with health or medicine,' he bureaucrated.

'Do you believe that okra as an augment to their present diet would be good for their health or bad for their health?' Adam asked.

'I shall not be entrapped with your word games, Doctor. Land usage is clearly in my department, sir, clearly. Right here on page seven hundred and two of the regulations,' and he read the long rule as Jack Lambert stifled a smile. Clifton-Meek temporarily closed the book filled with handy markers. 'I am, sir, making a survey for the Sarawak-

Orient Company for proper land use in the Second Division for the possibility of rubber plantations.'

'In the first place,' Adam said, 'the Ulus can't eat rubber. In the second place I don't know how you can make a survey if you haven't once travelled the Lemanak River.'

'I have maps and other methods.'

'Is it your recommendation then that okra fields should not be planted?' Adam asked.

'Yes, Lionel,' Lambert interjected, 'just what do you propose?'

'I am only saying,' he retorted, with voice rising, 'the book clearly defines the duties of both our offices. If the medical officer just pops about taking matters into his own hands chaos will result.'

'May I say candidly that if you were to take a trip down the Lemanak, as I have proposed to you on numerous occasions, common sense would show you there is no land available for rubber plantations. What you would know is that there is universal malnutrition due to insufficient farm land. And as for the rest of your ridiculous report only an ass would protest my purchase of water buffaloes and recommending new fishing methods.'

'The regulations clearly state that the agricultural officer is the sole judge in these matters,' Clifton-Meek screamed with veins popping in his neck and his ruddy cheeks becoming crimson.

'Gentlemen, gentlemen,' Lambert said, 'we are all officers of the crown here.'

'The crime I seem to have committed,' Adam Kelno said, 'is to try to better the lives of my patients and see them live longer. Why don't you take your report, Clifton-Meek, and shit all over it.'

Clifton-Meek sprang up. 'I demand this report be sent to the capital, Mr. Lambert. It is a pity we have to put up with certain foreign elements who do not understand the meaning of orderly administration. Good day, sir.'

A disgusted silence followed Clifton-Meek's departure.

'Never mind, don't say it,' Lambert said, filling a glass with water from his carafe.

'I will make a collection of native omens, taboos, gods, spirits, rituals, and rules of His Majesty's Foreign Office regulations, and I'll call it *Handbook for Idiots*. The Meeks shall inherit the Empire.'

'For some strange reason we've managed to muddle through for almost four centuries,' Lambert said.

'Down the river they fish with spears, hunt with blow-guns, and plough their fields with sticks. Once you get an idea through their savage skulls there is always a Lionel Clifton-Meek to bury it in his paper heap.'

'Well now, Kelno, you've only been out here awhile. You ought to know things go slowly. No use of all this tugging and hauling. Besides, most of the Ibans are nice chaps once you get on to the idea they have their own way of doing things.'

'Savages, damned savages.'

'Do you really think they're savages?'

'Well, what else is there to think?'

'That's rather strange coming from you, Kelno.'

'What do you mean, Lambert?'

'We don't pry into a man's past here but you were a prisoner in the Jadwiga Concentration Camp. What I mean to say is, having gone through all that in Poland, done by an allegedly civilized people, it is rather difficult to really say just who are the savages in this world.'

TEN

For the most part, Adam Kelno remained aloof from the small, stifling, repetitious, and dull clique of British civil servants at Fort Bobang.

His one meaningful friendship was with Ian Campbell, a

craggy Scotsman who supervised a co-operative of small rubber plantations with headquarters at Fort Bobang to oversee the warehousing and shipping operation. Campbell was an unpretentious man, yet steeped in the classics and literature nourished during long, lonely seasons. He was a drinking man, a chess-playing man, a man with terse words and no nonsense for the pale colonials and of wisdom of the jungle and the natives.

A widower, once married to a French plantation-owner's daughter, he was left with four small children who were cared for by a Chinese couple. He, himself, was cared for by a striking Eurasian girl in her late teens.

Campbell personally tutored his children with studies beyond their years inflicted with the zeal of a Baptist missionary. His own friendship with Kelno came into being when his children enrolled in the informal classes Angela taught the children of Fort Bobang.

His youngest son was Terrence, a year older than Stephan Kelno, who in short order formed a friendship that was destined to span their lifetimes.

Both Stephan and Terrence made remarkable adaptations to this remote place and both seemed capable of overcoming the disadvantages of their removal from civilization. The boys were like brothers, together most of the time and dreaming aloud of places beyond the sea.

And during those periods when Adam Kelno skidded into a tropical depression, it was always Ian Campbell whom Angela called upon to bring her husband around.

The monsoon season came. The rivers raged to impassability. And with it, MacAlister's prophecy of doom unfolded. In that second year, Angela had a third miscarriage and they had to go about the business of seeing to it that she could not become pregnant again.

Wilted by the heat and turned soggy by the rain and caged in Fort Bobang Adam Kelno took to heavy drinking. His nights were filled with a kind of madness, the recurring dreams of the concentration camp. And that nightmare he had known since boyhood. It always took the form of a large animal, a bear or a gorilla or an unidentifiable monster, chasing him, entrapping him, and then crushing him. The spear or weapon he carried or his own strength was totally impotent in stopping the attack. As he was powerless to move, breathing became more and more difficult and always on the brink of death by suffocation he awakened sweating, heart pounding, gasping, and at times crying out in terror. And the parade of the dead at the Jadwiga Concentration Camp and the blood of the surgery never stopped.

The relentless rain showed no pity.

Each morning he took longer to lift his head from the pillow from the effects of alcohol and quaking after another night of horror.

A lizard flitted across the floor. Adam picked at his food listlessly. He was in the usual bleary-eyed state of this time of evening and his face showed a six day growth of stubble.

'Please eat, Adam.'

He grunted an indistinguishable answer.

Angela dismissed the servants with a nod of her head. Stephan Kelno was still a child, but he knew the reek of liquor from his father's breath and turned his cheek as Adam kissed him when he left the table.

Adam blinked and narrowed his eyes to get them into focus. Angela, poor Angela, sat in sallow sorrow. There were grey hairs in her head now. He had put them there with his own paint brush of misery.

'I really think you ought to shave and bathe and make an effort to come over to the Lamberts' and welcome the new missionaries,' she said.

'Lord God, will you stop trying to pawn off your only begotten son on these cannibals? Missionaries. Do you really think Jesus comes to places like this? Jesus avoids places like this ... concentration camps ... British prisons. Jesus knows how to stay out of trouble. Tell the missionaries ... I hope the head-hunters get them.'

'Adam.'

'Go sing your hymns with Mercy Meek. What a friend we have in Jeeeeesus. Hail Mary. Mother of God. Keep your nose out of Sarawak.'

Angela pushed back from the table angrily.

'Get me a drink first. No lectures. Just a drink. Even the goddam British gin will do. Aha, says the temperate and long suffering wife, the one thing you don't need is another drink.'

'Adam!'

'Subject of the next lecture. My husband hasn't made love to me for over a month. My husband is impotent.'

'Adam, listen to me. There is talk going around of dismissing you.'

'Where'd you hear that?'

'Clifton-Meek was very happy to slap me with that news,' she said. 'When I heard it I wrote to MacAlister in Kuching. They are gravely concerned.'

'Hurray. I'm sick of cannibals and Englishmen.'

'Where do you think you can go after this?'

'So long as I have these,' he said, thrusting his hands before her face, 'I'll find a place.'

'They aren't as steady as they used to be.'

'Where's my damned drink?'

'All right, Adam, you might as well hear the rest of it. I've reached the saturation point. If they sack you here ... if you don't pull yourself together, Stephan and I will not go on with you.'

He stared.

'We've taken all of this in silence and we've not complained about Sarawak. Adam, the one thing you've never had to question is my loyalty, and I'll stay here forever if need be. But I shall not go on living with a drunk who has completely given up on life.'

'You mean that, don't you.'

'Yes, I do.' She turned and left for the Lamberts'.

Adam Kelno grunted and held his face in his hands. The sheets of rain plunged the place into darkness until the servants bathed it in swaying lamplight. He continued to sit to force rationality back to his fuzzed brain, then staggered to his feet and shuffled to a mirror. 'You stupid bastard,' he said to himself.

Adam went to Stephan's room. The boy looked from his

bed half asleep and apprehensive.

Oh my God, he thought. What have I done? He is my life, this child.

When Angela returned she found Adam asleep in a chair in Stephan's room with the boy asleep in his lap. A storybook, worn from re-reading, had fallen to the floor. Angela smiled. Adam's face was clean-shaven. He awakened to her kiss and silently and gently put Stephan in his bed. He placed the mosquito netting around him and put his arm about his wife and led her to the bedroom.

Ian Campbell returned from an extended stay in Singapore at a sorely needed time. He gave himself to his friend to bring him through a soggy brained monsoon rot. It came over long chess games, with children scrambling underfoot. After all, Adam came to realize, Campbell had done it as a widower with four children. And he found the iron.

'It's never so bad, Adam, that it's worth turning one of your children into a drunk or leading them to a life of darkness. After all, man, they didn't bargain for this place.'

Adam Kelno decided he owed Ian Campbell very much and the way to pay it came through young Terrence. Often as not Terrence Campbell's curious brown eyes peered over the window-sill of the dispensary, mouth agape.

'Come on in, Terry. Don't stand there like a Lampur monkey.'

The boy would ease into the room and watch for hours as Dr. Adam, the magic Dr. Adam, made people well. As Terry's reward, Dr. Adam would ask him to fetch something or assist in some small way. And he dreamed of being a doctor.

When Dr. Adam was in a good mood, and Terry knew them all, he would ask a never-ending stream of questions about medicine. More than once Adam wished it were his own son, Stephan. But Stephan was outside doing something with a hammer and nails ... a raft, a tree house.

'God works in strange ways,' Adam thought, accepting but not accepting.

One thing was obvious and that was if Terrence Campbell had half a chance, he would be a doctor.

ELEVEN

The monsoon season ended. Adam Kelno had returned to life.

A small surgery was installed with a capability of minor operations. MacAlister came from Kuching to attend the dedication and remained for several days. What he saw in the operating theatre was a revelation. With Angela assisting, Adam performed a number of operations. MacAlister witnessed a complete change in Kelno with the surgeon's knife in his hands. Extraordinary skill, exquisite movements, command, and concentration.

A short time thereafter the police station radio received a request from the capital at Kuching to have Dr. Kelno come to perform an emergency surgery. A light plane was dispatched to Fort Bobang for him. It soon became fashionable for the British colony in Kuching to have Adam Kelno as their surgeon instead of travelling to Singapore.

As soon as the river was passable, Adam headed up the Lemanak. This time his son, Stephan, travelled with him. He came upon the Ulu long houses to find that disaster had struck during the monsoon season in the form of raging cholera.

Bintang was in mortal grief over the death of his two eldest sons. Pirak had used water from sacred jars, magic oil, specially prepared pepper, and ordered gongs and drums beaten for days to drive away the evil spirits. But it came. Diarrhoea followed by unbearable cramps and vomiting, dehydration, and the sunken eyes and fever and the leg pains and the apathetic wait for death. As the epidemic mounted, Bintang and those who were not stricken fled to the hills and left the sick to die.

The twenty families of the tribe who had taken Dr. Adam's medicine lived in six different long houses, and none of them fell to the sickness. Out of his own great sorrow, Bintang began to change his attitude. Although he still disliked the terse, cold doctor he now had to respect his medicine. Bintang called his Turahs together and with the disaster still fresh in their minds, they agreed to make changes.

The cemetery, a chief cause of contamination, was moved. It was a brazen step. Then, the long debated okra fields were planted and bullocks brought to plough the fields. The buffalo were able to turn the earth much deeper than their own crude hand ploughs and the crops of yams and vegetables became larger and finer in taste. Dr. Adam brought a fishing expert from Kuching who was able to replace the spear with netting methods. The chickens and pigs were fenced and the place to make human refuse was moved away from each long house. Much new medicine was given through Dr. Adam's needle.

And as the year wore on, Bintang noticed a change in Dr. Adam himself. In one way he was like the Ulu in his love for his child. With the young son and Terrence Campbell travelling with him, the doctor seemed much more kind. And on the second trip, Dr. Adam brought his wife, who also knew much of medicine and did much to take away the shyness of many of the women.

On the fourth and final trip to the Ulus before the monsoon, Dr. Adam's boat turned the bend to Bintang's long house and tied ashore just before nightfall. Something seemed strange. For the first time there was an absence of the greetings of gongs and a gathering of the villagers. Mudich, the translator, alone awaited him.

'Quick, Dr. Adam. Bintang's little son very sick. Crocodile bite.'

They raced the path to the long house, climbed the notched steps, and as they reached the veranda he could hear low, rhythmic chanting. Adam shoved his way through the crowd to where the child lay groaning on the floor. The leg wound was covered with wet herbs and sacred healing stones. Pirak had chanted himself into a trance waving a pole topped with beads and feathers over the child.

Adam knelt and abruptly uncovered the wound. Fortunately he had been bitten in the fleshy part of the thigh. Some of the flesh had been torn away, the teeth marks went deep. Pulse, weak but steady. He flashed a light into the child's eyes. No serious haemorrhaging but the wound was dirty and débridement and drainage were needed along with surgery on a severed muscle. Temperature ... very hot, a hundred and four degrees.

'How long has he been lying there?'

Mudich could not answer properly because the Ulus had no sense of hourly time. Adam fished through his bag and prepared a penicillin shot. 'Have him removed to my hut, immediately.'

Suddenly Pirak emerged from his communion with the spirits. As Dr. Adam gave the boy an injection he screamed in anger.

'Get him the hell out of here,' Adam snapped.

'He say you are breaking the magic spell.'

'I hope so. He's twice as sick as he need be.'

The Manang Bali picked up his bag of magic potions, magic stones, tusks, roots, herbs, ginger, pepper, and he rattled it over the child yelling that he was not finished with his treatment.

Adam snatched the bag and flung it over the veranda.

Pirak, who had been already disgraced by the cholera epidemic and with his power in the village slipping, realized he had to make a bold stand. He grabbed Adam's bag off the floor and flung it away.

Everyone backed away as Adam came to his feet and hovered over the old fakir. He controlled the impulse to strangle Pirak. 'Tell Bintang,' he said in an uneven voice, 'the boy is becoming very sick. Bintang has already lost two of his sons. This child will not live unless he is given to me immediately.'

Pirak jumped up and down and screamed. 'He is breaking my spell. He will bring back evil spirits!'

'Tell Bintang that Pirak is a fraud. Tell him that now. I want him ordered away from this child.'

'I cannot tell that,' Mudich said. 'The chief cannot throw out his own magician.'

'This child's life is in the balance.'

Pirak argued with Bintang heatedly. The chief looked from one to the other in confusion. Centuries of his society and culture weighed on him, and he was afraid of either decision. The Turahs would never understand such a thing as casting out his Manang. But the child. He will die, Dr. Adam say. Ulus have uncommon love for their children. When his own two sons died of the fever he adopted two little Chinese girls as his own for the Chinamen often gave away the unwanted females.

'Bintang says, Manang must heal son in the way of our people.'

Pirak thrust out his chest arrogantly and beat it with his fist and strutted as someone returned his bag of sticks and stones to him.

Adam Kelno turned and walked off.

Adam sat in naked futility under the waterfall below the river. He could hear the gongs and chanting from the long house. On the bank, Mudich and his boatmen kept guard for crocodiles and cobras. Poor Dr. Adam, Mudich thought. He will never understand.

He dragged himself, with weighted weariness, to a small separate hut that housed his clinic, and his own private room, which held a low palleted bed over the matted floor. He uncorked a bottle of gin and went at it until the sound of goings and drums faded under the beat of evening rain, and then he stretched on his pallet and groaned to semi-sleep.

'Dr. Adam! Dr. Adam! Wake! Wake!' Mudich said.

With years of medical training he came awake instantly. Mudich stood over his pallet with a torch.

'Come,' he said urgently.

Adam was on his feet, buttoning his shirt and tucking it into his trousers. In the next room Bintang stood with the child in his arms.

'Save my son,' Bintang cried.

Adam took the boy and laid him on a crude examination table. The fever raged. It's bad, Adam thought, it's very bad. 'Hold the torch closer.'

As he set the thermometer into the child's rectum the boy went into a convulsion.

'How long has he been doing this? Before or after the sun?'

'When sun fall boy jerk around crazy.'

That would mean three or more hours. He withdrew the thermometer. One hundred and nine degrees. The child frothed and writhed. Brain damage! Irreparable brain damage! Even if he could pull the child through he would be an imbecile.

The little olive-skinned man looked up to the doctor with begging eyes. How to explain that the chief's son would be a hopeless idiot?

'Tell Bintang there is very little hope. He must wait outside. Mudich, set the torch in the holder and wait outside also. I will work alone.'

There was no choice but to let the child go off to sleep.

Adam Kelno was back in Jadwiga Concentration Camp. The surgery ... Barrack V. He leaned down close to the child and was compelled to untie the string that held in place a tiny cloth covering the boy's genitals.

IF THESE OPERATIONS ARE NECESSARY, I WILL DO THEM. DO YOU THINK I ENJOY IT?

Adam fondled the tiny pair of testicles, kneaded them in his fingers, ran his hand up the scrotum.

IF THEY MUST COME OFF FOR THE LIFE OF THE PATIENT.

He backed away suddenly and went into a violent trembling, looking somewhat mad, as the boy went into another agonized spasm.

An hour later, Adam emerged from the clinic and faced the anxious father and a dozen waiting tribesmen.

'He went to sleep peacefully.'

When a primitive, as Bintang, emits the sound of grief it is the cry of a wounded animal. He screamed and threw himself on the ground and beat upon himself in a tantrum of exquisite torment. And he wailed his hurt until exhaustion overcame him and found him face down in the mud bleeding from self-inflicted fury. Only then was Adam able to render him unconscious.

TWELVE

The police radio advised Kuching that the flying weather was marginal so MacAlister came to Fort Bobang by boat. He tied up to the main pier amid a small forest of dugouts, where Chinese and Malayans and Muruts and Ibans jabbered in a multitude of tongues in furious barter. Along the shore, women beat their wash clean and others drew water, carrying it in cans hanging from ox-like yokes.

MacAlister jumped ashore and walked up the dock past the main corrugated tin warehouse, where his nostril was pelted with the odour of slabs of freshly pressed rubber, pepper, and sacks of bat dung collected from the caves by the ingenious Chinese and sold as fertilizer.

The old Asian hand marched stiffly up the dirt road, past the Chinese shops and thatched huts of the Malays, and into the British compound. MacAlister grumbled through a gargantuan moustache, as he slowed for his umbrella-bearing servant, who raced to keep the sun from his master's head. Knee-length stockings were met by long khaki shorts, and his cane popped in cadence to the crisp step.

Adam stood up from the chess game to greet him. MacAlister studied the board, then looked to Adam's opponent, his seven-year-old son, who was giving his father a trimming. The boy shook MacAlister's hand and Adam shooed him off.

'The lad plays quite a game.'

Adam could scarcely conceal his pride in Stephan, who at this early age could read and speak English, Polish, and a smattering of Chinese and Malay.

After a time they settled on the screened veranda with the ever constant green view of the flowing rivers of Borneo. Their drinks came and soon the new sounds and smells of dusk invaded along the blessed relief from the heat. Out on the lawn, Stephan played with Terrence Campbell.

'Cheers,' said MacAlister.

'Well, Dr. MacAlister, what's the occasion?' Adam asked with his usual abruptness.

He laughed vaguely. 'Well, Kelno, seems that you've made quite a success in Kuching. Governor's wife's tonsils, Commissioner of Native Affairs' hernia, to say nothing of our leading Chinese citizen's gallstones.'

Adam waited through the trivia. 'Well now, why am I in Bobang, eh?'

'Yes, why?'

'To come right out with it, Sir Edgar,' he said in reference to the governor, 'and I have charted out an entirely new medical facility for the future of Sarawak. We want to move some of the newer men into meaningful positions as quickly as we are able to put the old-timers out to pasture. We'd like you to transfer to Kuching and take over as chief surgeon of the hospital. I think you'll agree it's becoming quite a good facility.'

Adam drank slowly these days. He took it all in deliberately.

'Traditionally,' MacAlister continued, 'whoever is the chief surgeon is automatically assistant chief medical officer of Sarawak. I say, Kelno, you don't seem too pleased by all of this.'

'It sounds very political, and I'm not one much for administrative work.'

'Don't be so modest. You were the C.M.O. at the Polish army hospital at Tunbridge Wells.'

'I never got used to filling out reports and playing politics.'

'What about Jadwiga?'

Adam paled a bit.

'We're not pushing you up past a dozen men in the dark. Nor are we bringing up a past you want to forget, but your responsibilities were for hundreds of thousands of people there. Sir Edgar and I think you're the best man.'

'It has taken me five years to get the trust of the Ulus,' Adam said. 'With Bintang and his Turahs I have been able to get many projects started and just now we are able to draw comparative results. I have become quite caught up in the problem of malnutrition. A surgeon you can get in Kuching, and the British will never be short of administrators, but I feel that eventually something important may come to light out of my work. You see, Dr. Mac-Alister, in Jadwiga we had to depend entirely on what the Germans provided us to support life. Here, no matter how bad the land is and no matter how primitive the society, one can always better oneself, and we are coming close to proving it.'

'Ummmm, I see. I suppose you've considered the fact that Mrs. Kelno would be more comfortable in Kuching. She could pop over to Singapore a few more times a year.'

'I must say, in all candour, that Angela is as excited about my work as I am.'

'And the boy? His education?'

'Angela teaches him daily. I will put him against any boy his age in Kuching.'

'Then you are quite definite about turning this down?'

'Yes.'

'Shall we let our hair down,' MacAlister said.

'Of course.'

'How much of all this is your fear of leaving the jungle?'

Adam set his drink down and sighed deeply, as Mac-Alister found him at his source.

'Kuching is not the middle of London. No one is going to find you there.'

'The Jews are everywhere. Every one of them is a potential enemy.'

'Are you going to keep yourself locked up in the jungle for the rest of your life?'

'I don't wish to talk about it any more,' Adam Kelno answered with tiny beads of perspiration breaking out all over his face.

THIRTEEN

Stephan Kelno was the apple of his father's eye and an unusually gifted boy. Perhaps no single thing impressed the natives more than the presence of Dr. Adam's son on the river trips.

Adam stood on the wharf, steeped in sorrow as the ferry to Kuching pulled away, and Angela and his son waved to him until they were out of sight. From Kuching they would take a steamer to Singapore and then on to Australia, where Stephan would begin his formal education in a boarding school.

Adam was filled with more than the usual parental fear that something might happen to his child. For the first time in years he prayed. He prayed for the boy's safety.

To fill the terrible void, the relationship with young Terrence broadened. From an early age Terry spoke in medical terms and assisted in minor surgery. There could be no doubt that he would make an extraordinary doctor and to make this possible became Adam's goal. Ian Campbell was for it, though he doubted that a boy from the jungle could compete in the outside world.

Kelno turned his enormous energy to a series of new programmes. Adam asked Bintang and the other Turahs of the tribe to send a promising boy or girl in his teens from each long house to Fort Bobang. This took a bit of convincing, for the elders, who had always lived communally, did not wish to give up any manpower. Ultimately Adam was able to convince them that with special training they would be of more value.

He started with fifteen youngsters who built a miniature long house. The first programmes were kept very simple. The reading of time, basic first aid, and sanitation programmes for each long house. Out of the first group two of the boys were sent to the Batu Lintang Training School in Kuching for more sophisticated schooling.

Within the year Angela was teaching them how to read and write English, as well as some nursing. Even L. Clifton-Meek got caught up in it and opened an experimental plot of land just beyond the compound. At the end of the third year there was a major breakthrough, when one of the boys returned from the Batu Lintang School qualified to operate a radio. For the first time in their thousand year existence, the Ulus were able to speak to and hear from the outside world. During the monsoon season, the radio became a godsend to diagnose and treat a variety of ills.

Terrence Campbell turned out to be the hidden jewel in the programme. His ability to communicate with the Ulu youngsters made things happen that awed everyone in the British compound. As more sophisticated textbooks arrived, Terrence devoured them. Adam was now more determined than ever to qualify Terry for a top English college. Perhaps some of Kelno's zeal lay in the realization that his own son would never choose medicine. But there it was, Kelno the mentor and idol and Terry the determined and brilliant student.

Mass inoculation of Bintang's people reduced age old scourges. Bintang's long houses were cleaner, the earth yielded more, and there was a little more time to live with a little less pain. Soon, other chieftains and Turahs petitioned Dr. Adam to send children to Fort Bobang and the centre grew to forty students.

The budget meetings in Kuching were always a hassle, but MacAlister generally gave Kelno what he wanted. It was no secret that the Sultan of Brunei wanted Dr. Adam as his personal physician and offered a lavish new hospital. After two years, he got his helicopter, which increased his movement capability a hundredfold. The Ibans made up a song about the wingless bird and the doctor who came from the sky.

All of this was but a grain of sand. Adam knew that given all the resources he could command and all the money he could spend, there was little that would really change, but each small step forward renewed the determination to continue.

The years passed by and the work continued. But what Adam Kelno really lived for was the return of Stephan on the summer holidays. To no one's surprise the boy was skipping ahead in his classes. Although he fared well in Australia, Fort Bobang was his home, where he could take those wonderful trips on the Lemanak with his father.

And then Adam received news that distressed him more than he believed possible. MacAlister was retiring and moving to England. There had never been either intimacy or affection between the men, and he wondered why it bothered him so.

The Kelnos went to Kuching, where a farewell dinner was given for MacAlister and Sir Edgar Bates, the governor, who was departing for England to attend the coronation of the new queen. Sir Edgar would also remain in England and a new governor assigned to Sarawak.

Even in places so remote, the British knew how to conduct their affairs with flourish and fanfare. The ballroom was white with colonial uniforms and coloured with sashes and medals.

There were a multitude of toasts filled with true and mock sentiment. Things were changing quickly these days. The sun was setting on that Empire where the sun was never supposed to set. In Asia, and Africa, and America it fell like a house of dominoes. The Malayans in Sarawak had picked up the cadence of the freedom wind.

As the evening reached its zenith, Adam turned to his wife and took her hand. 'I have a surprise for you,' he said.

'We leave in the morning for Singapore, and we will fly to Australia to visit Stephan and perhaps a short vacation in New Zealand.'

The long night of Adam Kelno was coming to an end.

FOURTEEN

The new governor was a persuasive fellow and convinced Adam to take the appointment as chief medical officer of the Second Division. With freedom in the air there was an urgent attempt to leap forward. The training of civil servants and upgrading the medical and educational facility took priority. Development of forests and mines by Sarawak-Orient ran parallel to an infusion of new teachers, nurses, airfields, and ports.

In the Second Division Adam was able to remain in Fort Bobang but inherited over a hundred thousand persons, mostly Ibans with a smattering of Chinese and Malayans in the population centres. Adam had four doctors and a dozen nurses and assistants and of course Terrence Campbell, with primitive aide stations at the long houses. They were badly understaffed to cope with the range of diseases and problems, but he still had a higher ratio than the other Division Medical officers, who could only claim one doctor to every thirty-five thousand people.

His long suit remained the utilization of the land. There simply was not enough grazing land or farmland, so the threat of famine always lurked. Even as taboos were being broken he was unable to penetrate the ones forbidding the eating of deer and goats. It was the Iban belief that these animals were reincarnations of dead ancestors. Conversely he was unable to stop them from eating rats.

In searching United Nations bulletins and other works on the subject, Kelno became entranced by similar work in the new state of Israel. Although they were entirely different in make-up, Israel and Sarawak shared the fate of land shortage and acute deficiencies of beef and protein.

Israel had filled the protein gap with crops requiring very little land. Intense chicken hatcheries worked on a twenty-four hour basis. This idea was not suitable for the Ibans. The buildings required electricity to light them so the hens would lay around the clock. Also, the chicken itself was a disease prone fowl requiring a more advanced mentality to raise properly.

It was the second idea that caught Kelno's fancy, the artificial fish ponds. Israel had a consulate in Burma, her first diplomatic exchange in the Far East, and a number of Israeli agricultural experts were sent to establish experimental farms. He was sorely tempted to go to Burma and study the fish farms, but his fear of being recognized by a Jew overruled it.

He gathered the available literature and near Fort Bobang had his students build a half dozen ponds supplied with water from natural sources with simple canals to feed them and outlet valves for overflow. Each pond was stocked with a different variety of fish and cultured with self-perpetuating algae and plankton.

A half dozen years of trial and error were required to determine the most reliable and hardiest crop. A variety of Asian carp did the job along with imported New Zealand lobster, which flourished in fresh water.

And then came the years of persuasion before fish ponds began to pop up near the fields of the Ulus on the Lemanak.

My Dear Kelno [wrote MacAlister]

Not much is happening in Budleigh-Salterton. I am so pleased we have stayed in correspondence. It is difficult to believe you have been in Fort Bobang over a decade.

I have read your paper on the fish ponds, and your new experiments in grinding whole trash fish from the ocean as a protein supplement. May I say right off that I consider this one of the most dynamic possibilities to do something about the most pressing problem in Sarawak. I'm glad now I didn't convince you to come to Kuching to practise at the hospital.

I fully agree that your paper should be read to the British Academy. However, I cannot go along with your idea obscuring the authorship to that of an unnamed 'research team'. The paper should, and must, have your name on it.

Pursuant to this, I have travelled to London on numerous occasions and working quietly with old friends in Scotland Yard and the Foreign Office we have delved discreetly into the matter of your past unpleasantness with the Polish Communists.

We have even been able to extend our inquiries to Poland itself through our diplomats in Warsaw. The results are all quite positive. All the Poles who were in the embassy in London are long since gone, and since you now have British citizenship there is no request for extradition on war crime charges of any kind.

Furthermore, I have spoken to Count Anatol Czerny, a charming chap, and it is also his opinion that it is all water over the dam and you have nothing to fear.

I am pleased to hear that Stephan is doing so well 'down under'. Count Czerny assures me also that Terrence Campbell with his superior grades in special examinations and the fact you applied for entry several years ago will be admitted to Magdalen College. I think it is the most beautiful in Oxford, dating all the way back to the fifteenth century.

Dear Kelno, please look favourably on my request to read the paper in your name before the academy. My kindest regards to your charming wife. In friendship,

Yours sincerely,
J. J. MacAlister, M.D.

Adam reached the decision to allow MacAlister to read his paper without too much searching. He had travelled on numerous occasions to Singapore, New Zealand, and Australia without incident. His nightmares had all but faded. It was his love of Stephan that cast the deciding vote. He wanted to have his boy proud of him, and that desire outweighed his fears. He owed that much to Angela, too. And so the paper was read under the authorship of Dr. Adam Kelno.

These were the days of the new enlightenment, when it became fashionable for white men to ponder about the unproductive fields and life of squalor of black and yellow men and mass death by starvation. A conscience stirred far too late with far too little to save more than half of the world that went hungry. Adam Kelno's paper created a ripple.

As a pure scientist he had to resort to a method believed by many to be extremely cruel. Half the Ulu long houses received his medicine, fish ponds, sanitation programmes, and new crops and farming methods. The other half went without these things in order to furnish the comparative statistics. The higher death rate, lower longevity, and level of physical development and vitality dramatized the impact of his programme.

The use of human guinea pigs was something the scientists did not like but understood. A secondary part of the paper that concerned the breaking down of ancient taboos particularly proved interesting to those who had struggled in the colonies.

The paper was widely published and acclaimed and became a standard reference for those teams of doctors, scientists, and agricultural experts who were wrestling with hunger throughout the world.

The best of it all was that no adverse reaction was heard anywhere to Adam Kelno's name.

Eighteen months after the paper, 'Artificial Fish Ponds, and Their Effect on the Diet and Health of Primitive Peoples: Use of Ground Whole Trash Fish as a Protein Supplement: Comparative Diet and Vaccine Charts', an internationally manned UNESCO team arrived in Sarawak and made to Fort Bobang for a firsthand look at Kelno's work. A month later a report was filed that 'United Nations funds and personnel should be committed to Fort Bobang to join the study'.

Adam now looked forward to Singapore as a place for joyous reunions with Stephan. This was to be an occasion among occasions. Stephan had been accepted at Harvard and would soon be travelling to America to study architecture.

'I have news, son,' Adam said, unable to constrain himself. 'Mother and I have talked things over. Fifteen years in the jungle is quite enough. We are going to return to England.'

'Father, I'm speechless! It's marvellous, just marvellous. Strange how it all works. Terry in England with you. Me in America.'

'One doctor, one architect from Fort Bobang. Not so bad,' Adam said with just a tinge of sadness. 'The United Nations people really have taken things over at Bobang. In a manner of speaking, my work is done. The medical facility of Sarawak has more than doubled and a lot is going on. I'm pleased to say that when Sarawak becomes part of the Malayan State, Sir Abdel Haji Mohamed, the prime minister apparent, wants me to remain.'

'They're no fools.'

Stephan knew it was his father's dream that they be together and he didn't want to dampen the moment but inside him he felt he had to do his stint in some faraway place.

The Kelnos travelled from Singapore to Kuching in the highest spirits. The capital was something out of Somerset

77

Maugham. Lady Grayson, the governor's wife, sent the Kelnos an invitation to join them at a formal garden party in honour of the Queen's birthday.

As they arrived at the governor's mansion, Lord Grayson met them and escorted them to the lighted garden into an array of the top government officials in their whites and the Malayans and Chinese, who would soon be administering the state. As they entered a hush fell over the lawn and everyone stared at Adam.

The governor nodded and the native orchestra played a ceremonial fanfare.

'What's going on, Lord Grayson?' Adam asked.

He smiled. 'Ladies and gentlemen, refill your glasses. Last night I was advised by the Colonial Office that the Queen's Birthday List has been published in London. Among those chosen for honour to the Empire, Dr. Adam Kelno has been awarded the Order of Knight's Bachelor.'

'Oh, Adam, Adam.'

'Ladies and gentlemen. A toast. To Sir Adam Kelno.'

'Hear, hear!'

FIFTEEN

Oxford—1964

Beyond the limits of greater London, England and Wales are divided into several legal circuits and numerous times each year, the judges leave London to dispense justice in the assize towns.

The circuit system was founded after the Norman invasion in the eleventh century, when the kings began the custom of sending their justices into the countryside.

Henry II, the first great legalist and reformer, formalized

78

the assize system in the twelfth century and the procession of rulers continued to refine it.

Such a system is possible because England accepts London as the seat of the royal power with one set of laws for the entire country. In America, for example, there are fifty separate sets of state laws, and a man from Louisiana would hardly want to be tried by a judge from Utah.

Several times each year, the counties are visited to dispense justice in the name of the Queen, where the judges try the most difficult and major legal issues.

Anthony Gilray, who was knighted and named a judge fifteen years earlier in the Queen's Bench Division, arrived in Oxford on assize.

Gilray had a commission in the form of a letter from the Queen, which bore the great seal, and he travelled to Oxford with his marshal, his clerk, his cook, and his valet. It was a time for pomp and ceremony. On the first day in Oxford, Gilray and a fellow-judge attended an Assize Service at the cathedral, entering the church behind the under-sheriff of the county, the high sheriff's chaplain, the high sheriff in military uniform, the judge's clerks in morning dress of tails, and then the judges attired in full-bottomed wigs and ermine-lined scarlet capes.

Here, they prayed for guidance in the administration of justice.

The courtroom. The ceremony continues.

Everyone rises and the commission is opened. The sheriff, chaplain, and under-sheriff are on Gilray's right, and his clerk on his left. Before him sits the traditional tricorne hat and the clerk, a portly and distinguished-appearing man, reads the commission naming 'beloved and faithful counsellors, Lord Keeper of our Privy Seal and the Lord Chief Justice of England, most dear cousin counsellors, most noble knights' in their full and lengthy titles.

The clerk bows to the judge, who places the tricorne hat on his head for a moment, and the reading continues that all who have grievances can now be heard.

'God save the Queen,' and the court is in session.

In the rear of the court an eager young premedical student, Terrence Campbell, poised his pencil. The first case concerned a medical malpractice suit and would be used in his paper, 'Medicine and the Law'.

Outside the courtroom there was the milling of spectators, barristers, journalists, jurors, all adding to the excitement of the opening of court.

Across the street, Dr. Mark Tesslar stopped for a moment on his way and watched the scene and the line of pompous old, highly polished, flag-bedecked ceremonial automobiles lined up before the courthouse.

Tesslar was now a citizen of England and a permanent member of the Radcliffe Medical Research Centre at Oxford. He was curiously drawn over the street and into the courtroom. For a moment he stood at the rear as Anthony Gilray nodded to the wigged black-robed barristers to commence.

Tesslar observed the eager row of students, who always were present at such cases, then turned and limped from the building.

SIXTEEN

Angela Kelno, who was born and raised in London, was the most anxious about the return and the most shocked. No sudden arctic blast ever chilled more deeply.

AT FIRST, EVERYTHING SEEMED IN ORDER WHEN WE LANDED IN SOUTHAMPTON. I THINK I CRIED DURING THE ENTIRE DRIVE UP TO LONDON. ON EVERY MILE OF THE WAY I REMEMBERED SOMETHING AND MY TENSION GREW. AT LAST WE CAME TO LONDON. MY FIRST IMPRESSION WAS THAT LITTLE HAD CHANGED IN FIFTEEN YEARS.

OH, THERE WERE A FEW NEW SKYSCRAPERS HERE AND THERE AND A NEW WIDE DUAL CARRIAGEWAY INTO LONDON AND SOME ULTRAMODERN BUILDINGS, PARTICULARLY WHERE CENTRAL LONDON HAD BEEN BOMBED OUT. BUT THE OLD WAS THERE. THE PALACE, THE CATHEDRALS, PICCADILLY, MARBLE ARCH, AND BOND STREET. NONE OF THAT HAD CHANGED.

WHEN I FIRST LAID EYES ON THE YOUNG PEOPLE I WAS UNABLE TO RELATE. AS THOUGH THIS WAS NOT LONDON AT ALL. STRANGE PEOPLE FROM A WORLD I NEVER KNEW TRANS-PLANTED HERE. SOME FRENZIED KIND OF UPHEAVAL HAD TAKEN PLACE. YOU KNOW, YOU RECOGNIZE IT QUICKLY IN ENGLAND. THINGS HAD BEEN SO STEADY BEFORE.

MIND YOU, I'VE BEEN A NURSE FOR THIRTY YEARS AND I DON'T SHOCK EASILY. THIS THING ABOUT NUDITY IN THE STREETS. IN SARAWAK NUDITY WENT WITH THE HEAT AND THE COLOUR OF THE NATIVES. IT WAS RATHER SILLY TO EQUATE IT WITH THE LILY-WHITE PALENESS OF ENGLISH GIRLS IN CHILLY, STAID LONDON.

AND THE COSTUMES. IN SARAWAK THEY WERE BASED ON TRADITION AND CLIMATE BUT HERE THEY MADE NO SENSE WHATSOEVER. THE HIGH LEATHER BOOTS COULD ONLY REMIND ONE OF WHIP-WIELDING SADISTS IN THE SEVEN-TEENTH CENTURY PARIS BROTHELS. THE WHITE THIGHS TURNED BLUE AND GOOSE FLESHY IN THE BITING COLD SO THEY COULD SPORT HEMLINES AT THEIR BUTTOCKS. WHAT WE ARE BREEDING IN THIS GENERATION OF ICY BACKSIDES IS A FUTURE HISTORY OF ENGLISH HAEMORRHOIDS. MOST RIDICULOUS ARE THE CHEAP IMITATION FURS THAT DON'T EVEN COVER THEIR BOTTOMS. WITH THEIR SKINNY WHITE LEGS POKING OUT OF THE GHASTLY PINK AND LAVENDER BUNDLES. THEY LOOK LIKE SOME SORT OF MARTIAN EGG ABOUT TO HATCH.

IN SARAWAK, THE MOST PRIMITIVE IBAN COMBED HIS HAIR NEATLY AND KNOTTED IT. THE DELIBERATE ATTEMPT AT SLOPPINESS AND ANTI-BEAUTY APPEARS TO BE SOME SORT OF PROTEST AGAINST THE OLDER GENERATION. YET, IN THEIR MANIA TO PROCLAIM THEIR INDIVIDUALITY AND BREAK WITH THE PAST THEY ALL NOW LOOK AS THOUGH THEY HAD BEEN

CAST FROM THE SAME MOULD. BOYS LOOK LIKE GIRLS AND GIRLS LOOK EXCEEDINGLY DRAB. RATHER AN OBVIOUS ATTEMPT TO LOOK UGLY BECAUSE THEY FEEL UGLY AND A WITHDRAWAL SO THEY WILL NOT BE IDENTIFIED BY SEX. HAVE EVERYTHING ONE BIG NEUTER.

THE FRANTIC DRESS OF THE MEN IN BELL BOTTOMS AND LACES AND JUNK JEWELLERY AND VELVET ALL APPEARS LIKE A CALL FOR HELP.

ADAM TELLS ME THAT WHAT IS HAPPENING IN HIS CLINIC INDICATES A TOTAL COLLAPSE OF OLD MORALS. THEY HAVE MISTAKEN SEXUAL FREEDOM FOR THE ABILITY TO GIVE AND RECEIVE LOVE. AND MOST SAD OF ALL IS THE BREAKING UP OF THE FAMILY UNIT. ADAM TELLS ME THE NUMBER OF PREGNANT GIRLS IN THEIR TEENS IS UP FIVE OR SIX HUNDRED PER CENT AND THE STATISTICS ON BARBITURATE AND DRUG USERS ARE FRIGHTENING. AGAIN, THIS SEEMS TO INDICATE AN OVERWHELMING URGE OF THESE YOUNG PEOPLE TO WITHDRAW INTO A FANTASY WORLD, LIKE THE IBANS DID, IN TIMES OF STRESS.

I COULDN'T BELIEVE THE MUSIC. ADAM TELLS ME THERE ARE MANY CASES OF PERMANENT HEARING DAMAGE. THE GARBLED POETRY AND DOUBLE MEANING OF FILTHY LYRICS ARE FAR LESS COHERENT THAN THE IBAN SINGERS. THE MONOTONE AND ELECTRIC DEVICES ARE A FURTHER ATTEMPT TO DROWN OUT REALITY. THE DANCING AS THOUGH ONE WERE WATCHING PATIENTS IN A LUNATIC ASYLUM.

IS THIS REALLY LONDON?

ALL THAT I WAS RAISED BY IS BEING RIDICULED AND IT SEEMS THAT NOTHING IS BEING DONE TO REPLACE OLD IDEAS WITH NEW ONES. THE WORST PART OF IT IS THE YOUNG PEOPLE ARE NOT HAPPY. THEY HAVE ABSTRACT THOUGHTS ABOUT LOVING, MANKIND, AND ENDING WAR, BUT THEY SEEM TO WANT THE PRICE OF LIFE WITHOUT WORKING. THEY RIDICULE US, BUT WE SUPPORT THEM. THEY HAVE POOR LITTLE LOYALTY TO ONE ANOTHER AND ALTHOUGH SEX IS PRACTISED IN UNIVERSAL LOTS THEY DON'T UNDERSTAND THE TENDERNESS OF AN ENDURING RELATIONSHIP.

COULD ALL OF THIS HAPPEN IN ONLY FIFTEEN YEARS? THE DISMANTLING OF HUNDREDS OF YEARS OF CIVILIZATION

AND TRADITION. WHY DID IT HAPPEN? FOR STEPHAN'S AND
FOR TERRY'S SAKE, ONE MUST START TO LOOK AROUND FOR
ANSWERS.

LONDON, IN MANY WAYS, WAS LIKE WHEN I FIRST WENT
TO SARAWAK. IT IS A JUNGLE FILLED WITH STRANGE NOISES
AND CUSTOMS. ONLY, THEY ARE NOT AS HAPPY AS THE IBANS.
THERS IS NO HUMOUR TO IT ALL, ONLY DESPAIR.

SEVENTEEN

It was expected that Adam Kelno, having been knighted,
would have capitalized on the situation to build himself an
exclusive practice in the West End. Instead, he opened a
small clinic as a National Health Doctor in a working-class
section of the Borough of Southwark, close to the Elephant
and Castle in the brick-row houses near the Thames, where
most of his patients were warehousemen, longshoremen,
and the admixture of immigrants flooding in from India,
and blacks from Jamaica and the West Indies.

It was as though Adam Kelno did not believe his release
from Sarawak and wished to continue his anonymity by
living in modest seclusion close to his clinic.

Angela and her cousin walked themselves foot weary in
that magic quadrangle bounded by Oxford and Regent and
Bond Streets and Piccadilly now swarmed with hundreds of
thousands of Christmas shoppers in the gargantuan department stores and the ultra little shops.

Although she had been back in England for more than a
year the biting wet penetrating December cold bothered
her. The hunt for a taxi was futile. Orderly lines waited
with British patience outside the stores and at the bus
stops.

Down into the tube.

The underground crossed beneath the Thames to the Elephant and Castle and she made home by foot, bogged under a small hill of packages.

Oh, the wonderful weariness, the wonderful tempo of Christmas back in England. All those puddings, and pies, and sauces, and songs, and lights.

Mrs. Corkory, the housekeeper, unloaded her arms. 'Doctor is in his study, ma'am.'

'Has Terrence arrived?'

'No, ma'am. He phoned down from Oxford to say he was taking a later train and wouldn't be arriving until past seven or so.'

She poked her head in Adam's study, where he was in the familiar posture of scratching away at lengthy reports.

'Hello, dear, I'm home.'

'Hello, darling. Did you buy out London?'

'Almost. I'll help you with the reports later.'

'I think this paper work for the health service is worse than the Colonial Office.'

'Maybe you'll use a full-time secretary. We really can afford one, Adam. And a dictation machine.'

Adam shrugged. 'I'm not used to such luxuries.'

She thumbed through his letters. There were three requests for speeches. One was from the Union of African Medical Students and another from Cambridge. He had scribbled a note on each reading, 'decline with the usual regrets'.

Angela was against it. It was as though Adam were trying to downgrade his small measure of fame. Perhaps he had had his fill of blacks and browns. Then why did he choose Southwark to practise, when half the London Poles would have doted over a knighted Polish doctor. Well, that was Adam. In all their years of marriage she had come to accept it though the lack of personal ambition annoyed her, for his sake. But no pushy wife, she.

'Well, we're ready for the invasion from Oxford,' Angela said. 'By the way, dear, did Terrence say how many friends he would be bringing?'

'Probably the usual contingent of homesick Australians, Malayans, and Chinese. I'll be the epitome of Polish gallantry.' They exchanged a small kiss and he returned to his paper work, then threw the pen down. 'By God you're right. I'm going to get a secretary and a voice machine.'

Angela answered the phone ring. 'It's Mr. Kelly. He says his wife's pains are coming every nine minutes regularly.'

Adam was up quickly and out of his lounging jacket. 'This is her sixth so she'll be right on time. Have him bring her over to the clinic and call the midwife.'

It was almost midnight before Mrs. Kelly delivered and was situated overnight in the clinic. Angela had dozed in the parlour. Adam kissed her softly, and she automatically arose and went to the kitchen to heat water for tea.

'How did it go?'

'Little boy. They're naming him Adam.'

'Isn't that nice. Well, we have four infant Adams after you this year. In future years everyone will wonder why every male from Southwark was named Adam.'

'Did Terrence get in?'

'Yes.'

'Sounds rather quiet for five boys.'

'He came in alone. He's up in your study waiting for you. I'll bring the tea up.'

Terrence seemed stiff as they embraced.

'Where are all your friends?'

'They'll be down in a day. May I speak to you about something first?'

'You'll never make a politician. I've been able to read that grim expression since you were born.'

'Sir,' Terrence spoke haltingly. 'Well, you know how it's been with us. Because of you I was a doctor at heart since I can remember. And I know how good you've been to me. My education and how close we are.'

'What's wrong?'

'Well, sir, my father mentioned some little things about you being in prison and up for deportation once, but I never thought ... it never occurred to me ...'

'What?'

'It never entered my mind that you might have ever done anything wrong.'

Angela came in with a tray of tea. She poured in silence. Terrence looked at the floor and licked his lips as Adam stared ahead, hands tight on the arms of his chair.

'I've told him you've suffered enough,' she said, 'and not to pry into things we want to forget.'

'He has just as much right to know everything as Stephan does.'

'I haven't done the prying. Someone else has. This book here, *The Holocaust* by Abraham Cady. Have you ever heard of it?'

'It's quite well known in America. I haven't read it myself,' Adam said.

'Well, the damned thing's just been published in England. I'm afraid I have to show this to you.' He handed the book to Dr. Kelno. A marker was in page 167. Adam held it under a lamp and read.

'Of all the concentration camps none was more infamous than Jadwiga. It was here that SS Dr. Colonel Adolph Voss established an experimental centre for the purpose of creating methods of mass sterilization, with the use of human guinea pigs, and SS Dr. Colonel Otto Flensberg and his assistant carried on equally horrendous studies on prisoners. In the notorious Barrack V a secret surgery was run by Dr. Kelno, who carried out fifteen thousand or more experimental operations without the use of anaesthetic.'

Outside a dozen carollers pressed close to the window and with frosty breath sang out.

> '*We wish you a merry Christmas,*
> *We wish you a merry Christmas,*
> *We wish you a merry Christmas,*
> *And a happy new year.*'

EIGHTEEN

Adam closed the book and placed it on his desk. 'Well, do you think I did that, Terrence Campbell?'

'Of course not, Doctor. I feel like a bloody bastard about all this. God knows I don't want to hurt you but it's published and hundreds of thousands if not millions of people are going to read it.'

'Maybe I felt so strongly about our relationship I never felt the need to explain all of it to you. I suppose I was wrong.' Adam went to the bookcase across the room, unlocked a bottom cupboard drawer, and took out three large cardboard boxes filled with volumes of papers, files, press clippings, letters. 'I think it's time you knew everything.'

Adam started from the beginning.

'I think it is impossible to explain to someone exactly what a concentration camp is like or for them to comprehend such a thing could really exist. I still think of it in grey. We never saw a tree or flower for four years and I don't remember the sun. I dream of it. I see a stadium with hundreds of rows and each row filled with lifeless faces, dull eyes, shaved heads, and striped uniforms. And beyond the last row the silhouettes of the crematorium ovens, and I can smell the smoke of human flesh. There was never enough food or medicine. I looked from my clinic day and night to an endless line of prisoners dragging themselves to me.'

'Doctor, I just don't know what to say.'

Adam recounted the conspiracy against him, the torment of Brixton Prison, of not seeing his own son Stephan for the first two years of his life, the flight to Sarawak, the nightmares, the drunken stupors, all of it. Tears fell freely down both their cheeks as he continued in monotone until the first light of day cast a grey pall into the room and the first sounds of movement of the city could be heard. The wet tyres sung off the pavement and they were silent and motionless.

Terry shook his head. 'I don't understand it. I just don't understand it. Why would the Jews hate you so much?'

'You are naïve, Terry. Before the war there were several million Jews in Poland. We had only gained our own liberation at the end of the First World War. The Jews were always strangers in our midst, always attempting to overthrow us again. They were the soul of the Communist Party and the ones guilty of giving Poland back to Russia. From the beginning it was always a life and death struggle.'

'But why?'

He shrugged. 'In my village all of us owed money to the Jew. Do you know how poor I was when I got to Warsaw? For my first two years my room was a large closet, and my bed was of rags. I had to lock myself in the bathroom in order to have a place to study. I waited and waited to gain admittance to the university but there was no room because the Jews lied about themselves to find ways around the quota system. You think a quota system is wrong. If there hadn't been one they would have bought every seat in every classroom. They are cunning beyond imagination. The Jewish professors and teachers tried to control every facet of university life. Always pushing their way in. I joined the Nationalist Students Movement, proudly, because it was a way to combat them. And afterwards, it was always a Jewish doctor getting the prime positions. Well, my father drank himself to death and my mother worked her way to an early grave paying off the Jewish moneylender. All the way to the end, I stood for my Polish nationalism and because of it I have been driven to hell.'

The boy looked at his mentor. Terry was disgusted with himself. He could see Adam Kelno tenderly calming a frightened Ulu child and reassuring the mother. Dear Lord, it wasn't possible for Dr. Kelno to use medicine wrongly.

The Holocaust lay on the desk. A thick grey-covered volume with the lettering of the title and the author's name in red portraying devouring flames.

'No doubt the author is a Jew,' Adam said.

'Yes.'

'Well, no matter. I've been mentioned in other books by them.'

'But this is different. It has hardly been published and already a half a dozen people have asked me about it. It's only a matter of time until some journalist digs it up. With you knighted it will make a hell of a story.'

Angela appeared in a dowdy bathrobe.

'What am I to do,' he said, 'flee to some jungle again?'

'No. Stand and fight. Stop the sale of this book and show the world that the author is a liar.'

'You're young and very innocent, Terry.'

'Along with my father you're everything to me, Dr. Kelno. Did you spend fifteen years in Sarawak just for the privilege of carrying this mark to your grave?'

'Do you have any idea of what this involves?'

'I must ask you, Doctor, is there any truth to this at all?'

'How dare you!' Angela cried. 'How dare you say that!'

'I don't believe it either. Can I help you fight it?'

'Are you quite ready for the scandal and the barrage of professional liars they'll parade into the courts? Are you quite certain the honourable thing to do is not to hold our silence with dignity?' Angela said.

Terrence shook his head and walked from the room to hold back the tears.

Much beer and gin were consumed by Terry's mates and many bawdy songs were sung and many of the world's consuming issues were argued with a righteous wrath reserved for the young.

Terry had a key to Sir Adam Kelno's clinic a few blocks from the house, and after hours his chums dispensed of other frustrations by love-making with numerous young ladies on the examination table and the overnight cots amid the smell of medical disinfectants. A minor discomfort.

Christmas came and turkeys and geese were devoured and each guest opened a modest but well-chosen and humorous gift. Adam Kelno opened a number of worthless but sentimental offerings from his patients.

It all seemed Christmasy enough and the visitors were unable to detect the underlying tension. They returned to Oxford filled with the cheer.

Terry and Adam said good-bye with reserve. The train pulled out. Angela slipped her arm through her husband's as they left the Victorian loftiness of Paddington Station.

A week passed, then two and three. The listlessness of the student was matched by the listlessness and short temper of Adam Kelno.

It was the longest period of time the two had ever been out of communication.

And he was filled with the memory of the dugout struggling up the Lemanak with Stephan at the tiller and Terry on the bow chatting to the boatman in the Iban language. How warmly the Ulus greeted the boys. It was during the summer holiday, when Stephan was eleven years old, Bintang presented them with costumes and made them a member of the tribe, and they danced with the chief wearing ceremonial feathers and 'painted' tattoo marks.

Terry's bright eyes watched over the surgical mask as Adam operated. Adam always glanced at him. When the boy was there he always performed a better operation.

The hard days of clinic at the long houses would be over and they would all go to the stream and bathe or sit under a waterfall and they slept near each other, never fearing the sounds of the jungle.

All the rest of it flooded his thoughts day and night until he could no longer bear it. It wasn't only Terrence who filled his thoughts. What would happen when Stephan learned of this in America?

Sir Adam Kelno walked the narrow Chancery Lane, that artery of British law flanked by the Law Society on one side and Sweet and Maxwell, the legal publishers and booksellers, on the other side. The window of Ede and Ravencroft, Ltd., tailor of the profession, held its usual grim display of academic and black barristers' robes, unchanged in style since time remembered and garnished with a variety of grey barristers' wigs.

He stopped at 32B Chancery Lane. It was a narrow four storey building, one of the few survivors of the Great Fire centuries earlier. A warped and misshapen Jacobean relic.

Kelno glanced at the registry. The second and third floor held the law offices of Hobbins, Newton, and Smiddy. He entered and disappeared up the creaking stairs.

TWO

THE DEFENDANTS

ONE

The author of *The Holocaust* was an American writer named Abraham Cady, one-time journalist, one-time flyer, one-time ballplayer.

At the turn of the century the Zionist movement spread like a forest fire over the Jewish Pale of Settlement in Czarist Russia. Bent under universal suppression and pogroms of centuries standing, the groundswell to leave Russia found direction in the resurrection of the ancient homeland. The little Jewish village of Prodno sponsored the Cadyzynski brothers, Morris and Hyman, to go to Palestine as pioneers.

While working in the swamps of Upper Galilee on land redemption, Morris Cadyzynski fell prey to recurrent attacks of malaria and dysentery until he was taken to the hospital in Jaffa. He was advised to leave Palestine as one of those unable to adapt to the severe conditions. His elder brother, Hyman, remained.

It was usual in those days that a relative in America take on the responsibility of getting as many of the family over from the old country as possible. Uncle Abraham Cadyzynski, after whom the author was later named, had a small Jewish bakery on Church Street in the ghetto in Norfolk, Virginia.

Morris had his name shortened to Cady by a perplexed official trying to separate over a hundred 'skis' who immigrated on the same boatload.

Uncle Abraham had two daughters, whose eventual husbands were not interested in the bakery, so it was passed on to Morris when the old man died.

The Jewish community was tiny and close knit, hanging together unable to shake off all the ghetto mentality. Morris met Molly Segal, also an immigrant in the Zionist movement, and they were married in the year of 1909.

Out of deference to his father, the Rabbi of Prodno, they were married in synagogue. The party afterward at the Workmen's Circle Hall was in the Yiddish tradition of an endless parade of food, dancing the hora, and '*mazel tovfs*' until the middle of the night.

Neither of them were religious, but they were never able to break most of the old country ties of conversing and reading in Yiddish and keeping a mostly kosher kitchen.

Ben was the first born in 1912 and then Sophie came two years later as Europe was going up in flames. During the First World War business prospered. With Norfolk as a major troop and supply shipping point to France, the government gave Morris's bakery a contract to augment over-burdened facilities. The output of the bakery tripled and quadrupled but in doing so it lost most of its Jewish identity. The bread and cakes had come from old family recipes and now they had to conform to government specifications. After the war Morris got some of the old flavour back. He was so popular all over Norfolk that he began to ship out to grocery stores, some in all gentile neighbourhoods.

Abraham Cady was born in 1920. Although it was a prosperous family it was difficult to tear away from the little row house with the white porch on Holt Street in which all the children were born.

The Jewish section started in the one hundred block of Church Street at St. Mary's Church and ran for seven blocks to where the Booker T. Pharmacy started the Negro ghetto. The streets were lined with little shops out of the old country and the children were to remember the smells and sounds of it all their lives. Heated discussion in Yiddish where the two newspapers, the *Freiheit* and New York *Vorwärts*, vied for opinion. There was the marvellous odour of leather from Cousin Herschel's shoe repair shop and the pungent aroma of the cellar of the 'pickle' man, where you could have a choice of sixty different kinds of pickles and pickled onions from briny old vats. They cost a penny each, two cents for an extra.

In the back yard behind Finkelstein's Prime and Fancy Kosher meats the kids liked to watch the *shochet* kill chickens for a nickel each to conform to religious requirements.

There was endless barter at the vegetable stalls and at Max Lipshitz's Super Stupendous Clothing Mart; Max himself, measuring tape around his neck, pulled potential customers off the street, and just a little ways down Sol's Pawn Shop held a junk yard of tragedy, mostly from coloured customers.

Much of what Morris Cady earned went either to the families in the old country or to Palestine. Aside from the black Essex parked before the house there was little to testify to their nominal wealth. Morris did not play the stock market so when the crash came he had enough cash to buy out a couple of sinking bakeries at thirty cents on the dollar.

Despite their simplicity, their affluence caught up with them and after a year of discussion they bought a big shingled ten-room house on an acre of land at Gosnold and New Hampshire Streets with a view to the estuary. A few Jewish families, upper-middle-class merchants and doctors, had penetrated Colonial Place but further down the line around Colley Street and Thirty-first. The Cadys had moved into an all gentile neighbourhood.

Not that the Cadys were black, but they weren't exactly white. Ben and Abe were 'the Jew boys'. The Hebes, Yids, Sheenies, Kikes. Much of this was changed at the big circle at Pennsylvania and Delaware, where they played ball near the pumping station. Ben Cady was handy with his dukes and a definite risk to provoke or attack. After Ben established an understanding to live by with the neighbourhood kids they all discovered the never-ending delights that came from the oven of Molly's kitchen.

Abe had to go through it all again in J. E. B. Stuart Grammar School, filled with youngsters from the nearby

Turney Boys' Home, consisting mainly of problem children from broken families. All they seemed to want to do was fight. Abe had to defend some unknown honour until his brother Ben taught him 'all the dirty Jew tricks' to acquit himself.

Fists gave way to a different kind of anti-Semitism at Blair Junior High but by the time Abe was a teen-ager he had a running commentary with the unpleasant aspects of his birth.

It was Ben who brought them honour by becoming a three letter athlete at Maury High by bombing baseballs out of sight in the spring, sharpshooting baskets and plunging for hard yardage in the fall and winter.

After a time the neighbours pointed with certain curious pride to the Jewish family. They were good Jews. They knew their place. But the strangeness of entering a gentile home never exactly wore off.

What Abe Cady remembered the most about his father was his devotion to the family in the old country. His restlessness to get them all out of Poland. Morris brought a half dozen cousins to America and paid passage for another half dozen to Palestine. But try as he might, he could never induce his father, the Rabbi of Prodno, and his two younger brothers to leave. One was a doctor and the other a successful merchant, who were to remain in Poland until the tragic end.

Sophie, the daughter, was plain. She married a plain guy with a promising sales route in Baltimore, where most of the Cadyzynski family had settled. It was a nice to travel to Baltimore for family reunions. One couldn't complain. America had been good. They were reasonably successful and always close in a pinch despite the usual family squabbles and feuds.

It was Ben who gave Morris and Molly the heartaches. They were proud enough of their athlete hero son. Such glory he had brought them, they could not deny. There was a school cheer for Ben even after he graduated. BASH EM, BAM EM, BEN, BEN, BEN!

98

Ben Cady was a child of the thirties. He never saw a coloured person without feeling pain for him. Sensitive to the suffering of the depression, despising the ignorance of the South, he leaned more and more to the clever and fanatic voices that promised liberation of the toiling masses. It made more sense to him than anything in the world. The Earl Browders and Mother Bloors and James Fords who came down from the North and dared preach their gospel in mixed meetings with the blacks in tiny black halls of black town.

'So look, son,' Morris said to Ben, 'you don't want to be a baker and that's fine by me. I don't want my sons to be bakers. We can hire a foreman, we can hire book-keepers so there should always be income from the business. Don't do me favours. Don't be a baker. Ben, look already, nine colleges, including the University of West Virginia, are on their knees begging humbly to give you an athletic scholarship.'

Ben Cady had black eyes and black brows and black hair, and when not bursting from his intensity on the athletic field it burst from his being in a manner that no one could fail to understand.

'I want to screw around for a few years, Dad. You know, just look things over. Maybe sign on a ship.'

'You want to be a bum.'

Abe turned off the Jack Benny radio show because they were starting to talk loud in the next room. He stood in the door, gangly. He looked about half the size of Ben.

'Abe, go do your homework.'

'It's July, Pop. I don't have any homework.'

'So you've got to come in and take Ben's side and gang up on me.'

At this point Morris Cady went through the story of his youth in Poland and his struggle in Palestine and his continued struggle for the family. All of this led up to his wife, Molly, the finest woman God ever created and then came the children.

About Sophie, what's to complain? A plain girl with a plain boy. Only three years married and two gorgeous children. Such *nachas* I get from the grandchildren. Maybe her husband Jack is a putz but he's a good provider, and he treats Sophie like she's pure gold.

Abe, look at the grades he gets in school. Nobody in the entire family denies Abe is a genius. Someday he will be a great American Jewish writer.

'Ben,' Morris bargains, 'Ben, let's put *tochis afn tisch.* You got through school through one method, brute force. So, you don't want to be a baker. Honkey dorey with me. But with fifteen colleges, including the University of West Virginia, humbly begging your presence for God's sake get yourself a degree. I'm asking too much that you should educate yourself?'

Ben's face radiated blackness.

'How do you think your mother and I feel when you go to that *goyim* airfield and do those crazy things in an airplane? Spelling out names in the sky with smoke. That's what we struggled to raise you for? Let me tell you, Ben, you should see the look on your mother's face waiting for your footsteps to come on the porch. Your mother dies every minute you're up there in the sky. Some consideration. She cooks the meal, and she says to me, Morris, I know this food will never be eaten by Ben. Look at me, son, when I'm talking to you.'

Both Abe and Ben have their heads hung and wring their hands.

'What's bothering you, son?'

Ben looked up slowly. 'Poverty,' he said, 'fascism, inequality.'

'You think I didn't hear all that Commie crap in Poland. You're a Jew, Ben, and in the end the Communists will betray you. I know from firsthand what kind of butchers they are in Russia.'

'Pop, stop picking on me.'

'Not until you educate yourself. All right, son, it's fashionable for young people to go into the coloured section and dance with *schwartzes*. First you dance with them, then you bring them home to your mother.'

100

Morris held his hand up for silence before Ben could answer.

'Look at this business. Flying. Becoming a Commie, fraternizing with *schwartzes*. Ben, I don't have a prejudiced bone in my body. I'm a Jew from the old country. Don't you know I know how these black people suffer. Who, after all, are the most liberal thinkers and the most decent to the coloured people? The Jews are. And if something goes wrong, if the blacks explode ... who do you think they'll turn on ... us.'

'Are you finished, Pop?'

'Deaf ears,' Morris opined. 'I'm talking already to the wall.'

TWO

WE DIDN'T LEARN ABOUT MY BROTHER BEN GETTING KILLED BY A TELEGRAM OR ANYTHING LIKE THAT. WE GOT A LETTER FROM ONE OF HIS BUDDIES IN THE LACALLE SQUADRON, A GROUP OF AMERICAN VOLUNTEERS FLYING FOR LOYALIST SPAIN. SOME WERE MERCENARIES AND SOME, LIKE BEN, WERE TRUE ANTI-FASCISTS. IT WAS A RAG-TAG GANG. ANYHOW, IT SEEMED KIND OF STRANGE THAT THE LETTER WAS FILLED MORE WITH TALK ABOUT THE CAUSE FOR WHICH BEN DIED AND THE FACT THAT THE FASCIST FLYERS WERE COWARDS.

BEN WAS FLYING A RUSSIAN CHATOS BIPLANE. IT WAS OUT-DATED AND THEY WERE ALWAYS OUTNUMBERED BY THE SWARMS OF GERMAN HEINKELS AND ITALIAN FIATS. ON THIS PARTICULAR MISSION BEN HAD DOWNED A JUNKER BOMBER, WHEN THEY GOT INTO A DOGFIGHT. THREE AMERICANS WERE JUMPED BY THIRTY-FIVE HEINKELS, THE LETTER SAID.

BEN'S DEATH WAS LATER CONFIRMED BY A GUY WHO CAME

TO VISIT US IN NORFOLK, WHO HAD BEEN A VOLUNTEER IN THE LINCOLN BATTALION OF THE INTERNATIONAL BRIGADE. HE HAD BEEN WOUNDED AND LOST AN ARM, AND WAS SENT BACK TO THE STATES AS A RECRUITER.

ALL THE RELATIVES CAME DOWN FROM BALTIMORE WHEN THEY HEARD BEN HAD BEEN KILLED AND ALL THE OLD FRIENDS CAME FROM CHURCH STREET. THE HOUSE WAS FILLED DAY AND NIGHT.

THERE WERE OTHER PEOPLE TOO. SOME OF BEN'S TEACHERS AND COACHES AND CLASSMATES AND NEIGHBOURS, SOME OF WHOM HAD NEVER SAID HELLO OR SET FOOT IN OUR HOUSE BEFORE. EVEN TWO MINISTERS, A BAPTIST PREACHER AND A CATHOLIC PRIEST, CAME TO VISIT MOMMA AND POPPA. POPPA ALWAYS GAVE DONATIONS TO ALL THE CHURCHES IN THE NAME OF THE BAKERY.

FOR THE FIRST TWO WEEKS MOMMA NEVER STOPPED COOKING. SHE KEPT SAYING OVER AND OVER THAT THE COMPANY SHOULDN'T GO HUNGRY. BUT WE ALL KNEW SHE WAS WORKING TO BURN UP THE NERVOUS ENERGY AND KEEP BUSY SO SHE COULDN'T THINK ABOUT BEN.

AND THEN SHE CAME APART AND HAD TO BE PUT UNDER SEDATION. SHE AND POPPA WENT AWAY FOR A LONG REST TO SOPHIE'S IN BALTIMORE AND LATER TO THE CATSKILLS AND MIAMI. BUT EACH TIME THEY CAME BACK TO NORFOLK IT WAS LIKE THEY HAD COME HOME TO A MORTUARY. MOMMA AND POPPA WOULD GO TO BEN'S ROOM AND SIT BY THE HOUR LOOKING AT HIS SCHOOL PICTURES AND TROPHIES AND READ AND REREAD HIS LETTERS.

I DON'T THINK THEY WERE EVER THE SAME AFTER BEN DIED. IT SEEMED THEY STARTED GROWING OLD THE DAY THEY HEARD THE NEWS. FUNNY, UP TILL THEN I NEVER THOUGHT OF MY PARENTS GROWING OLD.

SOME COMMUNIST FRIENDS OF BEN'S CAME TO OUR HOUSE AND TOLD MOMMA AND POPPA THAT BEN'S DEATH SHOULD NOT BE IN VAIN. THEY PERSUADED THEM TO ATTEND A RALLY FOR LOYALIST SPAIN IN WASHINGTON. I WENT UP WITH THEM. BEN WAS EXTOLLED AND THEY GLORIFIED MOMMA AND POPPA FOR GIVING A SON TO THE CAUSE OF ANTI-FASCISM. WE ALL

REALIZED THEY WERE JUST USING US AND WE NEVER ATTENDED ANOTHER OF THOSE MEETINGS.

I GUESS MY BROTHER BEN WAS THE MOST IMPORTANT PERSON IN MY LIFE.

I REMEMBER SO MANY THINGS ABOUT HIM.

HALE'S UNDERTAKING PARLOUR HAD THIS BIG BOAT THAT HELD MAYBE FORTY OR FIFTY PEOPLE. YOU COULD RENT IT FROM THEM FOR $15.00 A DAY AND GET UP A BIG PARTY AND CRUISE UP THE CHESAPEAKE. EVEN THOUGH I WAS THE KID BROTHER HE ALWAYS INCLUDED ME. I HAD MY FIRST DRINK OF WHISKY ON ONE OF THE SCHOOL PARTIES. I GOT SICKER THAN HELL.

ON THE BACK END OF OUR LOT WE HAD A GARAGE AND OVER THAT, A LITTLE APARTMENT. THE PEOPLE WHO OWNED THE HOUSE BEFORE US HAD A COLOURED COUPLE LIVING IN IT. BUT MOMMA LIKED TO DO HER OWN HOUSEWORK AND ONLY HAD A CLEANING LADY ONCE A WEEK, SO WE USED THE APARTMENT AS A KIND OF HIDEAWAY.

WHEN BEN WAS FLYING HE'D PLAY SEMI-PRO FOOTBALL ON SUNDAYS AT THE OLD LEAGUE PARK FOR THE NORFOLK CLANCY'S. MAN, I'LL NEVER FORGET THE DAY HE MADE TWO TOUCHDOWNS AGAINST RED GRANGE'S VISITING ALL-STARS AND CUT GRANGE DOWN ON THREE OR FOUR OPEN FIELD TACKLES. BEN WAS REALLY SOMETHING. MOST OF THE KIDS DID THEIR NECKING ON MAYFLOWER DRIVE ALONG THE LAFAYETTE RIVER, BUT WE HAD THE APARTMENT AND WE SURE HAD SOME GREAT PARTIES.

THE YARD BY THE GARAGE WAS PRETTY BIG AND WE'D FUNGO FLIES AND GROUNDERS TO EACH OTHER. USING THE SIDE OF THE GARAGE AS A BACKSTOP BEN TAUGHT ME HOW TO PITCH. HE PAINTED A TARGET OF A BATTER ON THE WALL AND MADE ME THROW AT IT UNTIL MY ARM NEARLY FELL OFF. HE WAS REALLY PATIENT.

HE'D PUT HIS HAND ON MY SHOULDER AND TALK BASEBALL TO ME. WHEN BEN TOUCHED ME IT WAS LIKE BEING TOUCHED BY GOD.

'LOOK, ABE,' BEN WOULD SAY, 'YOU'RE NOT GOING TO DAZZLE ANYBODY WITH YOUR SPEED OR BLOW THEM OUT OF THE

BOX. SO YOU HAVE TO PITCH WITH YOUR JEWISH HEAD.' I WAS TAUGHT A VARIETY OF SLOW CURVES AND CHANGE-UPS AND A SLIDER. IN THOSE DAYS A SLIDER WAS CALLED A SCREWBALL. WELL, BEN TAUGHT ME TO BE A REAL JUNK PITCHER WITH JUST ENOUGH MUSTARD ON THE FAST BALL TO KEEP THE BATTER HONEST. I WAS NEVER AN OVERPOWERING TYPE PITCHER, BUT BEN TAUGHT ME ENOUGH TO BE FIRST STRING FOR MAURY HIGH AND GET A SCHOLARSHIP TO THE UNIVERSITY OF NORTH CAROLINA. OFTEN WE'D PLAY TILL DARK, THEN KEEP GOING UNDER THE STREET LIGHTS.

THERE WAS A DIRT AIRFIELD WHERE GRANBY STREET CURVED AROUND THE BEND NEAR THE CEMETERY AT DEAD MAN'S CORNER ON THE WAY TO THE BEACH AT OCEAN VIEW. THE WHOLE AREA WAS IN TRUCK FARMS, AND YOU HAD TO MAKE YOUR APPROACHES RIGHT OVER THE TOMBSTONES. IT'S ALL PART OF THE NAVAL AIR BASE NOW BUT ONE OR TWO OF THE OLD BUILDINGS REMAIN. ANYHOW, THERE WAS THIS RICH JEWISH DEPARTMENT STORE OWNER NAMED JAKE GOLD-STEIN, WHO WAS A BIG FAN OF BEN'S AND OWNED A COUPLE OF AIRPLANES, ONE A WACO TAPERWING. IT COULD SHAKE YOUR TEETH OUT BUT COULD YOU EVER DO STUNTS IN IT. BEN STARTED FLYING THE WACO, AND I STARTED HANGING AROUND THE FIELD.

BEN WAS THE ONLY JEWISH PILOT EXCEPT FOR MR. GOLD-STEIN BUT EVERYONE RESPECTED HIM. HE WAS A LOT LIKE THEM. YOU KNOW, A BREED APART SO BEING JEWISH DIDN'T MATTER, AND WE DIDN'T HAVE TO GO THROUGH ALL THOSE FIGHTS AGAIN.

JAKE GOLDSTEIN SPONSORED BEN AT A LOT OF AIR RACES, AND HE'D GO OFF AND BARNSTORM AND STUNT FLY AT FAIRS. WHEN HE WAS GONE I'D RUN ERRANDS FOR THE PILOTS AND CHOCK DOWN PLANES AND THEN I GOT TO TINKERING WITH ENGINES AND ONCE IN A WHILE I'D GET MY REWARD. A PLANE RIDE.

BEN WOULD LET ME TAKE THE STICK AND LIKE EVERY-THING ELSE, HE TAUGHT ME HOW TO FLY. BUT WHEN HE WAS GONE SOME OF THE OTHER GUYS REALLY SHOOK ME UP. I KNOW THEY WERE JUST CLOWNING, BUT THEY'D START

LOOPING AND SNAP ROLLING AND WOULDN'T STOP UNTIL I WAS READY TO PASS OUT. I'D STAGGER OUT OF THE COCKPIT AND RUN FOR THE TOILET AND PUKE MY GUTS OUT.

THERE WAS ONE ANTI-SEMITE IN THE CROWD. A GUY BY THE NAME OF STACY. ONCE WHEN BEN WAS GONE HE STUNTED ME UNTIL I FAINTED. SOME OF THE GUYS TOLD BEN ABOUT IT, AND BEN AND I QUIETLY WENT TO WORK. HE TAUGHT ME EVERY TRICK IN THE BOOK.

THEN, ONE DAY BEN SAID, 'HEY, STACY, WHY DON'T YOU GO UP WITH ABE FOR A RIDE. I THINK HE'S ABOUT READY TO SOLO AND MAYBE YOU OUGHT TO CHECK HIM OUT INSTEAD OF ME.' STACY FELL FOR IT. WE GOT INTO THE TWIN COCKPIT WACO, BUT WHAT STACY DIDN'T KNOW WAS THAT HIS SET OF CONTROLS HAD BEEN DISCONNECTED.

BEN GOT EVERYONE OUT TO WATCH. POW! WHAP! ZAM! DID I LET THAT SONOFABITCH HAVE IT. I FLIPPED HER OVER ON HER BACK AND BARREL ROLLED RIGHT OVER THE RUNWAY, THEN ANGLED HER UP SO STEEP SHE POWER STALLED AT THREE G'S RIGHT AT THE HANGAR. I LOOKED BACK. I THOUGHT STACY WOULD SHIT HIS PANTS. ANYHOW, I KEPT IT UP UNTIL HE BEGGED ME TO SET HER DOWN. THEN I LET HIM HAVE A LITTLE MORE, A FEW OUTSIDE LOOPS.

STACY NEVER CAME BACK TO THE AIRSTRIP AGAIN.

I WAS THE YOUNGEST FLYER OF THE GANG AND EVERY-THING WAS GOING FINE UNTIL I HAD TO DO A BELLY LANDING IN A CORNFIELD ONE DAY WHEN THE ENGINE QUIT. I WASN'T SCARED ALL THE WAY IN UNTIL THE PLANE STOPPED DEAD AND NOSED OVER. I GOT SCARED WHEN I CLIMBED OUT AND STARTED CRYING, 'PLEASE DON'T TELL MOMMA AND POPPA.'

I WAS BANGED UP REAL GOOD AND TOLD A WHOPPING LIE ABOUT FALLING OFF THE ROOF OF THE GARAGE, BUT THEY LEARNED THE TRUTH FROM AN INSURANCE ADJUSTER AND INVESTIGATORS.

JESUS, WAS POPPA MAD!

'IF YOU WANT TO BREAK YOUR GOD-DAMNED NECK, BEN, THAT'S FINE BY ME, BUT WHEN YOU TAKE A SENSITIVE CHILD LIKE ABE AND MAKE A GANGSTER OUT OF HIM, I'M GOING TO FORBID IT!'

MY POPPA, GOD REST HIS SOUL, HARDLY EVER FORBID ANY-

THING IN HIS LIFE. HIS WAS THE FIRST BAKERY TO UNION-
IZE WITHOUT A STRIKE OR BLOODSHED JUST BECAUSE HE
WAS A LIBERAL THINKER. THE OTHER BAKERY OWNERS WERE
READY TO LYNCH HIM, BUT POPPA DIDN'T SCARE EASILY. AND
HE WAS THE FIRST TO HIRE A COLOURED BAKER. A LOT OF
PEOPLE MIGHT FORGET ABOUT HOW MUCH GUTS IT TOOK
TO DO THAT IN THOSE DAYS.

WELL, I DIDN'T FLY FOR A LONG TIME AFTER THAT. NOT
UNTIL BEN GOT KILLED IN SPAIN. THEN I HAD TO FLY AND
POPPA UNDERSTOOD.

I GUESS WHAT I REMEMBER MOST ABOUT MY BROTHER BEN
WERE THOSE QUIET DAYS WE JUST HORSED AROUND. MAYBE
WE'D GO TO THE MARSH BEHIND J. E. B. STUART SCHOOL AND
CATCH A COUPLE OF FROGS. THERE WOULD ALWAYS BE KIDS
FROM THE TURNEY HOME THERE AND WE'D HAVE FROG RACES
... OR MAYBE WE'D BOWL A FEW GAMES OF DUCKPINS AT
THE OLD BUSH STREET ALLEY. IT WAS THE ONE THING I WAS
BETTER AT THAN BEN.

BEST OF ALL WERE THE TIMES AROUND THE CREEK. WE'D
GET UP EARLY IN THE MORNING AND TAKE OUR BICYCLES
DOWN TO THE DOCKS AND BUY US A WATERMELON FOR A
NICKEL. THEY SOLD THEM TO THE KIDS CHEAP BECAUSE THEY
HAD SPLIT IN SHIPMENT.

THEN WE'D BIKE TO THE CREEK. I HAD MY DOG IN THE
FRONT BASKET AND BEN CARRIED THE WATERMELON IN HIS.
WE'D SIT ON THE BANK AND PUT THE WATERMELON IN TO
COOL IT AND WHILE IT WAS COOLING WE'D WALK TO A SMALL
PIER AND FISH FOR SOFT SHELL CRABS. WE'D TIE A PIECE
OF ROTTEN OLD MEAT ON A STRING AND HOLD IT RIGHT ON
THE TOP OF THE WATER AND WHEN A CRAB WENT FOR IT,
BEN WOULD SWOOP IT UP WITH A NET. THOSE CRABS WERE
PRETTY DUMB.

MOMMA DIDN'T KEEP A KOSHER KITCHEN, BUT SHE
WOULDN'T LET US BRING CRABS HOME SO WE'D COOK THEM
ON THE BANK WITH A PIECE OF CORN OR A POTATO AND
WE'D HAVE THE WATERMELON AS DESSERT AND JUST LIE IN
THE GRASS AND LOOK AT THE SKY AND TALK THINGS OVER.

WE TALKED A LOT OF BASEBALL. THAT WAS LONG BEFORE
BEN STARTED FLYING. BETWEEN US WE KNEW THE BATTING

AVERAGE OF EVERY PLAYER IN THE MAJOR LEAGUES. THEY REALLY HAD BALLPLAYERS THEN. JIMMY FOXX AND CARL HUBBELL WERE MY IDOLS. MAYBE BEN WOULD READ A STORY I WAS WRITING.

WELL, WE ALWAYS ATE SO MUCH WE GOT BELLYACHES, AND MOMMA WOULD RAISE HELL BECAUSE WE COULDN'T EAT DINNER.

EVEN WHEN WE GOT OLDER WE'D ALWAYS LIKE TO WANDER DOWN TO THE CREEK TOGETHER. THAT WAS THE FIRST TIME BEN TOLD ME HE WAS GOING TO BE A COMMUNIST.

'IT'S SOMETHING POPPA WILL NEVER UNDERSTAND. HE DID THINGS HIS WAY WHEN HE WAS A KID. HE LEFT HOME TO WORK IN THE SWAMPS IN PALESTINE. WELL, I CAN'T DO THINGS THE WAY HE DID THEM.'

BEN HURT FOR THE COLOURED PEOPLE, AND HE FELT COMMUNISM WAS THE ONLY ANSWER. HE USED TO TALK ABOUT THE DAY THEY WOULD HAVE EQUALITY, AND GUYS LIKE JOSH GIBSON AND SATCHEL PAIGE WOULD BE PLAYING IN THE MAJORS AND THERE WOULD BE COLOURED SALES PEOPLE AT RICE'S AND SMITH AND WELTON'S DEPARTMENT STORES, AND THEY'D BE ABLE TO EAT IN THE SAME RESTAURANTS AND NOT HAVE TO RIDE ON THE BACK OF THE BUS, AND THEIR KIDS WOULD BE ABLE TO GO TO WHITE SCHOOLS, AND THEY'D BE ABLE TO LIVE IN WHITE NEIGHBOURHOODS. IN THE MIDDLE OF THE NINETEEN-THIRTIES, BEN'S DREAMS SEEMED PRETTY HARD TO BELIEVE.

I REMEMBER THE LAST TIME I SAW BEN.

HE LEANED OVER MY BED AND TAPPED ME ON THE SHOULDER, THEN HELD HIS FINGER TO HIS LIPS, AND HE WHISPERED SO AS NOT TO WAKE UP MOMMA AND POPPA.

'I'M GOING AWAY, ABE.'

I WAS HALF ASLEEP AND GROGGY AND DIDN'T UNDERSTAND AT FIRST. I THOUGHT HE WAS GOING ON A FLYING TRIP. 'WHERE YOU GOING?'

'YOU'VE GOT TO KEEP IT A SECRET.'

'SURE.'

'I'M GOING TO SPAIN.'

'TO SPAIN?'

'TO FIGHT FRANCO. I'M GOING TO FLY FOR THE LOYALISTS.'

I GUESS I BEGAN TO CRY. BEN SAT ON THE EDGE OF THE BED AND HUGGED ME. 'REMEMBER SOME OF THE THINGS I TAUGHT YOU AND MAYBE THEY'LL HELP YOU GET ALONG. BUT MAINLY, POPPA IS RIGHT. YOU STICK TO YOUR WRITING.'

'I DON'T WANT YOU TO GO, BEN.'

'I'VE GOT TO, ABE. I'VE GOT TO DO SOMETHING ABOUT ALL THIS.'

STRANGE, ISN'T IT? I WASN'T ABLE TO CRY AFTER BEN'S DEATH. I WANTED TO, BUT I COULDN'T. THAT HAPPENED MUCH LATER, WHEN I DECIDED TO WRITE A BOOK ABOUT MY BROTHER BEN.

I TOOK THE SCHOLARSHIP TO THE UNIVERSITY OF NORTH CAROLINA BECAUSE OF THEIR JOURNALISM COLLEGE, AND THOMAS WOLFE AND ALL THE OTHER WRITERS, REALIZING TWO OF MY AMBITIONS, TO WRITE AND TO PLAY BALL. CHAPEL HILL HAD THE MOST BEAUTIFUL CAMPUS YOU COULD IMAGINE.

I WAS THE ONLY JEWISH BALLPLAYER ON THE FRESHMAN TEAM AND YOU'VE GOT TO KNOW SOMEONE WAS ALWAYS TRYING TO STICK A FAST BALL IN MY EAR OR CUT ME IN HALF WITH THEIR SPIKES.

THE TEAM COACH WAS A WASHED-OUT RED NECK, WHO NEVER GOT HIGHER THAN THE B LEAGUES AND EVEN CHAWED HIS TOBACCO LIKE A BUSHER. HE DIDN'T LIKE ME. HE NEVER MADE ANY ANTI-SEMITIC REMARKS TO MY FACE BUT THE WAY HE SAID, 'ABIE,' WAS ENOUGH. I WAS THE BUTT OF ALL THE LOCKER ROOM JOKES AND HEARD THEIR CRUEL REMARKS SUPPOSEDLY OUT OF EARSHOT.

I WAS THE BEST FRESHMAN PITCHER IN THE CONFERENCE, AND WHEN THEY ALL LEARNED I COULD HANDLE MYSELF OFF AND ON THE FIELD, THANKS TO BEN, I STARTED GETTING ALONG. EVEN THAT SONOFABITCH OF A COACH KNEW HE'D BETTER TREAT ME TENDER BECAUSE WITHOUT ME THAT BUNCH OF MACKERELS WOULD BE AT THE BOTTOM OF THE STANDINGS.

THE TEAM HUSTLED FOR ME BUT IT WAS THE OPPOSITION THAT GOT TO ME. YOU SEE, I LOOKED EASY TO HIT, BUT I WASN'T. I PLAYED SOME PRETTY GOOD SEMI-PRO BALL IN

NORFOLK AGAINST A LOT OF GUYS WHO HAD ONCE BEEN PROFESSIONAL PLAYERS AND HELL, THESE COLLEGE FRESH-MEN WERE A BUNCH OF WILD ASS SWINGERS ALWAYS SHOOT-ING FOR THE FENCES. THEY CROAKED WITH FRUSTRATION, WHEN THEY COULDN'T HIT MY JUNK AND SOFT STUFF. AFTER I SAW THEM SWING A COUPLE OF TIMES I USUALLY HAD THEM EATING OUT OF MY HAND.

ANYHOW, MY HEAD BECAME THE BIGGEST TARGET IN THE CONFERENCE. IN THE FIRST FOUR GAMES—I WON THEM ALL BY SHUTOUTS—I WAS HIT BY OPPOSING PITCHERS SIX TIMES. FORTUNATELY I CAUGHT THEM ALL IN THE LEGS AND RIBS. BUT NONE OF THEM COULD MAKE ME BACK AWAY AT THE PLATE. I GUESS YOU MIGHT SAY I DARED THEM TO HIT ME.

'ABIE,' OLD RED NECK SAID, 'YOU'RE A RIGHT-HANDED PITCHER AND A LEFT-HANDED HITTER. WHEN YOU CROWD THE PLATE YOU'RE EXPOSING YOUR PITCHING ARM. I DON'T WANT YOU TO BE NO HERO. DON'T CROWD THE PLATE. YOU'RE BEING PAID TO PITCH, NOT HIT.'

HELL, I KNEW I WAS A BANJO HITTER. LOUD SINGLES AND AN OCCASIONAL DOUBLE, BUT I HUNG IN THERE. I GUESS IT HAD TO HAPPEN. ONE DAY A STRONG-BACKED SCATTER-ARMED LEFTY FROM DUKE CAUGHT ME WITH A BLAZER RIGHT ABOVE MY ELBOW AND BUSTED IT.

WHEN I CAME OUT OF THE CAST, I EXERCISED UNTIL I CRIED. THE DAMAGE WASN'T PERMANENT, BUT I COULDN'T REGAIN MY PINPOINT CONTROL. ALL THOSE BALLS I THREW AT THE GARAGE DOOR, ALL THE DAYS OF CATCH WITH BEN WERE DOWN THE DRAIN. THE ATHLETIC DEPARTMENT KINDLY INFORMED ME THAT MY SCHOLARSHIP WASN'T AVAILABLE ANY LONGER.

POPPA WANTED ME TO STAY IN COLLEGE, BUT I WAS GET-TING THE FEELING THAT YOU CAN'T LEARN TO WRITE FROM COLLEGE PROFESSORS. ESPECIALLY PROFESSORS WHO DIDN'T KNOW MY BROTHER BEN, OR ANYTHING ABOUT THE THINGS I WANTED TO WRITE. AND MY BASEBALL CAREER WAS OVER, WHICH WAS NO GREAT LOSS.

I QUIT AFTER MY FRESHMAN YEAR AND AFTER NAGGING A LOT OF NEWSPAPERS I WAS HIRED BY THE VIRGINIA PILOT AS THE AVIATION EDITOR AT THIRTY BUCKS A WEEK. AT NIGHT I

WROTE FOR THE PULP MAGAZINES LIKE 'DOC SAVAGE' AND 'DIME WESTERN' FOR A PENNY A WORD UNDER THE NAME OF HORACE ABRAHAM.

AND THEN ONE DAY I GOT TIRED OF THE PULPS AND BEGAN TO WORK ON MY NOVEL, THE ONE ABOUT BEN.

THREE

David Shawcross was more than a publisher. He was an editor of near legendary proportions running what was tantamount to a one-man house. He had emerged from the ranks of the English publishing dynasty, starting as errand boy at five shillings a week and working up to editor in chief over a period of two decades.

When he was twenty-one Shawcross headed the popular publication division for the notable sum of thirty shillings a week. In order to exist he devilled on the side synopsizing incoming manuscripts for other publishers.

David Shawcross survived all of this through sheer brilliant editorial talent. He refused to become a company henchman although named to the board.

Shawcross quit at a time of his own choosing and began his own small publishing firm.

Shawcross rarely published more than a dozen books a year but each carried a special merit and it seemed that once a year one of his books dented the best-seller lists. Good writers were attracted to the house because of its quality reputation and the desire to have David Shawcross as their editor.

As a small publisher he had to stay afloat through new talent, which not only required sharp instincts but endless digging. Americans were the most popular writers in the

110

world, but he was unable to bid against the large British firms for them. He did it in another way.

By astute analysis he knew that the major American editors ran on a treadmill that gave them little or no time to pursue and develop new talent and, moreover, no American publisher had an adequate system of covering unsolicited manuscripts or nursing along a promising talent.

The senior editors were consumed with manuscripts of their published writers plus a never ending round of sales conferences, making contracts, swimming the sea of cocktail parties, giving lectures, attending the necessary Broadway plays, and entertaining visiting 'firemen'. Junior editors had nearly no power to push a promising manuscript. Furthermore, the pressurized atmosphere of New York generally led to two or three martinis at lunch and watered down any desire to delve into unpublished manuscripts from unknown authors. David Shawcross commented that publishing was the only business in the world that did nothing to perpetuate itself. Every publisher had a history of allowing eventual best-sellers to slip through his hands, mainly through stupidity.

Somewhere in every sludge pile there was a publishable book or a potential author who needed a hand to 'cross the line'. So he made an annual trip to America and dug. In a decade Shawcross discovered a half dozen new American authors including the sensational Negro James Morton Linsey, who became a major literary figure.

Abraham Cady's manuscript sat on an agent's desk on a day he was visited by David Shawcross. It had been taken on by the agent on the recommendation of one of his authors, who was a columnist on the *Virginia Pilot*, where Abe worked as aviation editor. The book had been rejected seven times for seven different reasons.

That night at the Algonquin Hotel, Shawcross arranged a half dozen pillows around his back, adjusted the lamp, and laid out an array of tobacco. He perched his specs on his nose and balanced the blue-covered manuscript on his belly. As he turned the pages he dribbled ashes down his front, an absent-minded smoker of cigars, who left a tell-

111

tale calling card of matches, ashes, burn holes, and an occasional flash fire in a wastebasket. At four o'clock in the morning he closed the manuscript of Abraham Cady's *The Brothers*. There were tears in his eyes.

Abe drew a deep breath as he entered the lobby of the Algonquin Hotel, that famed panelled domain of writers and actors. His voice was shaky as he asked for Mr. Shawcross's suite.

Abe knocked on the door of 408.

'Please come in.' A plump, ruddy-cheeked tailored Englishman took his raincoat and hung it up. 'Why, you're no more than a boy,' he said as he plopped into a high-backed chair with the manuscript spread on the coffee table before him. He thumbed through page after page, dripping a few ashes, brushing them off, then looked at the lad glued to the corner of the sofa and snatched off his glasses with a deliberate gesture.

'There's a million would-be writers in this world to every writer,' he said, 'because they're thick-headed and too much in love with their own words to listen. Now, I think what you've got here shows promise but it needs work.'

'I came to listen, Mr. Shawcross. I'll try not to be thick-headed but maybe I am, I don't know.'

Shawcross smiled. Cady had his own mind, all right.

'I'll spend a few days working with you. The rest will be up to you.'

'Thank you, sir. I got some time off from the paper in case it was needed.'

'I am going to caution you, young Cady, that I've tried this many times and rarely succeeded. Most writers resent criticism and those who don't mind and seem to understand what I'm driving at lack the ability to comprehend and translate it into publishable material. It's all very, very difficult.'

'You'd better believe I'm going to make it,' Abe said.

'Very well. I've booked a room for you down the hall. Unpack your things and let's have a go at it.'

For Abraham Cady, it was a luxurious experience. David Shawcross showed why he was one of the world's best editors. Not to write through Cady's pen but to get the best out of Cady. Basic story-telling was the key most authors never learn. Get the hero up a tree and cut the limb behind him. Pace. Stopping a chapter at an exquisite instance of suspense. Overwriting, the cardinal curse of all new authors. Underwriting ... throwing away in two lines a situation that could be milked for several chapters. It is all right to lecture as long as you lecture subtly but never let a speech interfere with the flow of the story.

And the key trick that few novelists know. A novelist must know what his last chapter is going to say and one way or another work toward that last chapter. Too many writers start with a good idea and carry it through the first chapters, then fall apart because they had no idea where the top of the mountain was in the first place.

At the end of three days, Abraham Cady had listened carefully and questioned without anger. Abe returned to Norfolk and began his rewrite. This, Shawcross told him, the rewriting and rewriting, separated the authors from the would-be authors.

When a young man sets sail on the sea of authorship he is alone with little knowledge of the winds and tides and swells and storms. There are so many questions that can only be answered by persistence. And he went through it again, the awful loneliness, the exhaustion, the rare instances of exhilaration. And his book was done.

'Abe,' Morris called over the phone. 'There's a cablegram for you.'

'Read it, Poppa.'

'O.K. It says, "Manuscript received and read. Well done. I will be pleased to publish it straight away. My regards and congratulations. Signed, David Shawcross." '

The Brothers by Abraham Cady had an excellent reception in England. Old Shawcross had come up with another of his sleepers. It was a simple story, the author was not finely polished, but he struck at the heart. The novel said that because the Western Allies had betrayed Loyalist Spain there would be a great war. The price of diplomatic obscenity would be paid in the blood of millions of English, French, and Americans.

In America *The Brothers* was published by a firm who had originally rejected it (on the grounds it had nothing important to say) and it received an even greater acclaim, for it was published on the eve of the Second World War.

FOUR

FROM THE TIME OF THE SELLOUT AT MUNICH POPPA TRIED EVERYTHING TO GET THE RELATIVES OUT OF POLAND BUT IT WAS IMPOSSIBLE. IN ADDITION TO HIS FATHER AND TWO BROTHERS THERE WERE SOME THIRTY OTHER COUSINS AND AUNTS AND UNCLES. AND THEN GERMANY ATTACKED POLAND. IT WAS A NIGHTMARE. FOR A SHORT TIME WE BREATHED EASIER, WHEN THE SOVIET UNION TOOK THE EASTERN PART OF POLAND WHICH HELD THE TOWN OF PRODNO. THEN THAT HOPE DIED WHEN GERMANY ATTACKED RUSSIA AND PRODNO FELL INTO GERMAN HANDS.

POPPA'S ATTITUDE ABOUT FASCISM CHANGED. BEN'S DEATH AND THE FEAR FOR HIS FAMILY TURNED HIM INTO A MILITANT. I KNEW IT WOULD BE TERRIBLE FOR THEM WHEN I DECIDED TO GO TO WAR, BUT I COULDN'T WAIT.

IN THE FALL OF 1941 I ENLISTED IN THE ROYAL CANADIAN AIR FORCE IN ORDER TO GET TO ENGLAND AND JOIN THE EAGLE SQUADRON OF AMERICAN VOLUNTEERS. LIKE BEN'S LACALLE SQUADRON IT WAS A HELL-BENT GANG, BLAKESLEE, GENTILE, CHESLEY PETERSON, AND A LOT OF OTHERS WHO MADE NAMES AS FIGHTER PILOTS. FUNNY PART OF IT WAS THAT MANY OF THEM HAD WASHED OUT OF THE AMERICAN ARMY

AIR CORPS FOR INABILITY TO FLY.

POPPA MADE A SMALL PROTEST ARGUING THAT AMERICA WOULD SOON BE IN THE WAR SO WHY SHOULD I GO OUT SPORTING FOR TROUBLE. MOMMA WAS WORSE. SHE FEARED SHE WOULD END UP LOSING BOTH OF HER SONS. THEY GAVE IN. POPPA CONFIDED THAT HE WAS PROUD AND MOMMA SAID THINGS LIKE, 'TRY TO BE CAREFUL AND DON'T BE A HERO.'

I WAS PRETTY SCARED WHEN I KISSED THEM GOOD-BYE AND BOARDED THE TRAIN FOR TORONTO. A FEW MONTHS AFTER I STARTED TRAINING AS A SPITFIRE PILOT, AMERICA WAS ATTACKED AT PEARL HARBOR.

August 19, 1942

Seven thousand Canadian and British Commandos poured ashore at the French beach resort of Dieppe on a reconnaissance raid to test the German coastal defences.

Engineers moving behind the infantry reached and spiked some large German guns but the operation ran into serious trouble quickly. One flank was hit by a German flotilla and in the centre Canadian tanks were hung up on the sea wall, and then the German counter-attack turned the raid into a disaster.

Overhead, a blizzard of Spitfires and Messerschmitts raged in a massive dogfight while other allied planes came in low to cover the disaster on the beach. Among them were the American Eagles and their youngest pilot, twenty-two-year-old Abraham Cady flying his fifth mission.

As the planes ran low on fuel and ammunition they streaked back to England to refuel and load and return to the action. Abe came back to Dieppe on his third sortie of the day as the airmen desperately attempted to stall the German counter-attack.

Working at treetop level he made pass after pass at a German company crawling out of the woods. With communications largely broken and squadrons scattered all over the sky it became increasingly difficult to warn comrades in trouble. They were all on their own.

Abe swooped down on a bridge and sprayed it clean of the enemy, when a trio of Messerschmitts pounced on him from the cover of a cloud. He peeled off deftly to evade and just as he felt he had slipped away his plane shuddered violently under the impact of a string of machine-gun bullets. The controls jerked his arms half out of their sockets, and he started to spin. Abe muscled her back into control, but she veered crazily like a toy glider in a wind-storm.

JESUS H. CHRIST ON A CRUTCH! MY TAIL'S SHOT UP. DITCH HER? HELL NO, NOT OVER WATER. SHAG ASS FOR ENGLAND. LORD, GIVE ME THIRTY MINUTES.

Abe jockeyed his swerving craft a few hundred feet over the Channel racing for England. Fifteen minutes to land, ten . . .

'Zenith, Zenith, this is Dog Two Dog on red alert. I'm shot up.'

'Hello, Dog Two Dog. This is Zenith. What are your intentions?'

SONOFABITCH!

A Messerschmitt came up behind Abe. Using every ounce of his strength he pulled the nose of his plane up and into a deliberate stall. The startled German was unable to duplicate the manoeuvre and passed beneath him. Abe let her dive and pressed the triggers.

'I've got him! I've got him!'

HANG ON. THANK GOD . . . COAST OF ENGLAND. CHRIST, I CAN'T HOLD MY ALTITUDE. EASY BABY, EASY, YOU'RE RIPPING MY ARMS OUT.

He veered at the mainland at a sharp angle.

'Hello, Dog Two Dog. This is Drewerry. We see you now. We're advising you to ditch.'

'I can't. I'm too low to jump. I'm going to have to land her.'

'Cleared to land.'

The sirens at Drewerry set off a scramble of activity. Fire wagons and an ambulance and a rescue squad inched up the apron next to the runway as the wounded bird augered in.

'Poor devil, he's really out of control.'

'Hang on there, Yank.'

BOY, I DO NOT LIKE THIS ANGLE. I DO NOT LIKE IT AT ALL.

116

COME ON, SWEETHEART, LINE UP WITH THAT RUNWAY. THAT'S
A GOOD GIRL. NOW JUST HOLD IT.

Three hundred, two hundred, cut engine, glide, glide.

'Look at that lad fly!'

COME ON, GROUND, LET ME FEEL YOU. COME ON, GROUND.
OH BOY, DOES THAT FEEL ... JESUS! MY FUCKING LANDING
GEAR IS BUSTED.

Abe pulled up his landing gear and set her down on her
belly. The Spitfire careened off the runway with sparks
flying. At the last instant he veered away from a barracks
and tore for the woods, then mangled to a halt in the trees.
The sirens screamed and bore down on him. Abe shoved
the canopy back and crawled out on the wing. Then after a
beat of silence a terrible explosion was followed by billow-
ing flames!

FIVE

OH MY GOD! I'M DEAD! I KNOW I'M DEAD! GOD! I CAN'T
SEE! I CAN'T MOVE! MY HEAD IS BLURRED!

'Help me!' Abe cried.

'Lieutenant Cady,' a woman's voice penetrated the darkness, 'can you hear me?'

'Help me,' he cried, 'where am I? What's happened to
me?'

'Lieutenant Cady,' the voice said again. 'If you hear me,
please say so.'

'Yes,' he gasped.

'I'm Sister Grace, a nurse, and you're in the RAF Hospital near Bath. You've been badly hurt.'

'I'm blind. Oh God, I'm blind!'

'Will you try to get control of yourself so we can speak?'

'Touch me so I know you're here.'

He forced himself to gain control.

'You've undergone a serious operation,' Sister Grace said, 'and you're all bandaged up. Don't be frightened because you can't see or move. Let me go and get the doctor, and he'll explain everything to you.'

'Please don't go away for long.'

'I'll be right back. You must remain calm now.'

He sucked in air deeply and quivered in fear. His heart raced to urgent footsteps he could hear coming toward him.

'Woken up, have you,' a commanding British voice said. 'I'm Dr. Finchly.'

'Tell me, Doctor, tell me if I'm blind.'

'No,' the doctor answered. 'You've had quite a bit of sedation and your mind is apt to be rather fuzzy. Are you able to comprehend?'

'Yes, I'm a little cuckoo, but I understand.'

'Very well, then,' Finchly said, sitting on the edge of the bed. 'You've lost the sight of your right eye, but we're going to be able to save the other one.'

'Are you sure?'

'Yes, we're quite certain of it.'

'What happened?'

'Let me explain it to you in simple terms. Your aircraft exploded shortly after you ran into the woods. You were crawling on the wing at the time and at the instant of explosion your hands went up over your face to protect it.'

'I remember that much.'

'The backs of your hands took most of the shock and were severely burned. Third degree burns. Now, you have four tendons on each hand like rubber bands to each finger. These may be damaged. If the burns don't heal properly we will have to do a skin graft and if the tendons have been damaged we'll do tendon grafts. Do you understand me so far?'

'Yes, sir.'

'In any event we will be able to restore full use of both hands. It may take time, but we're very, very successful

118

with both skin and tendon grafts.'

'What about my eyes?' he whispered.

'With the explosion, some minute fragments hit both your eyes perforating your cornea. The cornea is a thin membrane that covers the eye. Now, each eye is filled with a substance that appears somewhat like egg albumen that keeps it inflated like air in a tyre. Your right eye was deeply penetrated, the fluid leaked and the entire eyeball collapsed.

'As for the other eye, everything was intact except for the perforation of the cornea. We had to replace it with substitute cornea. The way we did this was to dissect the upper membrane of your eyelid and cover the eye with it, stitching it to the bottom of the lid. The stitches are thinner than a strand of human hair.'

'When can I know if I can see?'

'Well, I promise you, you have vision in your left eye but there are two problems you're going to have to face up to. A fatty embolism can form from the damage to your hands and move up to your eye and destroy further tissue. Secondly, you are suffering from a rather severe concussion from the blast which would put normal vision out of focus. We'll allow you to see for a few minutes each day, when we change bandages and treat your eye and hands.'

'O.K.,' Abe said, 'I'll be good . . . and thanks, Doctor.'

'Quite all right. Your publisher, Mr. Shawcross, has been waiting here for almost three days.'

'Sure,' Abe said.

'Well, Abe,' Shawcross said, 'they said you did some fancy flying to get back across the Channel and that was quite a trick getting your landing gear up and avoiding the barrack.'

'Yeah, I'm a hell of a flyer.'

'Is it all right if I smoke, Doctor.'

'Certainly.'

Abe liked the smell of Shawcross's cigar. It reminded him of those days in New York, when they worked day and night on his manuscript.

'My parents know about this?'

'I induced them not to inform your mother and father

until you could send word, personally.'

'Thanks. Jesus, I sure bought the farm.'

'Bought a farm?' Dr. Finchly asked.

'It's an American phrase. It means he got a bashing about.'

'Yes, rather, I'd say.'

Dear Momma and Poppa:

You shouldn't be alarmed because this letter isn't in my handwriting. The reason I'm not personally writing for a while is that I got into a slight accident and burned my hands a little.

Let me assure you I'm otherwise in good health, in a fine hospital, and there is no permanent damage of any kind. Even the food here is good.

I had a little trouble landing my plane and so forth. I probably won't be flying any more because they're so sticky about perfect health.

There's a nice young lady here who takes my letters and she's happy to let me write to you every few days.

Mainly, you're absolutely not to worry for a minute.

Love to Sophie and everyone.

Your devoted son,

Abe

SIX

PATIENCE.

IF I EVER HEAR THAT WORD AGAIN, I'M GOING TO FLIP MY LID. PATIENCE, THAT'S WHAT THEY TELL ME TWENTY TIMES A DAY. PATIENCE.

I LIE FROZEN ON MY BACK IN TOTAL DARKNESS. WHEN THE EFFECT OF THE DRUGS WEARS OFF THE PAINS IN MY HANDS BECOME EXCRUCIATING. I PLAY GAMES. I PLAY OUT A BASEBALL GAME PITCH BY PITCH. I'M THE RED SOX PITCHER. IN ONE GAME I STRUCK OUT THE WHOLE YANKEE LINE-UP. RIZZUTO, GORDON, DICKEY, KELLER. DIMAGGIO WAS LAST. WE GOT TO THREE AND TWO. HE'S DUG IN TO SAVE THE YANKEE REPUTATION. I GIVE HIM A LOT OF MOTION AND DISH UP A SLOW CURVE. IT TAKES GUTS TO THROW THAT PITCH IN SUCH A SITUATION. DIMAGGIO NEARLY BROKE HIS BACK DIVING AFTER IT. NINE STRAIGHT YANKEES. IT'S A FEAT THAT WILL STAND IN THE RECORD BOOKS FOR YEARS.

I THINK ABOUT THE WOMEN I'VE SLEPT WITH. I'M STILL A KID SO A DOZEN ISN'T BAD. BUT I CAN'T REMEMBER MOST OF THEIR NAMES.

I THINK ABOUT BEN. GOD, I MISS BEN. WHAT A WINNER I AM. I WANTED THREE THINGS IN MY LIFE; TO PLAY BALL, TO FLY, AND TO WRITE. TWO OF THEM ARE GONE FOREVER AND HOW CAN I WRITE, WITH MY PECKER?

ANYHOW, THESE PEOPLE HERE ARE REALLY WONDERFUL. THEY TREAT ME LIKE A PORCELAIN DOLL. EVERYTHING I DO BECOMES AN INVOLVED CHORE. IF SOMEONE LEADS ME TO THE BATHROOM AND SETS ME ON THE POT I CAN DO MY BUSINESS BUT THEN SOMEBODY'S GOT TO WIPE ME. I CAN'T EVEN AIM TO TAKE A LEAK. I'VE GOT TO SIT LIKE A WOMAN. IT'S ABSOLUTELY HUMILIATING.

EVERY DAY THEY LET ME OUT OF MY MUMMY CAGE FOR A FEW MINUTES. MY GOOD EYE IS USUALLY GLUED SHUT. BY THE TIME I GET IT INTO FOCUS THEY'RE WRAPPING ME UP AGAIN.

I KEEP TELLING MYSELF IT COULD BE WORSE. EVERY DAY THE EYE IS LESS BLURRED AND I'M STARTING TO GET SOME MOVEMENT IN MY HANDS.

DAVID SHAWCROSS COMES FROM LONDON ONCE OR TWICE A WEEK. HIS WIFE, LORRAINE, NEVER FAILS TO BRING A PACKAGE OF FOOD. SHE'S AS BAD AS MOMMA. I KNOW IT'S COSTING HER VALUABLE RATION COUPONS, AND I TRY TO TELL HER THEY'RE FEEDING ME LIKE ROYALTY.

HOW I WELCOME THE SMELL OF THAT STINKY CIGAR. SHAWCROSS HAS ALL BUT GIVEN UP PUBLISHING TO WORK FOR THE GOVERNMENT TO NEGOTIATE A BOOK EXCHANGE PROGRAMME WITH THE RUSSIANS. HIS STORIES OF THE PARANOID BEHAVIOUR AT THE SOVIET EMBASSY ARE A RIOT.

MY BUDDIES VISIT ONCE IN A WHILE BUT IT'S A LONG TRIP FOR THEM. THE EAGLE SQUADRON HAS BEEN TRANSFERRED OUT OF THE RAF INTO THE AMERICAN AIR CORPS. SO, I DON'T KNOW WHAT I AM. I'M NOT MUCH USE TO ANYONE, ANYHOW.

A MONTH PASSES. PATIENCE, THEY TELL ME. JESUS, I HATE THAT WORD. THEY'RE GOING TO START SKIN GRAFTS SOON.

THEN SOMETHING HAPPENED AND THE DAYS DIDN'T SEEM SO LONG OR AGONIZING AFTER THAT. HER NAME IS SAMANTHA LINSTEAD, AND HER FATHER IS A SQUIRE WITH AN OLD FAMILY FARM IN THE MENDIP HILLS NOT FAR FROM BATH. SAMANTHA IS TWENTY AND A RED CROSS VOLUNTEER AIDE. AT FIRST SHE CAME IN ON ROUTINE THINGS LIKE TAKING LETTERS AND SPONGING ME OFF. WE GOT TO TALKING A LOT AND PRETTY SOON SHE BROUGHT HER PHONOGRAPH AND SOME RECORDS AND A RADIO SET. SHE'D SPEND A GOOD PART OF THE DAY IN MY ROOM, FEEDING ME, HOLDING MY CIGARETTE, AND SHE READ A LOT TO ME.

CAN A MAN FALL IN LOVE WITH A VOICE?

I NEVER SAW HER. SHE ALWAYS CAME AFTER MY MORNING TREATMENT. ALL I KNEW WAS HER VOICE. I SPENT HALF MY TIME NOW IMAGINING WHAT SHE LOOKED LIKE. SHE INSISTED SHE WAS VERY PLAIN.

ABOUT A WEEK AFTER SHE CAME I WAS ABLE TO TAKE SHORT WALKS WITH HER LEADING ME AROUND THE HOSPITAL GROUNDS. AND THEN, SHE GOT TO TOUCHING ME MORE AND MORE.

122

'Light me up Sam,' Abe said.

Samantha sat near the bed and held the cigarette carefully as he puffed. When she snuffed it out, she slipped her hand through the opening of his pyjamas and rubbed the tips of her fingers over his chest, barely making contact.

'Sam, I've been thinking. Maybe you'd better not come back to see me, any more.' Her hand drew away from him suddenly. 'I don't like the idea of anyone feeling sorry for me.'

'Do you think that's why I come here?'

'You lie in darkness all day and all night and your mind can play tricks. I'm starting to take things more serious than I ought to. You've been a real wonderful person and shouldn't be a victim of my fantasies.'

'Abe. Don't you know how wonderful it is for me to be with you? Maybe when we see each other you won't care for me, but I don't want to change anything now. And you're not going to get rid of me that easily, and you really aren't in much of a condition to do anything about it.'

Samantha's car passed onto the circular driveway of Linstead Hall. The tyres crunched over the gravel and then halted before a small manor house of two centuries ago.

'There's Mommy and Daddy. This is Abe. You can't see too much of him, but his photographs are quite handsome.'

'Welcome to Linstead Hall,' Donald Linstead said.

'Pardon my gloves,' Abe answered, holding up his bandaged hands.

She led him carefully through a wooded land and then found a soft place in a meadow looking down on the manor and she described the scene to him.

'I can smell cows and horses and smoke and all kinds of flowers. It must be beautiful up here. I can't tell one flower from the other.'

'There's heather and roses and the fires are coming from the peat bogs.'

Oh Abe! she thought. I do love you.

123

On the third visit to Linstead Hall the family received the happy news that Abe's eye bandages would be removed for a few hours each day.

Samantha seemed edgy during the walk. In the darkness, one can sense things fiercely. The tone of her voice was different, the vibrations were tense.

It had been a long day and Abe was tired. A male nurse came in from the village to bathe and change him. Afterward he stretched out on the bed, grumbling over his entombed hands. Patience. To be able to shave, to be able to blow my nose, to be able to read.

To be able to see Samantha.

He heard the door open and close and could tell by the turn of the knob it was Samantha.

'I hope I didn't awaken you.'

'No.'

The bed sank as she sat beside him. 'It's going to be a great event when they take those bandages off your eyes. I mean your eye. You've been very brave.'

'Like I had a choice. Well, we sure know what humility is.'

Abe could hear the soft sobs she was trying to stifle. He wanted to reach out for her as he had wanted to a hundred times. What did she feel like? Were her breasts large or small? Was her hair soft? Were her lips sensuous?

'What the hell are you crying for?'

'I don't know.' They both knew. In a sad strange way they had experienced something totally unique and it was going to come to an end and neither of them knew if the ending was final or would ignite a new beginning. Samantha was afraid she would be rejected.

She lay beside him as they had done after their walks, and her fingers unbuttoned his shirt, and she laid her cheek on his chest and then her hands and lips became like whispers all about his body.

'I talked to the doctor,' she said. 'He told me it would be all right,' and she reached between his legs. 'Just be still, I'll do everything.'

She undressed him and flung her own clothing off and

locked the door.

Oh, fantastic darkness! Every sensation was so vivid, the gentle slaps, the kissing of his feet, the feather soft whip of her hair. Samantha was in a controlled frenzy as he succumbed to her.

And then she cried and told him she had never been so happy, and Abe said he was really a better lover but under the circumstances he was glad some part of him worked. And then the love talk became silly, and they laughed because it was really quite funny.

SEVEN

David Shawcross's phone rang angrily. He groped for the bed lamp, yawned his way to a sitting position. 'Good God,' he mumbled, 'it's three in the morning.'

'Hello!'

'Mr. Shawcross?'

'Yes, this is Shawcross.'

'Sergeant Richardson, Military Police attached to the station in Marylebone Lane, sir.'

'Richardson, it's three o'clock in the morning. Get on with it, man.'

'So sorry to disturb you, sir. We've picked up an officer, RAF chap, a Lieutenant Abraham ... C ... A ... D ... Y, Cady.'

'Abe in London?'

'Yes, sir. He was rather intoxicated when we picked him up. Drunk as a lord if you don't mind me saying, sir.'

'Is he all right, Richardson?'

'In a manner of speaking, sir. There was a note pinned to his uniform. Shall I read it?'

'Yes, by all means.'

' "My name is Abraham Cady. If I appear to be drunk, don't be confused. I am having a case of bends due to tunnel work on a secret project and must be decompressed slowly. Deposit my body to David Shawcross, 77 Cumberland Terrace, NW 8." Will you accept him, Mr. Shawcross? Don't want to press charges on the chap, just out of the hospital and all that.'

'Charges. For what?'

'Well, sir, when we got to him he was swimming in the fountain in Trafalgar Square ... nude.'

'Bring the bugger over, I'll take him.'

'So you were a German U-boat, were you now?' Shawcross taunted.

Abe groaned through one more cup of black coffee. At least the British call it coffee. Ugh!

"Flaunting your up-periscope in the middle of our stately fountain. Really, Abraham.'

'Shawcross, put out the goddam cigar. Can't you see I'm dying.'

'More coffee, dear?' Lorraine asked.

'God no. I mean, no thanks.'

She tinkled a bell for the maid and helped her clear the dishes. 'I've got to be trotting off. The queues are still dreadful and I've got to stock up. Our kiddies are coming down from Manchester tomorrow.' She kissed Abe's cheek. 'I do hope you're feeling better, dear.'

When she left, David grumbled. 'I suppose I love my grandchildren as much as the next grandfather, but frankly, they're spoiled little bastards. I keep writing Pam and telling her how dangerous it is here in London but damned if she'll listen. Anyhow, I've been thinking seriously about taking Geoff into the business after the war. Now what's all this nonsense about you and this girl, Pinhead, Greenbed ...'

'Linstead. Samantha Linstead.'

'Are you in love with her or what?'

'I don't know. I've never seen her. I've made love to her,

126

but I've never seen her or touched her.'

'Nothing really strange about that. All lovers are blind in one way or another. I've seen her. She's rather attractive, in an outdoorsy sort of way. Sturdy type.'

'She stopped coming to the hospital when they took the bandages off my eyes. She was afraid I wouldn't like her. I was never so damned miserable in my life. I wanted to go beat the manor house door down and claim her, then I got all choked up, too. Suppose she was a real dog? Suppose she got a good look at me in the daylight and got sober? Stupid, isn't it?'

'Very. Well, you'll have to take a look at each other sooner or later. In the meanwhile do you have any company to forget Samantha with?'

'No, I'm out of touch in London,' Abe said. 'The first four calls I made last night, two were married, one pregnant, and on the fourth call a man answered.'

'Well, let's see,' Shawcross said, diving his pudgy fingers into his vest and fishing out an address book. As he thumbed it he grunted in delight a few times. 'Why don't you meet me for lunch at Mirabelle's at two. We ought to be able to come up with something.'

Abraham Cady, sobered and reassembled, turned Curzon Street all filled with the electricity of wartime London and into the plush sanctuary of Mirabelle's. The maître d' was expecting him. Abe stood a moment and looked over the room to Shawcross's traditional table. He had come up with a redhead. Very British looking. Nice body from what he could see. Didn't look too stupid. Seemed nervous. That was par. Everyone gets nervous before meeting a writer and usually disappointed afterward. They expect nothing but gems to flow from the writer's brilliant mind.

'Ah, Abraham,' Shawcross said, struggling out of his seat. 'Meet Cynthia Greene. Cynthia is a secretary to one of my colleagues in the publishing business and is an admirer of your book.'

Abe took the girl's hand warmly as he always took a woman's hand. It was a bit damp with nerves but otherwise firm. A handshake told so much. He detested the wet limp fish so many women gave. She smiled. The game was on. He sat down.

Nice going, Shawcross, Abe thought.

'Waiter, a little nip of the hair that killed the dog for my friend here.'

'Whisky, over ice,' Abe ordered.

Shawcross commented that ice was barbaric and Abe told about an English girl he knew who drank a pint and a half of Scotch each and every day but would never take ice because she was afraid it would wreck her liver.

Cheers. They sipped and studied the fragile wartime menu. Abe surveyed Miss Greene.

The first thing he liked aside from her general looks and firm handshake was that she was obviously an English lady and kept her mouth shut. All women have volcanoes. Some compulsively erupted from the mouth with unending dribble. Other women kept their volcanoes dormant and exploded them at the right time in the right way. Abe liked quiet women.

The head waiter handed David Shawcross a note. He adjusted his specs and grumbled. 'I know this sounds like an obvious ploy to get you two alone but the Russians have called me. Uncivilized bastards. Try to muddle through without me. Now, don't you try to steal my writer for your house. He's due for a good book, soon.'

They were alone.

'How long have you known Shawcross?' Abe asked.

'Since he began visiting you in the hospital.'

There was no mistaking that voice. 'Samantha?'

'Yes. Abe.'

'Samantha.'

'Mr. Shawcross loves you like a son. He phoned me this morning and told me you cried half the night. I'm sorry I ran. Well, here I am. I know you're terribly disappointed.'

'No ... no ... you're just lovely.'

EIGHT

From a meadow in the Mendip Hills Abe and Samantha watched wave after wave of airplanes flying toward the Continent. The sky was black with them. Lumbering bombers and swarms of fighters. They passed and their sounds faded and the sky was blue. Abe stared pensively down to Linstead Hall.

Samantha felt a sudden chill. She placed her sweater on her shoulders. The flowers bent to the breeze and her soft red hair danced. She went so well with the countryside. Samantha looked as though she were born riding a horse.

The hospital agreed that he could take a furlough as long as he reported for twice weekly treatments. Dr. Finchly also strongly advised Abe to stay out of London. He needed the peace of Linstead Hall. Heather and horse manure. But the daily flights of planes constantly reminded him that there was a war out there.

'So pensive,' Samantha said.

'The war is passing me by,' he said.

'I know you're restless but when all is said and done perhaps you were never meant to be anything but a writer. I know you've a book churning inside you.'

'My hands. They start to hurt after just a few minutes. I may have to have one more operation, yet.'

'Abe, have you ever thought of me being your hands?'

'I don't know if you can write a book that way ... I just don't know.'

'Why don't we try.'

The thought of it brought Abraham Cady to life. It was very awkward at first and difficult to share a novelist's thoughts. Each day he became better able to organize his mind. He learned to dictate until he was capable of pouring out a torrent of words.

The furlough ended. Abe was discharged from the Air

Corps. A farewell bust at the Officers' Club with his old buddies and back to Linstead Hall to write.

Samantha became the silent partner and privileged observer to one of the unique of all human experiences, the writing of a novel. She saw him detach himself from the first world of reality and submerge into the second world of his own creation and wander through it alone. There was no magic. There was no inspiration that people always look for and imagine in the writer. What there was was a relentless plodding requiring a special kind of stamina that makes the profession so limited. Of course there came those moments when things suddenly fell into a natural rhythm and even more rare, that instant of pure flying through creative exhilaration.

But what Samantha witnessed most was the uncertainty, the drain, the emotional downs, the exhaustion. Those times he did not have the strength to eat or undress himself.

David Shawcross stood in the wings, a happy man knowing exactly when to make Abe turn it off with a blast in London. A roaring drunk. A flushing out, and a return to the blank sheet of paper. He told Samantha that Abe had within him the key to greatness on one major premise. He was aware of his weaknesses as a writer as well as his strengths; Shawcross said few writers had the ability of introspection because they were too vain to admit weakness. This was Abraham Cady's power, and he controlled his second novel. He was in his twenties and writing like sixty.

The Jug (a nickname for the P-47 Thunderbolt) was a simple and classical story of men at war. The hero was Major-General Vincent Bertelli, a second generation street fighter of Italian-American descent. An officer in the early thirties he rose quickly in the war that had become air oriented. Bertelli was a relentless and apparently heartless driver who was ready to take heavy losses in dangerous raids on the thesis that 'war was war'.

The general's son, Sal, flew as a squadron commander in his father's command. The deep love between them is camouflaged by what appears to be father/son hatred.

130

General Bertelli orders a raid and places his son's squadron in a suicide position. The news of Sal's death is delivered by Barney, the sole survivor in the Squadron.

Bertelli listens without emotion and is spat upon by Barney.

'You're tired,' the general said, 'I'll forget about this.'

Barney turned on his heel. 'Barney!' the general commanded and he halted. Bertelli wanted desperately to show his son's transfer order and to tell him he pleaded with Sal to quit. His boy had refused despite everyone knowing he had flown himself into exhaustion.

'Never mind,' General Bertelli said.

And suddenly Barney knew. 'I'm sorry, sir. He just had to go on proving himself, like he had no choice.'

'It's a fucking war,' the general answered, 'people are going to get hurt. Get some rest, Barney. You're going up again in a few hours. Big target. U-boat pens.'

The door closed. General Bertelli opened the top drawer of his desk and swallowed a nitroglycerin tablet for the attack that was coming on. 'Sal,' he said, 'I loved you. Why couldn't I tell you.'

'The end,' Abe's hoarse voice rasped. He stood behind Samantha and watched her type those two beautiful last words.

'Oh, Abe,' she cried, 'it's lovely.'

'I need a belt,' he said.

When she left he took her place at the typewriter and pecked out with stiff fingers, 'Dedicated to Samantha with love,' and then the words ... 'will you marry me?'

NINE

Little by little full use of Abe's hands returned. An eye patch covered his deformity. Abraham Cady was a one-eyed, broken winged eagle, but an eagle, nonetheless. After his discharge and with his book, *The Jug*, selling well, he signed on with United Press in London.

London was a vital place, the heartbeat of the free world building up to burst upon the European Continent aware fully of its own importance and rife with the colours of Allied and Empire troops and those of governments in exile. The smoke of German incendiaries had long died out in the gutted centre of London. The nights in the tubes were over but there were still queues, the eternal British queues and sandbags and balloon barrages and blackouts and then the buzz bombs.

Abraham Cady joined a fraternity of those men charged with the mission of telling the story and in these days in London it was a legendary roll call from Quentin Reynolds to Edward R. Murrow on their news beats from the American Embassy to Downing Street to BBC House to the great press artery of Fleet Street.

The Linsteads had traditionally kept a small town house in London in Colchester Mews off Chelsea Square. The mews were once carriage houses and servants quarters behind the stately five-storey homes bordering London's green squares. After the First World War, when horses faded from the scene, the mews were converted into doll house quarters that were particularly attractive to writers, musicians, actors, and visiting squires.

Abe and Samantha moved into the mews after their wedding at Linstead Hall, and he went searching for a part of the war.

At a time and place that distinguished journalism was commonplace Abe Cady was able to carve a distinctive

132

niche as the flyer's correspondent.

From those first floundering days of the Battle of Britain, all of England became a massive airfield. The British owned the night and the American Eighth Air Force mastered the European skies by day with raids deep into Germany now escorted by swarms of Mustang fighters.

Abe flew with the Halifaxes by night and Flying Fortresses by day, and he wrote of a sort of fairyland war of seemingly harmless puffs of smoke down 'flak alley' and the great swirling ballets of the dogfights. He wrote of the blissful numbness of total exhaustion to the lullaby of five thousand droning engines. And blood. A tail or belly gunner cut in half and men struggling to free him from his prison. Of long streams of smoke and crippled birds struggling in a place out of their element to find the earth again. And sentimental songs around the bars, of silent stares at the empty bunks. Of varnished officers poring over blown-up maps of Germany with a crisp detached vernacular. And the view from the sky as their loads of death rained down on miniature sets that were the cities of Germany.

WE'LL BE OVER BERLIN IN A HALF HOUR. THE ARMADA OUTSIDE HAS BLACKENED THE SKY LIKE A SWARM OF LOCUSTS. WE ARE CLOAKED WITH FIGHTER PLANES OF THE WOLF PACK FLYING RAMROD TO ESCORT THE BOMBERS.

A STARTLED COMMUNICATION. 'LOOK OUT, TONY, MESSERS AT SEVEN O'CLOCK.'

A SHORT, WILD DOGFIGHT BELOW US. A SCARLET-NOSED MUSTANG BELCHES SMOKE AND SPIRALS EARTHWARD WITH A MESSERSCHMITT ON HIS TAIL. OUR KID MUST HAVE BEEN GREEN. THE MESSERS ARE NO MATCH FOR THE MUSTANG. THE KRAUT HAD TO BE GOOD TO HAVE SURVIVED THIS LONG. THE MUSTANG ERUPTS. IT'S DONE. NO PARACHUTE.

LATER I LEARNED HE WAS A SECOND YEAR ENGINEERING STUDENT AT GEORGIA TECH. WHAT WILL IT BE LIKE TOMORROW IN ATLANTA WHEN THE CABLEGRAM ARRIVES AND THE LIVES OF A DOZEN PEOPLE FALL TO A GRIEF-STRICKEN WHISPER. HE WAS THE ONLY MALE HEIR. THE ONE WHO WAS GOING TO CARRY THEIR NAME INTO THE NEXT GENERATION.

133

THE KRAUTS HAVE BEEN BEATEN OFF. IT COST FOUR MUS-
TANGS AND TWO BOMBERS. BOMBERS DIE SLOWER. WRITHE
IN AGONY, TWIST AND ROLL HEAVILY. DESPERATE MEN TUG
AT CANOPIES. AND THEN, DISINTEGRATION.

TENSING UP AND ALERT AS WE NEAR BERLIN. ALL EXCEPT
THE CO-PILOT ASLEEP TWISTED LIKE A PRETZEL THAT ONLY
A YOUNG MAN COULD MANAGE. I'M INVITED TO TAKE THE
CONTROLS.

MY HANDS ITCH WITH JOY AS I TAKE THE CONTROLS. THE
BOMBS FLOAT DOWN SLOWLY, DESCENDING LIKE A MANTLE
OF BLACK SNOW AND THEN GREAT GUSTS OF ORANGE BILLOW
FROM THE TORTURED CITY.

I AM SICK AT MY OWN ECSTASY AS OUR BATTERED FLEET
LIMPS BACK. WHY DOES MAN PUT HIS GREATEST ENERGY AND
TALENT INTO DESTRUCTION?

I AM THE WRITER. I MAKE IT ALL A MORALITY PLAY.
WE'RE WHITE UP HERE, LIKE ANGELS. THEY'RE BLACK DOWN
THERE LIKE DEVILS. DEVILS, ROAST IN HELL!

AND THEN I WONDER WHO I KILLED TODAY. AN ENGINEER
LIKE THE BOY FROM GEORGIA, A MUSICIAN, A DOCTOR, OR A
CHILD WHO NEVER EVEN HAD A CHANCE TO ASPIRE. WHAT A
WASTE.

Samantha set the receiver down and grunted down-
heartedly. Her pregnancy had made her ill. She had been
queasy all day. She made her way up the narrow stairs to
the tiny bedroom where Abe lay in sprawled exhaustion.
For a moment she considered ignoring the phone call, but
he would be very angry. She tapped his shoulder.

'Abe.'

'Uhhhh.'

'We just got a call from Wing Commander Parsons at
Breedsford. They want you there by fourteen hundred.'

I smell it, Abe thought. Ten to one they're going for the
ball-bearing works outside Hamburg. It will be one hell of
a show. The night raids were more vivid in their sharp
black and white contrasts. And after their pass, the carpet
of red fires on the burning from the target. Abe popped off
the bed and read his watch. Time for a shave and a bath.

Samantha appeared piqued and drawn. Her whiteness was even more apparent in London. 'You mustn't be late,' she said, 'I'll draw your bath.'

'You'll be all right, won't you, honey. I mean, about taking you out tonight. This raid must be a big one or Parsons wouldn't call.'

'As a matter of fact, I'm not all right. Decent of you to ask, though.'

'O.K., let's have it,' Abe snapped.

'I'd rather you wouldn't speak to me as if I were on the carpet before the colonel's desk.'

Abe grunted and tied on his robe. 'What's wrong, honey?'

'I've been sick every morning for two weeks, but that's to be expected, I suppose. To escape the confinement of these four walls I get to stand in queues for hours on end or dive into the tube for my life ahead of the buzz bombs. And after living on scraps I'm jolly well homesick for Linstead Hall. I suppose it would be bearable if I saw anything of my husband. You crawl in, write your story, and fall flat until the phone rings for the next raid. And those rare evenings you are in London you seem obsessed with shooting the breeze all night with David Shawcross or in some Fleet Street Pub.'

'Finished?'

'Not really. I'm bloody bored and unhappy, but I don't think it means very much to you.'

'Now, just hold on, Samantha. I happen to think we're goddam lucky. With fifty million men and women separated by this war we're plenty lucky to have a few hours together.'

'Perhaps we would be if you weren't on a crusade to make every bombing mission out of England.'

'That's my job.'

'Oh, they all say you love your job. They say you're the best bomber jockey in both air forces.'

'Come off it. They let me take the controls once in a while as a gesture.'

'Not according to Commander Parsons. It's got to be a sign of luck if the old one-eyed eagle leads them in. Steady

135

Abraham, he was known far and wide.'

'My God, Samantha! What in the hell is so hard for you to understand. I hate fascism. I hate Hitler. I hate what the Germans have done to the Jewish people.'

'Abe, you're shouting!' Samantha stiffened, breaking off the assault and quivering and sobbing to blunt male logic. 'It's the loneliness,' she cried.

'Honey, I . . . I don't know what to say. Loneliness is the brother of war and the mother of all writers. He asks his wife to endure it graciously because she will come to know that her ability to endure it can be her greatest gift.'

'I don't understand you, Abe.'

'I know.'

'Well, don't act as if I'm some kind of clod. We have gone through a book together, you know.'

'I didn't have hands so you owned me. Your possession of me was complete. When I had no sight and we made love you were your happiest because your possession was complete then, too. But now I've got my hands and eyes and you don't want to share me or understand what your end of this bargain consists of. It's going to be like this till the end of our lives, Samantha. It will always demand sacrifice and loneliness of both of us.'

'You're great at twisting things to make me look very little.'

'We're just starting out together, honey. Don't make the mistake of standing between me and my writing.'

Samantha returned to Linstead Hall. After all, she was pregnant and life in London wasn't easy. Abe assured her he understood and then he went on with his war.

On D-Day, Ben Cady was born at Linstead Hall. His father, Abraham, wrote at the navigator's desk of a B-24 Liberator sent up from Italy for a saturation raid in conjunction with the invasion.

TEN

There are no J. Milton Mandelbaums, Abe thought. He's only a fiction from a bad Hollywood novel. He's only trying to act like a J. Milton Mandelbaum.

Mandelbaum, the young producing 'genius' of American Global Studios, arrived in London to stir the hearts of man and produce the greatest aviation film of all times based on Abraham Cady's novel, *The Jug*.

He pitched tent in a three bedroom suite at the Savoy; the Oliver Messel Suite wasn't available at the Dorchester because of all the goddam brass and royalty in exile and that crap.

It was stocked to the gunnels with booze and broads and the kinds of things Englishmen had not seen in five years of war.

A 4-F in the draft (ulcers, eye astigmatism, psychosomatic asthma) he conned himself a 'technical war correspondent's' rating and had a Savile Row tailor do him up a half dozen officer's uniforms.

'After all, Abe,' he explained, 'we're all in this thing together.'

Abe suggested that if that was the case it would be good for Milton to fly a few bombing missions for firsthand insight.

'Somebody's got to hold the old fort down here and get the old production rolling,' Milton explained in passing on Abe's kind offer.

Milton always mentioned his own film first, the one which won an Oscar, somehow overlooking the fact it was based on a Hemingway story with the best director and screen writer in Hollywood working on it, and during most of the production he was in the hospital with an ulcer. An assistant (who was fired shortly after the film for disloyalty) had truly done the producing.

There were lengthy dissertations by him on his creative ability, his sincerity, his importance, the women (among them most of the NAME actresses) he had banged, his immaculate taste in all matters, his astute story instinct (if the studio would only get off my back I'd go back to writing. You and me are writers, Abe, we know the importance of the story), his house in Beverly Hills (pool, broads, limo, broads, sports cars, broads, servants, broads), the number of suits he owned, the extravagant gifts (he charged to the studio), his piousness (when I put up a window in the synagogue for my beloved father, I gave the temple an extra five thou), the people he knew by first name, the people who knew him by first name, the way the studio leaned on him for milestone decisions and his high ethical standards and his prowess at gin rummy and, of course, his modesty.

'Abe, we'll make them laugh, cry, die with those boys up there. I got a call into the front office. I'm pitching for Cary [Grant], Clark [Gable], or Spence [er Tracy] for the lead.'

'But, Milt. Maybe Tracy but Grant and Gable aren't my ideas of Italian fathers.'

'Cary and Clark don't play anyone's father. You got to know actors, kid. They don't like growing old. Actually I had in mind using Cary for the part of Barney.'

'Cary Grant, a twenty-three-year-old Jewish boy from the slums of New York?'

'We got to update a little. I was thinking of this General Bertelli character. Reads nice in the book, but do we really want to glorify wops when we're at war with them?'

'Bertelli is American born...'

'Sure, I know that, you know that. But he's still a wop to the great American Midwest. If we make the Bertellis heroes the boys in the front office in New York will have a haemorrhage. After all they're banking and distributing the flick. There's rules. Don't glorify wops, nigs got to be dumb like animals, krauts have got to be comic, and most of all, don't say you're Jewish on the screen.'

'But Barney is a Jew.'

'Look, Abe, and I say this with all sincerity and thinking back to a similar story line I licked on the Hemingway flick, let's don't get the father–son thing in the way of the action. I draw on my experience to tell you this with honesty. Barney as a Jew won't go.'

'The book is about two Italians and one Jew.'

'Yeah. We got to kick it in the head. It won't play. The public likes ... Irishmen. What we need is a big tough Irishman with a screwy little side-kick. Frank McHugh type. The way I see, Cary [Grant] or Jim [James Cagney] or Duke [John Wayne] as a hot pilot always beefing with his colonel, a fine character actor like Alan [Hale.]

It went like this for several weeks and one day Abe said, 'Milton. Go fuck yourself.'

What Cady did not know was that Mandelbaum was fighting for his life. After a dozen flops, enormous and dubious expenses charged to his productions, a scandal with a sixteen-year-old starlet, the self-proclaimed saviour of American Global was on the ropes. *The Jug* was to be his last con job. Cady could write. Mandelbaum couldn't read. In London there was no button to press to give the script a once-over from a tried and true hack. He had to make it go with Cady, or else.

As Abe started to stomp from the suite, sincere, ethical Milton Mandelbaum said, 'Sit down. We've been going at it hard. Let's talk things over.'

'Who can talk with you in the room? It's greasy crumbs like you who've lied and cheated Hollywood into its state of a low mentality insult. Get yourself another writer.'

J. Milton hissed in a snake's voice, 'Sit down, Abe. We've got a contract, sweetheart, and if you pull a stunt like this you're blackballed for life. What's more you'll never sell another one of your books.'

'But, Milton, you told me that any time I was unhappy and wanted out, just to walk through the door.'

'Now wait a minute, Cady. I had a lot of trouble selling you. The committee knows your brother was a Commie.'

'You son-of-a-bitch.'

He grabbed Mandelbaum by the lapels of his war correspondent's jacket and shook him with such fury his glasses flew off his face. He flung him to the floor, where Milton crawled around like a blind man, found his glasses, doubled over with pain from his ulcer and cried.

'Abie, don't leave me! My enemies at the studio will fry me. We've got eight hundred thou on the line, starting dates, actors, sets, costumes. All my life I've fought for principle, and I get crapped on.'

Abe stayed on the film. Strangely, Mandelbaum let him write what he wished. What he did not know was that Mandelbaum picked up a pair of stumble bums and paid them a few thousand dollars to write behind Abe's back. The pair would remain anonymous, taking Cady's scenes and warping them into Mandelbaum's jibberish.

When Abe left the film, he felt a great sense of relief.

'Every great script, every great film,' J. Milton Mandelbaum said, 'is written with sweat. We got to have a few lovers' quarrels. No, Abe, it would be better if you don't come around the set. Your job is done. We'll carry the ball now. Directors get jittery with writers around. They're damned prima donnas. But ... we got to have them. Frigging actors are dog meat. Those people don't know how to treat a writer with respect, like I do.'

Mercifully, the title of the film was changed to *The Screaming Eagles* and no one really remembered it as based on the Cady novel. Abe quietly had his name removed. The film made money. It was in a time that any dogfight piloted by Flynn or Cagney was box office. And so, flushed with a success and a new lease on life, Mandelbaum returned to resume his honourable career.

ELEVEN

I ENDURED THAT MOST AWFUL MOMENT WHEN I RETURNED TO NORFOLK AFTER THE WAR AND REALIZED MOMMA AND POPPA HAD GROWN VERY OLD. THE STEP WAS SLOWER, THEIR GLASSES WERE THICKER, THEIR HAIR WAS GREYER, AND THERE WERE SPELLS OF ABSENT-MINDEDNESS. ON MANY OCCASIONS MOMMA CALLED ME 'BEN'.

NORFOLK HAD GROWN SMALL. ABSENCE HAD MADE MY MIND PLAY TRICKS. THE HOUSE THAT I REMEMBERED AS SO LARGE AND AIRY WAS REALLY LITTLE AND MY ROOM WAS TINY. DISTANCES AROUND THE CITY WERE SHORT, PARTICULARLY IN CONTRAST TO THE VASTNESS OF LONDON.

SAMANTHA WAS A FISH OUT OF WATER, AND I WAS GETTING TO FEEL HER ATTEMPTS AT READJUSTMENT IN AMERICA WERE NOT TOTALLY HONEST. NONETHELESS, WE ANTICIPATED STARTING LIFE TOGETHER. NEW CHILD, A FEW THOUSAND DOLLARS IN THE BANK, NEW CAR. SHAWCROSS HAD BROUGHT OUT A BOOK OF MY WARTIME UNITED PRESS COLUMNS, AND THEY WERE BEING RECEIVED BETTER THAN WE ANTICIPATED.

ANYHOW SAMANTHA AND THE BABY AND I WOULD FIND OUR PLACE. THE SOUTH WAS OUT. BEN'S DREAM HAD NOT COME TRUE. THERE WERE FAINT STIRRINGS. SEVERAL HUNDREDS OF THOUSANDS OF NEGROES WERE HAVING THEIR FIRST CHANCE AT AN EDUCATION THROUGH THE G.I. BILL OF RIGHTS AND THEY'D NEVER GO BACK TO THE WAY THINGS WERE. AT THE END OF THE SECOND WORLD WAR THE FREEDOM SMELL WAS NOT YET IN THE AIR, BUT I FELT IT WAS GOING TO HAPPEN IN MY LIFETIME AND WHEN IT DID I'D COME TO THE SOUTH AGAIN AND WRITE ABOUT IT.

FROM THE DAY THE WAR ENDED, POPPA AND HIS BROTHER HYMAN IN PALESTINE PUT ON A DESPERATE SEARCH FOR THEIR FATHER, TWO BROTHERS, AND OVER TWO DOZEN RELATIVES LAST HEARD FROM IN POLAND SIX YEARS AGO.

BY THE TIME I ARRIVED FROM ENGLAND WITH SAMANTHA

AND THE BABY SOME OF THE HORROR STORY HAD ALREADY FILTERED BACK. MY FATHER'S HOME, PRODNO, WAS WALLED OFF AS A GHETTO. LATER, THE JEWS WERE ROUNDED UP AS CATTLE AND SLAUGHTERED IN THE JADWIGA CONCENTRATION CAMP.

AFTER A TIME CONFIRMATION CAME FROM THE HANDFUL OF JEWISH SURVIVORS THAT MADE ALL HOPE DIMINISH. THEY HAD BEEN MURDERED, ALL OF THEM. MY GRANDFATHER, THE RABBI OF PRODNO, WHOM I NEVER KNEW, MY UNCLES AND THIRTY MEMBERS OF THE FAMILY.

ONLY ONE CADYZYNSKI, A COUSIN, SURVIVED BY FIGHTING IN A PARTISAN UNIT. AFTER THE HOLOCAUST HE WAS MADE TO UNDERGO A NIGHTMARISH ODYSSEY IN AN ATTEMPT TO GET TO THE ONLY PLACE IN THE WORLD THAT WOULD TAKE HIM, JEWISH PALESTINE. HE TRIED TO RUN THE BRITISH BLOCKADE IN A TUGBOAT ONLY TO BE TURNED BACK AND INTERNED IN GERMANY. ON THE THIRD TRY, HE MADE IT.

WHEN THE STATE OF ISRAEL WAS DECLARED IN 1948 MY UNCLE HYMAN HAD THREE SONS IN THE WAR. ONE OF THEM WAS KILLED FIGHTING FOR THE OLD CITY OF JERUSALEM.

THE GRIEF OF MY FATHER OVER THE HOLOCAUST WOULD REMAIN WITH HIM TILL THE END OF HIS LIFE.

AFTER SPANNING THE VASTNESS OF AMERICA AND LEARNING MY OWN COUNTRY FOR THE FIRST TIME I FELL IN LOVE WITH SAN FRANCISCO AND THE BAY AREA. MONTEREY, MARIN, ALL OF IT. A WRITER'S MAGNET FROM JACK LONDON TO STEINBECK TO SAROYAN TO MAXWELL ANDERSON. THIS WAS THE PLACE. SAUSALITO, I THOUGHT. UP IN THE HILLS LOOKING DOWN TO THE WATER AND OVER THE BAY TO THE IVORY SAMARKAND OF SAN FRANCISCO.

SAMANTHA WAS ONE WOMAN I COULD READ. SHE SUFFERED A LOT AWAY FROM LINSTEAD HALL.

I THOUGHT I'D BETTER COMPROMISE AND BEGAN LOOKING FOR PROPERTY IN THE CARMEL VALLEY. IT WAS A FAIR BARGAIN. THE VALLEY WAS FILLED WITH WHITE OAKS AND OLD THICK SPANISH RANCH HOUSES THAT STAYED COOL EVEN IN MIDSUMMER. THE COASTLINE PLUNGED DOWN TO A ROARING SEA ALONG BANKS OF WILD FLOWERS AND CYPRESSES TORTURED BY THE WIND. CARMEL WAS ARTSY-CRAFTSY AND THERE

WAS A TOUCH OF CLOSENESS WITH STEINBECK IN THE CREAK-
ING FISHING BOATS OF MONTEREY AND THE GLORIOUS AROMAS
OF CANNERY ROW. AND ALL OF IT WAS WITHIN REACH OF SAN
FRANCISCO. WELL, SAMANTHA . . . WHAT ABOUT IT?

SO, I RATIONALIZED WITH MYSELF. NOBODY MAKES A PER-
FECT MARRIAGE, RIGHT? WITH ALL HER MOANING I HAPPENED
TO LOVE MY WIFE. AND GOD KNOWS, I'D NEVER ENTER THE
THOUGHT OF SEPARATING FROM MY SON.

SAMANTHA HAD A POINT. HER ONLY BROTHER HAD BEEN
KILLED FIGHTING IN FRANCE. SHE WAS THE HEIR TO LINSTEAD
HALL AND AFTER HER, LITTLE BEN. HER PARENTS WERE AGEING
AND IT WOULD HAVE BEEN TRAGIC TO THINK OF THE TWO
HUNDRED-YEAR TRADITION OF LINSTEAD HALL COMING TO AN
END.

GOT IT? I'M TALKING MYSELF INTO SOMETHING.

GRANTED, I DON'T LIKE HORSES. ALL THEY WANT IS TO BE
FED. IN RETURN, THEY ARE UNFAITHFUL, THEY'LL KICK YOU
IN THE HEAD, THROW YOU, AND MAKE PILES OF HORSE SHIT.
BUT ON THE OTHER HAND, I DON'T HAVE TO SLEEP WITH
THEM, NOT EVEN IN LINSTEAD HALL. I INTEND TO HAVE A
MOTORCYCLE.

THE THOUGHT OF BEN GROWING UP WITHOUT KNOWING
THE BEAUTY OF BASEBALL IS A BIT ANNOYING, BUT HE'S GOING
TO FRIGGING-A KNOW HOW TO FLY A PLANE BY THE TIME
HE'S SIXTEEN. SAMANTHA ISN'T GOING TO WEEP ME OUT OF
THAT ONE.

AFTER ALL, WHAT'S SO BAD ABOUT ENGLAND? I'D COME TO
LOVE IT ALMOST AS MUCH AS AMERICA. LONDON? ONLY THE
GREATEST CITY IN THE WORLD. WHEN YOU GET RIGHT DOWN
TO THE NITTY-GRITTY I'VE DONE MOST OF MY WRITING IN
ENGLAND AND MY MOST CHERISHED DREAM IS TO WRITE A
BOOK ABOUT ISRAEL, SOMEDAY.

I WAVERED A LOT. SOME DAYS I GOT LIVID WITH THE IDEA
THAT SAMANTHA HAD THE RIGHT TO TELL AN AUTHOR WHERE
HE HAD TO WORK. AND THEN I GOT A CALL FROM MY SISTER
SOPHIE THAT MOMMA HAD DIED IN HER SLEEP FROM A STROKE
AND WE ALL RUSHED BACK TO NORFOLK.

I CONVINCED POPPA HE SHOULDN'T RATTLE AROUND IN THAT HOUSE ALL BY HIMSELF. SOPHIE OFFERED TO TAKE HIM IN IN BALTIMORE BUT THE OFFER WAS HALF ASSED. I'VE GOT TO SAY SAMANTHA WAS A GOOD DAUGHTER-IN-LAW. SHE INSISTED HE COME BACK WITH US TO ENGLAND. THERE WAS ALL KINDS OF ROOM IN LINSTEAD HALL, AND HE COULD HAVE HIS OWN LITTLE COTTAGE. POPPA WAS ULTRA SENSITIVE ABOUT BEING A BURDEN BUT IT MADE SENSE.

WHEN HE SOLD OUT THE BAKERY DURING THE WAR, HE GOT TAKEN BY A COUPLE OF GONIFFS WHO LET IT RUN INTO THE GROUND AND IT FINALLY WENT INTO BANKRUPTCY. WHAT LITTLE MONEY POPPA HAD WAS GONE. HE HAD GIVEN MOST OF IT AWAY DURING HIS LIFETIME FOR RELATIVES AND THE JEWS IN PALESTINE.

FOR A WHILE EVERYTHING WAS FINE. WE RESETTLED IN ENGLAND, AND I BEGAN WORK ON A NEW NOVEL WHICH WAS GOING TO BE MY BEST. THE LINSTEADS WERE BEAUTIFUL PEOPLE AND POPPA WAS THE GRANDFATHER TO END THEM ALL.

IN 1947 SAMANTHA GAVE US A DAUGHTER. PERSONALLY, I WANTED TO NAME HER AFTER MOMMA, BUT I GOT TO NAME BEN SO I DIDN'T KICK TOO MUCH. VANESSA CADY. NOT BAD.

I NOTICED HALFWAY THROUGH WRITING MY NOVEL THAT POPPA STARTED TURNING RELIGIOUS. IT HAPPENS TO A LOT OF JEWISH PEOPLE WHO GO AWAY FROM THE FAITH. IN THE END, IT SEEMS, THEY ALL WANT TO BE JEWS AGAIN. THE CLOSING OF THE CIRCLE.

WHEN I SUGGESTED HE GO TO ISRAEL HE BROKE DOWN AND CRIED. I NEVER SAW MY FATHER CRY BEFORE, EVEN WHEN BEN AND MOMMA DIED. I ASSURED HIM IT WOULDN'T BE A BURDEN ON ME. MY UNCLE HYMAN HAD A PLACE IN TEL AVIV AND HE WOULD BE WELCOMED WIHT OPEN ARMS.

ACTUALLY THINGS WEREN'T GOING WELL AT LINSTEAD HALL. JOE FARMER, I'M NOT. I WAS THINKING OF PUTTING A TORCH TO THE PLACE AND COLLECTING THE INSURANCE BUT YOU HANG ON. TRADITIONS DIE VERY SLOWLY IN ENGLAND. AND MOTHER OF PEARL, AM I HUNG WITH A TRADITION! SO, I BORROW AND PLOUGH FORWARD ON MY NOVEL. I DON'T FEEL PIOUS ABOUT SENDING MY FATHER TO ISRAEL. HE GAVE TO

EVERYONE ALL HIS LIFE, AND HE DESERVED IT. I ARRANGED HIS PASSAGE AND BOUGHT A SMALL FLAT FOR HIM AND SAW THAT HE HAD A LIVEABLE INCOME.

LET ME TELL YOU SOMETHING. THE SAME THING THAT WAS KILLING POPPA WAS KILLING ME. IT BURNED MY GUTS, TORE AT MY EYES, RIPPED AT ME DAY AND NIGHT. I WAS SICK AT HEART AT WHAT HAPPENED TO THE JEWS IN POLAND AND GERMANY.

THIS IS WHAT I CRAVED TO WRITE ABOUT. AS SOON AS THE NEW NOVEL WAS DONE, WE'D BE OUT OF THE HOLE AND I'D GO AND LIVE IN ISRAEL AND WRITE ABOUT IT. GOD I WANTED IT. GOD I WANTED IT!

POPPA DIED IN HIS SLEEP JUST AS I FINISHED MY BOOK. MY UNCLE HYMAN WROTE THAT SEEING ISRAEL REBORN ALLOWED HIM TO GO TO HIS REST IN PEACE.

ON MY FATHER'S GRAVE I SWORE I WOULD WRITE A BOOK TO SHAKE THE CONSCIENCE OF THE HUMAN RACE.

AND THEN THE WORST HAPPENED. MY NOVEL, 'THE PARTISANS' WAS PUBLISHED AND LAID AN EGG. ALL THREE AND A HALF YEARS AND SIX HUNDRED AND TWENTY PAGES OF IT BOMBED WITH CRITICS AND READERS ALIKE. ABRAHAM CADY WAS UP THE PROVERBIAL CREEK WITHOUT PADDLE ONE.

TWELVE

IF SAMANTHA HAD AN OUTSTANDING SINGLE QUALITY IT WAS HER ABILITY TO PUT A NEEDLE UP MY BUTT. SHE INSISTED SHE DIDN'T UNDERSTAND WHY 'THE PARTISANS' WAS A FLOP. IT WAS, AFTER ALL, HER VERY FAVOURITE OF ALL MY BOOKS.

I'LL TELL YOU WHY SHE LIKED IT. IT WAS A FAILURE AND BROUGHT ME DOWN TO HER LEVEL OF MEDIOCRITY. IT TOOK A LONG TIME, A MORTGAGE OVER MY HEAD AND TWO BEAUTI-

FUL CHILDREN TO COME RIGHT OUT AND ADMIT IT, BUT SAMANTHA WAS A DULL WOMAN WITH AN INFERIORITY COMPLEX AS DEEP AS THE GRAND CANYON AND AS IMPOSSIBLE TO FILL. SHE WAS INCAPABLE OF LIFTING THE INTELLECTUAL CONTENT OF ANY CONVERSATION OR EVENT, AND SHE WAS FRIGHTENED OUTSIDE THE FAMILIAR ELEMENT OF LINSTEAD HALL.

VERY EARLY IN THE MARRIAGE SHE STOPPED GROWING BUT COULD NOT COME FACE TO FACE WITH HER OWN INEPTNESS, SO THE WAY SHE COULD BECOME BIG WAS TO MAKE ME LITTLE. TEARING ME DOWN WAS AN OBLIQUE WAY OF LIFE.

CONSISTENT WITH HER PERSONALITY, SHE BUILT A HIGH DEFENSIVE WALL ABOUT HERSELF LASHING OUT AT ANYTHING THAT EVEN SMELLED OF CRITICISM. WITHOUT INTROSPECTION SHE WAS INCAPABLE OF ADMITTING MISTAKES OR WRONG-DOING.

BUT, YOU KNOW SOMETHING. I LOVED HER. IT WAS A PARADOX THAT SUCH A LIGHTWEIGHT COULD BE THE GREATEST SINGLE EVENT BETWEEN SHEETS OF A BED. AND THAT MAKES UP FOR A LOT.

STRANGE HOW SOME BRAINY BUSINESS WORLD, FEMALE LAWYER TYPES CAN BE SUCH LOUSY LAYS. LIKE STICKING YOUR PECKER IN GROUND GLASS. AND SIMPLE OLD SAMANTHA, THE QUEEN OF THE BALLERS.

SAMANTHA HAD ANOTHER ENDEARING QUALITY, AN UNCANNY ABILITY TO ALWAYS SINK LOWER THAN ME AND NEVER LIFT ME UP. SHE WAS, IN ANY SITUATION, SADDER, SICKER, AND MORE DEPRESSED.

I WAS IN MORTAL PAIN AFTER 'THE PARTISANS' BOMBED. SAMANTHA SIMPLY COULDN'T UNDERSTAND IT. ANYHOW, MY DRUNK STARTED AT AN RAF REUNION IN LONDON AND ENDED THREE DAYS LATER IN A BROTHEL IN SOHO. MY POCKETS WERE CLEANED AND MY CAR IMPOUNDED. BUT FOR THE BENEVOLENCE OF A GOOD-NATURED HOOKER I WOULDN'T HAVE HAD A TAXI FARE TO GET TO DAVID SHAWCROSS.

BACK AT LINSTEAD HALL THE SILENCE WAS HORRENDOUS. EIGHT DAYS OF TOTAL NIL UNTIL IT ALL HIT THE FAN.

AND THEN STRANGE SALVATION CAME IN THE FORM OF RUDOLPH MAURER, A ONCE REMOVED ROUMANIAN WITH A PICKLE NOSE AND MOLE EYES REPRESENTING A LARGE HOLLY-

146

WOOD TALENT AGENCY. LO AND BEHOLD, AMERICAN GLOBAL STUDIOS WANTED TO BUY 'THE PARTISANS', AND THE PRODUCER ASKED IF MY SERVICES WERE AVAILABLE AS THE SCREEN WRITER.

IT DIDN'T TAKE LONG TO TOTE UP THE BOTTOM LINE. I COULD KEEP SAMANTHA'S GODDAM HORSES IN HAY FOR FIVE YEARS.

DAVID SHAWCROSS ARGUED VEHEMENTLY AGAINST MY GOING TO HOLLYWOOD, AND HIS REASONS LATER PROVED RIGHT. BUT FRANKLY, AFTER THE FAILURE OF THE NOVEL I WAS GUN SHY, IN HOCK, AND DAMNED GLAD TO HAVE FOUND AN OUT.

MOMMA ALWAYS USED TO TELL ME, 'ABE, IF YOU HAVEN'T GOT ANYTHING NICE TO SAY, SO KEEP YOUR MOUTH SHUT.' WELL I'M NOT GOING TO SAY MUCH ABOUT MY YEARS IN THAT FUR-LINED MADHOUSE.

I LOVE MOTION PICTURES AND I BELIEVE IN THE MEDIUM. HOLLYWOOD CAN BOAST OF THE GREATEST CONCENTRATION OF TALENT IN THE WORLD ALONG WITH THAT LEGION OF SILKY CON-MEN AND QUASI-MINI-ARTISTS.

BUT THE SUM TOTAL OF ALL OF THEM IS A BLATANT DISRESPECT FOR WRITERS, THE WRITTEN WORD, AND THIS WILL SOME DAY ERODE THE SAND CASTLE AND THEY CAN ALL GO OUT TO DEATH VALLEY AND FRY IN THE AUGUST SUN.

IT IS BITTER FOR ME TODAY TO HAVE THE MEANS OF STRIKING BACK AND HOLD MY SILENCE IN DIGNITY. I BELIEVE THAT THE USE OF THE TYPEWRITER FOR PERSONAL VENGEANCE IS EVIL AND THE WRITER WHO DOES SO REDUCES HIMSELF TO THE LEVEL OF HIS TORMENTORS.

NEVERTHELESS, I'LL NEVER BE UP FOR SAINTHOOD AND I'M ENTITLED TO MY AUTOBIOGRAPHY. IT HAS BEEN WRITTEN ABOUT THOSE YEARS AND TUCKED AWAY. MY MEMORY OF EACH AND EVERY MONSTER IS VIVID. SO LET THEM SWEAT. IN THE END, ABE CADY IS GOING TO HAVE THE LAST WORD.

FOR A DECADE I DIVIDED MY TIME BETWEEN ENGLAND AND HOLLYWOOD. IN THE MEANWHILE SAMANTHA'S PARENTS PASSED AWAY. I MISS THEM. THEY WERE LOVELY PEOPLE AND SO KIND TO MY FATHER.

I WAS ABLE TO HIRE A GOOD FOREMAN, WHICH KEPT

SAMANTHA FROM RUNNING LINSTEAD HALL INTO THE GROUND.
COMING OFF TWO STRAIGHT BOX OFFICE SUCCESSES THERE
WAS MONEY IN THE BANK AND THE OLD HOMESTEAD WAS IN
THE BLACK. I MUST SAY I GOT A VICARIOUS THRILL OUT OF
TELLING MY HOLLYWOOD AGENT WHERE HE COULD STICK IT
AND IN WHAT MANNER.

I WAS BACK TO WHAT I SHOULD HAVE BEEN DOING . . . WRIT-
ING NOVELS. I STARTED THE NEW ONE DETERMINED NOT TO
MAKE THE MISTAKES OF 'THE PARTISANS'.

THIRTEEN

'I'm coming on home early, love,' David Shawcross said
over the phone to his wife in a voice that literally trembled
with excitement.

'Is everything all right, David?'

'Right! Right as rain. I've just received Abraham's new
manuscript.'

Within the hour, Shawcross unwedged himself from the
back seat of his Jaguar and stormed past his chauffeur.
Lorraine met him at the door.

'Look!' he said, holding up a cardboard carton. 'By
George, it's taken over a decade to get this. There were
times I thought he'd never come through. Turn off the
bloody phones. No calls, no interruptions.'

'Everything's ready, dear.'

His reading chair was encircled with note pads, sharp
pencils, tobacco, liquor, lamp adjusted just so, special
glasses. As she unlaced his shoes and replaced them with
soft slippers he was already tugging out a voluminous
manuscript of over a thousand pages. On the musty treadmill of reading mediocre manuscripts day in, month out, a

148

new Cady book was a king's reward. Lorraine hadn't seen him so happy and excited in years.

THE PLACE by Abraham Cady.

It was not until well after midnight that she found herself dozing in bed, her magazine fallen to the floor. It was uniquely quiet. Not a stir from the connecting study. Usually, when David locked in, he would roar out when something annoyed him, or break into laughter, or give out audible reactions to what he read. Tonight, there was not a peep.

She tied on a robe and approached the study door and knocked softly. No answer. She shoved it open. The leather chair was empty and the manuscript mostly read. David Shawcross stood at the window, hands clasped behind him.

'David?'

He turned. She saw him pale and watery eyed. He walked to his desk slowly, sat with his hands holding his face.

'How bad is it?'

'At first I couldn't believe it. Not of Abraham. I kept saying, he's leading us on. Pretty soon the real Cady will burst out.'

'What's gone wrong?'

'It's a work of slick, pornographic filth for the sake of pornography. Abraham was always a raw writer who gave off heat and swamped you with his passion. He's learned his lessons in California well. He's become polished and glib and plastic. The whole book is dishonest but the tragic part of it is that it will become a smash best seller and grab a fortune from the motion pictures. And the critics will rave ... it's dirty enough.'

'But why? Why on earth?'

'Why do they all eventually do their mattress dance on paper? The money is too bloody tempting. Now that they've succeeded blowing the lid off any moral restraint and anything goes, they masturbate in public under the guise of new freedoms and art. They're all nothing but a gang of mercenary whores. And the bloody critics are just as dishonest. I could just die ...'

149

He crossed the room wearily and stretched out on the sofa. Lorraine knew there would be no sleep for him tonight. She covered him with a robe. 'Tea or brandy?'

'No, love.'

'Are you going to publish it?'

'Of course. Shawcross Limited announces with great honour the return of that remarkable talent Abraham Cady to the literary scene . . .'

'David, Abraham called. He's quite anxious to get your reaction. He came down from Linstead Hall, and he'd like to see you tomorrow.'

'Yes, we might as well get it over with. Call the office in the morning and tell them I'll be working at home.'

'You look haggard,' Abe said; 'that's quite a dose to swallow in one reading. Took me three weekends to knock it off you know,' he joked. 'Well, Shawcross, what's the verdict?'

He stared across the desk at Cady. He looked and dressed the way he wrote . . . polished . . . like he had been plucked out of a Savile Row tailor's ass.

'We'll bring it out in the fall,' Shawcross said. 'I called New York and co-ordinated with your American publisher.'

'What's the good word?'

'My personal advice was to go a hundred thousand copies on the first edition in the States. I'm ordering paper for fifty thousand.'

Abe grabbed the desk, sighed deeply, and shook his head. 'Jesus. I didn't think it was that good.'

'It's not. It's that bad.'

'What's that?'

'You told me you wanted to do three things in this world, write, fly, and play baseball. As far as I'm concerned you can't do any of them.'

Abe was on his feet. 'You're sanctimonious. I knew this was going to come up, Shawcross. Your problem, old man, is that you're out of touch with the twentieth century.'

'Abraham. Fly into any kind of rage you wish. Call me any kind of names you'd like but for God's sake don't try to justify this piece of trash.'

'Well, you damned well don't have to publish it!'

'As long as you don't mind being a prostitute, why should you mind if I pander for you.'

Abe's face was violently hued. He shook his fist under Shawcross's nose and shook with desire to smash him, then threw up his hands. 'What the hell, it would be like hitting my father.'

'You've hurt me very deeply. I really haven't been surprised by the writers who have taken this trip, but I never would have believed it of you. If you want to go to another publishing house, all right, I won't hold you. I'll find you an eager young editor who will tell you all the right things, what new boundaries you've opened, how clean and succinct your phrasing is, how magnificently you weave character and plot.'

'Cut ... cut ... cut. Maybe I did play it a little close but this kind of thing is all the vogue now. Christ, if I could only get out of Linstead Hall.'

'You're not going to blame this abortion on Samantha.'

'In part. Damned well in part. She says, don't be grim, Abe, the world needs a laugh. That and those goddam horses and the goddam hay they eat. If I'd have had a woman willing to sacrifice I might have risked something else. All right, Shawcross, you've knocked me flat on my ass. I was cautious about writing another one like *The Partisans.*'

'I was proud of that book. It cost us both but it seems to have cost you more. Your courage, your anger.'

'Hell, you sound like a goddam literature professor. Starve, writer, starve.'

'You're a frightened man, Abraham, and you're writing scared.'

Abe slumped and hung his head. 'You're right. Ten years in nightmare city. Oh God, what I was going to do with my writing. You're disgusted with me.'

'I can't help but loving my own son,' Shawcross answered. 'I hope there's enough left in you to get disgusted with yourself.'

'I've got to cool down for a few weeks and think about things. I've got to get some sun.'

'Splendid idea.'

'Call Samantha for me, will you. I don't want to get into a hassle with her. She doesn't understand that I've got to dry out by myself, sometimes. Always takes it like I'm trying to run away from her.'

'Aren't you?'

'Maybe. Tell her I've written myself out and just have to break away.'

'Very well. I'm giving a cocktail party tonight at Les Ambassadeurs for a new author. There'll be some interesting women. Do come.'

'See you tonight, Shawcross.'

FOURTEEN

Les Ambassadeurs, a posh private dining and gambling club, stood on Hamilton Place, Park Lane, in an old converted mansion. The maître d' welcomed correctly over Abraham Cady, a well-known eye patch around London.

'Mr. Shawcross's party is in the Hamilton room, Mr. Cady.'

'Thanks.'

He breathed deeply and entered. He was greeted by a warm blast of tattle, tattle, tattle. Abe scanned the room like a cyclops searching out a friendly face for palatable conversation, when his eye came to a sudden stop on a chic, poised, raven-haired beauty in her mid-thirties. Will I still love her, Abe wondered, when she opens her mouth and attempts to talk.

'Oh, hello, Abraham.'

'Hi, Shawcross.' Abe nodded in the direction of the woman. 'Who is she?'

'Laura Margarita Alba. Lovely, charming girl. International jet setter. I understand she has quite a collection of jewellery in exchange for her favours. Usually found on the arm of a Greek shipping tycoon or a munitions dealer or someone in that crowd.'

'She here alone?'

'She comes to London from time to time representing clients and sponsors to bid on certain antiques, gems, art, at Christie's and Sotheby's. Frankly, Abe, I think she's a bit pricey for the likes of us. Want to meet her anyhow?'

'Let me consider the possibilities.'

About that time both Shawcross and Cady were whisked off into separate circles of tattle, tattle, tattle. Abe feigned listening and mulled. Then, across the room, she smiled directly to him and nodded.

There were several alternatives of attack, he thought. With a tramp, a bum, a whore, one must always treat them as ladies.

With that great pool in the middle rung, the established actress, the flustered housewife, the oversexed secretary, the ambitious starlet, one had to indulge in a silly game of double entendre, nuances, clever bubbles, promises that were not promises.

But here was an elegant lady. Laura Margarita Alba was that rare courtesan whom men paid dearly to be seen with and who felt it was the best hundred thousand they ever spent. Abe decided to gamble. He oozed out of his trap and moved toward her. She was chatting with some young stud with a lemon rinse, strong-posed jaw, penetrating blue eyes, and a velvet and lace suit. She was politely bored and watched Abe coming from the corner of her eye. Abe found out the name of the stud, tapped his shoulder, and told him Shawcross was looking for him.

'Madame Alba,' he said, 'I'm Abraham Cady. I'd like to fuck you.'

'What a lovely idea,' she answered, 'here's the key to my

153

place. Harlequin Suite on the Roof Gardens at the Dorchester.'

Abe stared at the key. 'You're kidding,' he said.

'I did my own reconnaissance before I came. If you hadn't asked me I intended to ask you ... or would you prefer to go through a few days of games before you make your conquest?'

'You're the end.'

'I admired you when you used to be a writer.'

'Very funny. Did Shawcross put you up to that?'

'No. I read the books, then I saw the movies. I'm leaving in a half hour. Why don't you follow in another half hour. I'll be waiting for you.'

The young lemon-rinsed stud burst back into the scene. 'I say, Shawcross didn't want to see me at all. Rather cheeky of you,' he said indignantly.

Abe turned his back to Madame Alba and faced the stud. He lifted his eye patch revealing an ugly sight. 'Want to make something of it, junior,' he asked.

The stud fled.

'Jesus Christ,' Abe said, 'lavender walls, lavender carpet, lavender bedspread.'

'I adore this suite. It goes with my black hair.'

'Before I sweep you off your feet, how about buying me a drink.'

Abe stared at the rug, sipped, then looked to the settee opposite where she was neatly blended in soft flowing lace.

'Mind if I call you Maggie?'

'No, I rather like it.'

'Well, Maggie, no bore in the world like someone with a long, sad story and I've got one. I'm afraid you picked lousy company. Frankly, I ought to be with a hooker in Soho. I can't afford you.'

'I go down for one of two reasons. Mostly for diamonds as you know. My last sponsor, a French aircraft manufacturer, was very un-French in his jealousy and kept me under virtual lock and key for two years.'

'Here's to all our plush prisons. Why me, Maggie?'

'Of course you must know how attractive you are. Besides, I have a thing about writers. They're all little boys in need of mothering, and you are the saddest little boy I've ever seen.'

'Will you hold me all night and tell me not to be scared and all those words I've longed to hear from my wife?'

'Yes.'

'Christ, the dialogue between us is worse than the book I just wrote.'

'What the critics never seem to learn is that the world runs on a few dozen clichés. We spend our lives repeating ourselves.'

'It's 1962 already,' Abe said, 'I'm forty-two years old. I've got a son eighteen and a daughter fifteen. I'm married almost twenty years to a decent woman who had no business being a writer's wife. You can't put into someone what the Lord didn't give them. She's let me down. I've had numerous affairs and have long since ceased to feel guilt, but I know that we all pay for what we do and someday it's going to come crashing down on me. On the other hand I get almost no satisfaction from my affairs because I'm really not seeking bodies. I'm looking for peace and the conditions to write what I really want to write.

'I was twenty years old when I did my first novel. Yesterday, twenty-two years later I turned in a manuscript that was pure unadulterated crap. What little dignity and self-respect I had I surrendered by writing this book.

'Look at me, Maggie, monogrammed shirt and tailored eyepatch. You know, two days ago was Yom Kippur, a Jewish holiday, the Day of Atonement, when we're supposed to meditate about ourselves and our lives. My dad, God rest his soul, passed away on Yom Kippur. I promised him something and I lied. Look at my goddam monogrammed shirt.'

In the morning it was Laura who was pensive and misty-eyed. She poured his coffee. 'There's nothing more exquisite than contemplating an affair,' she said, 'and nothing more sobering than having it, unless you run into Abraham

Cady. It's lovely to have a man who knows how to take care of you. You said as much when you looked through me at the cocktail party last night.'

Abe shrugged. 'You've got to establish who's boss.'

'Only one other man was able to treat me that way, my husband. I was very young, just over twenty, and Carlos was fifty when we met. I was already playing musical yachts. I thought the marriage would be dull but worth the security. But the bed was a battlefield and he was a master tactician in his kind of warfare. Abe, I have a lovely villa on the Costa del Sol at Marbella and two free weeks. Let me pamper you.'

'I've got a thing about going to Spain,' he said.

'Your brother's been dead almost twenty-five years. Perhaps it might be a good idea to see his grave.'

'One by one I seem to have given up most of my ideals. Even being with a woman like you is wrong. Consort of munitions dealers, widow of a prominent fascist.'

'I know. The underlying hatred is what makes us so exciting. Do you know how I learned about you? From a German actress who was your mistress. What vicarious thrills come from love–hate. Darling, I've said please. We won't even have to leave the villa.'

'All right, let's go.'

'Tomorrow, noon flight to Madrid. I have a car there. We'll drive to Málaga for the night and then on down the coast to Marbella.'

He turned over inside him at the mention of the names on the Spanish land, and he was unaccountably thrilled at the idea of seeing it.

'I have to go,' she said; 'there's an important painting going on auction at Sotheby's after lunch.'

He grabbed her waist. 'Phone your bid in for someone else to make. I'm taking you back to bed.'

They stared at each other for a long period, neither of them yielding. 'Very well,' she said at last.

FIFTEEN

The Villa Alba, outside Marbella, rose from the moody
sea as an intricate part of a massive rock on a myraid of
levels, cavelets with waterfalls spilling into shimmering
pools, and the traditional Spanish white arches and red
tiled roofs and floors were enhanced by expansive use of
glass and flying wings and jutting patios. It was a violently
coloured place of great splashes of modern art which were
abruptly muted by an ancient tapestry or a wormwood religious statuette.

The villa was set in a baked, terrace land outlined by tall
spikes of cypresses that ran to the ragged shores and their
long golden stretches. The sands had been trampled under
by the hordes of Hannibal and the hordes of bikini clad
tourists. A place inundated with lore and Roman walls and
the yachts of a fast-paced international set. Of Gothic and
Moorish pillage and rape and latter-day orgies.

For all the splendour of her home, Abe found an intrinsic
sadness about it for nowhere was there to be found a
portrait or remembrance of another human being. This was
Laura Margarita Alba, strange and lonely as the sea.

Nearby, the swirl of high social nothingness was centred
at the Marbella Beach Club of Prince Max von Honenhole-
Langenberg. In other times Laura made her presence felt
there, and she was a most fascinating hostess of bronzed
sun people and rotted old aristocracy whose incredible
dribble rarely went beyond who was sleeping with who.

For now she wanted Abe alone. They ravaged each other
with a controlled fury born out of physical and spiritual
starvation. The long years of emptiness found sudden fulfil-
ment and they squandered it on each other until they had
exhausted themselves into spending their time in a magnificent daze. The selfish woman now lavished upon him un-
selfishly, her will commanded by his.

At times in the middle of the night when both of them were restless they would sit in the shallow end of the pool and watch the machinations of the sea or walk down to the thatched hut in a private cove and talk until dawn. And in the morning they would lay in a half shuttered room in semidarkness with a soft breeze over their bodies as the only intruder. The servants moved around like whispers wondering about this man in the señora's life.

In the middle of the second week mutual thoughts began creeping in of why this shouldn't go on forever though neither of them spoke about this.

The tryst was invaded in the person of Lou Pepper, executive vice-president of International Talent Associates, a monolithic agency representing a lion's share of the creative people in show business.

Lou was a tall, thin man with a sleepy face whose dominating feature was seventy Sy Devore suits, all dark.

'Maggie, meet Lou Pepper, a wart on the ass of humanity.'

'Save the incredibly funny dialogue for your next screenplay. I didn't fly here because you are exactly my favourite person. Well, are you going to offer me a drink?'

'Give him a glass of water. Well, how'd you find me?'

'Most writers have two eyes so nobody recognizes them in public. Everybody knows the eye patch.'

'Let's go out to the patio. You come too, Maggie. I want you to hear all this. Mr. Pepper is a very important executive. He doesn't travel thousands of miles to see a mere writer.'

'You see, Señora Alba, Abe and I didn't part on the best of terms when he stomped out of Hollywood two years ago after being handed the best three picture deal any writer was ever offered.'

'Tell Maggie that you told me that any time I didn't want your services you'd tear up the contract you wrung out of me.'

'Abe has a long memory but even agents have to live.'

'Why?'

'At any rate, I'm still selling your new novel.'

158

Laura looked from Abe to Lou Pepper, distressed at the harsh language and the hostility between them and angry at the intrusion. Even with Abe, who overtly hated him, Lou Pepper would have to go into an egocentric advertisement of himself before getting into the details. He settled with a drink and droned.

'As soon as Milton Mandelbaum took over as head of American Global Studios he called me in. "Lou," he said, "I'm going to lean on you heavily." Milt is high on you, Abe, always has been. He keeps talking about the wonderful times you had together in London during the war, the bombing missions he flew with you, the whole schmear. I told him a Cady novel is coming. He put ten thousand on the line just to read the book and have first refusal rights. Mind if I take my jacket off.'

Out popped the cuff links. Abe knew it was a big deal because Lou always gave himself away. His armpits went on him. Deals were the way agents got their sex. Lou remained calm. That indicated he was certain of his ground. The begging and crying and breast beating would come later.

'Milt is interested in you as a total person. He wants to see you flourish. He's talking participation in profits.'

'The way that studio keeps books they wouldn't have had a profit if they had produced *Gone with the Wind*.

'As writer-producer it's a different ball game.'

'But, daddy, I don't want to be a producer.'

'You're sanctimonious, Abe. What the hell did you write that piece of crap for, posterity? You had dollar signs from bedroom scene one through fifty. You want to hear the deal?'

Abe had been cut down, suddenly, cruelly. *The Place* wasn't going to fool anybody. 'What's Mandelbaum got in mind,' he said in almost a whisper.

'Two hundred thousand for *The Place* plus escalation clauses based on sales. Two hundred thousand for your services as a writer and producer and ten per cent of the profits. We'll throw a few bones to the publishers to keep it up on the best-seller list.'

Abe shoved his hands in his pockets and walked out toward the precipice and looked down where a calm sea merely swelled in and out of the rocks. 'I guess this makes me one of the highest paid hookers in the world,' he mumbled to himself.

Lou Pepper, sensing the kill, swiftened the pace. 'You get a producer's cottage with your own can and bar and privileges in the executive dining room and a parking space in the private lot.'

'I'm moved, sincerely.'

Lou continued to talk at Abe's back. 'Plus first class travel to L.A. and twenty-five hundred a month living expenses. Samantha has agreed to come to L.A. with you.'

Abe whirled around. 'Who in the hell gave you permission to see her. You set me up.'

'You happen to live in England, where should I go, to China?'

Abe laughed sadly, returned to his chair and clapped a hand in a fist over and over. 'Lou Pepper doesn't travel halfway around the world for a piddling forty thousand-dollar commission. Who else have you got locked into the deal, male star, female star, director, cameraman, composer ... all who just happened to be represented by your agency.'

'Don't act like there's anything underhanded. Studios don't like to keep payrolls with big stars. It's up to the agencies to put the package together and lay it in their laps. Mandelbaum was interested in an entire deal he can sell his board.'

'You think your crowd plays rough, Maggie. What Mr. Pepper has here is a two million-dollar package. That's two hundred thousand dollars in commissions plus pieces of the picture. But, there's a hitch. No star or director will commit to a property without a screenplay ... that is, unless Lou Pepper can deliver the most commercial writer in the business, namely me. So he knocks down two hundred thousand in commissions, fifty thousand of which will be paid to the International Talent Associates' Geneva office and eventually find its way into a numbered account belonging to J. Milton Mandelbaum.'

'You've got a great imagination, Abe, that's what makes you such a fine writer. Hand a man a half million dollars and he spits on you like you're dirt.'

'Did you give Mandelbaum an option on my next book?'

'Your next three, Abe. I told you, Mandelbaum likes you as a total person. We all want to see you become a rich man. I've got to put in some calls to L.A. and New York. I'll be at the Marbella Club. Torture yourself on your own time. I'll tell you about reporting dates tomorrow.'

Abe paced the patio spitting out epithets, then crumpled. 'He knows I haven't got the guts to blow this deal. If I did, he'd see to it *The Place* never sold to another studio. Anyhow, I'll become the kind of writer Samantha always envisioned.' He filled a half tumbler full of Scotch.

Laura took the glass out of his hand. 'Don't get drunk tonight.'

'I'm busting! Let's drive up the coast.'

'You'll get us killed.'

'Maybe I want to—I'm going alone.'

'No, I'll drive with you. Let me pack a few things for overnight.'

They did not return to the villa until late the next evening after a wild ride in her Porsche along the treacherous twisting sea road to Málaga. There were a dozen messages to call Lou Pepper.

Laura flung open the door to the living room where a haggard David Shawcross waited.

'What the hell is this,' Abe said, 'the General Assembly of the U.N.?'

'I phoned David last night before we left.'

'I must say, Abraham, I've received warmer greetings from German prisoners of war.'

'Maggie tell you the whole story?'

'Yes.'

'Comments?'

'Your behaviour is about as much comment as anyone needs. You see, Laura, he loves his family and would go on with his wife forever if she let him pursue the thing that's eating him alive. He's a Jew and he wants to write about Jews. He loathes the contaminated air of the studios. I've seen a lot of writers get caught in that trap. One day, they simply stop writing. Abe smells that day at hand. It's his death warrant and he knows it.'

'What about the alternative, Shawcross. There'll be no movie sale on *The Place*. Lou Pepper will see to that. Samantha will never agree to a book that means two years' research out of England. By the time we finish dividing up with lawyers, I'll be down to zero again. What are we going to do gang, ask Maggie to hock her diamonds?'

'I've spoken to my bank and your American publishers. We'll keep you floating one way or the other.'

'You will?'

'Yes.'

'You think I've got enough stomach left?'

'You write, I'll pay the bills.'

Abe turned away. 'It may be past midnight,' he said. 'I may let you down. I don't know, Shawcross, I just don't know.'

'I always felt you were one Jew who wouldn't be taken to the gas chamber alive.'

The houseboy entered and said Mr. Pepper was calling again.

'What are you going to tell him?' Shawcross demanded.

'If you want the truth, I wasn't this scared when I crashed my Spitfire.'

Abe wiped a wet palm, lifted the receiver, and drew a deep breath to stabilize the pounding and trembling.

'Abe, I talked to Milt this morning. He wants to demonstrate his sincerity. Another twenty-five thou on the novel rights.'

Abe was sorely tempted to end it all on a note of profanity. He looked from Shawcross to Laura. 'No dice,' he said softly and hung up.

'I do love you, Abe. Ask me to come with you. Order me not to go away with him.'

'You think I haven't thought about this. We've had a

look at paradise. Only a damned fool could believe he could spend his whole life this way. All we can expect is a moment of peace between battles. We've had that. The places I'm going to are hot and sticky. You won't like them after a while. If it means anything, I love you too.'

SIXTEEN

SAMANTHA POSSESSED ENOUGH NATIVE FEMALE SHREWD-NESS TO MAKE ME MARCH TO HER TUNE FOR TWENTY YEARS. SHE DID NOT HOLD ME BY COMPASSION OR SACRIFICE OR TAK-ING A PARTNERSHIP IN MY WORK.

I WAS HELD BY BLACKMAIL.

SHE UNDERSTOOD THAT MY GREATEST FEAR WAS THAT OF LONELINESS. LONELINESS HAD DRIVEN ME INTO THE ARMS OF WOMEN I DID NOT CARE FOR OR WISH TO SPEND AN EVENING WITH ... ONLY TO AVOID BEING ALONE.

SHE ALSO UNDERSTOOD THAT MY GREATEST LOVES WERE MY SON AND MY DAUGHTER, BEN AND VANESSA. SAMANTHA PARLEYED THIS LOVE AND THIS FEAR INTO A CONSTANTLY DANGLING THREAT THAT I WOULD BE LEFT ALONE WITHOUT MY CHILDREN.

IN HER COCKSURENESS SHE ALWAYS BRAGGED THAT I WAS FREE TO GO ANY TIME AND SHE WOULDN'T DEMAND A THING. I WAS FREE TO LEAVE HER JUST AS I WAS FREE TO RID MYSELF OF LOU PEPPER AND MILTON MANDELBAUM.

WHEN I BOTTOMED OUT, WHEN I WAS DEPRESSED AND DISGUSTED WITH THE WAY MY LIFE WAS TURNING, SHE HAD A STANDARD TACTIC OF GETTING ME INTO BED AND MAKING SAVAGE LOVE TO ME. IT WAS A PACIFICATION, LIKE SCRATCH-ING A DOG'S CHEST. BUT SAMANTHA WAS SOMETHING IN BED AND RARELY FAILED TO BLUNT MY ANGER.

FOR TWO DECADES I PRAYED FOR THE MIRACLE THAT
THINGS HAD TO CHANGE AND THAT ONE DAY SHE WOULD TELL
ME SHE REALIZED I WAS UNHAPPY AND I SHOULD GO OUT AND
FIGHT WINDMILLS AND SHE WOULD STAND BESIDE ME.

WHEN I RETURNED FROM HOLLYWOOD WITH MY BRAINS
SCRAMBLED AND PLEADED WITH HER TO LEASE LINSTEAD
HALL. PACK UP THE CHILDREN AND COME WITH ME TO FAR
OFF LANDS THAT CHALLENGED THE WRITER'S IMAGINATION.

WHO WAS I KIDDING?

THE FEW TIMES SAMANTHA TRAVELLED WITH ME SHE WAS
MISERABLE ABOUT THE DISCOMFORTS, MY SCHEDULE, THE
SOCIAL OBLIGATIONS. SHE SPENT HER DAYS SHOPPING. AT
NIGHT I WAS SO WORRIED ABOUT POOR BORED SAMANTHA
BEING LEFT AT THE HOTEL WHILE I CONDUCTED INTERVIEWS I
WAS UNABLE TO CARRY ON MY WORK PROPERLY. EVERYTHING
HAD TO BE PRESENTED TO HER WITH AN APOLOGY.

I WANTED TO WRITE AT LINSTEAD HALL. EVEN THAT PIECE
OF CRAP, 'THE PLACE'. BUT SAMANTHA INSISTED MY PRESENCE
AT HOME DISRUPTED THE ROUTINE AND TIED HER DOWN. IT
WAS ALWAYS TOO PAINFUL FOR HER TO ENTERTAIN MY COL-
LEAGUES AND BUSINESS ASSOCIATES.

AND NOW I LISTENED TO HER WITH UTTER DISBELIEF. SHE
HADN'T LEARNED A THING IN TWENTY YEARS.

'Thank God,' Samantha said, 'for dear friends like Lou
Pepper. Your behaviour put him in the hospital in London
with severe colitis.'

I DIDN'T REALIZE YOU COULD GET COLITIS OF THE MOUTH
BUT IN LOU PEPPER'S CASE IT WAS CONSISTENT. HE HAD RE-
TURNED TO LONDON BEFORE ME AND WORKED HER OVER,
COMPLETE WITH DISCLOSURES OF LAURA. HE HAD TOLD HER
THAT THIS NEW ASSIGNMENT WAS THE MOST IMPORTANT
EVENT OF MY LIFE AND SPELLED OUT THE MONEY. IF SHE WAS
TO SAVE ME FROM FUTURE LAURA ALBAS I SHOULD NOT GO TO
LOS ANGELES ALONE. WHAT HE MEANT, OF COURSE, WAS TO
HAVE A BUILT-IN ALLY TO ALWAYS BE READY TO SIT ON MY
HEAD IN CASE I GOT OUT OF LINE.

SO, SAMANTHA WAS WILLING TO FORGIVE ME AND MAKE
THE SACRIFICE TO COME AND LIVE WITH ME IN A BEVERLY
HILLS MANSION. SHE ROUNDED OUT HER ESSAY WITH A DIS-

SERTATION ABOUT HER POOR HEALTH, HOW HARD SHE WORKED, HOW FRUGAL SHE WAS, AND FINALLY, HOW SHE HAD ALWAYS STOOD BY ME AND ENCOURAGED MY WORK.

IT WOULD DO ME NO GOOD TO GO INTO A RAGE. I'VE DONE THAT. I LOOKED AT HER AND REALIZED THAT IT WOULD NEVER CHANGE. SAMANTHA WAS AS SHALLOW AS HER HORSES, AND I NOW ADMITTED THAT I DID NOT BECOME A WRITER BECAUSE OF HER, AND I HAD REMAINED A WRITER DESPITE HER.

'I want a divorce,' I said.

AT FIRST SAMANTHA TRIED TO SOOTHE ME OUT OF IT. I HAD HAD A LONG FLIGHT, I WAS TIRED, ETC. I PRESSED THE ISSUE. THEN SHE BROUGHT OUT THE FEAR TACTICS. I WOULD BE ALL ALONE. THE CHILDREN WOULD TURN AGAINST ME. MY GUILT WOULD OVERWHELM ME.

WHEN SHE REALIZED I WASN'T GOING TO BUDGE SHE BECAME DESPERATE.

'I'm drowning, Samantha. If I continue on this way of life, I'm done. I have chosen, madam, the alternative of going down fighting.'

AT THIS POINT SAMANTHA, WHO NEVER WANTED ANYTHING, THREATENED TO STRIP ME OF EVERY SHILLING.

'I'm going to make it very easy for you,' I said. 'You can have everything, including the rights to *The Place*, which, I suspect, was really inspired by you. I leave here without a nickel. It's yours ... all of it ... everything.'

THEN I HAD TO TELL BEN AND VANESSA WHAT HAD HAPPENED. I TOLD THEM THAT I WOULD START TRAVELLING SOON IN EASTERN EUROPE AND IF ALL WENT WELL I'D BE IN ISRAEL FOR THE FOLLOWING SUMMER AND THAT THEY SHOULD COME.

A STRANGE THING HAPPENED. THEY INSISTED ON COMING TO LONDON WITH ME AND SEEING ME OFF.

WHEN I LEFT LINSTEAD HALL, IT WAS SAMANTHA WHO WAS ALONE.

SEVENTEEN

The odyssey of Abraham Cady began in the Soviet Union, where he was given a canned tour of model factories, new housing, the ballet, museums, children's pioneer homes, and dialectic acrobatics at the writers' union.

In the subways, before loud blaring radios, in the parks, there were clandestine meetings with Jews.

His request to visit Prodno was lost in a bureaucratic maze. He travelled to Kiev to the infamous pits of Babi-Yar, where thirty-five thousand Jews were rounded up and murdered to a chorus of cheering Ukrainians. The large, persecuted Jewish minority of Kiev was more willing to speak to Cady.

His visit was abruptly halted and he was asked to leave Russia.

Starting from Paris with a new passport he travelled to Warsaw, which was intent on selling the point of view that the Poles were blameless in the genocide of the Jews and there now existed under communism a new and liberal attitude.

Abraham made the sorrowful pilgrimage to the Jadwiga Concentration Camp, the place of the murder of nearly all of the Cadyzynski family. It was intact, a national shrine. And the visit was to set off years of nightmares of the gas chamber and crematorium where he viewed it from the viewpoint of the SS murderers as well as the murdered Jews.

He went through the medical barracks where the maniacal experiments in surgery were carried out.

Again, he was talking to too many people and too many were willing to talk to him. He was picked up at the Bristol Hotel in Warsaw in the middle of a meal, detained for three days at the secret police headquarters as a Zionist spy, then ejected from Poland.

It was the same in East Berlin where the prevailing propaganda was that the Eastern Germans had redeemed themselves by turning to communism while the Western Germans remained the true Nazis. On his third trip into East Berlin he was warned not to return.

Next, Abraham Cady took the path of the surviving refugees of the Second World War from Eastern Europe to the main staging centre in Vienna. From Vienna to the camps in Italy and France along the sea where the illegal immigration agents purchased leaky, ancient, unfit boats and tried to cross the Mediterranean into Palestine against the British blockade.

He wandered the fabled island of Cyprus like the resurrected Lazarus had wandered it, for it was here that the British established mass detention camps filled with those refugees turned away from Palestine.

He went to Germany and interviewed dozens of former Nazis, none of whom knew the words to the 'Horst Wessel' song, their marching anthem in the Hitler era. Nor did anyone living near Dachau detect any strange smells.

Over the streets of Munich and Frankfurt and Berlin he re-created the 'Night of Crystal', the dreaded mass assault on German Jewry by the Brown Shirts.

At the end of seven months, Abraham Cady arrived in Israel for a reunion with the few remaining relatives and then, twenty thousand miles of travel within that tiny state. The interviews ran over a thousand backed by three thousand reference photographs. Hundreds of hours were logged in the archives of death. He compiled a mountain of books and documents and he read until his eye nearly collapsed.

And his debt to David Shawcross mounted.

Vanessa and Ben arrived during the first summer. Abe welcomed it because he was wearying of a rather wild Hungarian mistress who stormed out at the infringement of her 'territory'.

At the end of the summer, they announced candidly they were not returning to England.

'Why? What will your mother say?'

'Mom is a bit tired from her devoted service as a mother, she won't mind,' Vanessa said.

'Cut it, Vinny,' Ben said. 'The reason we want to stay is that we've found what you're hoping other people will find through your writing.'

It was pretty hard to argue even though Abe knew his son intended to train to fly for the Israeli Air Force. But the unsaid reason, and he felt it keenly, was that the children didn't want him alone during the writing of the book. All the research had been gathered and consumed and one could feel the tension mount as the actual writing was to begin.

For the next sixteen months Abraham Cady wrote and rewrote and rewrote some two million words.

David Shawcross
77 Cumberland Terrace
London NW 8

December 15, 1964

Dear Uncle David:

I have some disturbing news, but fortunately everything is going to turn out well. We found my father on the beach a week ago, collapsed from exhaustion. He is resting in a hospital in Tel Aviv for what is described as a minor heart seizure. All told, we are quite fortunate for this served as a warning.

During the past three months Dad has been writing himself into a frenzy, almost totally detached from the world. He is obsessed with this book and would only quit when his fingers fell off the keys and his mind ceased to

168

function. Often as not he fell asleep over the type-writer.

This has been an experience we shan't forget. Each day, at sunset, we would sojourn to the outside patio and Vanessa would read the day's work, aloud. Dad would listen without interruption, jotting down notes for changes. In a small measure we were able to feel some of the emotional upheaval he was undergoing.

The manuscript is ready except for the last three chapters, which Dad wants to rewrite. I'm sending it, save those three chapters, under separate cover.

My Hebrew is coming along fine. I hope it will be sufficient to begin flight training soon. Vanessa has graduated from the English-speaking gymnasium and may be called into the Army for a year's national service. Technically, she doesn't have to serve, but I don't believe anything will keep her out.

Please don't worry about Dad. He's under good care.

Our affection to Aunt Lorraine.

Ben Cady

NIGHT LETTER
ABRAHAM CADY
KFAR SCHMARYAHU BET
ISRAEL

JANUARY 15, 1965

I HAVE READ YOUR MANUSCRIPT STOP I BELIEVE THAT YOU HAVE ACHIEVED WHAT EVERY WRITER ASPIRES TO AND FEW REALIZE STOP YOU HAVE WRITTEN A BOOK THAT WILL LIVE, NOT ONLY BEYOND YOUR MORTAL TIME ON EARTH, BUT FOR ALL TIMES. YOUR DEVOTED FRIEND, DAVID SHAWCROSS.

Abe had been in Israel for well over a year, but he had avoided the cemetery outside Haifa. With the receipt of Shawcross's cable he felt that he could visit his father, at last.

EIGHTEEN

'THE HOLOCAUST' WAS PUBLISHED IN THE SUMMER OF 1965. IT HAD TAKEN ME ALL MY LIFE TO BECOME AN OVERNIGHT SUCCESS. NOW THAT I HAD SPILLED MY BLOOD IN WRITING THE BOOK THE VULTURES AND PARASITES SWARMED IN TO GET THEIR CUT. MOST NOTABLE WAS LOU PEPPER, WHO WAS WILLING TO LET BYGONES BE BYGONES.

WHEN I TURNED THE MANUSCRIPT IN EARLIER IN THE YEAR I WAS FILLED WITH AN INSATIABLE DESIRE TO RETURN TO AMERICA. I SETTLED WITH A LONG TERM LEASE IN A LOVELY GLASS AND WOOD CONCOCTION IN THE HILLS OF SAUSALITO WITH A BREATH-STOPPING VIEW OVER THE BAY TO SAN FRANCISCO. THIS DRIVE TO RETURN TO AMERICA HAD GROWN OVER THE YEARS WITH MY DEEPENING CONCERN ABOUT THE THING THAT WAS SHAKING EVERYONE, EVERYWHERE, AND THAT WAS THE ABILITY OR INABILITY OF MAN TO CONTINUE TO EXIST ON PLANET EARTH.

THE BAY AREA WAS THE 'NOW' PLACE WHERE MUCH OF IT ALL WAS HAPPENING AND MUCH OF THE FUTURE FOR OTHER PLACES COULD BE PREDICTED.

IN ORDER TO FALL INTO A STATE OF DEPRESSION THESE DAYS ONE ONLY HAD TO THINK ABOUT THE MASSIVE DISINTEGRATION OF THE EARTH AND AIR AND WATER AND THE MORAL ROT, THE GREED, AND CORRUPTION, AND THAT ENDLESS LIST OF HUMAN FAILURES THAT WE WERE SUDDENLY BEING MADE KEENLY AWARE OF.

MAN THE PREDATOR, THE PLUNDERER, THE DESTROYER WAS COMING FACE TO FACE WITH THE THOUSANDS OF YEARS OF SINS AND CRIMES AND THERE WOULD BE AN ARMAGEDDON IN THIS CENTURY. IT WAS ALL RUSHING TO A TERRIFYING CLIMAX.

IF WE WERE TO CATALOGUE AND MAKE CHARGES OF THE ABUSES OF THE HUMAN RACE, IF WE WERE TO CALCULATE WHAT MAN HAD TAKEN AND WHAT HE OWED, THEN HE WOULD HAVE HAD TO DECLARE BANKRUPTCY.

WE WERE NOW FACED WITH THE FRIGHTENING QUESTION OF WHETHER OR NOT WE WERE COMING TO THE END OF OUR PURPOSE TO EXIST ANY LONGER. THE OLD GODS AND WISDOMS FAILED TO PROVIDE THE ANSWERS. AND A HORRIBLE SENSE OF FUTILITY AND DESPERATION INVADED THE UPCOMING GENERATION.

GREAT AND GRAND WARS WERE NOW A THING OF THE PAST. THERE WERE TWO SUPER POWERS IN THE WORLD, EACH CAPABLE OF RAINING TOTAL DESTRUCTION. THEREFORE, FUTURE WARS WOULD HAVE TO BE FOUGHT IN COMPACT AND LIMITED BOUNDARIES AND UNDER STRINGENT RULES.

NOW THAT A GREAT WAR WAS OUT OF THE QUESTION, MAN SEEMED TO NEED SOMETHING TO REPLACE WAR. THE CRUX OF THE PROBLEM IS THAT THERE EXISTS A BASIC FLAW IN THE HUMAN RACE AND THAT IS MAN'S INEVITABLE DRIVE TO-WARD SELF-EXTINCTION.

INSTEAD OF WAR, HE HAS REPLACED WAR WITH THINGS AS DEADLY. HE INTENDS TO DESTROY HIMSELF BY CONTAMINA-TING THE AIR HE BREATHES, BY BURNING AND RIOTING AND PILLAGING, BY MAKING A SHAMBLES OF THE INSTITUTIONS AND RULES OF SANITY, BY MINDLESS EXTERMINATION OF BREEDS OF ANIMALS AND THE GIFTS OF THE SOIL AND THE SEA, BY POISONING HIMSELF INTO A SLOW LETHARGIC DEATH THROUGH DRUGS AND DOPE.

THE FORMAL AND DECLARED WARS HAVE GIVEN WAY TO A WAR DIRECTED AGAINST HIMSELF AND HIS FELLOW-MAN THAT IS DOING THE JOB FASTER THAN IT WAS EVER DONE ON A BATTLEFIELD.

YOUNG PEOPLE HAVE BRUSHED ASIDE AND TRAMPLED DOWN MANY OLD MORES AND ETHICAL CODES. IN MANY CASES IT WAS

OVERDUE THAT OUR SOCIETY BE STRIPPED OF HYPOCRISY AND RACISM AND FALSE SEXUAL VALUES. BUT IN THEIR RAMPAGE TO RING OUT THE OLD, THE YOUNG HAVE ALSO BROUGHT DOWN THE GREAT VALUES AND WISDOMS AND FAILED TO REPLACE THEM.

WHAT CAN I DO ABOUT THIS AS A WRITER? VERY LITTLE, I FEAR. AMONG OTHER THINGS I HAVE WATCHED A KIND OF INSANITY PERVERT LITERATURE AND ART AND MUSIC TO WIN FALSE PRAISE BY FALSE PROPHETS. WE HAVE IN MUCH OF IT THE SYMBOLS OF DESPAIR AND CONFUSION. LOOK AT A DANCE FLOOR. HEAR THE LOVELY MUSIC.

WELL, MY THING IS TO WRITE. ALL I CAN HOPE TO DO IS PUT A SINGLE FINGER IN A DAM WITH A MILLION LEAKS.

I FELT THAT IF I COULD CREATE A SINGLE FICTITIOUS AMERICAN CITY AND WRITE ITS HISTORY AND OF ITS PEOPLE FROM EVERY POSSIBLE ASPECT FROM ITS BEGINNINGS TO ITS RISE TO THE DECLINE IT COULD BE MY MOST VALUABLE CONTRIBUTION. WHAT I WANTED TO ACHIEVE IN FICTION WAS TO ISOLATE AND EXAMINE A COMPLETE ENTITY AND THROUGH LOOKING AT ONE TOTAL SEGMENT GAIN SOME INSIGHT INTO THE OTHER THOUSAND SEGMENTS.

ALL OF THIS WILL TAKE THREE OR FOUR YEARS TO RESEARCH AND EVOLVE INTO A NOVEL. VANESSA WILL BE FINISHED WITH HER MILITARY SERVICE IN ISRAEL SOON AND WILL JOIN ME IN SAUSALITO AND TAKE HER COLLEGE IN BERKELEY, WHICH HAS BECOME A RICH SOURCE OF MY OWN RESEARCH, INCIDENTALLY.

BEN? BEN IS SEGEN MISHNE/LIEUTENANT CADY OF THE ISRAELI AIR FORCE. I'M PROUD. I'M FRIGHTENED. BUT I BELIEVE THAT WITH THE TRAINING HE'S GOTTEN HE'LL BE THE BEST AVIATOR OF THE THREE OF US.

IT IS A COMFORT THAT IN FINDING ISRAEL THE CHILDREN HAVE A PURE AND UNCLUTTERED GOAL IN LIFE, THE SURVIVAL OF OUR PEOPLE.

AFTER ALL, THE ONLY THING THAT IS GOING TO SAVE MANKIND IS IF ENOUGH PEOPLE LIVE THEIR LIVES FOR SOMETHING OR SOMEONE OTHER THAN THEMSELVES.

I AM A SOUGHT AFTER SPEAKER THESE DAYS. I GOT INVITED

TO A WRITERS' SEMINAR AND FOR THREE DAYS I GOT QUES-
TIONS.

'SURE, ANYBODY CAN BE A WRITER. I'LL PUT YOU IN BUSI-
NESS. HERE'S A SHEET OF PAPER.'

'HOW? APPLY THE SEAT OF THE PANTS TO THE SEAT OF
THE CHAIR.'

OR

'I'M A WRITER TOO, BUT I DIDN'T GET AS LUCKY AS YOU,
MR. CADY.'

IT CAME MY TIME TO SPEAK AT THE BANQUET. I STUDIED
THE TENSE, EAGER FACES AS I APPROACHED THE ROSTRUM.
'WHO HERE WANTS TO BE A WRITER?' I ASKED. EVERYONE IN
THE ROOM RAISED HIS HAND. 'WHY THE HELL AREN'T YOU
HOME WRITING?' I SAID, AND LEFT THE STAGE. THAT ENDED
MY CAREER IN WRITERS' SEMINARS.

HOWEVER, THE JEWS DISCOVERED ME. JEWISH CHARITY
WAS ALWAYS A WAY OF LIFE WITH MY FATHER AND MY
FAMILY. TAKING CARE OF OUR OWN HAS BEEN OUR KEY TO
SURVIVAL. IT IS THE ESSENCE OF ISRAEL. I REMEMBER IN
THE BEGINNING IN THE JEWISH SHOPS ON CHURCH STREET
IN NORFOLK THERE WAS ALWAYS A 'PUSHKE'—A LITTLE
COLLECTION CAN FOR SOMETHING IN PALESTINE.

WELL, LET ME TELL YOU, JEWS NEVER RUN OUT OF CAUSES
FOR WHICH TO RAISE MONEY AND IN 1965 I SPOKE FOR ONE
HUNDRED AND SIXTEEN OF THEM. THE WHOLE SPEAKING
SCENE IS A BAD ONE. I DON'T LIKE IT FROM THE WELCOMING
COMMITTEE AT THE AIRPORT TO THE TV INTERVIEWS TO THE
INTIMATE DINNERS WITH THE BIG DONORS AND I'M SO TERRI-
FIED WHEN I APPROACH THE ROSTRUM I HAVE TO BE LOADED
WITH BOOZE AND TRANQUILLIZERS. ANYHOW, SINCE 'THE
HOLOCAUST' I'M THE HOT NUMBER THESE DAYS, AND IT'S VERY
HARD FOR ME TO SAY NO TO THESE PEOPLE.

Abe's secretary, Millie, let in Sidney Chernoff, who represented Einstein University, which was the second fully
accredited Jewish educational facility in Chicago.

'Mr. Cady phoned that he would be a few minutes late.
Would you like to wait in his office?'

So, this is where he worked! Chernoff gloried and drank it in. The ageing leather chair, the battered typewriter, the desk filled with trinkets, photographs of his two children in Israeli uniform. It was food for a week's conversation! There was a floor to ceiling corked wall. MARK TWAIN CITY, CALIFORNIA. Pinned to the wall were sheets of dates and statistics and names of characters and family groups and the educational, political, industrial, and cultural make-up of the city.

Imagine! A city born out of a man's mind.

A long table opposite held stacks of books and documents and photographs covering every possible facet of urban life. Reports on the influx of minorities, riots and floods, strikes, police, and fire methods.

Sidney Chernoff's trek through the inner sanctum was abruptly halted by the loud sound of an approaching motor-cycle. He looked out of the window down to the driveway where some roughneck gunned the bike, switched it off, and dismounted. My God! It was Abraham Cady!

Chernoff tried to be nonchalant as the booted, leather-jacketed Cady introduced himself, plopped into the seat behind his desk and propped his feet up, and ordered a Bloody Mary from Millie.

'That's quite an interesting piece of machinery,' Chernoff said, trying to say SOMETHING cool about the bike.

'Harley C. H. Sportster 900,' Abe said, 'that mother takes off like a striped ass ape.'

'Yes, it appears very powerful.'

'I've got to bust loose and clear my head now and then. I've been riding with the narcotics squad for over two months. It's an ugly scene. We found two kids, age twelve and fourteen, dead from an overdose of heroin last night.'

'That's ghastly.'

'Only trouble with a bike is that it doesn't fly. The CAB is giving me a lot of static about a private pilot's licence. The eye, you know.'

Abe's Bloody Mary and Chernoff's tea arrived.

Chernoff sipped and nodded in approval with large puckered lips. He oiled his way into the subject of his visit, speaking in the deep melodious voice of the practised super intellectual. Cady had an idiosyncrasy with the motorcycle, but he was a great novelist who understood the lofty language of a fellow cultured creature. Chernoff sprinkled his presentation with Hebrew phrases, wisdoms of the Talmud, and quotes from personal conversations he had had with other great men. He explained why a man of the stature of Abraham Cady should identify with Einstein University, the second major Jewish institute in the country. There were a number of chairs in the arts and letters that Abe could raise funds for. In turn, Abraham Cady would receive great spiritual reward in knowing he was advancing the cause of Jewish education and intellectualism.

Abe dropped his feet from the desk with a thud. 'I'll be glad to appear for Einstein,' he said.

Sidney Chernoff could not conceal his unabashed joy! Cady was not the monster he had been painted. A Jew is a Jew and if he is appealed to correctly his Jewishness will shine through.

'I have one small condition,' Abe said.

'Of course.'

'The money I raise is to be used for the sole purpose of recruiting a major football team, hiring a big name coach, and working toward a schedule against the top teams in the country.'

Chernoff was puzzled. 'But Einstein has a fine programme of inter-mural sports.'

'It's like this, Mr. Chernoff. We've got enough scholars, learned men, doctors, scientists, essayists, lawyers, mathematicians, musicians, and fund raisers to stock every underdeveloped country in the world, including Texas. The way I see it is like this. The Jews have engaged in conversation for two thousand years without notable success in matters of human dignity. A few thousand of our people in Israel went out and kicked the piss out of somebody and that is where our respect comes from. I want Einstein University to put eleven big buck Jews on the field against Notre Dame. I want Jews who can knock other people down, face mask, pile on, get penalties for unnecessary roughness. I

175

want a Jew who can throw a ball fifty yards to another Jew who can catch it with three monsters hanging on his back.'

After a long siege of research at the longshoremen's hall, debating with the scholars on civic upheaval, looking for action in the ghetto of Fillmore Street, hobnobbing at the Pacific Union Club, riding with the police on emergency calls, freaking with the beatniks, marching with and against campus rebels at Cal ... Abe would find respite sailing his boat over the bay to San Francisco and going out with the fishing fleet. A few days in rough water bending his back on a salmon run, letting the beard grow, leaking over the rail, drinking with the Italians, all flushed him for another run at his work.

He was at sea for four lovely days on the *Maria Bella II* in the chilled buffeting January wind and waves. He was sad as she chugged through the Golden Gate into the arms of the great bay.

Dominick, the skipper of *Maria Bella II*, handed Abe a sack of crabs.

'If my mother saw these crabs she'd turn over in her grave.'

'Hey, Abe,' Dominick yelled, 'when you going to write something about me?'

'I already have. It's a one page book called the *Complete Encyclopedia of Italian War Heroes.*'

'Very funny, Jew writer. You're lucky you only got one eye.'

'I've got two. I wear an eye patch because I'm yellow.'

Maria Bella II wobbled in the swells, veered right before Alcatraz, and eased toward Fisherman's Wharf and the magic alabaster city that rose up behind it.

Dom's father was on the pier as they tied up. 'Hey, Abe, your secretary, she call up. She say for you to call her right-away.'

'Millie, Abe. What's up?'

'A cable arrived from Shawcross in London two days ago. I didn't know whether to radio out to the boat or not.'

'Read it.'

'Libel proceedings launched against *The Holocaust* naming author, publisher, and printer by Sir Adam Kelno, former inmate doctor in Jadwiga Concentration Camp over reference to him on page 167 stop Kelno involved in extradition case in London nineteen years ago and freed and later knighted by British government stop Send us all your sources of information immediately stop He is demanding all books on sale be withdrawn stop Unless you can support allegations we are in extremely serious trouble. And it's signed, David Shawcross.'

THREE

BRIEF TO COUNSEL

PREFACE

Greater London encompasses the city of London and thirty-two boroughs, among which are the former city of Westminster, and the former Royal Borough of Kensington, and such other famous areas as Chelsea, Harrow, Hammersmith, Lambeth, and the picturesquely named Tower Hamlets.

THE CITY of London is a tiny fiefdom of one square mile running along the Thames Embankment from about Waterloo Bridge to Tower Bridge. The City is autonomous and each year with great pomp renews its status by payment to the crown of six horseshoes, sixty-one horseshoe nails, a hatchet, and a bill hook. Within its seven hundred acres, the Lord Mayor is sovereign only to the crown and when the king or queen enters its boundaries, they must pause for official permission and welcome of the Lord Mayor.

The numerous wigged and gowned ceremonies clash with a twinge of humour with the mini-skirted young ladies of the financial district.

In ancient times the various guilds of fishmongers, ironmongers, grocers, vintners, and the like, selected London's officials, who wore robes and carried maces and sceptres and swords of state denoting their positions.

The boundaries of The City are marked, the most prominent being the statue of the griffin where the Strand becomes Fleet Street before the Royal Courts. Tradition called for a father to take his son to the boundary and whack him on the backside so he could always remember the limitations of his travelling, a ceremony called 'beating the bounds'.

Within its magic mile, The City holds Fleet Street, the newspaper centre of the world, the Old Lady of Threadneedle Street, as the Bank of England is known, Lloyd's, Petticoat Lane, the Tower of London, St. Paul's Cathedral, Old Bailey, blackly renowned as the world's most famous criminal court, the great fish markets, all under the protection of ceremonial pikemen and in day to day life of six foot bobbies with distinctive marking on their hats to distinguish them from other London bobbies.

There is yet another great institution in The City, the Royal Courts of Justice and three of the four Inns of Court. As The City is autonomous from greater London, so are the Inns of Court autonomous from The City.

The Inns of Court came into existence centuries ago when the Knights Templar, holy brothers in arms, were given a habitation in 1099 to 'carrie on their vows of chastity and poverty' intermixed with some bloody doings. They were abolished by order of the Pope in 1312 but the Templars survive today through the Masonic Fraternity whose Freemasons cherish the distinction of the degree of Knight Templar.

With the demise of the Templars the lawyers drifted into The Temple in the 1200s. Lawyers as well as doctors in those days were priests and the law was canon in nature.

The Magna Carta and King Henry III ended much canon law and after a time converted to common law. The Inns were then to take permanent possession of legal education and the legal world.

There is an ancient verse that sums up the Inns.

> Gray's Inn for walks,
> Lincoln's Inn for a wall,
> The Inner Temple for a garden,
> The Middle Temple for a hall.

Middle Temple Hall is staggering in heraldry. It was here that the first performance of Shakespeare's *Twelfth Night* was held. The serving table below the dais is made of

182

timber from Sir Francis Drake's *Golden Hind* and Elizabeth and her admirals were its patrons. Under its sign of the Holy Lamb Oliver Goldsmith and Dr. Johnson and Blackstone worked and Chaucer resided and wrote the *Canterbury Tales*. No less than five members of the Middle Temple signed the American Declaration of Independence. In its gardens the thirty-year War of the Roses commenced.

Yet it is the hall that remains the overpowering and magnificent mark of Middle Temple. A hundred feet in length it soars fifty feet with a timbered carved roof of Elizabethan hammered beams. In the year of 1574, some time before the Spanish Armada, a magnificent hand-carved wooden screen was erected to span the forty-five-foot girth of the hall. Rows of ponderous tables run the length of the hall toward the dais flanked by a wainscoted wall holding the coats of arms of Treasurers and Readers. At the dais the Benchers of Elders of the Temple preside over sombre dinners and wild revelry. Over the side and end walls are fourteen stained glass windows with coats of arms of the Lord Chancellors from Middle Temple. Royal patrons painted by Hogarth and Van Dyke stare down on it all.

Crossing a narrow lane one leaves Middle Temple and enters Inner Temple, whose best-known landmark is the Knights Templar Church dedicated in 1185. It miraculously escaped the periodic fires which levelled The City during the Middle Ages but was gutted in the Blitz. Now, brilliantly restored, it is one of England's few round churches, modelled after the Holy Sepulchre in Jerusalem with floors covered with thirteenth-century marble effigies of knights and an arcade of grotesque stone heads representing souls in hell. Near them were the cells where paupers, debtors, and other sinners starved to death watching the knights in their holy prayer. Christopher Wren beautified it with a rectangular nave.

Much of the Inner Temple had been destroyed and rebuilt because of fire and war, but it is her names that make her glory permanent. Charles Lamb and William

Makepeace Thackeray and Boswell and Charles Dickens. And rich are the names of its buildings and lanes of Hare Court and Figtree Court and Ram Alley and King's Bench Walk with its immensity of lawn flowing down to the Thames.

Both segments of the Temple, Middle and Inner, are cut off from the outside world and the bustle of Fleet Street and the Victoria Embankment by Christopher Wren gates and walls.

On the rear side of the Law Courts, between High Holborn and Carey Street, stands Lincoln's Inn on a site once occupied by the Friars on what is now known as Chancery Lane. When the Archbishop of Canterbury changed their name to Blackfriars, their houses were chartered to Henry de Lacy, Earl of Lincoln in 1285. Heart of the pastoral fields of Lincoln's Inn is Old Hall, erected in 1489, and it is still intact and used as a lecture room. This is the Inn of William Pitt and Disraeli and Cromwell and the martyr Thomas More, who were among its nine prime ministers and twenty Lord Chancellors.

Across High Holborn, a street named for a path burned by the Great Fire, and just beyond the reach of The City, lies the quadrangle of the fourth Inn, Gray's. This is the place of Sir Francis Bacon. Gray's is mostly inactive today as a base for practising barristers, with most of its offices leased to solicitors.

The Four Inns are part and parcel of English history and greatness. They form the Law University and in addition to their own particular individuality they have enormous libraries, conduct moots or mock trials, are recipients of royal patronage, are filled with students, and hold the formal dinners where new barristers are called to the bar.

While the world swirls around them they continue to live in a quasi-monastic serenity, gowned in their distinctive robes and traditionally going to war together in a single Inns of Court Regiment.

In each building, a Queen's Counsel or senior barrister 'leads' the juniors in a set of chambers. Often two barristers from the same chamber argue from opposite sides of the courtroom.

Some say this is a private debating society and that these two thousand barristers are too privileged and that the thousands upon thousands of examples of common law are too archaic and intricate.

Yet, here is law for law's sake. The barrister argues the case for a set fee and is not allowed to take a portion of a client's judgement. He may not be sued for what he says in court. On the other hand he is not permitted to sue a client for fees.

Within the Inns corruption is unknown.

The barrister is judged by a man who has been chosen from the ranks of Queen's counsels in a no nonsense courtroom.

A new student taken into a chamber to study is fearfully admonished that he is in the home of the Knights Templar, in the midst of kings and queens, statesmen and judges, and philosophers and writers. He is to be governed by the Benchers or elders and receives the wisdom of the Reader or chief lecturer.

A young man or many older people possessing a standard diploma and a few hundred pounds may enter an Inn and be taken by a master in chambers.

Many a brilliant barrister in the courtroom is impatient in drafting his pleadings and here a new pupil can worm his way into his master's good graces. Doing research and drafting immaculate, painstaking, technically perfect pleadings can endear the pupil to the master.

The pupil makes as little an ass of himself as possible. He reads his master's papers, looks up points of law for him, accompanies him to court, and works hard and late.

The pupil learns to have every point of law at his master's finger tips. He develops the skill of taking fast and accurate notes in court and anticipating the master's questions.

This goes on for a year or so. There is study, attendance at a number of required dinners at the Inn, and the arguing

185

of a moot or mock trial.

A few things fall the student's way. Some overly busy junior in the chambers may need a hand to 'devil' or prepare his work or even argue a minor case in the county.

Each set of chambers, numbering from two to twenty barristers, is managed by a clerk, an all important man who can speed the pupil on his career or keep him mouldering. He deals on the barristers' behalf with the solicitors' offices, assigns cases, sets the fees, and works for a portion of them.

Having devilled, argued minor cases, and shown diligence, the clerk will begin to throw a few things to the bright young man.

To advance his progress the student writes for law journals and puts his name in with the legal aid people.

After the call to the bar and assignment to a decent set of chambers the new junior is with ten or so other juniors and led by an eminent Q.C. Good juniors are in demand. In five years he may be able to afford a larger room in chambers. One day, after a particularly brilliant showing, the Q.C. rewards the junior with a red bag to carry his gown, wig, and books in.

After fifteen or so years as a junior the crown may appoint the junior to be a Queen's Counsel. The robe made of 'stuff' is discarded and the Q.C. 'takes silk'.

As a Q.C. one merely has to argue the case with all the preparation being done by the juniors.

At the age of fifty or more a prominent Q.C. may be appointed to the bench as a judge and automatically knighted. It is the pinnacle of the legal career.

On the other hand, he may remain a junior barrister until his dying day.

ONE

Parliament Square was inundated with the clang of great bells to ring in a new legal year with ancient majestic pageantry.

The war was over and England had survived with the empire intact. Englishmen were going about the business of cleaning up the rubbish in the centre of London where the Hun had left his mark and soon all of that would be in the past. There would be the return to order and tradition as it had been before. There was talk of brave new worlds but this kind of talk followed every war, it seemed. No dynamic changes would be in store for England. They liked things tidy without the dramatic upheavals of the Latins and Levantines. Yes, the new era would be exactly like the old one.

If one doubted that, they had only to be there on this day and they would understand what England was all about. Within the walls of Westminster Abbey, the Lord Chancellor, resplendent in black and gold robes, led the judges of England and the barristers in a sacred service. As they worshipped in pursuit of divine guidance in dispensation of the law, their Roman Catholic counterparts conducted a Red Mass in their cathedral.

The great doors of the Abbey swung open. The procession is begun. It is led by the mace bearer, a tall thin grim chap, and then the bearer of the great seal. Each is attired in knee breeches, buckled shoes, and a cascade of lace embroidery.

Behind them, Lord Ramsey, the Lord Chancellor, wearied by the burden of office. The train bearer follows the Lord Chancellor's stately pace as they cross the great way toward the House of Lords.

There then followed a flamboyantly cloaked array of the

Lord Chancellor's judges: the scarlet-robed Lord Chief Justice whose ermined collar bore the heavy golden chain of the House of Lancaster. Thence the Master of the Rolls, the traditional deputy of the Lord Chancellor and head of the Chancery Courts, and the others in order of their rank, all dressed in breeches, buckled shoes, full-bottomed wigs. Now the President of the Probate, Divorce, and Admiralty Division and the Lords Justices of Appeal in cumbersome black and gold and the flaming-robed Justices of the High Court.

A long line of the senior barristers, the King's Counsel, in black silk gowns and great wigs born of the Queen Anne era. Lastly came the junior barristers.

They are received in the Royal Gallery in the House of Lords after crossing from the east end of the Abbey.

In this time of talk of dramatic change one hears that the law is archaic, living in a private sanctuary of its practitioners, in shocking need of reform, and choking on its own ancient rituals. One hears that common law is filled with symbols of other times. Yet, nearing its thousandth year of use it would be difficult to argue that any other system devised by man surpasses it and it would be equally difficult to contend that it doesn't fulfil the modern needs of justice with surety and dispatch.

The soul of English law is the Lord Chancellor and in this time it is Cyril Ramsey who has reached the epitome of his profession and taken an office which seems far too demanding for a single man. His head wears three crowns.

The Lord Chancellor is one of the few men in the world who hold positions in all branches of government. As the ranking judge of England, Lord Ramsey is the leader of the entire legal structure. He recommends the judges and appoints the junior barristers to the exalted inner realm of King's Counsel.

He is the Speaker of the House of Lords and presides over that body, sitting on the ancient Woolsack, symbol of his office in Parliament.

He is the chief legal adviser to the Crown.

He is a member of the cabinet.

In Parliament he helps in the passage of the laws. As an adviser and cabinet member he helps execute them. As a judge, he enforces them.

He is imprisoned in the grandeur of an apartment in the Parliament looking out on the Thames. From here he heads over a hundred committees for legal reform, for trustee of public funds, for overseeing legal education, for obtaining legal aid, for patronage of hospitals and colleges and law societies and charities. As though this were not enough Lord Ramsey and all the Lord Chancellors before him are bound and tied with constant ceremonial demands. For all of this he receives the annual salary of some thirty-five thousand dollars.

Yet, as traditional 'keeper of the King's conscience' he is inheritor of an era of greatness bowing neither to tension or tragedy, nor showing public exuberance. Dignity, that is the keynote. The keeper of tradition.

Yes, the average Londoner who saw all of this on this day could scarcely believe that any dynamic changes were in the making.

The new legal year was formally under way. Ramsey greeted all of his judges and all of his barristers, whom he knew from long personal and professional association. He was approached by Anthony Gilray, King's Counsel.

Ramsey had on his desk the nomination of Gilray to judgeship in the High Court. He thought it would be a good appointment. Gilray was as sound as the pound sterling. Ten years earlier, one of Ramsey's first duties as Lord Chancellor had been to promote Gilray from junior to K.C. 'Takes silk' they called it when one became a King's Counsel. Gilray had been far above average in his parade of court hearings. When his appointment as judge went through in an automatic manner, Gilray would be knighted as all of England's high judges are and he would be sworn in to a seat in King's Bench Division of the High Court.

'Lord Ramsey,' Anthony Gilray said, holding out a thin hand.

'Hello, Tony, good to have you back from the Army.'
'Good to be back.'
'How does it look to you?'
'Oh, about the same. England never changes.'

TWO

January 1966

Mr. Bullock, the managing clerk of Hobbins, Newton, and Smiddy, contacted Mr. Rudd, the clerk of Sir Robert Highsmith, Q.C., and arranged a consultation in chambers at 4 Essex Court, Middle Temple.

In the years that had passed, Robert Highsmith had risen in stature to one of the greatest libel lawyers in England and because of his continued work with political prisoners had attained knighthood.

Despite his status, he doted on impoverished furnishings in a room with peeling walls, a broken-down over-stuffed sofa, threadbare carpet, and a portable electric heater to augment the inadequate gas burner. The one item of elegance, as in most barristers' chambers, was the desk, a great leather-topped Victorian partner's desk.

However, parked in his space below was a new Rolls-Royce.

Sir Robert Highsmith and Sir Adam Kelno penetrated the barrier of years with searching looks of remembrance. Sir Robert was greyer, heavier, and not quite so dishevelled. A copy of *The Holocaust* lay on the desk. 'There seems to be very little question but that you've been libelled. Offhand one would think it would be impossible for them to defend. However, we must take into consideration that the offending passage occupies one paragraph of a seven hundred page book. Would the general public identify you, a knighted English citizen, as the same person mentioned in passing as a doctor of unidentified nationality in Jadwiga?'

'Perhaps not,' Adam answered, 'but my son recognized me as well as my ward.'

'In seeking damages the sting of the libel will weigh heavily and may be exceedingly nominal.'

'The damage is inside ... here ...' Adam said, pointing to his heart.

'What I am saying is that we may be opening up a Pandora's Box. If, mind you, the other people decide to fight, are we certain that we will come out of this untainted? Are our hands completely clean?'

'No one should know that better than you,' Adam answered. 'I think these words were deliberately put into the book as part of the same plot to harass me to my death. At least now, I have a chance to fight back, not in a mock court in Poland, but under British justice.'

'Isn't it rather unlikely they are going to fight this?' Richard Smiddy asked.

'If we make our demands too heavy, they may be forced to fight. It depends on what Sir Adam is really seeking.'

'Seeking? Aside from the hell of Jadwiga I am in Brixton Prison and in exile in Sarawak for seventeen years. I am there because of them. I have done no wrong. What do you think I should be seeking?'

'Very well,' Sir Robert said, 'but I'm going to have to take the position of tempering your passion with the reality of the situation. Do you understand that?'

'Yes.'

'I'm sorry you have to go through it all again, Sir Adam. Let's hope they'll be sensible.'

In the anteroom, Smiddy made mention to Mr. Rudd to contact his clerk, Mr. Bullock, to set the fees. Smiddy and Adam Kelno walked from the Temple and stopped before the onrush of black taxis and red double decked buses racing up and down the Strand past the statue of the griffin marking the Temple Bar. Over the street the ominous grey stone of the Law Court seemed to glare at them.

'Mark my words, Sir Adam, it will never get into that court.'

> Abraham Cady &
> Shawcross Publishers, Ltd.
> & Humble, Ltd. Printers
> c/o David Shawcross
> 25 Gracechurch Street EC 3

Hobbins, Newton & Smiddy
Solicitors
32B Chancery Lane
London WC 2

Sirs:

Since our initial communication we have been instructed by our client, Sir Adam Kelno, M.D., to inquire:

1. If you are prepared to make a statement of apology in open court.

2. What proposals you have to make to indemnify Sir Adam Kelno for expenses incurred in this matter.

3. What are you prepared to do in removing all copies of *The Holocaust* from all bookstores and ensuring that no mention of Dr. Kelno is made in any future editions.

4. What proposals you have to make by way of damages for the grievous injury done his honourable name.

In that these charges against Sir Adam Kelno are totally without foundation it is impossible to imagine a graver libel upon a professional man in his position.

Since our client requires a statement in open court it is

mandatory to issue a writ and we would like to ask you to give us the name of your solicitors who will accept service.

Yours faithfully,
Hobbins, Newton, and Smiddy

THREE

In Sausalito, Abraham Cady scrutinized his voluminous notes, then wrote to archives, individuals, and historical societies in Vienna, Warsaw, New York, Munich, and Israel for information. The name Kelno had meant little or nothing to him in the context of the massive book.

In London, the small conference room of Shawcross Publishers was converted into a sort of war room. First, Shawcross dug up all the history of the extradition proceedings against Kelno.

His first major discovery was that Dr. Mark Tesslar was still alive and on the permanent staff of the Radcliffe Medical Centre in Oxford. The years had neither diminished nor blunted his feeling. Looking beyond Tesslar's accusations, he felt they were basically truthful and this spurred him to widen his own investigation.

Shawcross turned most of the publishing operation over to his son-in-law, Geoffrey Dodd, and his daughter, Pam. Their son, Cecil, was just beginning in the business. Shawcross took young Cecil as his own personal staff on the investigation.

The staring point was the war crimes indictment of SS Colonel Dr. Adolph Voss, chief medical officer of the prisoners of Jadwiga Concentration Camp. Unfortunately,

193

Voss never came to trial, he committed suicide in prison. None the less the prosecutor in Hamburg had a list of two hundred prospective witnesses.

The indictment and the prospective witness list were almost twenty years old. Many on the list had died, others had moved or disappeared. Yet Shawcross took a crack at everyone in a correspondence carried out in ten languages. Huge charts blanketed the wall of the conference room plotting the progress and answers to every inquiry.

A smattering of information drifted to London. Most of it was discouraging and shed no light. No one seemed to be willing to state they could identify Adam Kelno and they were even more positive on the point that the surgery in Barrack V was a total secret.

Inquiries to Poland went unanswered. The Polish Embassy in London was evasive. Shawcross concluded that a policy was yet to be set by the Poles in the matter. Cautious bureaucrats from the embassies of the Eastern European countries drowned the inquiries in red tape. After all, Abraham Cady was a known anti-Communist writer.

Four months passed. The wall charts were dead-ending the majority of inquiries. Only a few threads, the meagrest clues from Israel, kept the project from collapsing.

And then came a staggering body blow.

Archibald Chárles III of Charles, Ltd., the monolithic printing combine, puffed away in his immaculately panelled office in The City, contemplating this nasty piece of business.

The Charles empire had four great printing plants in the British Islands, a forest for paper pulp in Finland, and a conglomerate of partnerships all over the Continent.

The actual business flowing from David Shawcross amounted to a fraction of a single percentile. None the less, Shawcross occupied a special place. It was the same kind of special place he held in the publishing world as a great editor and literary master. Archibald was a close chum of Shawcross and said on more than one occasion that this was the kind of man a publisher ought to be.

While the business relationship was unimportant in terms of the Charles dynasty, the personal camaraderie had carried over when Archibald took over as managing director and, later, chairman of the board. Shawcross could count on his printers to fill his paper orders and to give special treatment to any of his pet books.

No doubt but that Archibald Charles was a credit. The stockholders were pleased at the steady rise in earnings. He thought in modern terms of mergers and conglomerates more like an American than an Englishman.

'I have Mr. Shawcross on the phone,' his secretary said.

'Hello, David, Archie here.'

'How are you?'

'Good. Mind if I pop over this afternoon?'

'Fine.'

Coming out of his magnificent skyscraper to the drab rooms of Shawcross's on Gracechurch Street was a singular act of respect. He was pin-striped and bowlered because that's what the stockholders expected.

He arrived at Shawcross's, was led down the corridor past stuffy little cubicles of the editors and secretaries to the 'war room'. Archibald studied the walls papered with charts. 'Phased out' was encircled in red lettering. Blue stars marked some sort of progress.

'Good Lord, what do you have here?'

'I'm looking for a needle in a haystack. Contrary to public belief, if you look long enough you'll find the needle.'

'Are you intending to publish books any more?'

'Geoff and Pam are running things out there. We'll have an autumn list of some kind. Tea?'

'Thank you.'

Shawcross erupted a cigar as the tea arrived.

'It's the Kelno affair,' Archibald said. 'As you know I've assigned one of my best people full time to analyse everything you've sent over. You've had numerous meetings with old Pearson about this.'

'Yes. Very decent chap.'

'We've put everything in the hands of our solicitors and have had consultations in chambers with Israel Meyer. I

195

think you'll go along with me when I say he's one of the best barristers practising. Moreover, we picked Meyer because he is a Jew and would be extremely sympathetic to your point of view. At any rate we've reached a decision.'

'Well, I don't see what decision there is,' Shawcross said. 'Every day we learn another fragment about Kelno. There can be no decision when there is no choice.'

'We have a very marked difference of opinion, David. We're pulling out of the case.'

'What!'

'We sent our solicitor over to see the Smiddy people. They're willing to settle now for under a thousand pounds and an apology in open court. I suggest you do the same.'

'Archie, I don't know what to say. You can't be serious.'

'Dead serious.'

'But don't you see that picking us off one by one means they'll demolish Abraham?'

'My dear David, you and I are innocent victims of a fool writer who didn't get his facts straight. Why should you be responsible because Cady has libelled a distinguished British doctor?'

The chair screeched on the bare wooden floor as David pushed away from the conference table and walked to the charts. 'See this, Archie. Just in the past few days. A statement from a man who was castrated.'

'Now, David, I'm not going into a debate with you. We've done the proper thing. Pearson, our solicitors, our barrister, and my board have studied all the information and have a unanimous decision.'

'Is that your personal feeling also, Archie?'

'I am the head of a public company.'

'In that event, Archie, you have a public duty.'

'Rot. All stockholders are the same. I've restrained myself while you've turned your house into a detective agency. I have not lifted a finger and said that you've got us into this. And I say again, get out of it.'

Shawcross whipped the cigar out of his teeth. 'Apologize to a ruddy bastard who cut the nuts off healthy men! Never, sir! Too bad you don't read some of the words that come from your presses.'

Archibald Charles opened the door. 'Will we be seeing you and Lorraine for dinner and theatre tomorrow?'

No answer.

'Come now. We're not going to let this stand in the way of our friendship, are we?'

FOUR

For several weeks there had been a cooling in the relationship between Shawcross and his daughter Pam and her husband, Geoffrey Dodd. It was obvious they thought he was spending too much time on the Kelno affair. Shawcross felt it would be a good idea to have them down to the beach house at Ramsgate in Kent for the weekend and mend things up.

The autumn list of new books was very thin and there wasn't much in prospect for the spring. During these lean periods in the past Shawcross had the uncanny knack of coming up with a dark horse and would make the bestseller list. But these days every moment went into the volumes of correspondence, the translations, and the attempt to crack the doors at the Communist embassies. There would be no recurrence of the annual Shawcross miracle.

The whole Kelno affair had come at a poor time for Shawcross. He was getting along in years and wanted to spend more and more time at Ramsgate just editing and working with new writers.

Geoff and Pam were doing a good job and now with their son, Cecil, in the firm the family continuation looked secure.

Geoff and Shawcross walked beneath the chalk cliffs as they had done on many occasions for a decade, tossing about company business, paper orders, personnel, layouts, bindings, contracts, printing schedules, the Frankfurt Book Fair, the new list.

Shawcross poked his walking stick in the sand. 'I'm still reeling from this shock from Archie.'

'Perhaps it's an omen, David,' Geoff said.

David looked concerned. He had always taken Geoffrey Dodd so much for granted and expected unqualified loyalty.

'Let's have at it. What's on your mind, Geoff?'

'We haven't had a big winner since, well, *The Holocaust*. Abraham is a year away from starting a new novel, another year to write it and six months for us to get it ready. Usually when we'd get into a situation like this, you'd shake the tree and come up with something.'

Shawcross grumbled and flipped his cigar into the breakers. 'I know what you're going to say, merger. Well, who do we talk merger to? The sanitary napkin manufacturer, the soup company, or the oil tycoon who thinks his idiot son should be a publisher.'

'It would be a case of beefing up the present ten books to thirty books a year and giving us the reserves to bid on the Micheners and Irving Wallaces.'

'I'd always hoped we'd be able to keep things in the family, but I suppose it's not very realistic, is it?'

'The point is,' Geoff said, 'no one will talk merger or partnership so long as we have this lawsuit hanging over our heads.'

'I am not going to abandon Abraham so long as he remains in this case.'

'Then I've got to tell you something, quite candidly. Lambert-Phillips has offered me a directorship.'

'Those cheeky bastards daring to raid me.'

'I had my hand in the courtship.'

'I . . . I see.'

'It's the position of managing editor, seat on the board, stock options. Almost a thousand more than I'm making. Quite frankly I was astonished.'

'You shouldn't be. You're a good man, Geoff. And what about Cecil?'

'He would want to come with me.'

David tried to conceal a convulsing sensation. All of a sudden a lovely little world he had built with dedication and integrity was splitting apart. 'Pam, of course, goes along with all this?'

'Not exactly. She's for us taking a partner and keeping on with Shawcross. But you've got to make up your mind about this business with Kelno. I've got to tell you why I talked this over with Lambert-Phillips. It's not the money really. It's because David Shawcross has a pair of shoes so large, no one can fill them properly. Sure, I'm a good managing editor but God almighty, David, you've run a one man show that neither Cecil nor I could cope with in to-day's world.'

They reached the beach house.

'Thanks for the chat, Geoff. I'll think about it.'

The ash on David's cigar was four inches long. The galleys were balanced on his stomach, but he had stared aimlessly for an hour without reading them.

Lorraine sat on the edge of the bed and removed his cigar and fed him his pills.

'Pam told me today when you and Geoff took your stroll,' she said. 'What do you think we ought to do, love?'

'Difficult to say. We'll have to make a decision fairly soon. Abraham will be on his way to London next week.'

FIVE

The room Abraham Cady loved most in the world was David Shawcross's library and its smell of the plush leather of the rich maroon and green and blue bindings of an incredible collection of first editions. Almost every important writer of the twentieth century was represented. Abe was most proud that *The Holocaust* was the most prominently displayed as the greatest single volume ever published by Shawcross.

In a moment, Shawcross's insurer, Allen Lewin, arrived. He was fine, as insurers went, Abe thought, and completely loyal to Shawcross.

'Before we get into our business,' Lewin said, 'I'd like to clear up one point. What are your recollections now of the offending paragraph. How did it get into your book?'

Abe smiled. 'When I give a newspaper interview to a journalist he may end up writing three or four hundred words about me. There's always a dozen errors. In a seven hundred page book of over four hundred thousand words, I made one. I'll admit, it was a dilly. This same information had been published about Kelno before. He was on the list of wanted war criminals. After researching as I did and particularly reading the records of the war crimes trials of doctors I think anyone was willing to believe anything about any of them. What I read about Kelno, in sources that had been totally reliable till then, was completely in keeping with other facts of German atrocities. This doesn't excuse me, of course.'

'Abraham is the most thorough and accurate writer in fiction today,' Shawcross said. 'This mistake could have happened to anyone.'

'I wish it had happened to someone else,' Lewin said, 'preferably from another house.' He unsnapped his briefcase and they ordered whisky all around.

'You and Mr. Shawcross have been in close communication so you know our independent findings pretty well coincide. As for the situation inside the house, Geoff and Cecil are planning to leave unless there is a merger or a partnership and this is impossible until the case is settled.'

'I didn't realize that,' Abe said.

'We have to familiarize you with the financial situation from our point of view so you'll understand how we are coming to our decision.'

'Sorry to have to give you all this rubbish, Abe,' Shawcross said, 'but matters are too grave.'

'Shoot.'

'I'm a Jew, Mr. Cady,' said Lewin. 'I approached this with all the moral overtones. We have spent months at it and now we have to take a cold-blooded look at the risk and our possibilities. We have a number of vague statements of people operated on in Jadwiga, but no one except Dr. Tesslar who claims to be an eyewitness. I've had three barristers go over Tesslar's statement. They all feel he would be an extremely vulnerable witness, particularly in the hands of such an examiner as Sir Robert Highsmith. Then we got into questions of whether or not any others will actually come to London, and if they do their value is questionable. In a British courtroom we don't have much of a chance ... if any.

'And there are other factors,' Lewin said. 'Kelno has a large reputation. The cost factors in fighting such a case are staggering. Technically, Mr. Shawcross is held harmless of libel by your contract with him. However, if he remains as a co-defendant and there is a judgement against you, Kelno will go after Shawcross first because his money is in England. And that means after us, as his insurers.

'At the present moment, Richard Smiddy is ready to adopt a reasonable attitude. Just getting Mr. Shawcross out of this with a damage settlement plus calling in thirty thousand copies of *The Holocaust* is going to take a heavy toll. But at least he'll then be able to get back to running a publishing business instead of a detective agency. My own intuition tells me that Kelno wants personal exoneration

201

more than money and in the end will settle reasonably with you. If you are stubborn and lose in England he'll go after some twenty foreign publishers to whom you have a great responsibility.'

'You're suggesting settlement for me?'

'Yes.'

'All right,' Abe said, 'I'd like to hire you as my personal adviser.'

Lewin smiled and nodded.

'Now that you're my adviser, you're fired,' he said and left the library.

SIX

I WANT MY MOTOR-CYCLE. I WANT THE WIND TO TEAR THROUGH ME AT A HUNDRED MILES AN HOUR. I WANT MY KIDS. BEN IS NERVELESS. THAT'S WHAT MAKES HIM SUCH A GOOD FLYER. BEN KEEPS ME CALM AND VANESSA IS SOFT. EVEN THE ISRAELI ARMY DIDN'T HARDEN HER.

I LOVE LONDON. EVEN NOW I FEEL WARM HERE. I HAVE A MEMORY OF EVERY STREET IN THE MAYFAIR.

IN MY NEXT LIFE I'M GOING TO BE AN ENGLISHMAN. NO, A TOUGH POET PLAYWRIGHT FROM WALES. I'LL CLAW INTO LONDON, THEN INTO THE WEST END THEATRES. I'LL HAVE A MAD FLAT IN CHELSEA AND BE RENOWNED FOR CRAZY BRAWLING PARTIES IN WHICH I RECITE MY POETRY AND OUT-DRINK ANY MAN IN THE ROOM.

WELL, THAT'S MY REINCARNATION ORDER, LORD. AS FOR THIS LIFE, I'M ABRAHAM CADY, WRITING JEW. LOOK AT ME CAREFULLY, GOD. I DRINK TOO MUCH. I COMMITTED ADULTERY TEN MILLION TIMES. I FORNICATE WITH OTHER MEN'S WIVES. NOW SERIOUSLY, GOD, DO I LOOK LIKE JESUS'S BROTHER TO

YOU? SO WHY ARE YOU TRYING TO NAIL ME UP ON ONE OF YOUR GODDAM CROSSES?

WHY ME?

I'VE PLAYED BALL WITH MY PROFESSION. DID YOU SEE THE CONTRACT I GAVE UP TO WRITE THIS GODDAM BOOK? SO NOW THAT I HAVE A FEW DOLLARS IN THE BANK IS IT FAIR THAT I GET BUSTED?

GOD, I WISH THE KIDS WERE HERE. I WISH I WERE A WELSHMAN.

'All right,' Abe said, 'I give up. Where am I?'

'In my flat,' a woman answered.

'Soho or Chelsea?'

'Neither. West one, Berkeley Square.'

'I'm impressed.'

Abe had worked his way upright and slipped on his eye patch, then got the good one into focus. The bedroom was a display of wealth and taste. The woman ... forty-five, handsome, pampered, preserved. Thick brown hair and large brown eyes.

'Anything go on between us? I mean, don't take it personally, but I lose my memory when I get too drunk.'

'You didn't do much of anything.'

'Where'd you find me?'

'The Bengal Club. Tucked away in a corner, stiff. It was the first time in my life I've seen a man sitting up straight and looking directly at me and completely unconscious. So I said to my companion, who is the funny man with the one red eye and my companion said, why it's the famous writer, Abraham Cady, and well, one just doesn't leave Abraham Cady sitting upright and unconscious with his one red eye shining like a stop light.'

'God, you're amusing.'

'As a matter of fact, some mutual friends told me to look after you.'

'What friends?' Abe asked suspiciously.

'Our friends at Two Palace Green.'

At the mention of the address of the embassy of Israel, Abe became serious. In his travels he always knew where to reach a 'friend' and 'friends' knew how to contact him. Often the meetings were indirect.

'Who are you?' Abe asked.

'Sarah Wydman.'

'Lady Sarah Wydman?'

'Yes.'

'Widow of Lord Wydman, London branch of Friends of the Hebrew University, Friends of Technion, Friends of the Weizmann Institute?'

She nodded.

'I'd like to meet you again, under happier circumstances.'

Her smile was lovely and warm. 'What can your tummy hold?'

'Orange juice. Gallons of it.'

'You'll find an assortment of things in the guest bathroom.'

'All prepared for me.'

'Never can tell when you'll run into a distressed writer.'

Abe pulled himself together. The guest bathroom was extremely well equipped, especially for a lover. A guy wouldn't have to pack a thing. Razor, after shave lotion, new toothbrush, Alka-Seltzer, talcum, terry cloth robe, slippers, and a deodorant. He showered his way back to life.

Lady Wydman set down the *Times*, letting her glasses fall to her bosom, where they were held by a thin gold chain, and poured the first of Abe's orange juice.

'What's up, Lady Sarah?'

'Sarah will do. There is a prevailing feeling among our friends that Kelno is guilty of some pretty nasty goings on at Jadwiga. They asked me if I would look into the matter. I'm quite active in the Jewish Community.'

'Well, Sarah, I've got a problem.'

'Yes, I know. Does the name Jacob Alexander mean anything to you?'

'Only that he's a prominent Jewish solicitor here in London.'

'He's quite involved with Jewish affairs. There's a great

204

deal of interest in keeping you in this case.'

'Why? The Jews are looking for a new martyr.'

'There seems to be some interesting new evidence.'

Lady Wydman's Bentley passed along Lincoln's Inn Fields, one of the largest squares in Europe. Near the centre gazebo nurses from the Royal College of Surgeons played netball during the noon hour and doctors got in a quick set of doubles on the grass courts. At the wall at Searle Street there were posts marking the place where a turnstile once stood to keep the cattle from grazing on Holborn.

They passed into Lincoln's Inn through the New Gateway and just beyond the Great Hall the magnificent gardens and walkways unfolded.

Much of Lincoln's Inn was leased to solicitors. Solicitors had offices. Barristers had chambers. The law offices of Alexander, Bernstein, and Friedman occupied the basement, ground level, and first floor of 8 Park Square. A top-hatted assistant porter waved Lady Wydman's Bentley into a reserved parking space and Abe followed her into a maze of cubbyholes, creaking floors, endless stacks of papers, walls of books, hidden nooks and stairs that made up the quaint offices of Alexander, Bernstein, and Friedman, Commissioners of Oaths.

Alexander's secretary, a mini-skirted young lady named Sheila Lamb, who had taken a lifelong ribbing for that name, entered the tiny waiting room inundated with back copies of *Punch*.

'Follow me, please,' she said.

Jacob Alexander arose from behind his desk, a tall slender man with bushy grey hair who could have been someone's conception of a Biblical prophet. He greet Cady warmly and spoke in the deep tones of a trained rabbi.

Sheila Lamb closed the door behind her as she left.

'We have spoken among ourselves at great length,' Alexander said. 'It would be unthinkable to apologize to Adam Kelno in open court. It could be taken in the same context as apologizing to the Nazis for our outrage over the extermination camps.'

'I'm well aware of the issues,' Abe said, 'also our

chances.' He went on to recite Lewin's disastrous predictions and that Shawcross was probably out of it.

'Unfortunately, Mr. Cady, you are an international symbol to Jew and non-Jew alike. The man who wrote *The Holocaust* must assume responsibilities he cannot divest himself of.'

'What kind of support am I going to get?'

Alexander shrugged. 'Maybe yes, maybe no.'

'I still can't foot the bill.'

'Neither can we,' Alexander said. 'But once we engage the action, I believe you'll find support.'

'And if a decision goes against us?'

'There's always bankruptcy.'

'I hear that word too often. I think you're asking too much. I am not positive in my own mind that Kelno is guilty.'

'And if I convince you Kelno is guilty.'

Abe was shaken. Through it all he had hoped for a loophole to get out with some sense of honour. But, if he were shown cold evidence there was hardly a way he could back off. Lady Wydman and Alexander looked at him and both of them searched. Is this the man who wrote *The Holocaust*? Was this courage merely paper courage?

'I guess,' Abe said, 'anybody can be a hero as long as it doesn't cost him anything. I'd better have a look at what you've got.'

Alexander pressed the buzzer and Sheila Lamb responded. 'Mr. Cady and I will be flying to Paris. Put us on a flight around six o'clock and book two singles at the Meurice. Call the I.F.J.O. representative in Paris, Mr. Edelman, and give him our arrival time and get him to contact Pieter Van Damm and tell him we will be in tonight.'

'Yes, sir.'

'Pieter Van Damm,' Abe whispered.

'That's right,' Alexander answered, 'Pieter Van Damm.'

Pieter Van Damm greeted them warmly in the foyer of his sumptuous apartment on Boulevard Maurice Barres. Along with Cady and Alexander there was Samuel Edelman, French representative of the I.F.J.O.

'I'm honoured,' Abe said, grasping the hand of the world-famed violinist.

'The honour is mine,' Van Damm answered.

The maid took their coats and hats. 'My wife and children are in the country. Come, come.'

An enormous study held a gallery of presidents and kings photographed with the man whom many believed to be the world's greatest violinist. A French walnut antique Pleyel grand piano was carelessly stacked with sheets of music near his practice stand. Van Damm showed off a pair of Amati Violins with the childish pride of one who obviously enjoyed his renown.

They grouped about on a sofa and chairs in an alcove looking down to the Bois de Boulogne, settling in with cognac and whisky.

'L'Chiam,' Van Damm said.

'L'Chiam,' they responded.

Van Damm set his drink down. 'I suppose I should start from the beginning. I was twenty-four when the war broke out, married, with a child and a first violinist with the Hague Symphony. My name at that time was Menno Donker. You know the story of how we were forced into hiding. Roundups began by the Germans in the summer of 1942 and then, the large scale deportations in the winter and spring of 1943.'

Van Damm halted a moment, pained with memory. 'I was deported in the winter of 1942 in an unheated cattle car. My child froze to death on the way and my wife was taken for gassing at the selection shed when we arrived at

Jadwiga.'

Abe bit his lip and clenched his jaw to hold back tears. No matter how many times he heard the story it tore at his soul.

'You told it all so well for all of us in your novel,' Van Damm continued. 'I was sent to work in the medical compound. Adam Kelno was the chief of the prisoner/doctors, and I was assigned more or less as a clerk/orderly. I kept records, ordered medicine, scrubbed floors, whatever.'

'So you had a day to day relationship of sorts with Kelno?'

'Yes. In the summer of 1943 I was approached by a Czech prisoner by the name of Egon Sobotnik. He was a member of the underground and solicited my help in forging death certificates, smuggling medicine, and things of that nature. I agreed, of course. Sobotnik's official job was to keep the surgical records so I learned of the experiments being carried on in Barrack V. Between us we kept a diary on Barrack V and smuggled it out of the camp in bits and pieces.'

'Were you ever in Barrack V, yourself?'

'Only to be operated on. Kelno got wind of my activities and I was transferred to Barrack III, which held the raw material for the experiments. At first I was to look after six younger Dutch boys who had their testicles irradiated by prolonged exposure to X-ray. It was part of an experiment to sterilize all the Jews. You wrote about that. We were on the upper floor of the barrack and the women below. It seems they had X-rayed a number of young women also.

'In the evening of November 10, 1943,' Van Damm's voice shook, 'fourteen of us were taken from Barrack III to Barrack V. Eight men, six women. I was the first to go. You see, Mr. Cady, I am a eunuch. Adam Kelno removed both of my testicles.'

Abe felt as though he were going to vomit. He stood up quickly and turned his back to the others. Van Damm stirred his cognac and gazed at its colour and took a small sip.

'You were healthy when he did this?' Alexander asked.

'Yes.'

'Was Dr. Mark Tesslar in the operating room?'

'As I said, I was the first one and Tesslar was not there then. I learned later that there was so much commotion they sent for him to keep the victims calm. Tesslar took care of the men afterwards. Without him I don't think I would have lived. A woman doctor, a Maria Viskova, took care of the girls on the floor below. And also, there was a French woman doctor who came from time to time, mostly with the girls.'

'We are in contact with both of them,' Alexander said.

Van Damm told the rest of his story in monotone. After the liberation he made his way back to Holland to learn that all of his family had been exterminated.

He drifted to Paris, sorely in need of medical attention, and was pulled together by a saintly doctor. At first he wanted to study for the rabbinate, but his mutilation and the results of it were so obvious it was not possible.

Menno Donker hovered close to insanity. He was made to take up the violin again as therapy. With the help of a constant and devoted physician he was able to receive shots and hormones to give him a semblance of masculinity; a little beard, a deeper voice. With the physician always in attendance he was able to play. The rare poignancy that marked his music was born from the pits of tragedy. In a short time, the public found his genius. It was a small miracle in itself that a eunuch could have such lust and vigour required of a great virtuoso.

After the war he met the daughter of a prominent Dutch Jewish family of Orthodox learning. They fell in love in a sort of a way that seemed lost in today's world. It was a spiritual and religious union. For a long time he was able to conceal his secret and then came that awful moment when he had to tell her.

It made no difference. She wanted to take the vows with him, regardless. After a bitter struggle with his conscience he went to her parents and as religious Jews, they agreed and made a secret marriage contract knowing the union could never be consummated physically.

It is said that there is no more devoted or happier couple alive than the Van Damms. Twice they left on sabbaticals of a year's duration and each time they returned with an adopted child. Insofar as the world and the children themselves knew, the Van Damms were their natural parents.

Alexander and Edelman wept openly as Pieter Van Damm finished his story. Abraham Cady, now returned to being the practised journalist, sat granite-faced.

'And you changed your name to Van Damm when you began your concert career.'

'Yes. It was a family name.'

'What became of Sobotnik, the diary you smuggled out, the surgical records?'

'Disappeared. Egon Sobotnik was alive when Jadwiga was liberated, but he simply disappeared.'

'We will turn over heaven and earth to find him,' Alexander said.

'What you have just told us,' Abe said, 'will bring another tragedy to yourself, your wife, and your children. It may bring great harm to your career.'

'I think I understand the consequences.'

'And you are willing to say all of this in a courtroom.'

'I'm a Jew. I know my duty.'

'When Kelno did this to you, did he have any consideration for you at all?'

'He was brutal.'

Abraham Cady was not the kind of man to live protectively, yet he felt both doomed and ashamed of having wanted to pull out. The strain plus the sorrow swept him.

'Do you have any further questions?' Alexander asked.

'No,' Abe whispered, 'no.'

EIGHT

Immediately upon his return from Paris a meeting with Shawcross, his insurers and Jacob Alexander was arranged. It was a nightmare. Haggling went on for hours.

Even with the evidence of Van Damm, Lewin was reluctant to let Shawcross enter the case. Jacob Alexander argued, in return, that Shawcross had made a great deal of profit from *The Holocaust* and other Cady books and should bear a part of the responsibility, if only a fraction.

A dozen side conferences were called.

'You've whittled them down enough,' Shawcross said. 'Abe is willing to take the full brunt of any damages against us. I don't think we can ask more.'

'He may sign a contract to that effect but suppose he decides not to honour it?'

'Come to your senses. Geoff Dodd's resignation is sitting on the desk.'

They convened in the cluttered conference room. Shawcross rejected Sheila Lamb's offer of tea. His unlit cigar hung limply as he avoided Abe's searching stare.

'I've been advised to pull out,' Shawcross said.

'What, no lecture about integrity? You're very good at giving those,' Abe said in rising anger.

Alexander grabbed Abe. 'Excuse us for a moment, gentlemen,' he said, and moved out into the hallway where they had conferred a dozen times during the day. Abe sagged against the wall.

'Oh, Jesus,' he moaned.

Alexander's firm hand was on his shoulder as they stood in silence for several moments. 'You've done your best,' Alexander said. 'I have been wearing two hats, the Jewish hat and the hat of a friend. I must speak to you now as a brother. We have no chance with Shawcross out.'

'I keep thinking about my trip to Jadwiga,' Abe said. 'I

saw the room where they were operated on. I saw the claw marks gouged out of concrete walls in the gas chamber in the last desperate second of life. Who in the hell has a choice? I keep thinking over and over it was Ben and Vanessa. I wake up and hear her screaming on the operating table. Where do I go from here, Alexander? A clay hero? My boy flies for Israel. What am I going to tell him? All over the world the kids are pointing a finger at us and demanding to know who stands for humanity. Well, at least I have more choice than Pieter Van Damm had. I will not apologize to Adam Kelno.'

Mr. Josephson, managing clerk of Alexander, Bernstein, and Friedman for nearly two decades, sat opposite his grim master.

'Cady is going to have a go at it alone,' Alexander said.

'Bit chancy,' the wise old figure answered.

'Yes, a bit. I'm thinking about our lead counsel. Thomas Bannister. He stood for extradition against Kelno two decades ago.'

Josephson shook his head. 'Tom Bannister is the best in England,' he agreed, 'but who can put the bell around the cat's neck. He's so deep in politics he hasn't done much in court in the past few years. On the other hand, Bannister would like the smell of this case.'

'Those were my thoughts. Give old Wilcox a call,' Alexander said in reference to Bannister's clerk.

'I can't promise results.'

'Well, have at it, anyhow.'

Josephson turned at the door. 'Is Abraham Cady daft?'

'The Americans would call it, ballsy.'

Wilcox was a shrewd barrister's clerk of forty years' standing, beginning as a messenger boy and working his way through menial jobs in The Temple from third assistant clerk on up.

For thirty-five years he had been in chambers in the Paper Buildings, Inner Temple, entering almost the same day as the young junior Thomas Bannister. Over the decades he had grown with his master, helping him achieve a near unmatched eminence at the bar, take silk as a Q.C., growing in the political field, being named a cabinet minister, and now groomed as a possible future prime minister of Britain. In chambers with seven thriving juniors, at a fee of 2½ per cent Wilcox was among the wealthier clerks in Inner Temple.

Thomas Bannister's name was synonymous with impeccable integrity even in a place where integrity was commonplace. A confirmed bachelor, he lived in an apartment in Inner Temple.

After having served successfully as a minister, he was in line to be the party's next leader. Bannister's name was spoken more and more often.

The two foxes, Wilcox and Josephson, fenced about in traditional protocol.

'Well, what have you got, Mr. Josephson?'

'Big one, indeed.'

Which brought on lovely thoughts of his commission. Wilcox continued to play it terribly cool.

'We are solicitors for Abraham Cady, defendant against Sir Adam Kelno.'

'That is a juicy morsel, all right. Didn't think he would defend that. Well, which of my gentlemen do you have in mind?'

'Thomas Bannister.'

'Come now, you can't be serious.'

'Extremely serious.'

'I could do right well by you with Devon. Brightest junior I've seen in the last twenty years.'

'We want Bannister. Any barrister is obliged to fight any case so long as his fees are met.'

'Don't be unreasonable,' Wilcox said. 'I've never barred anyone from your offices or any other solicitor.'

NINE

'Nightcap, Tom?'

'I'd love it.'

The chauffeur held the door open. Lady Wydman emerged followed by Thomas Bannister. 'Morgan, wait for Mr. Bannister and take him back to The Temple.'

'Oh, please let him go. I'd love to walk about a bit and take a taxi back. I don't get much chance to walk around London these days.'

'As you wish.'

'Good night, ma'am, Mr. Bannister. When will you be needing me?'

'Not till noon. I have a fitting at Dior.'

She handed Bannister a cognac. He warmed and paced the floor characteristically. 'Cheers.'

'Cheers.'

'Lovely evening, Sarah. I can't remember when I've enjoyed one more. I'm a cad for neglecting you and forcing you to ask me out but the work load has been extremely heavy.'

'I certainly understand, Tom.'

'Lucky for me I can't turn you down.'

'I hope not,' she said.

Bannister sat and let his legs stretch. 'Now that you've wined and dined me, I would like to know what particular thing you're going to ask of me that I can't turn you down for.'

'It's the libel suit between Sir Adam Kelno and Abraham Cady. I'm certain you know why I would be interested. Jacob Alexander is representing Cady.'

Bannister's usual deadpan betrayed him. 'Didn't I see Josephson in my chambers a few days ago?'

'Yes. We're having trouble getting to you these days. I

think the party wants to put you in plastic and deep freeze you until the elections.'

'I've raised hell about this with them before. I wonder what kind of prime minister they think I'll make by ducking controversies.'

'Will you look into it, then?'

'Of course.'

'One thing, Tom, if you decide to take the case they're going to be hard-pressed. It's the kind of thing a single man ought not to be asked to fight. Rather something that a great corporation or a government would undertake.'

Bannister smiled. His smiles were small and infrequent and, therefore, twice as meaningful. 'You are heavy in this. Tell me, Sarah, what kind of a chap is this Abraham Cady?'

'Manners of a dock worker in a boardinghouse, idealistic as a naïve child, bellows like a bull, drinks like a fish, and tender as a lamb. He's no English gentleman.'

'Yes, writers can be like that. Strange breed.'

One could not escape the feeling of entering a holy place when climbing the ancient stone steps of the Paper Buildings toward the chambers of Thomas Bannister.

His room was a bit more dandy than that of his fellow barristers. Richly and tastefully furnished save the gaudy portable electric heaters on the floor.

Bannister and Cady, two trained professionals, sized each other up as Alexander observed tensely.

'Well,' Thomas Bannister said, 'Kelno did it all right. We're not going to let him get away with it, are we?'

There was visible relief.

'We are all aware of how enormous and difficult the task ahead is going to be. Most of the burden in the next year will fall on you, Alexander.'

'It shall receive my full energies and we are not without allies.'

'Gentlemen,' Abe said, 'I believe I have the finest representation possible. I have no intention of telling you how to conduct this case. But there is one condition. Under no circumstances is Pieter Van Damm to testify. I know this places an added weight on us, but I think I'd rather lose. It's my first and only order.'

Alexander and Bannister looked at each other and mulled it along. Their admiration was confused by taking their strongest legal point from them. Yet, it's all on principle, isn't it, Bannister thought. I rather like this Cady chap. 'We shall do our best,' Bannister said.

'Must you really leave tomorrow?' Lady Wydman asked Abe.

'I want to see Ben in Israel. Vanessa is coming home with me. I've got to get to work.'

'I'm going to miss you like the devil,' she said.

'Me too.'

'Can I make a tiny scene?'

'You're a girl. It's your prerogative.'

'You know I adore you, but I'm too damned proud to be just another item in your collection, and I know I would be very silly, and fall in love with you, and be a jealous sow throwing temper tantrums bargaining for a commitment, and do all those bloody stupid things women do that I detest. I know I can't handle you and it really aggravates me.'

'That's very good for my morale,' he said, taking both her hands. 'I've got a problem, Sarah. I'm not capable of giving all the love I have to a woman, only to my children. And I'm not capable of receiving the kind of love a woman like you has. I can't commit, even in a game. What we have here between you and me are two chiefs and no Indians.'

'Abe.'

'Yes.'

'You'll need me when you come back for the trial. I'll keep you warm.'

'O.K.'

She flung her arms about him. 'Oh, I'm lying. I'm crazy about you, you bastard.'

He held her very gently. 'The first time I saw you I knew there was something very special about you. You are a lady. A gentleman leaves a lady with her dignity.'

216

'Have my bill prepared. I'll be leaving for the airport in an hour or so.'

'Yes, Mr. Cady. It's been a pleasure to have you with us. Oh, sir, some of the staff bought copies of your book. Would you mind terribly signing them, sir?'

'Sure. Send them up to my room and stick a piece of paper with their name in each book.'

'Thank you, Mr. Cady. There's a gentleman waiting for you in the bar.'

Abe took a seat opposite Shawcross slowly and ordered a scotch with ice.

'I changed my mind,' Shawcross said.

'Why?' Abe asked.

'Don't know really. Pieter Van Damm hasn't left my thoughts. Well, Abe, I mean fair play is fair play. It's the only proper thing to do. Damm it all, I am an Englishman.'

'L'Chiam.'

'Cheers. You give Ben and Vanessa my love, will you, and when you get back to Sausalito don't worry yourself about Kelno, get cracking on that novel of yours as soon as you can.'

'Shut up for a minute, will you.' Abe pondered. 'Shawcross, you're what the Lord had in mind when he made publishers.'

'Very kind of you to say. You know I told Geoff and Pam and Cecil I was going to go it with you. They withdrew their resignations. They're standing by me.'

'It doesn't surprise me. They're decent people. Before this is all over with a lot of men and women are going to have to show what they're made of.'

217

TEN

February 1966

Sir Adam Kelno's paper was studiously received and deeply respected by the Royal College of Surgeons in Edinburgh. Not an inspired speaker or fully in command of English, he was, none the less, an eminent authority on malnutrition, administration of mass medicine, and human durability under duress.

Although his personal practice continued modestly in Southwark among working class patients, he wrote and lectured at length in his speciality.

Speaking at the faculty in Edinburgh always came as an added pleasure and he scheduled those lectures so he could combine the trip with a motor holiday.

Once cleared of the population centre, the wildness and emptiness of the central lowlands fled by the window. Angela turned up the heater and poured some hot tea from the thermos. Adam could drive all day in the morbidity of Scotland with total enjoyment of the respite from the long hours in London.

They slowed for a thatched roof barren village, where black Angus cluttered the main street and a pair of husky Scots on horseback herded them toward the pasture.

The smell of dung penetrated into the car.

For a moment Adam was in Poland in his own village. It was not like this. His village had been flatter and greener and poorer and even more primitive. But all countryside and all peasants and all their villages stirred a sting of memory.

A third horseman clip-clopped in front of the car, bringing him to a complete halt. There was a boy of perhaps twelve on the horse and a pair of dogs raced at the ankles of the cows.

SO THERE I AM AND THAT BEAST OF A MAN OVER THE

ROAD WOULD BE MY FATHER. OH, THAT POOR BOY. WHAT CHANCE DOES HE HAVE IN THIS PLACE? WHAT CHANCE DID I HAVE? AND MY FATHER WITH A MIND AS BLEAK AS THE ROCKS IN THE LONELY FIELDS.

SPUR YOUR HORSE, LAD! SPUR IT AND GALLOP OFF. RUN TO THE CITY AND SAVE YOURSELF.

I HATE YOU, FATHER!

Adam shifted into low gear and inched his way behind the cattle.

I HIDE IN THE HAY. MY FATHER STOMPS INTO THE BARN AND ROARS MY NAME. HE KICKS THE HAY AWAY AND JERKS ME TO MY FEET. I CAN SMELL THE STINK OF ALCOHOL AND GARLIC FROM HIM. HE KICKS ME TO MY KNEES AND BEATS ME UNTIL HE MUST STOP AND WHEEZE TO CATCH HIS BREATH.

HE SITS ACROSS THE TABLE FROM ME REEKING WITH HIS ODOURS AND REELING. THE BORSCHT AND MEAT SLITHER DOWN HIS CAKED BEARD AS HE STUFFS HIS MOUTH LIKE AN ANIMAL. HE BELCHES AND LICKS HIS FINGERS AND COMPLAINS THAT HE OWES THE VILLAGE JEW MONEY. EVERYONE IN THE VILLAGE OWES MONEY TO THE JEW.

HE GRABS ME, SHAKES ME, AND LAUGHS AT MY FEAR. WHY DOESN'T HE BEAT MY BROTHERS AND SISTERS? WHY ONLY ME? BECAUSE MY MOTHER LOVES ME THE MOST, THAT'S WHY.

THROUGH THE CRACKS IN THE WALL THAT SEPARATE OUR ROOMS I SEE HIM STANDING NAKED. HIS PENIS IS ENORMOUS AND BLACK AND UGLY AND FILLED WITH VEINS. IT GLISTENS FROM WHAT CAME OUT OF MY MOTHER. HE SCRATCHES IT AND PLAYS WITH HIS HUGE HANGING TESTICLES.

I HATE HIS PENIS AND TESTICLES! IT MAKES MY MOTHER CRY WHEN HE DOES IT TO HER. HE GRUNTS LIKE A PIG WHEN HE IS ON HER.

IF I HAD MY WAY I'D TAKE A ROCK AND SMASH HIS TESTICLES. I'D CUT THEM OFF WITH A KNIFE.

I WANT TO SLEEP CUDDLED WITH MY MOTHER. LIKE SHE USED TO DO BEFORE I GREW TOO OLD. HER BREASTS WERE LARGE AND WARM AND I COULD BURY MY FACE IN THEM AND TOUCH THEM WITH MY FINGERS. SHE DOESN'T MIND BECAUSE I AM STILL LITTLE. I RUN AND HIDE IN HER SKIRTS AND SHE

LIFTS ME TO HER AND HOLDS ME AGAINST HER BREASTS.

THEN HE WILL FIND ME AND PULL ME AWAY FROM HER AND SHAKE ME AND BEAT ME. I AM ALWAYS FILLED WITH BRUISES.

I MUST RUN TO THE CITY, WHERE HE CAN NEVER FIND ME AGAIN.

THE SNOW COVERS THE GROUND AND I STAND BY MY MOTHER'S GRAVE. HE KILLED HER, AS THOUGH WITH HIS OWN HANDS.

HE IS OLD NOW AND UNABLE TO BEAT ME AND HIS FILTHY ORGANS NO LONGER FUNCTION.

'Adam! Adam!'

'What? Eh ... eh ...'

'Adam!'

'What?'

'You are speeding. You're driving almost a hundred miles an hour.'

'Oh, sorry. My mind must have wandered.'

The clinic was filled, as usual, but Terrence Campbell was down from Oxford for a few days so things were right. Terry would begin his medical training in Guy's Hospital in the fall. It would be so wonderful to have him always close at hand. The boy worked with him through the day giving shots, doing lab work, taking tests, consulting his guardian on diagnosis. He was a born physician.

The last of the patients were gone and they retired to his office.

'What do you make of this,' Adam said, putting an X-ray to the light.

Terry studied it. 'Shadows. A spot. T.B.?'

'I'm suspicious of cancer.'

Terry looked at the name on the envelope. 'That poor woman has five children.'

'Cancer has no conscience,' Dr. Kelno answered.

'I know, but what will happen to the children? They'll have to go to an orphanage.'

'I have been wanting to talk to you about this sort of thing. It is the one part of medicine where you show a marked weakness. In order to be a good physician you must build an intellectual reservoir that will enable you to stand the sight of a dead friend. The physician who gets emotionally involved with his patients cannot exist long.'

Terry shook his head that he understood but continued to stare at the X-ray.

'Well, on the other hand, she may not have cancer and if she does it may not be terminal. There's something else I want to show you.' He opened his desk drawer and handed Terry a legal document with a cheque attached to it, in the amount of nine hundred pounds.

'What is it?'

'An apology from the printers to be read in open court. What is more, the insurers for Shawcross are refusing to back a defence. I understand that Cady was in London and left rather frantically.'

'Thank God it will soon be over,' Terry said.

'Im glad you helped make me to it, you and Stephan. I'm going after Cady. I will take him to task in every country where his filthy book was published. The Americans in particular will pay dearly.'

'Doctor,' Terry said softly, 'when you went into this, you did it for a lofty purpose. It's beginning to sound as though you are bent on vengeance.'

'Well, what of it?'

'To seek revenge for the sake of revenge is an evil in itself.'

'Don't quote to me from the Oxford philosophers. What do you think this Cady deserves for what he has done?'

'If he concedes his mistake and wishes to purge himself you have to adopt a charitable attitude. You can't hound him to death.'

'The same kind of charity I received in Jadwiga, in Brixton. The same kind of hounding. No more, no less. They're the ones who say an eye for an eye.'

'But don't you see that if you adopt this attitude, you put yourself in a position of behaving like ... well, a Nazi.'

'I thought you would be proud of this,' Adam said, closing the drawer.

'I am, Doctor, but don't destroy yourself seeking revenge. I don't think Stephan would want that either.'

Sir Robert Highsmith snipped away at the myriad of rose stalks, leaving only the healthiest to grow later in the summer. He pottered with a particular detachment in his garden in Richmond, Surrey.

'Darling, tea is ready,' Cynthia said.

He tugged off his gloves and made to the conservatory of his small manor, which had been the gatehouse of a royal estate two centuries earlier.

'Roses should be lovely this year,' he mumbled.

'Robert,' his wife said, 'you've been rather far away all weekend.'

'Kelno affair. Strange happenings.'

'Oh? I thought it was almost over with.'

'So did I. Suddenly old Shawcross did a complete turn about when it appeared his insurers were on the verge of an apology in open court. The Cady chap has come to London and is going to fight the case. Shawcross has joined him. The most puzzling thing of all is that Tom Bannister has taken the case.'

'Tom? Isn't that rather risky of him.'

'Chancy, indeed.'

'Do you suppose Sir Adam has told you everything?'

'It would leave one to wonder, wouldn't it?'

ELEVEN

Jerusalem—April 1966

Dr. Leiberman responded to a ring of the bell in his flat on David Marcus Street.

'I am Shimshon Aroni,' the man before him said.

'I was expecting you'd find me,' Dr. Leiberman answered.

Aroni, the famed Nazi hunter, followed the doctor into his study. His sixty-eight years were deceptive. Aroni was keen and active behind a hard wrinkled face. By contrast Franz Leiberman was soft and fatherly.

'I have read the stories you have planted in the newspapers and magazines. Who did you find?'

'Moshe Bar Tov at Kibbutz Ein Gev. He gave me the names of the others. All told, four men, two women, whom you have treated over the years. You know what is going on in London. I have come to you because of your relationship with these people. It would be easier to convince them to testify if their doctor co-operated.'

'I won't co-operate. They've suffered enough.'

'Suffered? If you're a Jew you suffer. You never stop suffering. What about you and your family, Dr. Leiberman. How many did you lose?'

'My dear Aroni. What do you want? To put them on display like animals. To speak in a public courtroom about their mutilations. The women in particular will never be well. With careful treatment, the devotion of their families, they are able to carry on what appears to be a normal existence. But what has happened to them is buried in a dark room. They risk a dangerous traumatic shock if they have to bring it all up again.'

'It will be brought up again. We will never allow this to be forgotten. We will throw it up for the world to look at at every opportunity.'

'You are hardened by years of hunting war criminals. I

223

think you are a professional vengeance seeker.'

'Perhaps I went mad,' Aroni said, 'when my wife and children were torn from my arms at the selection centre at Auschwitz. What has to be done, has to be done. Do I see them separately or do you co-operate?'

Franz Leiberman knew Aroni was a relentless tracker. He would never let go. One by one he would drain and shame each of them into testifying. At least if they met together as a group, they could give each other courage.

Alexander, Bernstein & Friedman
Solicitors
8 Park Square
Lincoln's Inn
London WC 2

April 30, 1966

Shalom Alexander:

I report progress. I have met with six victims whose names and preliminary statements are attached. I have convinced them they have no choice but to come to London. Franz Leiberman will travel with them. He will be a calming influence.

Through discussions I have learned the names of two other victims, one Ida Peretz née Cardozo, who lives in Trieste. I leave to see her tomorrow.

Also, one Hans Hasse of Haarlemmerweg 126 in Amsterdam.

I suggest you supply this information to the I.F.J.O. in The Hague.

I will continue to report as events warrant.

Yours,
Aroni

Nathan Goldmark had aged seedily. When his position as an investigator for the secret police in the matter of war crimes ceased to exist he wormed his way into the hierarchy of the Jewish Section of the Polish Communist Party.

Most of Poland's Jews had been exterminated by the Nazis. Most of the survivors fled. A minute minority of a few thousand chose to remain for reasons of old age and fear of the hardships in beginning a new life. A few stayed as idealistic Communists.

Writers such as Abraham Cady took the view that the extermination camps would not have been possible in a civilized Western country that did not agree in spirit with what the Nazis were doing. There were no extermination camps in Norway or Denmark or Holland or France or Belgium despite their occupation nor in Finland or Italy despite the fact they were German allies. Poland, however, with its centuries' tradition of anti-Semitism was a practical place for the Auschwitzs and Treblinkas and Jadwigas.

In order to live down this reputation Poland later went through the motions of keeping a Jewish community in the country as a showpiece to the world that things had changed under communism. Intact were a few synagogues, a small Jewish press, and a national theatre kept as superficial and pitiful remnants of the once great community of three and a half million.

Using Nazi methods of forcing the Jews to do it to themselves, a separate Jewish branch of the Communist Party was invoked upon them with the mission of keeping and controlling some kind of Jewish population. They tried vainly to flog life into the theatre and press with Communist slogans.

Nathan Goldmark, a crafty politician whose sole ethics were survival and servitude, was put to good use as a tool of the regime.

His train had climbed into the Carpathian Mountains where the last snows of winter were retreating into the glacier fields. Zakopane, in addition to being a winter resort, was Poland's most important centre for tuberculars.

He had come to keep an appointment with Dr. Maria Viskova, chief medical officer of a worker's sanatorium and of the rarest breed, a Jewish Polish Communist out of belief. As a national heroine she had chosen to work away from Warsaw and the Nathan Goldmarks, whom she despised.

Her appearance, of one who has known enormous tragedy, had been softened by the years and translated into compassion. In her fifties, Maria Viskova was a silvered and handsome woman. She closed her office door behind her. A late spring storm of half rain, half heavy wet snow was falling.

Nathan Goldmark unbundled and crouched over her desk, hiding his bitten nails and tugging at the collar over the skin rash on his neck.

'I am in Zakopane to speak to you on the Kelno matter,' he said. 'It has been brought to our attention you have been contacted by certain Western elements.'

'Yes, by a firm of solicitors in London.'

'You know our position about international Zionism.'

'Goldmark. Don't waste my time or the time of my patients with this nonsense.'

'Please, Comrade Doctor. I have travelled a long way. Twenty years ago you made a statement against Kelno. The committee feels your position is no longer valid.'

'Why? You were eager enough to extradite him to Poland for trial. You yourself took my statement. What changed your mind? Kelno has never answered for what he did.'

'The matter became invalid when the Hungarian, Eli Janos, failed to recognize Kelno in a police line-up.'

'You know as well as I do, Goldmark, that Dr. Konstanty Lotaki was also doing these operations with Kelno and that in all likelihood it was Lotaki who castrated Janos.'

'Pure speculation. Besides, Lotaki has purged himself of guilt and totally rehabilitated himself as a dedicated Communist.'

'It is nothing short of criminal that Lotaki has never been

226

brought to justice. What is all this about, Goldmark? The guilty have suddenly become innocent. Twenty years or a hundred years do not absolve them of their crimes. And what of Mark Tesslar, who saw Kelno at his work?'

'The committee feels that the word of Tesslar cannot be relied upon.'

'Why? Because he defected? Does that make him a liar?'

'Comrade Doctor,' Goldmark argued, 'I can only convey the recommendations of the committee. In the days we were trying to extradite Adam Kelno the British were attempting to discredit the legitimate Communist government of Poland. Today we look to the West for co-operation. The committee feels that it is best not to stir up old hatreds. After all, Kelno has been knighted. For Poland to co-operate in this trial could be considered as an affront to the British . . .'

Goldmark chewed at his fingernails under the heat of the glare of Maria Viskova.

'There is another matter and it is that of Abraham Cady, a Zionist provocator and an enemy of the Polish people.'

'Have you read *The Holocaust*, Goldmark?'

'I don't wish to comment on that.'

'Don't worry, I won't report you to the committee.'

'It is filled with slanders, lies, provocations, and Zionist propaganda.'

The snow fell more heavily. Goldmark, the master at avoiding eyes, was all but shattered. He decided to walk to the window and comment on the weather. The courage of Maria Viskova was well known. Her dedication as a Communist was above question. One might think, for the good of the party, she would yield on the issue and save them embarrassment. How would he be able to report her attitude back to Warsaw? The thought occurred to him that the secret police should enter the matter and silence her. But then the Zionists would get wind of it and create an international scandal.

'I intend to go to London at the time of the trial, Goldmark. What are your intentions?'

'It is a question for the committee,' he answered.

Paris Rambouillet—June 1966

The home of Dr. Susanne Parmentier a few miles south of Paris was neat, quaint, and with a touch of elegance, as Jacob Alexander had envisioned it. He and Samuel Edelman, the French I.F.J.O. representative, were led by a bent old servant to the drawing room after which he fetched Madame Parmentier from the garden.

She was quite aged, in her mid- or late seventies, but there was a Gallic twinkle in her eye. She seated them in a room of high taste most prominently adorned with silver framed photographs of her late husband, their children, and grandchildren.

Alexander excused himself for his fractured French accent.

'When I received the letter from Maria Viskova stating she had given you my name I had very mixed thoughts on the matter. As you can see I am quite old and decrepit and not altogether well. I am not so certain I can be of much help, but Maria said to see you and so, here we are.'

'We've studied your situation as an inmate of Jadwiga and we definitely feel the importance of your testimony,' Alexander said.

She shrugged and gestured heavily with her hands and arms as she spoke. 'I only knew of Kelno's activities second-handed. I cannot swear to it through personal observation.'

'But you are close to Mark Tesslar.'

'We are like brother and sister.'

'Strange, he never gave your name.'

'He was only honouring my wishes. Until I received Maria Viskova's letter I saw no reason to bring up the past.'

'Let me ask you a direct question,' Alexander said.

'I will try not to give you an evasive French answer.'

'The case may largely depend on Tesslar's testimony. What is your opinion of his reliability? As a practising psychiatrist, Dr. Parmentier. I'd like a view detached from your personal friendship with him.'

'To speak to you in lay terms, Mr. Alexander, I would say something may have happened to him that day in November when he witnessed Kelno's surgery. The impact of the trauma may have caused him to cloud his judgement.'

'It is a gamble we must make, as you know. What about Kelno's charges that Tesslar was an abortionist before the war and later in the concentration camps?'

'A fantasy of Adam Kelno. Anyone who knows Mark Tesslar knows he is a humanitarian. He left Poland to finish his medical studies in Switzerland because of anti-Semitism. Both Maria Viskova and I will swear he never performed an abortion for the Nazis.'

'Will you come to London?'

'I have meditated for many hours. I have conferred with my pastor at great length and prayed for divine guidance. As a Christian, I have no choice but to testify.'

The sparkle left her eyes and she was weary. She plodded to a spray of flowers, nipped a pair of tea roses, and placed one in each of their boutonniere buttonholes.

'There is a woman in Antwerp who was operated upon on that day. After the war I gave her psychiatric care for several years. She is a person of great character. Her scar will never heal, but I know she would never forgive me if I did not take you to see her.'

TWELVE

Millie brought in the morning mail. Abe thumbed through the envelopes and smiled. There was a letter from Vanessa. He would save that for last.

He opened a letter from his French publisher, who

moaned prolifically but enclosed a cheque for two thousand dollars to help defend the libel suit.

All of his publishers had now been accounted for. The first to come through with five thousand dollars had been his German publisher, a militant anti-Nazi who had been sentenced to death for his implication in the plot to kill Hitler and who had cheated the gallows as a result of a bomb raid on Berlin, which allowed him to escape prison.

They all contributed something, except the Swedes. The smaller publishers beat their chests the loudest.

At last he opened Vanessa's envelope.

Kibbutz Sede Boker
July 25, 1966

10 Morningside Lane
Sausalito

Dear Daddy:

You have been reading between the lines since you left Israel last winter. Yossi and I have fallen deeply in love. The summer in the desert has been hot and oppressive, yet it has failed to dampen our spirits or our feeling for one another.

I don't know why this should make me feel sad except that taking on the commitment of him means ending a part of my past life. Yossi has another year to go in the Army and four years at the university. It is going to be a long pull and I don't feel I ought to burden him with a marriage.

I dread having to write my next words for they say that I won't be coming to America. With things getting worse again on the borders, I am reluctant to leave Israel even for a visit. The exception, of course, is to be with you in London during the trial.

230

Having shared with you the writing of *The Holocaust* I know what you will have to go through on an even more difficult new novel, and I feel as though I have let you down.

Ben asked me to write in his behalf as he will be on special manoeuvres for a fortnight. He's quite the Israeli officer, grown a large moustache, and is filled with sabra bluster and confidence. Ben's not serious about any girl in particular but all of them in general. Rather like his father in that respect.

He will also try to arrange leave in order to be in London so let us know when the trial is due.

Yossi has never been out of Israel. I hope he can also join us.

Daddy, I hope I haven't hurt you too much.

> Your loving daughter,
> Vanessa

August 3, 1966

My dearest Vinney:

I'd lie if I said I wasn't disappointed, but I agree with your decision one thousand per cent. The one thing we have never gone for is a daughter with a daddy hang-up. It's at this time of life I feel some guilt about all the months and years I've had to spend away in my work, but I think we've made it up during our times together and certainly in our relationship.

The closer I come to starting the book the more I realize the less I know. I'm not *young* enough to know everything. Only college kids are young enough to have all the answers and they seem very very intolerant.

It amuses me that this massive anti-establishment of today will be the establishment of tomorrow. In a few years the red hots will have to cool off and take over. Despite a number of innovations they will basically fall in love, marry, have children, struggle to raise their families, and search for a moment of peace. Very same bag I had.

But what is going to happen when *they* inherit the establishment? Will they be as tolerant of beats, junkies, rebels, rioters, and God knows what's coming up in the future. Well, I think they'd better start getting a little more tolerant of us old bastards who may have a little light to shed.

What I really wish is that they had a hero who wasn't an anti-hero. Something to live and strive for rather than the 'divine' mission of levelling everything to the ground. Something in this world like what you and Ben have found.

It appears that we won't come to trial until spring. I hang on every news broadcast gravely concerned over what appears to be an inevitable second round with the Arabs. Well, it's the price of our Jewishness, yours in Israel ... mine waiting for me in London. Will they ever let us alone?

My love to everyone. Tell your Yossi I wrote him to be sure to attend to his homework.

Dad

THIRTEEN

Mary Bates slipped a mini-skirt over her panty hose, then zipped up a pair of knee-length boots. Terrence Campbell propped up in bed on an elbow. He loved watching Mary dress, especially when she sat before the mirror without her bra, combing out her long blonde hair. Mini-skirts were crazy, he thought. They went about with freezing bottoms but if they wanted to show it, Terry would look.

Mary came over and sat on the edge of the bed. He opened the covers to invite her in. 'Love,' she said, 'I can't.'

'Quickie.'

'You are naughty. Up now. You'll be late for your first class.'

'One little taste.'

She threw the covers back and bit his bare behind gently.

'Jesus Christ, it's cold,' Terry cried.

'Look at his poor little shrivelled up thingie.'

'Wake him up.'

'Tonight.'

She spun off the bed before he could grab her and made to the tiny sink and stove on the opposite side of the room. It was only one room and a sort of bath, but Mary had managed to doll it up with odds and ends and clever sewing. Anyhow, it was theirs. After a year of Terry coming down from Oxford and making love in parked cars, on living-room couches, and in cheap hotels, at last they had some privacy.

The room was in a turning off the Old Kent Road, within walking distance of Guy's Hospital and Medical College, where Terry had begun his studies.

Terry shivered at the breakfast table. Mary was a lousy cook. It would be nice if Mary and Angela Kelno would become friends and she would learn to cook.

'We have a bloody uncivilized country,' Terry grumbled. 'Here in the middle of the twentieth century in an advanced Western nation you'd think the bloody flats would have hot water and central heating.'

'We'll have it someday,' she said.

Young love can overlook a lot of discomforts and they were strong for each other after more than a year.

'I'll be going straight from school to the Kelnos,' he said. It was a weekly ritual he looked forward to. A hearty augment to their thin diet. 'Will you be coming from work?'

'Can't come tonight, Terry. I talked to my sister yesterday and we made a date to take in a flick.'

Terry pouted. His toast was like a board. He broke it, smeared it in the egg yolks, and crunched it. 'This will make three weeks in a row you haven't been to the Kelnos.'

'Terry, let's don't get into an argument now.' Then she sighed and took his hand. 'Love, we've been all over it a thousand times. My family has disowned me. Sir Adam doesn't like me or our living together.'

'He's going to damned well respect you, Mary. I've written my father about you. Hell, he and mother had two children together before they were married and God knows they loved each other. Now, you just call your sister and break your date.'

'We haven't got a phone.'

'Call her from work.'

'Terry. What Sir Adam is really afraid of is that I *will* marry you. I'm just a plain little shop girl, really not good enough.'

'Rubbish.'

Or was it, Terry thought. A lot of their friends had the same arrangement. Students at Guy's. Their girls supporting them. When he graduated from Oxford and came to London they decided they weren't going to yield to the hypocrites, and they'd live together. The families of the girls invariably wanted marriage. Marriage meant respectability. An outdated notion of respectability.

The parents of the boys felt their sons could do better. After all, what kind of a girl would just leave her home and live with a student in a walk-up room? Not the kind they would want him to marry.

And all of the girls, despite their declarations of independence, really wanted marriage. So, in defying tradition they actually sought it.

Mary wanted to marry Terrence Campbell more than anything in life. There really wasn't much novel about it at all.

Dinner was late. Sir Adam Kelno attended a cocktail party in his honour. In the past six weeks there had been as many luncheons, dinners, and parties. The old Polish community of London was suddenly alive with a cause and even though they were permanently settled in England, they would continue to dream.

The libel case was a matter of Polish honour. His supporters were liberally sprinkled with high-standing British sympathizers. Adam silently gloried in this hero's role.

'I do hope,' Angela said, 'Mary knows she is welcome here.'

'I suggest you give her a call and tell her that,' Terry said.

'And teach her how to cook,' Adam said. 'You look like a scarecrow.'

'All medical students look like malnutrition victims,' Terry said. 'Remember?'

After dinner, things calmed. Adam had lectured at Guy's and was vitally interested in every aspect of Terry's studies. For the first year student it was mostly a concentration of chemistry, physics, and biology. Nothing really meaty for him yet.

Adam attempted not to bring up the subject of Mary Bates but instead made a general attack on the younger generation.

'Who,' he asked Terry, 'has to clean up the mess from overdoses of LSD and attempted abortions and venereal disease? I do. I have a clinic full of them. There is no morality left.'

235

'I have to get home now.'

'I don't understand Stephan, either. I don't understand any of you.'

FOURTEEN

One of the prime movers of the British legal machinery is the Master system. Masters are a kind of assistant judges or referees. The Master has been a barrister ten years or more before his appointment and sets the mode and preparation of a trial. They sit in chambers in the Royal Court of Justice doing away with much of the legal boon-doggle that lawyers use to plague courts in other parts of the world.

The Master will make rulings on the number of witnesses permitted, the approximate time a case should be scheduled, the pre-questioning of witnesses, rulings on amendments to complaints and pleadings, and issuance of orders to produce documents.

In certain instances the Master will try a case.

His rulings are quick and concise, accurate to the application of the law, and rarely overruled later in court.

The Masters Chambers border a large room called the 'Bear Garden' where solicitors gather to make an appearance. They come in pin stripes, young hopefuls, tired old shabby ones, long haired, short haired.

The Master is seated behind a counter-like affair, calling opposing solicitors before him every several minutes. He scans their briefs.

'Well, what is it you want?'

The solicitors argue. Often an astute Master will say, 'Some things are so clear they shouldn't be argued.'

At that point the solicitors retreat to the Bear Garden

having been subtly warned that one side is wasting his client's money and the court's time. An agreement may be made on the spot and a lawsuit stopped dead.

Before a lawsuit appears in court, the Master will have clearly set down the rules of verbal combat.

For an important trial such as the Kelno versus Cady affair, Master Bartholomew will take up the matter in his private chambers in deference to the appearances of barristers of the eminence of Thomas Bannister and Sir Robert Highsmith. In the chambers of Master Bartholomew came the first probings concerning the admissibility of certain witnesses and documents.

In the winter of 1966–67 formality was chucked. Tom Bannister's chambers and apartment were often too busy with political callers. Alexander's office in Lincoln's Inn was an impossible place of nooks and crannies unable to accommodate the mass of data flowing back from all over the world. There was a unanimous feeling that Shawcross's fabled library should become the command centre. In an unusual move they gathered every several days to fine-comb the correspondence, discuss strategy, and make the decisions.

The first bridge was the selection of a junior barrister. Traditionally the solicitor selected a junior but because of Bannister's eminence they casually waited for him to drop a name. That name was Brendon O'Conner; a flamboyant, brilliant, sentimental idealist. O'Conner and Bannister represented different styles of advocacy but the junior was an incredibly tireless worker and the soundness of his appointment became apparent very early.

Libel was one of six non-criminal categories in which either party could call for trial by jury. It was extremely rare in civil matters. The jury or not the jury has baffled lawyers since the inception of law. They could be astute or extremely dull or compromise poorly in the pressure of the jury room debates. Again, they yielded to Bannister, who said that twelve Englishmen could not be fooled, and the Junior applied to the Master for a jury. The application was automatically granted.

The list of potential witnesses grew. In the hands of Bannister and O'Conner a weak case could be turned into a strong case. The flaw, obvious to the astute observer, was only a single eyewitness, Dr. Mark Tesslar, who was highly vulnerable.

Pieter Van Damm held a mighty answer, but they remained under rigid instructions by Cady that he was not to testify.

There was a long shot that could bail them out, if Egon Sobotnik, the medical clerk at Jadwiga, were still alive, and if he could be found, and if he could be convinced to testify. If, if, if, if, if. All trails to find Sobotnik went cold. Even the dogged hunter Aroni, who was now putting his full time on the project, was unable to piece the clues together.

In his brief to counsel, Jacob Alexander prepared a massive document containing the statements of witnesses and all other relevant material.

The brief began with the year 1939 when Poland was attacked by Germany, then backtracked to a few slim facts on Kelno's prewar life. He was followed into Jadwiga Concentration Camp as a prisoner/doctor.

The document continued that in the middle of the war two Nazis, SS Dr. Colonel Adolph Voss and SS Dr. Colonel Otto Flensberg, induced Himmler to allow them to establish an experimental centre in Jadwiga with the use of human guinea pigs. Voss's main experiments were directed to finding a method of mass sterilization of Jews and others whom the Germans deemed 'unworthy of normal life'. Such sterilized persons could be used as a labour force for the Third Reich with controlled breeding to keep the slave ranks filled. All others would be exterminated.

The brief cited some fifty books and war crimes trials for reference. Voss had committed suicide before his trial and Flensberg had escaped to an African country where he now resides and practises. A number of minor doctors and orderlies including Flensberg's assistant stood trial. Half of them were hanged and the others sentenced to prison.

238

Assisting Voss in his experiments were named three prisoner/doctors, Adam Kelno, Konstanty Lotaki, and a Jew, Boris Dimshits.

The brief contained an exhaustive study of the medical experiments, the facility, the doctors who refused to co-operate.

When all the material had been gone over and all the discussions weighed and the various defences studied, a plea of 'Justification' was entered to the effect that what was said in *The Holocaust* was substantially true. The plea stated an admission that the defendants were the writer and publisher of the book. They further stated they could not support the figure of fifteen thousand experiments without anaesthetic. They contended that the number was unimportant in that many experiments were carried out and carried out in a brutal manner and therefore the plaintiff had not been seriously defamed.

In the first week of April 1967 Abraham Cady arrived in London. Vanessa was there to greet him. Her fiancé, Yossi, and Ben would come from Israel shortly.

Samantha had remarried a squire type, Reggie Brooke, who was good with horses and hay, and accounts. The years had mellowed her bitterness toward Abe. When she knew he was coming she offered the flat in Colchester Mews for his stay.

The Crown Office of the Supreme Court informed the Sheriff of London to summon seventy-five persons from the Jurors Book.

The undersheriff selected a panel by a random lottery and the prospective jurors were informed and the list of their names made public for inspection.

The challenging of a jury in England is rare because prima facie evidence must be produced against the juror. A lot of days and weeks of unnecessary courtroom haggling are thus avoided by the acceptance of the jury without challenge.

In Israel four frightened men and two women and their doctor continued to justify the coming trip.

In Warsaw, Dr. Maria Viskova picked up her visa.

In Rambouillet, in Brussels, in Trieste, in Sausalito, in Amsterdam ... doubts raged, nightmares recurred. It would all take place soon. The whole thing would be re-lived.

The time of trial was drawing near with neither side showing an inclination to negotiate a settlement. The case that would 'never go to court' was close at hand and each party wondered how much the other really knew.

The Cady camp was engaged in a huge and urgent man-hunt for the long disappeared Egon Sobotnik, the medical clerk of Jadwiga.

In Oxford, Dr. Mark Tesslar drew back from the microscope and set his glasses straight. His hand did not even tremble, which was rather remarkable for a man who had just seen the evidence of his own cancer.

'I'm sorry, Mark,' his colleague said.

'I guess we'll have to do an exploratory. The sooner the better.'

Tesslar shrugged. 'After two massive coronaries, I really don't think I'm going to escape this one. I want you to do the operation, Oscar. I'm not in great pain as yet whether the cancer is terminal or not. You are to keep me alive somehow, until I give my testimony. Afterwards, we'll dis-cuss what is necessary.'

FOUR

THE TRIAL

ONE

THE HIGH COURT OF JUSTICE   April 16, 1967
QUEEN'S BENCH DIVISION   QUEEN'S BENCH COURT VII
Before Mr. Justice Gilray
Sir Adam Kelno, M.D., vs. Abraham Cady and others.

Jesus, Solomon, and King Alfred rated status over the front entrance of the Royal Courts of Justice, which fronted five hundred feet where the Strand becomes Fleet Street at Temple Bar. These three were joined by twenty-four lesser bishops and scholars.

Moses brought up the rear entrance on Carey Street, a block away.

The bell tower, which soared a hundred and sixty feet over Bell Yard, looked down on an enormity that could be described as neo-Gothic, neo-monastic, and neo-Victorian. A seemingly aimless scramble of spires, towers, oriel windows, cone-shaped steepled buttresses, Norman ornamental mouldings, and ribs all in bulky grey stone blackened under years of soot.

On both sides of the entry stood the barristers' robing room. To the left, cameras are checked in. At the entrance to the mosaic-paved great hall is posted the Daily Cause List. The hall, two hundred and fifty feet in length, soars eighty feet in height and all of it is properly garnished with statues of the renowned. Running the length of a stone vaulted ceiling is a series of perpendicular tracery windows bearing stained glass coats of arms of all the Lord Chancellors of England.

The office of the Tipstaff stands on a balcony at the far

end of the great hall. Once an official who carried a tipped staff to denote his office, today he maintains order within the court as a sergeant at arms.

All of this cumbersome building stands on six acres of ground flanked by St. Dunstan's in the West and St. Clement Danes, churches of old and stately stature.

The court stands as a giant planet of law with its satellites, the surrounding Inns and Chancery Lane.

The first law court was in Westminster Hall, dating from the thirteenth century, the trial place where Charles I and the martyr Thomas More found mock justice, and from whose bowels thundered history from the installation of Cromwell to the condemnation of Guy Fawkes and Essex. It is here that the royal, the noble, and the eminent lay in state before burial in the abbey over the way. Westminster Hall became outdated and inconveniently located to the proximity of the Inns of Court and so the Royal Courts came into existence in the mid-Victorian times.

Thomas Bannister and Brendon O'Conner, already wigged and gowned, crossed the Strand past a busy knot of assembled journalists, into the court and up the stairs to the consultation room opposite QB VII where Jacob Alexander, Mr. Josephson, and Sheila Lamb had already assembled.

Now Sir Robert Highsmith and his junior, Chester Dicks, in bowler, pin stripes and carrying umbrellas and red and blue bags of stuff gowns and silk gowns, made off to the robing room.

Sir Adam Kelno arrived with his wife and Terrence Campbell pushing into the building abruptly. In his hand he clutched a cable from his son.

'There's Cady and Shawcross.'

'Mr. Cady, would you say a few words on . . .'

'Sorry fellows. Strict orders. No comment.'

'Who's the girl?'

'I think that's Cady's daughter.'

Samantha and Reggie Brooke arrived unnoticed.

Ushers, court reporters, associates, journalists, spectators buzzed around QB VII in a cold stone hallway as the hour approached.

A narrow polished hallway separates the row of judges' chambers from the rear of their courtrooms. Justice Gilray adjusted his wig and the ermine collar on his scarlet robe. Gilray, a hawk-faced man, was long trained to appear emotionless and seemingly bored, a judge's role he enjoyed. Many judges and barristers sought membership in the Garrick Club, where they could hobnob with theatrical people for they in turn used the courtroom as their own special stage. This was particularly true of libel lawyers, many of whom were frustrated actors.

The courtroom filled slowly through a twin entry of green draped alcoves. Dead ahead was the Queen's Bench on a raised dais looking down on austere wooden benches and tables for the associate, the solicitors, barristers, the press, jury, and spectators. It was all heavily panelled in oak, topped with a series of leaded cathedral windows high up on the balcony level. A pair of chandeliers with bell-shaped shades hovered from a stone ceiling and the monotony of the wood was broken here and there by a wrought iron rail, a row of lawbooks, a relentless clock.

Cady and Shawcross took their places behind Brendon O'Conner in the first row of the spectators' benches. David nudged Abe and nodded down their row to where Angela Kelno and a handsome boy, Terrence Campbell, were seated.

Abe smiled to Samantha and Vanessa, who moved up behind them with Lorraine Shawcross and Geoffrey, Pam, and Cecil Dodd. Then he looked down to the solicitors' table, where Adam Kelno sat with unwavering calm. Abe had interviewed thousands of people and was shrewd in finding a betrayal of that calm as Adam looked around for his wife and son.

Suddenly Kelno and Cady were staring at each other across the room. The first exchange was hostile and then they probed and pondered. Abe continued to feel anger, but Kelno had a sudden puzzled expression of 'What are we doing here?'

Their attention was diverted by the jury filing in. Eight

men, four women. They seemed totally nondescript. Twelve commonplace Englishmen and women to be found on any street.

A last flurry of whispers between barristers and solicitors and a shuffling of papers.

'Silence!'

Everyone arose as the Honourable Mr. Justice Anthony Gilray entered from a door behind the Queen's Bench. The entire court bowed to him as he took his seat in a deep, high-backed leather chair.

Sir Robert Highsmith bounced to his feet and informally chatted with the judge in reckoning it would be a long trial.

Thomas Bannister arose. Of average build and good English looks, the power generated from within him. His voice was soft and seemingly monotone until one began to find its rhythm. He agreed that the trial would be lengthy.

Gilray swung his chair toward the jury box and advised them in the matter of serving under undue hardship. No reply. 'I should like to ask if any of you lost relatives in a concentration camp?'

Both Bannister and O'Conner came to their feet. Bannister turned and looked over his shoulder to his junior to advise him he had the matter in hand. 'If his Lordship establishes this kind of condition for the jury then we will have to establish opposite conditions, namely any peculiar sympathy in behalf of physicians, knights, former Polish nationalists ... all kinds of conditions.'

'I meant,' the judge answered, 'I would not wish anyone who has lost a relative in a concentration camp to have to undergo undue suffering because of the revelations of this trial.'

'In that case, I have no objection to the question.'

It was asked without reply from the jury and they were sworn in.

The clock ticked audibly between rows of lawbooks on the left wall as Sir Robert Highsmith unfolded his notes on the rostrum on his table and stretched his back with his hands on hips. He studied the jury for a long moment and cleared his throat several times. In an English court the barrister is obliged to remain standing behind the rostrum which limits his physical gestures and mobility. Unable to parade all over the courtroom he must be a quick thinking orator whose elocution is clear and in a manner easily grasped.

'My Lord, members of the jury,' Highsmith began, 'this is an action for damages for libel. A libel, I suggest, as damning as ever came before an English court. We are going to be asked to take ourselves out of the comforts of London in 1967, for what we are concerned with is a nightmare of a Nazi concentration camp that existed over two decades ago against a background of the most incredible hell ever created by man.'

He held up a copy of *The Holocaust* and with deliberate slowness opened it to page 167. Another beat in time passed as he looked directly at every man and woman of the jury individually. He read, pausing carefully. ' "Of all the concentration camps none was more infamous than Jadwiga. It was here that SS Dr. Colonel Adolph Voss established an experimental centre for the purpose of creating methods of mass sterilization, with the use of human guinea pigs, and SS Dr. Colonel Otto Flensberg and his assistant carried on equally horrendous studies on prisoners. In the notorious Barrack V a secret surgery was run by Dr. Kelno, who carried out fifteen thousand or more experimental operations without the use of anaesthetic." Ladies and gentlemen of the jury, let me repeat this passage ... "fifteen thousand or more experimental operations without the use of anaesthetic." '

He slammed the book shut and let it drop from the rostrum to the table with a thud and stared at the ceiling.

'What,' he shouted, 'could be a more horrendous and defamatory and dastardly an insult!' he said, rolling his r's mightily and bouncing off his toes and jabbing at the air like a boxer. 'What greater libel to a physician whose reputation goes far beyond the confines of his clinic. I should like at this time to read the words we have set out in the Plaintiff's Statement of Claim. I suggest, therefore, you be given this bundle of pleadings.'

'Do you have any objection, Mr. Bannister?' the judge asked.

'Just what do you intend giving the jury?'

'Pleadings,' Highsmith answered, 'an agreed bundle of pleadings.'

Thomas Bannister took a bundle and handed it back to O'Conner, who thumbed through it, then whispered a few words. 'We are satisfied with reservation. There have been a number of interlocutory proceedings and addendums and there may be other relevant things.'

Each of the jury was given a bundle. Mr. Justice Gilray asked them not to read it on their own. It was the first in what was to be a number of confusing steps in their legal education.

'In a libel action, the plaintiff has to prove three things. First, did the defendants publish those words? Well they don't deny that. Secondly, did the words refer to my client? They're not contesting that either. And finally, were the words defamatory? We would have to prove that except the defendants admit they are defamatory. Technically, my case is over with, and I could say go on and prove your case. But I intend to call forward Sir Adam Kelno and let you judge the character of this man and therefore the extent to which he has been libelled.'

Highsmith became cynical. 'Oh well, the defence says, that figure of fifteen thousand is not really accurate and by the way we know he didn't really operate without anaesthetics. Well, they say, maybe several hundred or several dozen. You see, they really don't know. You will appreciate, of course, that Sir Adam Kelno was not a German, not a Nazi, but a Polish prisoner. An ally who was subjected to all sorts of terror served only by the fact he was a skilled physician, and he used that skill to help his fellow-creatures. He was an ally whose personal courage saved thousands. . . . Yes, I will use the number of thousands in clear voice, thousands from disease and death. The fact is, Sir Adam Kelno did perform or assist in some fifteen thousand operations, but they were proper, necessary operations, and moreover risked his own life as a member of the underground.'

Sir Robert Highsmith went into Kelno's escape to England, his knighthood, and his distinguished work.

'This man has come here to clear his name. The printers of this book,' he said, snatching it up and holding it high, 'recognized what they had done and had the sense to apologize in open court and you might think that Abraham Cady and David Shawcross would have done the same instead of forcing us to travel this bitter road. You are a British jury and it is your charge to determine the severity of what has been done in an admitted defamation of this innocent man.'

TWO

'Sir Adam Kelno.'

He arose from the solicitors' table and gave the tiniest smile to Angela and Terry and walked up to the witness box, which stood to the left of the Queen's Bench and directly over the filled press rows.

'On which Bible do you wish to be sworn?'

'I am a Roman Catholic.'

'The Douai Bible please.'

The judge turned to Kelno. 'I presume you will be in the witness box for quite a period. I suggest that the usher bring you a chair.'

'Thank you, my Lord.'

Sir Robert Highsmith established through Kelno a history from the graduation from medical school, the coming of the war, the joining of the underground, the arrest by the Gestapo, the fearful inquisition and the imprisonment in

Jadwiga Concentration Camp in the summer of 1940.

'We were registered, bathed, shaven clean all over, and issued striped uniforms.'

'What sort of work did you do when you first arrived?'

'General labour.'

'Did the Germans realize you were a doctor?'

'Perhaps, perhaps not. In the confusion of thousands of slave labour arriving, my records may have been overlooked. In the beginning I was afraid to say I was a doctor because of the German policy of destroying educated and professional Poles.'

'But you changed your mind later?'

'Yes. I saw the suffering and I felt I could help. I could not go on hiding my profession.'

'You yourself were a victim of the early conditions, were you not?'

'I came down with typhus from the lice. I was extremely sick for several months. When I recovered I made application for transfer to the medical compound and was admitted.'

'In addition to typhus, did you suffer otherwise?'

'Yes, personal indignities.'

'Once, twice?'

'On dozens of occasions. We were punished for real or imagined infractions. The corporal in charge ran us from place to place. We were not allowed to walk. For standard punishment we were made to squat and duck walk hundreds of metres and if we fell behind we were beaten. There was also a serious outbreak of dysentery which I contracted. That was actually when I revealed I was a doctor. The Germans could not handle the epidemic.'

'And after the epidemic subsided?'

'I was allowed to organize a surgical outpatient clinic in a couple of the medical barracks. I treated things that could be done simply such as boils, abscesses, minor injuries.'

'Now, we are speaking of late in 1940. Would you describe the general condition of the medical facility?'

'Bad. We were short on all supplies and even had to use paper bandages.'

'Were there any other qualified prisoner/surgeons working with you?'

'Not at first. I had some assistants. The hospital facility was soon overrun with haematoma cases.'

'Would you explain that?'

'Severe bruising, particularly in the buttocks, causing excess bleeding in the tissues. They became septic or infected. Sometimes they contained a pint of pus. This affected the muscles so that the patient could not walk, sit, or lie down. So, I performed surgery to alleviate the suffering by an incision, a draining, and a gradual healing.'

'What was the cause of these haematoma cases?'

'Beatings by the Germans.'

'Sir Adam, did you do any amputations in this early period?'

'Yes, mostly of small limbs such as fingers and toes due to frostbite or having been broken beyond healing by German beatings.'

Highsmith took off his glasses and leaned hard toward the witness box. 'Sir Adam,' he said in a rising voice, 'did you ever operate when it wasn't necessary?'

'Never. Not then or later. Never.'

'Now then, during this time from the end of 1940 into 1942, how were you treated?'

'I was beaten on numerous occasions.'

'And what was the effect of those beatings?'

'Enormous bruises, some the size of a soccer ball. The pain was excruciating. I ran a temperature and my legs swelled until I developed varicose veins and formed phlebolith stones, which were removed after the war.'

'When did things take a turn at Jadwiga?'

'In the middle of 1941 when the Germans attacked Russia. Jadwiga was a major camp of slave labour which manufactured many things essential to the German war effort. They realized they were losing too many days of work by their brutal treatment of prisoners so they decided to develop reasonably proper medical facilities.'

'Can you recall a particular event that triggered the building of proper facilities?'

'In midwinter of 1941 a cold wave struck and we had thousands of cases of pneumonia, frostbite, and shock from exposure on our hands. We had little to treat them with, only water to drink. They were stretched out on the barrack floors side by side with barely room to walk between them and they died by the hundreds. Dead people cannot work in factories so the Germans changed their minds.'

'I'm curious, Sir Adam, if the Germans kept count of the dead?'

'The Germans have a phobia about keeping meticulous records. During the epidemic they kept count by numerous daily roll calls that began at five-thirty in the morning. The living had to carry the dead outside. Everyone had to be accounted for.'

'I see, we'll get back to that later. So after the epidemic in the winter of 1941 you were allowed to build a proper facility.'

'More or less. We did not have enough materials so at night when the compound was clear of SS we went out on raiding parties. Later more supplies became available but never enough. However, it was made more bearable as other doctors were assigned to me. I was able to set up a fairly decent surgery in Barrack XX. The German doctors sent to work with prisoners were inferior and slowly the prisoner/doctors began taking over.'

'And what of your own personal position in all this?'

'For two years I was the chief surgeon and then in August of 1943 I was made titular supervisor of the entire medical facility.'

'Titular?'

'Yes, SS Dr. Colonel Adolph Voss was the true superior and any other SS doctor had command of my activities.'

'Did Voss come in to see you often?'

'He was mostly in Barrack I through V. I stayed away as much as possible.'

'Why?'

'He was carrying on experiments.'

Sir Robert slowed and changed the volume and pace of his voice to denote a key question. 'Were any records kept of your operations and treatments?'

'I insisted on accurate records. I felt it important so that there could never be doubts of my behaviour later.'

'In what manner were these records kept?'

'In a surgical register.'

'One volume?'

'Several volumes were filled.'

'Listing every treatment or operation?'

'Yes.'

'And signed by you?'

'Yes.'

'Who kept this register?'

'A medical clerk. A Czech. I forgot his name.'

Abe passed a note to Shawcross. I FEEL LIKE STANDING UP AND YELLING 'SOBOTNIK' AND SEE IF HE REMEMBERS.

'Do you know what became of the registers?'

'I have no idea. Most of the camp was in chaos when the Russians arrived. I wish to God we had the registers here now because it would prove my innocence.'

Sir Robert was struck silent. The judge turned slowly to Kelno. 'Sir Adam,' Gilray said, 'with reference to proof of your innocence. You are the plaintiff in this case, not the defendant.'

'I meant ... clear my name.'

'Continue, Sir Robert,' the judge said.

Highsmith jumped in quickly to erase the effect of Sir Adam's bumble. 'Now, all this time you were still a prisoner under German supervision.'

'Yes. Always a prisoner. The SS had orderlies to watch our every move.'

'Can you tell us the particular significance of Jadwiga West?'

'It was the extermination facility.'

'And you know that for a fact?'

'It was common knowledge. History has since proved it. I never personally saw Jadwiga West, but I was first informed by the underground.'

'And these German orderlies under Dr. Voss, did they have any other duties than to spy on you?'

253

'They selected from my patients ... victims for the gas chamber at Jadwiga West.'

A hush descended on the courtroom. And again, all that was heard was the clock. Englishmen had only heard of this in abstract. Here before them, Sir Adam Kelno, the colour of white paste, had drawn the curtain and was playing on a stage of memory and horror.

'Would you like a recess?' the judge asked.

'No,' Adam answered. 'Not a day passes in my life that I do not remember.'

Sir Robert sighed, clutched the lapels of his robe, and lowered his voice so the jury had to strain to catch his words. 'In which manner were these people selected?'

'Sometimes the German would just point a finger at people as he passed through the ward. Those who looked the least able to survive.'

'How many?'

'It depended on how many were shipped to Jadwiga West from the outside. They filled the gas chamber quotas from the hospital. A hundred a day. Some days, two or three hundred. When thousands of Hungarians were shipped in they left us alone for a time.'

'How far was Jadwiga West located from your compound?'

'Three miles. We could see it. And ... we could smell it.'

Abraham Cady was thrown back to his own visit to Jadwiga and it was all vivid again. For an instant he looked to Adam Kelno with remorse. How in the name of God could any man stand up against what was going on?

'What did you personally do about the German selections?'

'Well, when they made a selection they painted a number on the victim's chest. We found that it could be easily washed off. We would replace them with patients who had died during the night. Since the Germans did not personally handle the bodies we were able to get away with it for a time.'

'How many people were you able to save by this method?'

'Ten to twenty out of every hundred.'

'For how long?'

'Many months.'

'Would it be fair to say you saved several thousand people in this manner?'

'We were too busy saving lives to count.'

'And did you use other methods to trick the Germans?'

'When they suspected we were sending corpses to Jadwiga West, they made up lists of names so we switched names. Many people alive today carried the name of a dead person for years in the camp. We studied their plans through the underground and often knew in advance when selections were going to be made. I would clear out the hospital wards as much as possible by sending people back to work or hiding them.'

'When you did this, did you take into consideration the national or religious origin of these prisoners?'

'Lives were lives. We saved those we felt had the best chance of survival.'

Highsmith let all of this sink in for a moment turning to Chester Dicks, his junior, and fetching needed information. He turned back to the rostrum.

'Sir Adam. Did you ever give your own blood?'

'Yes, on numerous occasions. There were certain intellectuals, scholars, musicians, writers, we were determined to keep alive and at times we donated our own blood.'

'Would you tell the court what your own personal accommodations were like?'

'I shared a barrack with about sixty male staff.'

'And your bed?'

'A straw mattress stuffed inside with heavy paper. We had a sheet, a pillow, and a blanket.'

'And where did you take your meals?'

'At a small kitchen in one end of the same room.'

'What type of sanitation facility did you have?'

'One toilet, four sinks, and a shower.'

'And what kind of clothing did you wear?'

'A sort of striped denim.'

'With distinctive markings?'

'All prisoners had a triangle sewn over their left breast pocket. Mine was red denoting I was a political prisoner and there was a 'P' superimposed to denote I was Polish.'

'Now, in addition to the extermination facilities at Jadwiga West, were there any other kinds of killings?'

'In addition to the SS, German criminal prisoners and German Communists were put in charge of the others and were often as brutal as the SS. Anyone they wished to eliminate they simply beat to death, then hanged the victim with his own belt and registered the death as a suicide. The SS knew these brutes were doing their work so they turned their backs.'

'Were there any other killings, official or otherwise?'

'I mentioned earlier that in the medical compound Barrack I to V was the experimental centre. Between Barrack II and III there was a wall made of concrete. When the Jadwiga West facilities were overworked, a firing squad would execute dozens to hundreds.'

'Were there any other methods?'

'By a phenol injection in the heart. It caused death in seconds.'

'You saw the results of this?'

'Yes.'

'Were you ever ordered to give a phenol injection?'

'Yes, by an SS Dr. Sigmund Rudolf, assistant to Colonel Flensberg. He told me to administer injections of glucose to several patients, but I smelled carbolic and I refused. The patients became alarmed and SS guards beat them to submission and they were tied to chairs, and he gave them a dosage of about 100 cc. They died almost instantly.'

'As a result, were you punished?'

'Yes, Sigmund Rudolf denounced me as a coward and my teeth were smashed.'

'Let us go back for a moment, Sir Adam, to the experimental Barracks I to V. I believe it's been established that Colonel Voss and his assistant, Sigmund Rudolf, were the two primary doctors. Would you tell my Lord and the jury of your relationship with these two?'

'I had very little to do with Flensberg. Voss was experi-

256

menting on sterilization. One of the methods was through heavy exposure to X-ray of the female ovaries and the male testicles. He had working with him a Jewish doctor, a Boris Dimshits. Dimshits must have known too much for he was sent to the gas chamber. Shortly afterwards Voss summoned me and another Polish doctor, Konstanty Lotaki, and informed us we would be called upon to operate from time to time in Barrack V.'

At last, the door to Barrack V was opening with its awesome secrets. Bannister and O'Conner made swift notes of every word. Gilray concentrated to cover an obvious strange emotion sweeping through him.

'Continue please Sir Adam.'

'I asked Voss what kind of operations and he answered that I was to remove dead organs.'

'What was your reaction to all of this?'

'Lotaki and I were very upset. Voss made it clear that we would meet the same fate as Dr. Dimshits if we did not co-operate.'

'You would be sent to the gas chamber for refusal?'

'Yes.'

'Having earlier refused to inject phenol, did it occur to you to refuse?'

'This was an entirely different matter. Voss said that SS orderlies would perform the operations if we refused. We decided to discuss it with all the other prisoner/doctors. We all concluded together that it would mean certain death to all of Voss's victims and as skilled surgeons it was mandatory that Lotaki and I save these people.'

'You say you spoke to *all* the other prisoner/doctors?'

'All except Mark Tesslar. There was the personal chasm between us from the time we were students in Warsaw. Later at Jadwiga he worked with Voss in the experiments.'

'Just a moment,' Thomas Bannister said, rising.

Adam Kelno sprung off his chair, gripped the rail, and shouted. 'I will not be silenced! It is Tesslar and his lies who drove me from Poland! It is all a conspiracy of the Communists to hound me to my grave!'

'Obviously,' Thomas Bannister said coolly, 'this situation

calls for an objection; however, I don't think I'll make one at the present time.'

'Well, if you're not going to ask me to make a ruling,' Gilray said, 'then I won't make one. It seems that emotions are running rather high. I believe this will be a good time to recess for the day.'

THREE

It was almost midnight when Terry arrived at the Kelno home. 'Where have you been?' Angela asked.

'Walking, just walking.'

'Have you eaten?'

'I'm not hungry. Is Dr. Kelno still awake?'

'Yes, he's in his study.'

Adam Kelno was in a fixed waxen position. He did not hear the knock or see the boy enter.

'Doctor——'

Adam looked up slowly, then turned away.

'Doctor, I've been walking. I mean, I've been thinking about what I heard today or trying to understand it. I guess none of us really knew what that place was like. It's rather different than reading about it. I just didn't know.'

'A little hard for your stomach, Terry? What you heard today may be the only nice parts of it.'

'Oh God, Doctor.' He slumped down and put his head in his hands. 'If I had only realized what I was doing. I'm so damned ashamed of myself.'

'You ought to be. Maybe it's too much for you to hear. Maybe you shouldn't come into the court again.'

'Stop it, please. I feel like the most loathsome kind of bastard. Funny how someone like me who had been given every advantage gets so caught up in his own problems, his own world, his own selfishness, that he loses sight of other people's needs or feelings or suffering.'

'All young people are selfish,' Adam said, 'but your generation takes the prize.'

'Doctor, are you ever going to forgive me?'

'Forgive you? Well, you really didn't bring the Germans to Poland.'

'I'll make it up to you someday.'

'Just do your studies and become a good doctor. That's all your father wants. It's all the making up I want.'

'I had a long talk with Mary today after court. We reached an understanding. I'd like to live here at home during the trial.'

'Of course. I'm glad, Terrence. Mary?'

'I don't know. It would not be good to add to the tension by having her here. We'll just have to see how we feel afterwards.'

Angela entered. 'Come on both of you, you've got to have something to eat.'

Terrence held the door open. As Adam passed he touched the doctor's shoulder, then went into his arms and cried as he hadn't cried since he was a little boy.

Lady Sarah Wydman's plane landed at Heathrow Airport at two in the morning. The weary customs official yawned at her ten pieces of luggage and waved her through.

Morgan, the chauffeur, helped a porter load his cart as Jacob Alexander bussed her on the cheek. 'Jacob, you didn't have to come out here this time of the morning.'

'How was your flight?'

'Routine.'

The Bentley pulled away followed by a taxi carrying the excess baggage. They cleared the tunnel and cloverleaf and sped down the dual carriageway for London.

'How is it going?'

'Well, the opening round goes to Sir Robert, of course. Was your trip successful?'

'Yes. Any word about Sobotnik?'

'Not a trace of him. Aroni doesn't give us much hope, either.'

'Then Abe is simply going to have to allow Pieter Van Damm to testify.'

'We can't budge Abraham on that. I came to meet you tonight because I have to unload on someone, Sarah. I'm worried about Mark Tesslar. We went up to Oxford to take a new statement and we've discovered he is a very sick man. He's only recently recovered from a severe heart attack. At any rate, we've taken a gamble on this Lotaki chap, the one who did some of the operations with Kelno. He's in Lublin, Poland, surgeon at a hospital. Lotaki is a fair-haired Communist now, who has never had any action taken against him. We are going on the theory that if he helps us in London it may help him in Poland so on that basis he may come to testify.'

'On the other hand he may decide to testify for Kelno as the easier alternative of keeping his name clear.'

'We are aware of that risk, but we have to make some desperation moves.'

They pressed on into London to Berkeley Square.

'Jacob, I won't be in condition to show up in court tomorrow. Be a dear and tell Abe I'll phone him after court.'

'Sarah.'

'Yes?'

'Why won't you let me tell him about the money you've contributed and raised?'

'No. You see, he's taken so much on himself I want him to feel he has unseen friends behind him all over the world. Anyhow, he has a thing about Jewish fund raisers.'

FOUR

'Before I continue with my examination, my Lord, Sir Adam would like to address the court.'

'I wish to apologize for my outburst yesterday, my Lord,' he said shakily.

'These things are apt to happen now and again,' Mr. Justice Gilray said. 'I am certain that Mr. Smiddy and Sir Robert advised you on the severity of this sort of thing in a British courtroom. With all due respect to our friends in America, we shall not permit an English courtroom to be turned into a circus. The court accepts your apology and admonishes you that any repetition will be dealt with severely.'

'Thank you, my Lord.'

'You may continue your examination, Sir Robert.'

Sir Robert popped off the balls of his toes, rubbed his hands together, and otherwise warmed himself up. 'Yesterday at recess, Sir Adam, you testified that after Colonel Voss informed you and Dr. Lotaki that you would be operating to remove dead organs, you said you spoke to all the other prisoner/doctors save Dr. Tesslar. Is that correct?'

'Yes.'

'Precisely what kind of an opinion, or decision, or understanding was reached?'

'We had the example of Dr. Dimshits being sent to the gas chamber, and we had no reason to believe Voss was fooling when he threatened to send us, too. We had his threat that the patients would be mutilated by unskilled SS orderlies. We decided to save as many lives as possible and at the same time try to induce Voss to cut down on his experiments.'

'Yes. And then you were summoned to Barrack V with Dr. Lotaki from time to time to perform the removal of dead testicles and ovaries.'

'Yes.'

'How many times would you say this happened?'

'Eight or ten times. Surely under a dozen. I don't know about Dr. Lotaki. More than likely the same.'

'Did you also assist him?'

'On occasion.'

'Approximately how many operations were performed on each of these eight or ten visits you made to Barrack V?'

'Oh, one or two.'

'But not a dozen?'

'No, of course not.'

'Or hundreds?'

'No.'

'And did you succeed in getting these experiments stopped?'

'Not entirely, but we continued to make our reluctance known so that Voss carried on only enough experiments to justify continuation of the centre to Berlin.'

'Did Tesslar ever come into Barrack V while you were performing surgery?'

'No, never.'

'Never, never once? Never once did he see you operate?'

'Mark Tesslar never saw me operate.'

Highsmith mumbled long under his breath to give the jury time to digest the point. 'Never once,' he repeated to himself and played with the papers on the rostrum.

'So then, with the full understanding of your colleagues, you performed at very most two dozen of these necessary operations in the course of fifteen thousand other operations.'

'Yes. We only removed organs destroyed by X-ray. If we didn't remove them we feared they could cause tumour and cancer. In every single case I insisted the operation be entered into the surgical register.'

'Unfortunately,' Sir Robert said, 'the register is lost for ever. We shan't go into that. Will you tell my Lord and the jury the manner in which these operations were performed?'

'Well, the victims were in a wretched emotional state so I took exceptional care to comfort them and advise them that what I was doing was for their own good. I was going to save their lives. I used the best of my surgical skill and the best anaesthetics available.'

'On the matter of anaesthetics. This of course you know is part of the defamatory statement by the defendant that you did not use anaesthetics.'

'That is entirely false.'

'Would you explain what kind of anaesthetics were administered and how it was done?'

'Yes. For operations below the navel I felt a spinal preferable to an inhalant.'

'Did you also have that opinion in Warsaw, London, and Sarawak?'

'Yes, very much so. A spinal relaxes the muscles much better and usually causes less bleeding.'

'Did you have someone administer these spinals in Jadwiga?'

'I did them myself because of the shortage of trained people. First I gave a pre-injection of morphia to deaden the general area and then the spinal.'

'Does this cause the patient severe pain?'

'No, only a prick when done by a specialist.'

'Where did you give this anaesthetic?'

'In the operating room.'

'Now, what about post-operative care?'

'I told Voss that I must treat these patients until they made a full recovery and he agreed.'

'And you continued to visit them.'

'Yes, daily.'

'Do you recall any complications?'

'Only the normal post-operative conditions plus the poor facilities of Jadwiga. It was somewhat worse in these cases because of the trauma of losing a sex gland, but they were so happy to be alive I was warmly greeted and found them cheerful.'

'But they all survived, did they not?'

'No one died of these few necessary operations.'

'Because of your care and skill and post-operative attention?'

Thomas Bannister came up slowly. 'Aren't you leading your witness, Sir Robert?'

'I apologize to my learned friend. Let me rephrase the question. Did you do anything else special for these twenty or so patients?'

'I brought them extra rations.'

'Let us move on to another area for a moment. Sir Adam, were you a member of the underground?'

'Yes, I was in the Nationalist underground, not the Communist underground. I am a Polish Nationalist.'

'Then there were two undergrounds.'

'Yes. From the moment we entered Jadwiga the Nationalists organized. We arranged escapes. We kept contact with the Nationalist underground in Warsaw and all over Poland. We worked into key positions such as the hospital, the radio factory, in clerical positions to get more rations and medicine. We manufactured our own radio.'

'Was there co-operation with the Communist underground?'

'We knew the Communists planned to take over Poland after the war and many times they turned in our members to the SS. We had to be very careful of them. Tesslar was in the Communist underground.'

'What other accomplishments did your underground achieve?'

'We improved conditions with more rations and medicine and the building of more sanitation facilities. Mainly, twenty thousand prisoners worked in factories outside the camp and the underground on the outside smuggled things to them which they brought back into the camp. In this manner we got vaccine which stopped another typhus epidemic.'

'Would you say this saved many lives?'

'Yes.'

'Thousands?'

'I cannot estimate.'

'By the way, Sir Adam. You mentioned a radio for contact to the outside. Where was it hidden?'

'In my surgery in Barrack XX.'

'Hummmmm,' Highsmith mulled. 'What were your hours in Jadwiga?' he continued.

'Twenty-four hours a day, seven days a week. After regular out-patient hours set by the SS we continued to work in surgery and the wards. I took a few hours' sleep here and there.'

Abraham watched the jury as Sir Robert and Adam Kelno piled a mountain of heroism, courage, and sacrifice before them. He looked to O'Conner, who was all business, to Bannister, who was totally relaxed and fixed on the witness. Below, Jacob Alexander's secretary, Sheila Lamb, wrote feverishly. At the associates table, the shorthand writers changed periodically. The London *Times* law reporters, both of whom were barristers, were accorded a special place in the courtroom removed from the overcrowded press rows. These were jammed with more and more foreign journalists arriving on the scene.

'We have gone through the administering of anaesthetic by you in the operating room,' he repeated to ensure the point. 'Now did you in any way pride yourself in performing operations quickly?'

'No. But in Jadwiga there was so much surgery I trained myself to work fast but never so fast that it endangered a patient.'

'Did you wash your hands before every operation?'

'Of course.'

'And saw to it your patients were properly scrubbed.'

'My God, of course.'

'In the case of an ovariectomy, those performed on orders of Voss, what surgical methods did you adhere to?'

'Well, after the spinal took effect, the patient was taken off a trolley and strapped to the operating table.'

'Strapped? Forcibly?'

'For the patient's own safety.'

'Would you strap someone down for the same operation today in London?'

'Yes. It is standard procedure.'

265

'Continue, please, Sir Adam.'

'Well, the operating table may be tilted.'

'How much? As much as thirty degrees?'

'I don't think so. When performing an operation in the lower region, such as the pelvis, if you tilt the table the intestines roll back by themselves to give the surgeon an area to operate free from the loops of the intestines. I would make an abdominal incision, insert the forceps to lift the uterus, place a forceps between the tube and the ovary, and cut the ovary off.'

'What do you do with the removed ovary?'

'Well, I can't keep it in my hand. It is usually put on a dish or some sort of receptacle held by an assistant. When the ovary is removed it leaves a pedicle or stump. This stump is covered to prevent it from haemorrhaging.'

'The stump or pedicle is *always* covered?'

'Yes, always.'

'How long does such an operation take?'

'Under normal conditions, between fifteen and twenty minutes.'

'And all of this is done with sterile instruments?'

'Naturally.'

'And you are wearing rubber gloves.'

'I prefer to wear sterile cotton gloves over the rubber gloves to prevent slipping. It is an optional matter of the individual surgeon.'

'Would you tell my Lord and the jury if the patient, who is semiconscious and without feeling, is able to observe all this?'

'No. We place a screen made of a sterilized sheet so the patient is unable to observe.'

'What on earth do you do that for?'

'To prevent the patient from coughing or spitting into an open wound.'

'So then, the patient cannot see or feel. Would the patient be in a state of extreme distress?'

'Well, Sir Robert, no one is happy to be on an operating table, but they are not in what you would term, "extreme distress" at all.'

'And even though these operations were conducted in the Jadwiga Concentration Camp, would you be satisfied that normal surgical procedures were used.'

'It was more difficult there in many ways but it was proper surgery.'

After the luncheon adjournment, Sir Robert Highsmith took Sir Adam Kelno through his earliest meeting with Mark Tesslar as medical students in Warsaw.

They met again in Jadwiga, where Kelno claimed Tesslar continued to operate on SS prostitutes and later collaborated with the Germans on the experiments.

'Did Dr. Tesslar treat any patients or look after them in the general medical compound?'

'He lived in Barrack III in private quarters.'

'Private quarters you say. Not like yourself sharing with sixty others.'

'In Barrack III many of the victims of the experiments were kept. Tesslar may have looked after them. I do not know. I avoided him and when we met I made such meetings brief.'

'Did you ever brag to him about doing thousands of experimental operations without anaesthetic?'

'No. I am proud of my record as a surgeon and may have mentioned the thousands of operations performed in Jadwiga.'

'Proper operations.'

'Yes, proper. But my words have been distorted. I warned Tesslar about his own activities and told him he would have to answer for his crimes. It was like signing my own death warrant for when I returned to Warsaw he was already there and, to cover his crimes, he brought charges against me and I had to flee.'

'Sir Adam,' the judge interrupted. 'I would like to offer a bit of advice. Try to answer Sir Robert's questions and not volunteer any other information.'

'Yes, my Lord.'

'How long did you remain in Jadwiga?'

'Until early in 1944.'

'Would you tell my Lord and the jury under what circumstances you left the concentration camp?'

'Voss left Jadwiga to take over a private clinic of the wives of high German naval officers in Rostock near the Baltic and he took me with him.'

'As a prisoner?'

'As a prisoner. I was referred to as Voss's dog.'

'How long were you in Rostock?'

'Until January of 1945 when Voss evacuated into the centre of Germany. I was not taken with him. There was confusion among the Germans. I stayed in the area to treat many slaves and prisoners now roaming free. In April the Russian Army arrived. At first many of us were put into compounds for lack of papers, then I was relased and made my way back to Warsaw. I arrived on Easter Sunday of 1945 and immediately heard rumours of charges against me. The Nationalist underground was still in existence so I was given false papers to work as a labourer in a cleanup gang. I fled to Italy to join the Free Polish Forces as soon as I could.'

'What happened then?'

'There was an investigation to clear me. I came to England and served in the Polish Hospital in Tunbridge Wells. I remained until 1946.'

'What happened then?'

'I was arrested and put into Brixton Prison while the Polish Communists tried to extradite me.'

'How long did you remain in prison?' Sir Robert said, with a voice growing acid over the British treatment of his client.

'Two years.'

'And after two years in Brixton following nearly five years in Jadwiga Concentration Camp what happened?'

'The British government apologized and I joined the Colonial Service. I went to Sarawak in Borneo in 1949 and remained for fifteen years.'

'What were the conditions like in Sarawak?'

'Primitive and difficult.'

'Well, why did you choose that place?'

268

'Out of fear.'

'Then your testimony is that you have spent twenty-two years of your life either as a prisoner or in exile for crimes you did not commit.'

'That is correct.'

'What rank did you attain in the Colonial Service?'

'That of senior medical officer. I rejected higher positions because of my work with malnutrition and lifting the living standards of the natives.'

'Did you write papers on this subject?'

'Yes.'

'How were they received?'

'I was eventually knighted.'

'Hmmmmmmmm ... yes ...' Sir Robert glared at the jury almost in defiance. 'After which you returned to England?'

'Yes.'

'I'm curious, Sir Adam. Now, as a knighted British doctor, why you chose to practise in a relatively obscure clinic in Southwark?'

'I can only eat two chickens a day. I do not practise medicine for money or social standing. In my clinic I can serve the greatest number of needy people.'

'Sir Adam. Did you then or do you now suffer ill health from your years in Jadwiga, Brixton, and Sarawak?'

'Yes, I have lost almost all my teeth from beatings by the Gestapo and SS. I suffer from varicose veins, a hernia, stomach disorders from excessive recurrences of dysentery. I have neurological symptoms of anxiety and high blood pressure. I have insomnia and a bad heart.'

'How old are you?'

'I am sixty-two.'

'No further questions,' Sir Robert Highsmith said.

FIVE

Samantha backed into the door of the Colchester Mews with both arms filled with groceries in bags marked Harrods. A polite cabbie brought in the rest.

Abe was stretched out on the couch, a pile of newspapers strewn on the floor near him.

HERO OR MONSTER—*Evening News*

DILEMMA OF JADWIGA DOCTOR—*Herald*

HELL CAMP DOCTOR TESTIFIES—*Daily Worker*

SIR ADAM KELNO CONTINUES—*Times*

I HAD NO CHOICE—*Mail*

Mirror, Standard, Telegraph, Birmingham *Post, Sketch,* all careful to report accurately the events without editorial comment. Unlike some countries, the British press must be exceedingly careful not to try a man in the newspapers and magazines before he comes to court. In such cases when a newspaper becomes an accuser or prejudger, turning public sentiment, the paper can be named as a defendant to the action. It keeps journalism honest.

Abe yawned himself to his feet.

'Pay the driver, Abe,' Samantha said.

'Three bob on the meter, sir.'

Abe handed him a ten-shilling note and told him to keep the change. He liked London cabbies. They were polite. The cabbie liked Americans. They tipped well.

'What's all this, Christmas?'

'The cupboard was bare and knowing you, you'd starve first. Did Ben get in all right?'

'Yes. He's out on King's Road probably hustling for a broad.'

Samantha set the bags down on the kitchen counter and began to empty them. 'Well, how come old Dad isn't out there with him?'

'I'm ageing, Sam. I can't handle this young stuff any more.'

'Why, Abe. Vinny's young man is up at Linstead Hall. I don't see what she sees in him. Very argumentative sort.'

'Just a normal Israeli sabra. Most of them are defensively aggressive from too many years of living with their backs to the sea.'

'Abe, I heard a lot of the talk after court today. People are ... we ...'

'Wondering?'

'Yes.'

'There's two sides to this story.'

'Scotch?'

'That would be nice.'

'Dreadful, dreadful business,' she said, wrestling with an old model ice-cube tray. 'There's a lot of sympathy for Kelno.'

'Yeah, I know.'

'Are you going to be able to overcome it?'

'I didn't come to London to visit the Queen.'

The phone rang. Samantha answered. 'It's for you ... a woman.'

'Hello.'

'Hello, darling,' Lady Sarah Wydman beamed.

'Hi, good to hear you. Alexander said you got in very late last night.'

'Sorry not to be there at the beginning, but I simply got overbooked with theatre in New York. Dreary season. When do I get to see you?'

'Like tonight.'

'We can do one of the little restaurants in Chelsea or come to my place,' she said.

'I'd better stick close to the phone.'

'Good. I'll pick up something at Oakeshotts and make dinner for you at the mews.'

'I didn't know you could cook.'

'You don't know a lot of things. Seven-thirtyish?'

'Deal.'

Abe hung up. Samantha was pouting openly as she handed him his drink. 'Who was that?'

'Friend. Friend of the cause.'

271

'How friendly?'

'Lady Sarah Wydman. She's very big in the Jewish community.'

'Everyone has heard of Lady Sarah and her charitable works. Will you be making love to her here?'

He decided to play her silly game. 'The mews is too small, what with Ben in the next bedroom. I like to ball where I can yell and scream and run around bare-assed.'

Samantha turned crimson and bit her lip.

'Come on, Sam, we've been divorced for years. You can't still be jealous.'

'Oh, I'm just a silly. I mean, Abe, no one has been quite like you. After all we did conceive Ben right here. I always have the memory, when I come down from Linstead Hall, about us. Do you ever get a twinge about me?'

'Truth?'

'I don't know if I want the truth or not.'

'Truthfully, yes. Sam, we lived together for two decades.'

'I got quite excited when I knew you would be in London for a long stay. When Reggie and I offered you the mews I knew I'd come to London and ask you to make love to me.'

'Christ, Sam, we can't do that.'

'Old chums like us? What's so terribly wrong?'

'Reggie.'

'He suspects it anyhow and he'd never be convinced we didn't. Reggie is a dear sweet quiet stout type. As long as we don't throw it in his face, he wouldn't dare bring it up.'

'I've stopped sleeping with other men's wives.'

'Really, since when, darling?'

'Since I found out you can't fool the old man upstairs. You've got to pay off. Sam, please don't put me in the position of rejecting you.'

He handed her a handkerchief and she dabbed her tears. 'Of course, you're right,' she said. 'Frankly, I don't know who I like better, the old Abe or the new one.'

Lady Sarah, dressed in slacks and mink coat, arrived in her Bentley followed by Morgan carrying a sack of groceries.

She was a cordon bleu chef.

Abe turned tired very suddenly. He lay his head in her lap and she rubbed the back of his neck and his temples with a lovely practised skill, then she slipped down beside him. Sarah was nearing the line when a woman was suddenly no longer attractive, but she knew how to make the best of what she had. He decided she had not yet crossed the line.

'Christ, I'm tired.'

'You really will be by the weekend. Let's go to Paris.'

'I can't. The witnesses will be arriving from Israel. I should be on hand.'

'Paris.'

'I may not be able to resist,' he grunted.

'Don't worry, love. Things will go better when Tom Bannister gets started.'

'Funny, I haven't taken my mind off Kelno. Poor bastard. What he's lived through.'

'It doesn't justify what he did, Abe.'

'I know. But I keep asking myself if I would have done any differently if I had been in Jadwiga.'

Angela was awakened by a gagging noise. She could see the beam of light from the opened bathroom door and rushed to it. Adam was on his knees vomiting into the toilet. When he was finished she helped him to his feet and he fell against the wall gasping. She cleaned the mess and put him down and applied a cold towel to his clammy forehead and neck.

Then, she medicated him and held his hand until the spasm was gone. The scent of disinfectant flowed in from the bathroom.

'I am afraid of Bannister,' Adam said. 'For two days he has sat there never taking his eyes off me.'

'You're in an English court. He can't bully you. Sir Robert will watch his every move.'

'Yes, I suppose you're right.'

'Shhhh ... shhhhh ... shhhh ...'

SIX

Abe entered the now familiar courtroom and for an awkward moment found himself standing next to Angela Kelno and Terrence Campbell. They exchanged hard looks. 'Excuse me,' Abe said, and slipped down the row next to Sarah Wydman and Shawcross.

'The plane will be in from Tel Aviv after the weekend, but Alexander said we were not to go out and meet them. We'll see them in mid-week,' Shawcross said.

Bannister and a very weary appearing Brendon O'Conner filed in with Alexander and Sheila Lamb from the consultation room at the same moment the jury made its appearance. Two of the women and one of the men carried cushions to alleviate the discomfort of the long sit on hard wood.

'Silence!' the usher said.

Gilray entered and the ritual rise and bow was made.

A preliminary announcement was made from the bench. Sir Adam Kelno had received a number of threatening phone calls and Gilray issued a stern warning that it would not be tolerated. Then he told Thomas Bannister to proceed.

Bannister unfolded his legs as Adam Kelno returned to the witness box, seated himself, and set his hands on the rail, thankful his tranquillizer was taking effect. Bannister played with the 'fee bag' on his robe.

'Sir Adam,' he said in a voice softly contrasting Highsmith's. The entire tone of the room lowered. 'I appreciate the fact that English is not your mother tongue. Please ask me to repeat or rephrase any question you do not follow.'

Adam nodded and slowly sipped from the water glass to moisten his parched throat.

'What is the ordinary medical meaning of the term casus explorativus?'

274

'Ordinarily it is an operation performed in order to assist in a diagnosis, for example, to see the extent of a cancer.'

'Is that how you would describe the removal of a testicle or ovary?'

'Yes.'

'Sin referring to the left and dex to the right.'

'Yes,' he answered, remembering his instructions to keep his replies brief and not volunteer information.

'Would it not be correct to add that some kind of operation would be performed of this nature as the result of an X-rayed gland.'

'Yes.'

'For example, as part of Voss's experiments.'

'No,' he said sharply. 'I did not experiment.'

'Did you castrate?'

'A castration is done to a healthy man. I never performed a castration.'

'Weren't healthy men and women forced to be X-rayed?'

'Not by me.'

'Isn't it the usual practice to obtain the consent of a patient before you operate?'

'Not in a concentration camp.'

'From time to time weren't there German court orders to castrate a homosexual or other undesirables?'

'I recall no such incidents.'

HE'S FISHING, Chester Dicks wrote to Highsmith, who nodded to Kelno that he was doing fine. Adam became relaxed by the softness of Bannister's voice and the seemingly aimless line of questions.

'Had there been such cases, you would have certainly asked to see the court order.'

'I cannot speculate about something that did not happen.'

'But you would have refused to operate on a healthy man.'

'I never did.'

'Sir Adam, did any other prisoner/doctors ever leave Jadwiga Concentration Camp to work in private German hospitals?'

275

'Dr. Konstanty Lotaki.'

'Did he also perform operations in Barrack V in connection with Voss's experiments?'

'He did what he was ordered.'

'Was he ordered to remove testicles and ovaries?'

'Yes.'

'And he did that and he also left Jadwiga to work in a private German hospital.'

The first brief flush of comfort began to fade from Adam Kelno along with any ideas of an easy time with Bannister. I must be very alert, he thought, think out my answers with great care.

'Now, when you got to Rostock to work in the private clinic, you no longer wore prison clothing.'

'I don't think high ranking German naval officers would like their wives to be treated by a man in concentration camp stripes. Yes, I was given a suit of clothing.'

'Perhaps they wouldn't like being treated by a prisoner,' Bannister said.

'I don't know what they liked and didn't like. I was still a prisoner.'

'But a rather special prisoner with special privileges. I am suggesting that you co-operated with Voss to work your passage.'

'What?'

'Would you try again, Mr. Bannister?' the judge interjected. 'He does not understand the term.'

'Yes, my Lord. In the beginning you started as a labourer and took beatings and abuse.'

'Yes.'

'Then you became an orderly of sorts.'

'Yes.'

'Then a physician for prisoners.'

'Yes.'

'Then you were placed in charge of a very large medical complex.'

'In a manner of speaking. Under German control.'

'And finally, you became a doctor for German officers' wives.'

'Yes.'

'I suggest that you and Dr. Lotaki, the only two prisoner/doctors ever released from Jadwiga, were released for your co-operation with SS Colonel Dr. Adolph Voss.'

'No!'

Bannister stood motionless except for the repeating gesture of rolling his fee bag. He dropped the modulation of his voice even lower. 'Who wanted these operations performed?'

'Voss.'

'You knew full well he was experimenting on sterilization.'

'Yes.'

'By X-ray.'

'Yes.'

'In fact, Sir Adam, wasn't the removal of a testicle or ovary the second stage of the same experiment?'

'I am confused.'

'I'll try to clarify matters. Let's go through it step by step. These people were all Jews.'

'I believe so. Maybe a gypsy. Mostly Jews.'

'Young Jews.'

They were young.'

'Exactly when were they brought into Barrack V for surgery?'

'Well, they were all kept in Barrack III as material for the experiments. They were X-rayed in Barrack V and sent back for a month, then returned for the operation.'

'Aren't you omitting a step?'

'I don't recall.'

'I suggest that prior to their being X-rayed they were brought to Barrack V and had a piece of wood shoved up their rectums in order to induce an ejaculation and this sperm was analysed to see if they were potent.'

'I knew nothing about that.'

'Were they shaved before the operation?'

'Yes, they were prepared in a normal way.'

'Did they protest?'

'Of course they were unhappy. I spoke to them and told

them it was necessary to save their lives.'

'You testified, I believe, that you were removing dead glands.'

'Yes.'

'How did you know they were dead?'

'It was quite easy to assume by the large radiation burns.'

'And you testified that you were afraid the irradiation could develop into cancer.'

'Yes.'

'So you operated as a doctor fully convinced that what you were doing was for their welfare.'

'Yes.'

'You never said to any of them, if I don't get yours, the Germans will get mine?'

'I deny these kinds of lies with all my soul.'

'You never said that?'

'No, never.'

'On occasion, you testified to assisting Dr. Lotaki.'

'Maybe a dozen times.'

'Did you ever overhear him say that?'

'No.'

'You have stated a preference for spinal anaesthetic.'

'Under the conditions and for this type of operation.'

'And you testified that you gave a pre-injection of morphia.'

'Yes.'

'Even with morphia, isn't a spinal injection rather painful?'

'Not if given by a skilled surgeon.'

'Why the pre-injection of morphia?'

'To induce a feeling of peace and a state of semiconsciousness.'

'And this was all done by you in the operating room?'

'Yes.'

'Even though there is a screen between the patient's vision and the area of the operation, I suggest he can see it all from the reflection lamp overhead.'

'Reflection is very distorted as a mirror.'

'So then, you saw no reason to put the patient completely under.'

'I have so many operations of all kinds to do in a single day I must use the quickest and safest method.'

'What was the actual state of these patients?'

'Drowsy and semi-conscious.'

'I suggest, Sir Adam, they were quite awake because no morphia had been given.'

'I say I gave them morphia.'

'Yes. Well now, was Voss present at these operations?'

'Yes.'

'And he told you what he was doing. You were aware he was experimenting to sterilize healthy, potent men.'

'I knew.'

'And of course he was conducting those experiments because at that time no one really knew whether X-ray could or could not sterilize a sexual gland.'

Kelno gripped the rail and balked as Bannister's trap became obvious. He looked to his counsel quickly but they did not rise.

'Well?' Bannister pressed ever so softly.

'As a physician and surgeon I knew some of the harmful effects of X-ray.'

'I suggest that no one really knew about this. I suggest no work had ever been done in this field.'

'Voss may have consulted with a radiologist.'

'I suggest not. I suggest that no radiologist can tell what dosage of radiation will sterilize a potent man because no such work has been done in that field.'

'Any medical man knows radiation is harmful.'

'If this were known, then why was Voss carrying on his experiments?'

'Ask Voss.'

'He's dead but you, Sir Adam, were closely associated with him when he was doing this. I suggest that Voss wanted to know how much radiation was needed to sterilize a healthy man because he didn't know and no one else knew, and I suggest he told you what he was doing, and I suggest you didn't know either. Now, Sir Adam, what was

279

done with the removed testicles?'

'I don't know.'

'Weren't they, in fact, taken to a laboratory to ascertain if they were potent or not.'

'Perhaps.'

'I suggest that the removal of such testicles was the second step in the experiment.'

'No.'

'But when these men were X-rayed, the experiment wasn't over, was it?'

'I operated to save lives.'

'Concern for cancer? Who did the X-ray?'

'A German medical orderly by name of Kremmer.'

'Was he quite skilled?'

'He was not very skilled and that is why I feared cancer.'

'I see. Not too skilled. He was hanged for what he did, was he not?'

'I am going to object to that,' Sir Robert said, bouncing up.

'Objection sustained.'

'What became of Corporal Kremmer?' Bannister pressed.

'I object, my Lord. My learned friend is clearly trying to implicate Sir Adam as a willing accomplice. He was not a Nazi and he did not volunteer in this work.'

'The nature of my question, my Lord, is completely in order. I am suggesting that these operations were part and parcel of the experiments and therefore experimental surgery. Others were hanged for their participation in these experiments and I suggest Sir Adam Kelno need not have performed these operations and did so in order to work his passage.'

Gilray pondered. 'Well, we all know by this time that SS Corporal Kremmer was hanged. I ask the jury to receive this information with the gravest reservation. You may continue, Mr. Bannister.'

Sir Robert slipped to his seat slowly as Bannister thanked the judge.

'Now then, you saw these two dozen or so people in your

operating room and observed the results of heavy exposure to radiation.'

'Yes.'

'And you testified that Corporal Kremmer was not too skilled and you were fearful of the effects of the X-ray. Is that your testimony?'

'It is.'

'Now, Sir Adam, let us say that Corporal Kremmer did not do the X-ray but the most skilled radiologist did it. Wouldn't there be danger to the partner testicle and ovary?'

'I don't believe I understand.'

'Very well, let us clarify again. The male testicles adjoin each other in separate compartments but under a fraction of an inch apart. Is that correct?'

'Yes.'

'And the female ovaries are probably five to seven inches apart.'

'Yes.'

'In the case of a testicle exposed to an extremely heavy dosage of irradiation by a semi-skilled technician I suggest that the partner testicle would also be damaged. You testified they were badly burned and that was your concern.'

'Yes.'

'Well, if you feared cancer, why didn't you remove both testicles? Wasn't it in the interest of the patient to amputate both testicles?'

'I don't know. I mean, Voss told me what to do.'

'I suggest, Sir Adam, you first thought of this so-called cancer danger when you were being detained in Brixton Prison awaiting extradition to Poland.'

'That's not true.'

'I suggest you had no interest whatsoever in the welfare of the patients, or you would not have left in a cancerous testicle or ovary. I suggest you made it all up later.'

'I didn't.'

'Then why didn't you remove everything damaged?'

'Because Voss was standing over me.'

'Isn't it a fact that Voss told you and Dr. Lotaki on

several occasions that if you did these operations for him you would be taken away from Jadwiga.'

'Of course not.'

'I suggest it is improper and dangerous to operate on a person suffering from severe irradiation burns. What about that?'

'In London, perhaps, but not in Jadwiga.'

'Without morphia?'

'I tell you I administered morphia.'

'When did you first meet Dr. Mark Tesslar?' Bannister said, switching the subject suddenly.

The mention of Tesslar caused a physical flushing and crawling of flesh over Kelno and his palms became wet. One shorthand writer relieved the other. The clock ticked.

'I think this may be an appropriate time for a recess,' the judge said.

Adam Kelno left the witness stand with the first tarnish stain. He would never again take Thomas Bannister lightly.

SEVEN

A routine was forming. Sir Adam Kelno was able to skip across the river to take lunch at home while his counsel dashed off to a ready booth in a private club.

The Three Tuns Tavern on Chancery Lane at the alleyway of Chichester Rents had a small upstairs private room where Abe and Shawcross retired with whomever had joined them in court. The bill of fare at the Three Tuns consisted of the usual London pub selection of cold cuts, cold salad, and Scotch egg, a concoction of egg, meat, and breadcrumbs. After enlisting the bartender's help in making a dry, cold martini things were not so bad as they may have been. On the floor below, the bar was two and three deep with young solicitors, legal secretaries, students, and businessmen, all of whom knew Abraham Cady was upstairs but too British in their manners to annoy him.

And so it went each day. Court convened at ten-thirty in the morning until a one o'clock recess and in the afternoon from two until four-thirty.

After the first taste of Bannister, Adam Kelno felt that with all the insinuation he had not scored heavily and the others too felt that no real damage had been done.

'Now, Sir Adam,' Bannister continued after the recess, with a cadence in his voice becoming easier to follow. In the beginning it sounded dull but one could gather the rhythm of it and intonations within intonations. 'You told us before the recess you met Dr. Tesslar as a student.'

'Yes.'

'How many people lived in Poland before the war?'

'Over thirty million.'

'And how many Jews?'

'About three and a half million.'

'Some of whom had been in Poland for generations ... centuries.'

'Yes.'

'Was there a students' association for medical trainees at the University of Warsaw?'

'Yes.'

'As a matter of fact, because of the anti-Semitic views of the Polish officers clique, the aristocracy, intelligentsia, and the upper class, no Jewish students were allowed to be members of the association.'

'The Jews formed their own association.'

'I suggest that is because they were barred from the other one.'

'It may be.'

'Isn't it also a fact that the Jewish students were placed in separate parts of the rear of the class and otherwise segregated socially, as students and as fellow Poles. And isn't it a fact that the students' association had Jewless days and activated riots against Jewish shops and otherwise indulged in their persecution?'

'These were conditions I did not make.'

'But Poland did. Poland was anti-Semitic in nature, substance, and action, was it not?'

'There was anti-Semitism in Poland.'

'And you joined in it actively as a student?'

'I had to join the association. I was not responsible for its actions.'

'I suggest you were extremely active. Now, after the German invasion of Poland, you knew, of course, of the ghettoes in Warsaw and all over Poland.'

'I was already an inmate in Jadwiga, but I heard.'

Highsmith relaxed and jotted a note to Richard Smiddy. THIS LINE OF QUESTIONING WILL GET HIM NOWHERE. HE MAY HAVE EMPTIED HIS GUN.

'Jadwiga,' Bannister said, 'could accurately be described as an indescribable hell.'

'No hell could be worse.'

'And millions were tortured and murdered. You know that because you saw some of it first hand and because the underground gave you information.'

'Yes, we knew what was going on.'

'How many labour camps surrounded Jadwiga?'

'About fifty, holding up to a half million slave labourers for armament factories, a chemical factory, many other kinds of war plants.'

'Mostly Jews were used in this forced labour?'

'Yes.'

'From everywhere in occupied Europe.'

'Yes.'

What in the name of God is he getting at, Kelno wondered. Is he trying to build sympathy for me?

'You knew that the arrivals went to a selection shed and those over forty and all children were sent directly to the gas chambers of Jadwiga West.'

'Yes.'

'Thousands? Millions?'

'I have heard many figures. Some say over two million people were put to death in Jadwiga West.'

284

'And others were tattooed and wore various types of badges sewn on their clothing to divide them into various classes.'

'We were all prisoners. I don't understand what classes.'

'Well, what kind of different badges were there?'

'There were Jews, gypsies, German criminals, Communists, resistance fighters. Some Russian prisoners of war. I have testified to my own badge, a badge by nationality.'

'Do you remember another badge worn by Kapos?'

'Yes.'

'Would you tell my Lord and the jury who the Kapos were.'

'They were prisoners who watched over other prisoners.'

'Very tough?'

'Yes.'

'And for their co-operation with the SS they were quite privileged?'

'Yes ... but the Jews even had Kapos.'

'I suggest there were extremely few Jewish Kapos in proportion to the number of Jewish prisoners. Would you agree to that?'

'Yes.'

'Most of the Kapos were Polish, were they not?'

Adam balked for a moment, tempted to argue. The point had been slow in coming but it was quite clear. 'Yes,' he answered.

'Inside the main stammlager of Jadwiga some twenty thousand prisoners built the camp itself and manned the crematoriums of Jadwiga West. Later the number of prisoners increased to forty thousand.'

'I will trust your figures.'

'And those Jews arriving would carry their few valuables and family heirlooms. Some gold rings and diamonds and so forth among their little bits of luggage.'

'Yes.'

'And when they were sent to the gas chambers naked, their belongings were systematically looted. You knew all that?'

'Yes, it was horrible.'

'And you knew the hair was used to stuff mattresses in Germany and to seal submarine periscopes and that gold teeth were pulled from corpses and before the corpses were burned their stomachs were cut open to see if they had swallowed any valuables. You knew that.'

'Yes.'

Abe felt queasy. He covered his face with his hands wishing this kind of questioning were over with. Terrence Campbell was also chalky and the entire room stunned to silence even though it was a story they had heard before.

'At first there were German doctors but later on the prisoners took over. How many personnel did you have?'

'A total of five hundred. Sixty or seventy of these were medical doctors.'

'How many of them were Jews?'

'Perhaps a dozen.'

'But with lower ranking. Orderlies, scrubbers, that sort of thing.'

'If they were qualified physicians, I used them as such.'

'But the Germans didn't, is that not so?'

'No, the Germans didn't.'

'And their number was completely out of proportion to the number of inmates.'

'I used qualified doctors as doctors.'

'You didn't answer my question, Sir Adam.'

'Yes, the number of Jewish doctors was small by proportion.'

'And you know of some of the other things Voss and Flensberg were doing. Cancer experiments of the cervix, induction of sterilization through injection of caustic fluid into the Fallopian tubes. Other experiments to find the mental breaking point of victims.'

'I don't know exactly. I only went to Barrack V to operate and to Barrack III to see the patients afterward.'

'Well, did you discuss this matter with a French woman doctor. A Dr. Susanne Parmentier?'

'I recall no such person.'

'A French Protestant prisoner/doctor. A psychiatrist by the name of Parmentier.'

'My Lord,' Sir Robert Highsmith interrupted with a tone of sarcasm. 'We have all been educated as to the bestiality of Jadwiga. My learned friend is certainly trying to establish that Sir Adam was to blame for the gas chamber and other brutalities of the Germans. I cannot see the relevancy.'

'Yes, get on with it,' the judge said. 'What are you driving at, Mr. Bannister?'

'I suggest that even within the horror of Jadwiga Concentration Camp there were rankings of the prisoners and certain prisoners looked upon themselves as superior. There was a definite caste system and privileges given to those who did the Germans' work.'

'I see,' the judge said.

Highsmith slipped back, extremely wary of Bannister's oblique way of getting at it.

'Now then,' Bannister continued, 'I hold here in my hand a copy of a document prepared by your counsel, Sir Adam, called Statement of Claim. I have true copies, which I should like to give to his Lordship and the jury.'

Highsmith examined it, nodded his approval, and the associate handed copies to the judge, the jury, and one to Sir Adam.

'You state in your claim that you were an associate of SS Colonel Dr. Adolph Voss and SS Colonel Dr. Otto Flensberg.'

'By associate I meant——'

'Yes, exactly what did you mean by associate?'

'You are distorting a perfectly natural word. They were doctors and...'

'And you considered yourself as their associate. Now, of course you read this Statement of Claim carefully. Your solicitors did go over it with you line by line.'

'The word associate is a slip, an error.'

'But you knew what they were doing, you testified to that, and you know about the indictments against them after the war and you say in your own Statement of Claim they were your associates.' Bannister held another document up as Adam looked to the clock in hopes of a recess to organize himself. After a period of silence, Bannister spoke. 'I have here a part of the indictment against Voss. Will my learned colleague accept this as a true copy?'

Highsmith looked at it and shrugged. 'We have strayed afield. This indictment is again this horrendous business of trying to link together a prisoner with a Nazi war criminal.'

'One moment please,' Bannister said, and turned to O'Conner, who was shuffling through the stacks of papers on his table. He handed one to Bannister. 'Here is the affidavit, which you swore to, Sir Adam. You swore before a Commissioner for Oaths and you state the following; paragraphs one and two list the documents relating to your case. You're holding it in your hand. Is that your signature, Sir Adam?'

'I am confused.'

'Let us clarify it then. When you brought this action you disclosed a number of documents on your own behalf. Among the documents you disclosed was the indictment of Voss. You did it.'

'If my solicitors thought it necessary . . .'

'When you brought this document forth to support your case you thought it to be genuine, did you not?'

'I suppose so.'

'Now then, I shall read to the jury a portion of the indictment of Voss.'

The judge looked to Highsmith, who glanced at the indictment of Voss. 'No objection, my Lord,' he said between his teeth.

'"Headquarters of the Fuehrer, August 1942, Secret Reich matters, single copy. On July 7, 1942, a conference was held at Jadwiga Concentration Camp between Drs. Adolph Voss and Otto Flensberg and Reichfuehrer SS Heinrich Himmler on the matter of sterilization of the Jewish race. It was agreed upon that a variety of experiments would be performed on healthy, potent Jews and Jewesses." Now, Sir Adam, the second letter in your disclosure of documents is from Voss to Himmler in which Voss states he must carry out his radiation programme on a minimum of a thousand persons to get conclusive results.

Sir Adam, you have testified that between yourself and Dr. Lotaki you operated or assisted in perhaps two dozen such operations. What happened to the minimum of nine hundred and seventy-six other persons in Voss's letter?'

'I don't know.'

'What was the purpose of entering these letters in evidence?'

'Only to show I was a victim. The Germans did it, not me.'

'I am suggesting that in fact there were many more hundreds of these operations not accounted for.'

'Maybe the Jew, Dimshits, did most of them and that is why he was sent to the gas chamber. Maybe it was Tesslar.'

'You knew when you brought this action it would be your word against Dr. Tesslar's because the surgical record had disappeared.'

'I must rise,' Sir Robert said, 'and take the greatest exception. You cannot allude to a register that is not in existence. Mr. Bannister has asked Sir Adam how many operations he performed and Sir Adam has answered.'

'Mr. Bannister,' the judge said. 'May I call your attention to the fact that from time to time editorial comments creep into your questions.'

'I am sorry, my Lord. Speed in the mass sterilization programme was also essential to the German purpose. Could it be possible these operations were performed before Dr. Voss to demonstrate just how quickly they could be done?'

'I did not operate with such speed as to harm a patient.'

'Weren't you, in fact, proud of the speed with which you could remove Jewish testicles, and didn't you want to demonstrate it to Voss.'

'My Lord,' Sir Robert said, 'this objection is obvious. My client has testified he did not use undue speed.'

'I must admonish you again,' Gilray said. He turned to the jury with his first display of judicial authority. 'Sir Adam is being distressed through innuendo. I will advise you thoroughly at the proper time as to what is relevant and what is not.'

Bannister did not blink an eye. 'Do you recall a Dr. Sandor?'

'Sandor was a Jewish Communist.'

'No, as a matter of fact, Dr. Sandor is a Roman Catholic and not a member of any Communist Party. He was one of your doctors. Do you recall him?'

'Somewhat.'

'And do you recall a conversation in which you said to Sandor, "I've got twenty pairs of Jewish eggs for scrambling today."'

'I never said that. Sandor was a member of the Communist underground who will swear anything against me.'

'I think it may be a good time to explain to my Lord and the jury about these two undergrounds inside Jadwiga. You referred to your underground as a Nationalist underground, did you not?'

'Yes.'

'Composed of what sort of people?'

'Anti-Germans from every country in occupied Europe.'

'I suggest that is not true. I suggest that ninety-five per cent of your underground was made up of Poles and that no one held any position of authority who was not a former Polish officer. Is that not the case?'

'I do not recall.'

'Can you recall any Czech or Dutchman or Yugoslav who had any position of authority in your Nationalist underground?'

'No.'

'But you can certainly recall Polish officers.'

'Some.'

'Yes, some who are in this courtroom as spectators and prospective witnesses. I suggest, Sir Adam, that the nationalist underground was the same pre-war anti-Semitic Polish officers' clique inside Jadwiga.'

Kelno did not answer.

'You have testified to a Communist underground. Is this not the same as the international underground?'

'Yes, composed of Communists and Jews.'

'And non-Communists and non-Jews who outnumbered

290

the Polish officers' clique by fifty to one and whose ranks and officials represented every occupied country in equal proportion. Is that not so?'

'They were dominated by Jews and Communists.'

'Is one of the causes for haemorrhaging in the post-operative period the speed with which the surgeon operates?' Bannister said with his now patented change of subjects.

Kelno drank from the water glass and mopped his forehead. 'If a surgeon is qualified, speed can often reduce the possibility of shock.'

'Let us come to the time in mid 1943 when Dr. Mark Tesslar arrived at Jadwiga. You were no longer a labourer taking beatings from the Germans, but a doctor with a great deal of authority.'

'Under German direction.'

'But you made decisions completely on your own. For example, who could be admitted to the hospital.'

'I was always under a great deal of moral pressure.'

'But by the time Dr. Tesslar arrived you had a rapport with the Germans. You were trusted by them.'

'In a left handed way, yes.'

'And what was your rapport with Dr. Tesslar?'

'I learned Tesslar was a Communist. Voss sent for him from another concentration camp. One can draw one's own conclusions. I was polite on occasions we met but as you would say in England, I gave him a wide berth. I stayed clear of him.'

'I suggest there were numerous conversations between yourself and Tesslar because you really had no fear of him and he was trying desperately to get more food and medicine for post-operative victims he was taking care of. I suggest that you mentioned to him that you had performed some fifteen thousand operations with uncommon speed.'

'You may suggest until your head falls off,' Adam snapped.

'I intend to. Now then, Dr. Tesslar has made a statement that on one occasion in November of 1943 you performed fourteen operations at one session. Eight males, seven of

291

them Dutch, were either castrated or had a testicle removed. Six females had ovaries removed by you on the same occasion. There was so much commotion that the SS sent a medical clerk, an Egon Sobotnik, for Dr. Tesslar to come over to Barrack V and keep the patients calm while you operated.'

'It is a blatant lie. Dr. Tesslar never came into Barrack V while I operated.'

'And Dr. Tesslar has stated that you did not give the spinals and that they were not given in the operating theatre and that no pre-injection of morphia was given.'

'It is a lie.'

'Now then, let us consider the ovariectomies in Dr. Tesslar's statement. Forget for the moment what he has said and let us go through an ordinary operation of this sort. You make an incision in the abdominal wall. Is that correct?'

'Yes, after the patient has been scrubbed and given morphia and a spinal by me.'

'Even those who had serious irradiation burns.'

'I had no choice.'

'You put in the forceps, lifted up the uterus and put a forceps between the ovary and the Fallopian tube, and then snipped off the ovary and placed it in a bowl.'

'More or less.'

'I suggest, Sir Adam, when this had been done you did not stitch up the ovaries, uterus, and veins properly.'

'It is not true.'

'Are the raw stumps called pedicles?'

'Yes.'

'Isn't it proper to cover these pedicles by using the peritoneal flaps?'

'You are a good lawyer, Mr. Bannister, but not much of a surgeon.'

Bannister ignored the ripple of laughter. 'Then kindly educate me.'

'There is no peritoneum to cover the stump. The only way to keep it down is with a cross-stitch from the infundibulo-pelvic ligament. You cover the stump in that way to prevent inflammation and adhesions and excessive bleeding.'

'And you always did that?'

'Naturally.'

'Dr. Tesslar recalls that on six ovariectomies he witnessed by you, you didn't do that.'

'It is nonsense. Tesslar was never there. And even if he was in the operating room it is almost impossible to see my work unless he had X-ray eyes. With a theatre staff assisting me, with Voss and Germans present, and with a screen at the patient's head, where Tesslar claims he sat, it would be impossible for him to observe.'

'But if he sat by the side and there were no screen?'

'It is all very hypothetical.'

'Then it is your testimony that Dr. Tesslar didn't warn you the patients would haemorrhage or get peritonitis?'

'It is not so.'

'And Dr. Tesslar did not argue with you about not washing your hands between operations?'

'No.'

'Or using the same instruments without sterilization?'

'I am a proud and competent surgeon, Mr. Bannister. I resent the insinuations.'

'Did you keep notes to advise you whether to take out the left or right testicle or the left or right ovary?'

'No.'

'Isn't it true that doctors have amputated the wrong finger or toe or whatever because they didn't check their notes?'

'This was Jadwiga, not Guy's.'

'How did you know where to operate.'

'Corporal Kremmer, who did the X-ray, was in the room. He told me left or right.'

'Kremmer? Corporal Kremmer. The semi-skilled radiologist told you?'

'He did the X-rays.'

'And if Dr. Tesslar was not there then he could not have pleaded with you about the irradiation burns or the fact that no general anaesthetic was given.'

293

'I have repeated. I used morphia and a spinal, which I administered myself. I operated quickly as it was safer to prevent pneumonia, heart collapse, and God knows what. How many times do I have to repeat it?'

'Until everything is quite clear.' Bannister paused, studied the weariness of his witness. There is a natural breaking point beyond which the judge and jury are apt to gain sympathy for him. There is also a time that the clock says one must work to the climax of his examination.

'So all these things said by Mark Tesslar are invention.'

'They are lies.'

'Men and women screaming. In frightful pain.'

'Lies.'

'And handling patients in a rough and ready manner on the operating table.'

'I am proud of my record as a surgeon.'

'Why do you think Dr. Tesslar has told all these lies against you?'

'Because of our past clashes.'

'You have stated that on occasion when you practised medicine in Warsaw you sent a member of your family to Tesslar for an abortion without Tesslar's knowledge. I ask you now to identify the member of your family who had an abortion performed by him.'

Kelno looked around for help. Control yourself, he said, control yourself. 'I refuse.'

'I suggest no such abortions were ever performed. I suggest Dr. Tesslar left Poland to extend his medical experience because of the anti-Semitic activities of your association, and I suggest Dr. Tesslar never performed abortions or experiments for the SS in Jadwiga.'

'Tesslar said these lies against me to save himself,' Kelno cried. 'When I returned to Warsaw he was in the Communist secret police with orders to hound me because I am a Polish Nationalist who cries for the loss of his beloved country. The lies were proved as lies eighteen years ago when the British government refused to extradite me.'

'I suggest,' Bannister said in utter calm to contrast Kelno's rising outburst, 'that when you returned to Poland

and learned that Tesslar and several other doctors had survived, you fled and subsequently invented a total fiction against him.'

'No.'

'And you never struck a patient on the operating table and called her a damned Jewess?'

'No, it is my word against Tesslar's.'

'As a matter of fact,' Bannister said, 'it has nothing to do with Tesslar's word. It is the word of the woman you struck who is alive and at this moment on her way to London.'

EIGHT

Saturday evening was spent in the Paris countryside with Cady's French publisher, and Sunday Abe and Lady Sarah called upon Pieter Van Damm for a lovely dinner with Madame Erica Van Damm and the two children, both students of the Sorbonne.

The daughter, a homely quiet sort, went off to her room. Anton Van Damm excused himself for a date after promising to come to London to meet Ben and Vanessa.

'The trial does not go too well,' Pieter said.

'The jury seems to show no emotion. We have word from Poland that Dr. Lotaki will not testify for us and so far, no sign of Egon Sobotnik.'

'Time is growing short,' Pieter said. He nodded to his wife and on cue Erica asked Lady Sarah to have a look around the apartment so the two men were alone. 'Abraham, I have told my children everything.'

'I suspected so tonight. It must have been very difficult.'

'Strange. Not as hard as I thought. You put into your children all the love and wisdom you are able to yet you fear that in a crisis they have lost it. Well, they didn't. They wept, particularly for their mother. My son, Anton, was ashamed he did not know earlier so he could have helped me through difficult periods. And Erica explained to them that we have even greater compensations in our relationship than a sexual life.'

Abe pondered. 'I don't want you to think about testifying,' he said. 'I know it's on your mind.'

'I read your books, Cady. With us, we are able to rise to heights that normal couples cannot attain. Now, there are four of us who feel that strongly.'

'I can't let you do it. After all, the loss of human dignity is one of the things this case is all about.'

Anton Van Damm was waiting in the lobby of the Meurice when Abe and Lady Sarah returned. She whisked off in the open cage elevator, and they made into the bar.

'I know why you're here,' Abe said.

'It's on Father's conscience day and night. If it means losing the case, of having Kelno paid off, Father would suffer more than if he took the stand.'

'Anton, when I went into this I had some ideas about revenge. Well, I've changed that notion. Adam Kelno as a single person is not important. What some people do to other people is important. From this aspect, as Jews we must tell this story over and over. We must continue to protest our demise until we are allowed to live in peace.'

'You're looking for a victory in heaven, Mr. Cady. I want one on earth.'

Abe smiled and rumpled the boy's hair. 'I've got a son and a daughter about your age. I've never won an argument with them yet.'

'May I have your attention, please,' the loud-speaker of Heathrow Airport announced, 'El Al from Tel Aviv has just landed.'

As the door from customs opened, Sheila Lamb led the surge toward an uncertain little knot of passengers. Dr.

Leiberman introduced himself and the two women and four men. The Israeli witnesses.

'How good of you to come,' Sheila said, embracing them each. Jacob Alexander looked on in awe as the girl who had worked for him for five years in abstract suddenly felt the need to take charge to put everyone at ease. They had been numbers in a file but now they were here, the mutilated of Jadwiga.

Sheila passed out small bouquets of flowers and led everyone to a waiting line of cars.

'Abraham Cady was not able to come to meet you and sends his regrets. His face is well known and if he were here it might interfere with your anonymity. However, he is quite anxious to know you all and has asked you to dinner tomorrow evening.'

In a few moments they all seemed more certain and divided up into the cars. 'If they aren't too tired,' Sheila said to Dr. Leiberman, 'I think a little spin around London might be nice so they can get the feeling of our city.'

After Kelno's testimony, Dr. Harold Boland, a prominent anaesthetist, testified on behalf of Sir Adam Kelno that the spinal was a simple and reasonable method.

He was an old-timer who had given hundreds of spinals with and without pre-injection of morphia and supported in essence what Sir Adam had testified.

Brendon O'Conner cross-examined him only briefly.

'Then a spinal blockage, when properly injected, is a relatively simple piece of business?'

'Yes, in the hands of a physician with the experience of Sir Adam.'

'Provided,' O'Conner said, 'one has the full consent and co-operation of the patient. Would you care, Dr. Boland, to speculate if the patient was physically restrained against his will, screaming, kicking, biting for his freedom. Could not the spinal under those circumstances become quite painful?'

'I have never administered one under such circumstances.'

'If the needle slipped because of violent movement of the patient.'

'Then it could be painful.'

A parade of witnesses followed. First, the elder of the Polish community in London, Count Czerny, who recounted Sir Adam's successful fight against extradition. Then former Colonel Gajnow who conducted the initial investigation of Kelno in Italy, then Dr. August Novak, who had been the executive surgeon of the Polish Hospital in Tunbridge Wells, then three former Polish officers who were prisoners in Jadwiga and members of the Nationalist underground, and then four patients whom Kelno had saved in Jadwiga with particular skill.

O'Conner cross-examined each briefly.

'Are you Jewish?' he asked.

The answer was a uniform, 'No.'

But more interesting, 'When Dr. Kelno took out your appendix do you remember a sheet before your face?'

'I remember nothing. I was put to sleep.'

'Not injected in the spine?'

'No, I was put to sleep.'

J. J. MacAlister came up from Budleigh Salterton. He had difficulty in speaking because of a stroke, but his recounting of Kelno's years in Sarawak were most effective as a former colonial officer speaking the jargon of the jury.

Then another former inmate was called to the witness box.

'Sir Robert,' the judge said, 'to what point is your next witness addressed?'

'The same point, my Lord.'

'I can understand,' Anthony Gilray said, 'that you wish to impress on the jury that Dr. Kelno was a kind man. No one is suggesting he wasn't kind to certain patients.'

'I do not wish to seem impertinent, my Lord, but I have two more witnesses to this point.'

'Well,' the judge persisted, 'no one contests that Dr. Kelno was considerate of Polish men and women. What is suggested is that when it came to Jews, it was an entirely different matter.'

'My Lord, I must confess I have a witness who has just arrived from out of the country, and I shall agree that he will be my final witness if his Lordship would call an early recess today.'

'Well, I don't think the jury is going to object to an early adjournment.'

Cady, Shawcross, and his people rushed across the hall to the consultation room. In a moment Josephson came with the confirmation and they were shaken. Konstanty Lotaki had arrived from Warsaw to testify for Adam Kelno.

'We shall continue to do our best,' Bannister said.

NINE

The word spread like a brush fire that Konstanty Lotaki had arrived in London to testify for Kelno. It was a severe blow for Cady.

'I call to the stand as our last witness, Dr. Konstanty Lotaki.'

The associate led him up the three steps into the box and a Polish interpreter stood beside him. The jury was particularly alert at the sight of the new arrival and the press section spilled over into extra tables. The oath was issued to the interpreter.

Bannister arose. 'My Lord, since this witness will be testifying through an interpreter and since we have our own Polish interpreter, I should like to request that my learned friend's interpreter transmit all questions and answers loudly and clearly so that we are in a position to challenge if necessary.'

'Do you understand that?' Gilray asked.

The interpreter nodded.

'Would you ask Dr. Lotaki what his religious beliefs are and how he wishes to be sworn in?'

There was an exchange of conversation. 'He has no religious beliefs. He is a Communist.'

'Very well,' Gilray said, 'you may affirm the witness.'

The heavy-set pumpkin-faced man spoke low key, as though he were in a trance. He gave his name and his address in Lublin, where he was a chief surgeon of a government hospital.

He had been arrested on false charges in 1942 by the Gestapo and learned later the Germans used this method of pressing doctors into concentration camp service. He arrived at Jadwiga and was assigned to Kelno's section. It was the first time they had ever met. He worked with Kelno in a general way, having his own surgery, dispensary, and hospital wards.

'Did Dr. Kelno run a proper establishment?'

'Under the circumstances, no one could have done better.'

'And he treated his patients well and with personal kindness?'

'Exceptionally.'

'Did he discriminate against Jewish patients?'

'I never saw it.'

'Now, when did you first come into contact with SS Dr. Adolph Voss?'

'From the first day.'

'Do you recall a particular time when Voss ordered you down to his office and told you that you would be doing operations in Barrack V?'

'I will never forget it.'

'Would you tell my Lord and the jury about that?'

'We all knew about Voss's experiments. I was summoned in summer of 1943 after Dr. Dimshits had been sent to the gas chamber. Until then Dimshits had been his surgeon.'

'Did you go with Dr. Kelno?'

'We were called separately.'

'Please continue.'

'Voss told me we were to remove testicles and ovaries of persons he was experimenting on. I told him I didn't want to take part in this, and he said he would have an SS orderly perform the operations, and I would meet the same fate as Dimshits.'

There was a break-down in the translation and a member of the Polish press volunteered a half dozen words.

'Just a moment,' Anthony Gilray said. 'I am delighted to have members of the international press in my court, but I do rather they not take part in the proceedings.'

'Sorry, my Lord,' the reporter apologized.

'Mr. Interpreter, if you encounter any difficulty, kindly advise the court. You may continue, Sir Robert.'

'As a result of this meeting with Voss, what did you do?'

'I was distressed and looked to Dr. Kelno as my superior. We decided to call a meeting of all the doctors except Dr. Tesslar, and we decided it would be in the interest of the patients if we operated.'

'And you did.'

'Yes.'

'How often?'

'I think fifteen to twenty operations.'

'Proper operations?'

'With more than usual care.'

'And you had occasion to observe Dr. Kelno and on other occasions he assisted you. Was there ever, I repeat, ever on any occasion any abuse of the patients?'

'No, never.'

'Never?'

'Never.'

'Dr. Lotaki. In your learned opinion, is there danger to a patient in leaving in an organ that had been X-rayed?'

'I am not a qualified radiologist. I have no opinion. My concern is that the patients should not be operated on by less skilled people.'

'What kind of anaesthetic was administered on these occasions?'

301

'Larocaine by spinal blockage after a preliminary injection of morphia to comfort the patient.'

'Could you tell us who else was in the operating room?'

'A surgical team, someone to look after the instruments. Dr. Kelno and I assisted each other and Voss was present always with one or two other Germans.'

'Did you ever personally meet Dr. Mark Tesslar?'

'Yes, several times.'

'What was the general discussion about his activities?'

'In a concentration camp there are rumours about everything. I stayed clear of this business. I am a doctor.'

'Then you were not a member of the underground, either the so-called international underground or the Nationalist underground.'

'No.'

'So you had no malice toward Dr. Tesslar and he had none toward you?'

'That is right.'

'Did Dr. Tesslar ever attend any operations in Barrack V in which you either performed or assisted?'

'No, never.'

'And were any of these operations done with undue speed or in a haphazard manner?'

'No. They were done by standard procedures with almost no pain to the patient.'

'Now then, you were removed from Jadwiga Concentration Camp in 1944, is that correct?'

'I was taken out by Dr. Flensberg to a private clinic near Munich. He had me do surgery.'

'Were you paid?'

'Flensberg took all the fees.'

'But life was better than in Jadwiga.'

'Anything was better than Jadwiga.'

'You were dressed, fed decently, free to move about?'

'We had better clothing and food, but I was always under guard.'

'And at the end of the war you made your way back to Poland?'

'I have lived and worked there since.'

302

'Essentially, in Jadwiga you and Dr. Kelno performed the same kind of work for Dr. Voss. Did you know that Dr. Kelno was wanted as a war criminal?'

'Yes, I heard.'

'But you were not involved in the Nationalist underground so no charges were brought against you.'

'I did nothing wrong.'

'Now then, Dr. Lotaki, what is your present political conviction?'

'After what I saw in Jadwiga I have become a determined anti-fascist. I feel the best way to combat fascism is through the Communist party.'

'No further questions.'

Thomas Bannister adjusted his robe carefully, took his set stance, and studied Lotaki with a long period of deliberate silence. Abe passed a note to O'Conner, ARE WE IN TROUBLE?

YES, the return reply came.

'Do you agree, Dr. Lotaki, that before Hitler Germany was among the most civilized and cultured countries of the world?'

'Sterilized countries?'

A relief of laughter.

'You shall not laugh at any witness in my court,' Gilray said. 'Now, Mr. Bannister, as to this line of questioning ... you know your job and I'm not advising you ... never mind, continue. Explain the question again, Mr. Interpreter.'

'I agree that Germany was civilized before Hitler.'

'And if someone would have told you what this civilized country was going to do in the next decade you would have refused to believe that.'

'Yes.'

'Mass murders, experiments on human guinea pigs, forceful removal of sex organs for the eventual purpose of mass sterilization. You wouldn't have believed that before Hitler, would you?'

'No.'

'And would you say that any doctor having taken the

Hippocratic oath would not have taken part in these experiments?'

'I am going to intervene,' Gilray said. 'One of the problems of this case is that of voluntary acts as against involuntary acts in its context with human morality.'

'My Lord,' Thomas Bannister said with his voice rising for the first time. 'When I use the words "taken part in" I mean any surgeon who has removed sex organs. I mean that Dr. Lotaki knew what Voss was doing and why he was ordered to cut off testicles and hoick out ovaries.'

'I did it under duress.'

'Let me clarify this,' Gilray said. 'We are in the Royal Courts of Justice and this case is being dealt with according to the common law of England. Now then, is it your contention, Mr. Bannister, that you are putting a case before the jury on the grounds that an operation performed under duress still amounts to justification against libel?'

'That is my case, my Lord,' Bannister snapped back, 'that no doctor, prisoner, or otherwise, had any right to perform such operations!'

A gasp floated over the room. 'Well then, we know where we stand, don't we?'

'Now, Dr. Lotaki,' Bannister said. 'Did you really believe Voss would have used an inexperienced SS orderly to perform these operations?'

'I had no reason to doubt it.'

'Voss went to Himmler for permission to conduct these experiments. If these testicles and ovaries were not properly removed they were then useless to the experiment. How in the name of God could anyone believe this nonsense about an SS orderly?'

'Voss was not sane,' Lotaki sputtered. 'All of it was quite mad.'

'But he was bluffing. He had to submit reports to Berlin, and he had to have qualified surgeons.'

'So he would have sent me to the gas chamber like Dimshits and found another surgeon.'

'Dr. Lotaki, will you be so kind as to describe Dr. Dimshits to my Lord and the jury.'

'He was a Jew, older, perhaps seventy or more.'

'And living in a concentration camp aged him further?'

'Yes.'

'What of his physical appearance?'

'Very old.'

'And feeble and failing?'

'I ... I ... I can't say.'

'No longer able to function as a surgeon ... no longer of use to the Germans.'

'I ... can't ... say ... he knew too much.'

'But you and Kelno knew the same things and you didn't go to the gas chamber. You went to private clinics. I suggest that Dr. Dimshits went to the gas chamber because he was old and useless. I suggest that is the real reason, no other. Now then, Dr. Kelno has testified that he is a victim of a Communist plot. You are a Communist. Would you comment on that?'

'I am in London to tell the truth,' Lotaki cried out, shaken. 'What makes you think a Communist cannot tell the truth or testify for a non-Communist?'

'Have you heard of Berthold Richter, the high East German Communist?'

'Yes.'

'Are you aware that he and hundreds of Nazis are now in the Communist regime who were former concentration camp officials?'

'Now just a moment,' Gilray said, turning to the jury, 'I am certain Mr. Bannister is correct in his last statement but it doesn't mean that it is evidence unless it is offered as evidence.'

'What I am suggesting, my Lord, is that the Communists have a very convenient way to rehabilitate former Nazis and SS who are useful to them. No matter how black their past, if they throw themselves on the altar of Communism, and if they are of use to the regime, their past is forgotten.'

'You certainly are not suggesting Dr. Lotaki was a Nazi?'

'I suggest that Dr. Lotaki is a genius at the art of survival, and he has not only worked his passage once, but

305

twice. Dr. Lotaki, you say you went to Dr. Kelno as your superior and discussed the operations. What would you have done if Dr. Kelno had refused?'

'I ... also would have refused.'

'No further questions.'

TEN

Abe sat in the darkness. A car stopped before the mews, the door was unlocked.

'Dad?'

Ben felt around for the light switch and flicked it on. His father was across the room, legs stretched out straight, a stiff glass of whisky balanced on his chest.

'You drunk, Dad?'

'No.'

'Tipsy?'

'No.'

'Everyone's been gathered at Mr. Shawcross's for almost an hour. They're all waiting for you. Mrs. Shawcross has put on a beautiful spread, and they have a pianist playing for everyone ... and ... well, Lady Wydman sent me here to get you.'

Abe set the glass aside, pulled himself up, and hung his head. Ben had seen his father like this before, many times. In Israel he'd come into his father's bedroom, which also served as his office, after a long day of writing. His father would be wrung out, sometimes in tears about a character in the book, sometimes so tired he was unable to lace his shoes. He looked like that now, only worse.

'I can't face them,' Abe said.

'You've got to, Dad. From the minute you meet them,

you'll forget about their mutilation. They're a lively bunch, and they laugh and carry on and they want so badly to see you. The other man arrived from Holland this morning as well as the women from Belgium and Trieste. They're all here now.'

'What the hell do they want to see me for? For bringing them to London and putting them on display like freaks in a side show.'

'You know why they're here. And don't forget, you're their hero.'

'Hero, my ass.'

'You're a hero to Vanessa and Yossi and me, too.'

'Sure.'

'Don't you think we know why you're doing this?'

'Sure, we've done you a damned great service. Accept the gift of my generation to your generation. Concentration camps and gas chambers and the rape of human dignity. Now, accept our gift, you kids, and get in there and be civilized.'

'How about the gift of courage.'

'Courage. You mean fear of not going through with it and trying to live with yourself afterwards. That's not courage.'

'No one's in London because they're cowards. Now come along, I'll put your shoes on.'

Ben knelt before his father and laced his shoes up. Abe reached out and patted his son's head. 'What kind of a goddam air force would let you run around with a moustache like that. I wish to hell you'd shave it off.'

From the moment he arrived he was happy that Ben had made him come. Sheila Lamb continued to take the awkwardness out of the situation by whisking him to the six men and four women she had adopted as her wards. They were there with him, Ben and Vanessa to help his slipshod Hebrew, and Yossi was there adoring his daughter. The presence of the three young Israelis put a certain kind of courage into them all. There were no handshakes. There were embraces and kisses and they were all brothers and sisters.

307

David Shawcross presented each of them signed sets of Abraham Cady's collected works and the air was that of soldiers on the eve of battle. Abe became himself with Dr. Leiberman and joked about the fact he had only one eye and that made them all even closer.

Abe and Leiberman moved off by themselves. 'I was called in by your solicitor,' Dr. Leibermann said. 'He felt that because most of this testimony will be in Hebrew it would be better if I acted as the translator.'

'What about your medical testimony?' Abe asked.

'They feel, and I agree, that the medical testimony will be more effective coming from an English doctor.'

'They were reluctant at first,' Abe said. 'You know how doctors are about testifying against each other, but a number of good people came forth.'

It had been an evening of unexpected pleasantness, but a sudden weariness struck them all and, with it, an awkwardness. Everyone began looking toward Abraham Cady.

'I'm not drunk enough to give a speech,' he said.

And then without signal they were standing before him, looking at their non-hero, who in turn looked at the floor. Then he looked up. David Shawcross, his cigar stopped, and Lady Sarah, much like a saint. And soft Vanessa still much an English lady and Ben and Yossi, the young lions of Israel. And the victims . . .

'Our side of this case begins tomorrow,' Abe said, now finding strength to address those ten particular people. 'I know and you know the terrible ordeal before you. But we are here because we can never let the world forget what they did to us. When you are in the witness box remember, all of you, the pyramids of bones and ashes of the Jewish people. And remember when you speak, you are speaking for six million who can no longer speak . . . remember that.'

They came to him one at a time, shook his hand and kissed his cheek and filed from the room. And then there was only Ben and Vanessa beside him.

'God,' Abe said, 'give them strength.'

ELEVEN

'You may proceed, Mr. Bannister.'

Thomas Bannister turned his attention to the eight men and four women who had undergone their task as jurymen without visible emotion. Some were still wearing their 'one suit'. And nearly all of them filed into court with some sort of cushion.

Bannister played with his notes until the room hushed. 'I'm sure the members of the jury have suspected that there are two sides to this case. A great deal of what my learned friend, Sir Robert Highsmith, has said to you is entirely true. We do not dispute that the defendants are the author and publisher of the book or that the passage is defamatory and we agree that the person in the book is Sir Adam Kelno, the plaintiff.'

The press box was now so overfull, the front row of the three row balcony above was fixed with writing clipboards for those who had no room downstairs. Anthony Gilray, who had taken volumes of notes, continued burning out pencils.

'My Lord will address you on all questions of law. But, there are really only two issues. We say in our defence that the gist of the paragraph is true and the plaintiff is saying two things. He says the gist is untrue and because of that he is entitled to very large damages. Now our position is that because of what Dr. Kelno did, his reputation really hasn't been damaged, and even though he has been defamed he should not be awarded anything but the lowest coin in the realm, a halfpenny.

'A libel does not depend on what the author meant but how people who read it understood it. We assume that most of the people who read it never heard of Dr. Kelno or associated it with a Dr. Kelno practising in Southwark. Certainly, many people did know it was the same Dr. Kelno.

What did this mean to them?

'Now I agree with my learned friend that Dr. Kelno was a prisoner in an indescribable hell and under German domination. Quite easy for us in jolly, comfortable England to criticise what people did then, but when you consider this case, you must certainly bear in mind how you might have acted under similar circumstances.

'Jadwiga. How did something like this ever happen? Where in the world are the most civilized, advanced, and cultured countries? It would show no disrespect to the United States or our own Commonwealth to say, "The Christian countries of Western Europe were the flower of our civilization, the highest place to which man has come." And if you would have said, "Do you think it possible that within a few years one of these countries would drive millions of old people naked into gas chambers?" Well, everyone would have said, "No, it's not possible. Come now, be serious. The Kaiser and all that militarism have gone. Germany has an ordinary Western democratic government. We cannot conceive of why anyone would want to do anything like that. It would bring the loathing of the world on them." If it were peacetime and they did it, they'd soon be at war with those trying to stop it. And even in wartime, what could they possibly hope to gain with this kind of conduct?'

Thomas Bannister repeated his single gesture of rolling his fee bags and his voice now modulated with the subtlety of Bach counterpoint.

'You'd never get people to do it,' he continued. 'The German Army is made up of people from offices and factories and shops. They have children of their own. They would never get people with families to drive children into gas chambers. And ... if it had been suggested on top of all this that human guinea pigs would have their sexual organs removed in front of their eyes while they were conscious as part of experiments in mass sterilization, again we should have said, should we not ... "it's not possible" and furthermore, we should have said, "this kind of thing has to be done by doctors and you could never find any doctor who

310

would do it."

'Well, we would have been wrong because it did happen, all of it, and there was a doctor, an anti-Semitic Polish doctor who did it. And from the evidence it's clear that he had a dominating position and a dominating personality. You heard Dr. Lotaki say that if Dr. Kelno had refused, he would have too.

'We would have been wrong to think this could not have happened because there was a cause to support and justify what happened. That monstrous cause is anti-Semitism. Those among us who have no religion would rely on their intellect. But all of us, religious or not, have a concept of right and wrong.

'But once you allow yourself to think that there are some people, because of their race, their colour, or religion, who are really not human beings you have established a justification for imposing every sort of humiliation on them.

'This ploy becomes quite useful to a national leader who needs a universal scapegoat, someone to blame when anything goes wrong. And then you can whip the masses into a frenzy, put them in a state of mind that such people are animals ... well, we slaughter animals just the way it was done at Jadwiga. Wasn't Jadwiga West the logical end of this particular road?

'We should have been wrong,' Bannister went on with an oration that mesmerized every man and woman who heard it, 'because if you had ordered British troops to drive children and old people into gas chambers, none of whom had done anything wrong except they were the children of their parents, can you imagine British troops doing anything but mutiny against such orders?

'Well, as a matter of fact there were some Germans, soldiers, officers, priests, doctors, and ordinary civilians who refused to obey these orders and said, "I am not going to do this because I would not like to live and have this on my conscience. I'm not going to push them into gas chambers, and then say later I was under orders and justify it by saying that they were going to be pushed in by someone anyhow, and I can't stop it and other people will push them

311

more cruelly. Therefore, it's in their best interest that I shove them in gently." You see, the trouble was, not enough of these people refused.

'So there are three views, are there not, which may be taken by people reading this paragraph in this book.

'If we consider the case of the SS camp guard whom we hanged after the war. That SS guard would say in his defence. "Look here, I was conscripted and found myself in the SS, in a concentration camp and not realizing what was going on." But of course he learned what was going on and if he was a British soldier, he would have staged a mutiny. I am not suggesting these SS guards should have gone free after the war, but if we put ourselves in their place, conscripts in Hitler's army, perhaps hanging was a bit severe.

'Now, there is a second view. There should have been those who would have risked and taken severe punishment and even death by refusing because this is what we owe future generations. We must say to the future, if this thing happens again you cannot make the excuse that you feared punishment for there comes a moment in the human experience when one's life itself no longer makes sense when it is directed to the mutilation and murder of his fellow man.

'And the final view that this was not a German at all but an ally in whose hands were placed the lives of fellow allies.

'We know, of course, there were risks and punishments for prisoner/doctors. We have also learned, have we not, that the prisoners ran the medical facility and that one in particular, Dr. Adam Kelno, was held in high esteem by the Germans and he himself considered himself their associate. We cannot be made to believe that a German medical officer would have cut his own throat by disposing of the one most useful to him. And we know that the orders to remove this most valued doctor to a private clinic came from Himmler himself.

'The defence says that the gist of the paragraph was true and the plaintiff is only entitled to contemptuous damages of a halfpenny for if the paragraph had read so and so had committed twenty murders when in fact he only committed two, then how much real damage is done to the murderer's reputation.

'The paragraph was wrong to state that over fifteen thousand experiments were carried out by surgery. It was also wrong to state it was done without anaesthetic. We admit that.

'It is for you, however, to decide what kind of operations were performed, how they were performed in the case of Jews, and how much Sir Adam Kelno's character is worth.'

TWELVE

Because of the immediate and close relationship Sheila Lamb had established with the victims, she was questioned closely to determine a possible order of testimony. Bannister needed a woman first so that the men would be charged to courage, and he needed the one with authority, bearing, and common sense, who would not break on the stand. Sheila reckoned that Yolan Shoret, although the quietest of the lot, was the strongest.

Yolan Shoret, smallish and trimly attired, appeared much in control of herself as she sat and waited with Sheila and Dr. Leiberman in the second consultation room.

In the courtroom, Mr. Justice Gilray turned to the press. 'I cannot give directions to the press,' he said. 'All I can say is that I, as one of Her Majesty's Judges, would be appalled, simply appalled, if any of the witnesses who had undergone these terrible operations were identified or photographed.'

Sir Robert Highsmith winced at the words, TERRIBLE OPERATIONS. Bannister had certainly set up something in the judge's mind and perhaps in everyone else's.

313

'I have expressed my view and I am satisfied with the discretion of the press from my past knowledge.'

'My Lord,' O'Conner said, 'my instructing solicitors have just passed me a note saying that all representatives of the press have signed a pledge not to publish names or photographs.'

'That is what I expected. Thank you, gentlemen.'

'My witness will testify in Hebrew,' Bannister said.

There was a knock on the consultation room door. Dr. Leiberman and Sheila Lamb led Yolan Shoret over the hallway. Sheila squeezed her hand as she moved away to the solicitors' table to begin her notes. A hundred pairs of eyes turned to the door. Adam Kelno stared without emotion, as she and Dr. Leiberman mounted the steps into the witness box. Her dignity plunged the room into a hush as they were sworn in on the Old Testament and the judge offered them seats. She preferred to stand.

Gilray issued a few instructions to Dr. Leiberman on his translations. He nodded and said he spoke fluent Hebrew and English and that German was his mother tongue. He would have no trouble as he had known Mrs. Shoret for several years.

'What is your name?' Thomas Bannister asked.

'Yolan Shoret.'

She gave her address in Jerusalem, her maiden name of Lovino, and her birthplace as Trieste in 1927. Bannister watched her closely.

'When were you sent to Jadwiga?'

'In the spring of 1943.'

'And were you tattooed with a number?'

'Yes.'

'Do you recall that number?'

She unbuttoned her sleeve and slowly rolled it back to her elbow and a blow fell on the courtroom. She held out her arm with a blue tattoo. Someone in the rear of the court cried aloud and the jury showed its first reaction. 'Seven zero four three two and a triangle to denote a Jew.'

'You may roll your sleeve down,' the judge whispered.

The number was covered.

'Mrs. Shoret,' Bannister continued. 'Do you have any children?'

'None of my own. My husband and I adopted two.'

'What did you do in Jadwiga?'

'For four months I worked in a factory. We made parts for field radios.'

'Very hard work?'

'Yes, sixteen hours a day.'

'Did you have enough to eat?'

'No, my weight fell to ninety pounds.'

'Were you beaten?'

'Yes, by Kapos.'

'And what was your barrack like?'

'It was like a normal concentration camp barrack. We were stacked up in layers of six. Some three to four hundred to a barrack with a single stove in the centre, a sink, two toilets, and two showers. We ate from tin plates in the barracks.'

'After four months what happened?'

'The Germans came looking for twins. They found my sister and me and the Cardozo sisters with whom we grew up in Trieste and who were deported with us. We were taken by truck into the main camp to Barrack III of the medical compound.'

'Did you know what Barrack III was all about?'

'We soon found out.'

'What did you find out?'

'It held men and women who were used in experiments.'

'Who told you that?'

'We were put with another set of twins, the Blanc-Imber sisters of Belgium, who had been X-rayed and operated on. It did not take long to learn from everyone why we were there.'

'Would you describe Barrack III to my Lord and the jury?'

'The women were kept on the ground floor and the men on the upper floor. All windows facing Barrack II were boarded because there was an execution wall outside, but we could hear everything. The opposite windows were kept shut most of the time so we were always in darkness except for a few small light bulbs. The far end of the barrack was caged off and held about forty girls who were being experimented on by Dr. Flensberg. Most of them had been driven insane so they were mumbling and screaming all the time. Many of the other girls like the Blanc-Imber sisters were recovering from operations of Voss's experiments.'

'Did you have knowledge of any prostitutes or women receiving abortions?'

'No.'

'Did you know a Dr. Mark Tesslar?'

'Yes, he was with the men upstairs and from time to time helped treat us.'

'But so far as you knew, he did not operate on any women?'

'I never heard of it.'

'Who watched you in Barrack III?'

'Four women Kapos, Polish women armed with truncheons, who had a small room for themselves, and a woman doctor named Gabriela Radnicki, who had a little cell at the end of the barrack.'

'A prisoner?'

'Yes.'

'Jewish?'

'No, a Roman Catholic.'

'Did she treat you badly?'

'Quite contrary. She was very sympathetic. She worked very hard to save those who had been operated on, and she went alone into the cage holding the insane. She would calm them when they became hysterical.'

'What became of Dr. Radnicki?'

'She committed suicide. She left a note saying she could no longer bear to watch the agony and not be able to alleviate the suffering. We all felt we had lost our mother.'

Angela felt Terrence's hand grip hers so tightly she almost cried out. Adam continued to stare up at the witness box almost removed from what was being said.

'Was Dr. Radnicki replaced?'

'Yes, by Dr. Maria Viskova.'

'And how did she treat you?'

'Also like a mother.'

'How long were you kept in Barrack III?'

'A few weeks.'

'Tell us what happened then.'

'SS guards came and got us, the three sets of twins. We were taken to Barrack V to a room with an X-ray machine. An SS orderly spoke to us in German, which we did not understand clearly. Two other orderlies took off our clothing and one at a time a plate was fastened to our abdomen and our back. He took my number from my arm and recorded it and I was X-rayed for five or ten minutes.'

'What was the result of that?'

'A dark-coloured spot formed on my abdomen and I vomited very much afterwards.'

'All of you?'

'Yes.'

'Was this spot painful at all?'

'Yes, and it soon formed pus.'

'Then what happened?'

'We remained in Barrack III a few weeks to a month. Time was hard to keep track of. But I remember it growing colder so it must have been toward November. The SS came for us, the three sets of twins, and several men were brought down from upstairs and we were all marched over to Barrack V again and put into a sort of waiting room. I remember we were very embarrassed because we were undressed. ...'

'In one room?'

'There was a curtain separating us but soon we were all mixed together in confusion.'

'Naked?'

'Yes.'

'How old were you, Mrs. Shoret?'

'Sixteen.'

'From a religious family?'

'Yes.'

'With little experience with life?'

'With no experience. Until then I had not been seen

317

naked by a man, or seen a man's organ.'

'And your heads were shaved.'

'Yes, because of the lice and typhus.'

'And there you were all mixed together. Were you mortified?'

'We were being degraded like animals and we were terrified.'

'And then?'

'Orderlies held us down on some wooden tables and shaved our intimate parts.'

'And then?'

'Two men shoved me on a stool and held my head down between my legs and another man put a needle into my spine. I screamed for pain.'

'Screamed for pain? A moment please. Are you quite certain you weren't already in the operating room?'

'I am quite certain I was in the waiting room.'

'Do you know what an injection is? A small injection?'

'I have had many.'

'Well, didn't you have a small injection prior to the spinal?'

'No only the one.'

'Go on.'

'In several minutes my lower body went dead. I was thrown on a wagon and rolled out of the room. All around the men and women were screaming and struggling and more guards arrived with clubs and were beating them.'

'And you were the first taken out of the room?'

'No, I am sure a man was first. I was rolled into the surgery and strapped on the table. I remember the lamp over my head.'

'You were totally conscious?'

'Yes. Three men with masks stood over me. One wore the uniform of an SS officer. Suddenly, the door burst open and another man came in and began to argue with the surgeons. I could not understand too much of it because they were speaking mostly in Polish, but I knew the new man was protesting the treatment. At last he came to my side and sat near me and stroked my forehead and spoke to me in French, which I understood better.'

'What did this person say to you?'

'Courage, my little dove, the pain will soon pass. Courage, I will take care of you.'

'Do you know who this person was?'

'Yes.'

'Who?'

'Dr. Mark Tesslar.'

THIRTEEN

Sima Halevy was a striking contrast to her twin sister, Yolan Shoret. She appeared many years older, ill, and without the vigour or command of her sister. She spoke listlessly as she read her tattoo number to the court and told them she also lived in Jerusalem with two adopted children, orphaned immigrants from Morocco. She repeated the scene of the waiting room and the operation and the presence of Dr. Tesslar.

'What happened after the operation?'

'I was carried by stretcher back to Barrack III.'

'And what was your condition?'

'I was very sick for a long time. Two months, maybe longer.'

'Were you in pain?'

'In pain that I feel to this day.'

'What about the extreme pain?'

'For a week we all just lay in bed and cried.'

'Who looked after you?'

'Dr. Maria Viskova and often Dr. Tesslar would come from upstairs to see us. There was another doctor who came often, a French woman. I do not remember her name.

She was very kind.'

'Did any other doctor come to see you?'

'I vaguely recall one time when I was running a high fever that Dr. Tesslar and Dr. Viskova were arguing with a male doctor about more food and medicine. Only that once, and I am not so sure who it was.'

'Do you know what was wrong with you?'

'The wound had opened. We had only paper bandages. The smell from us was so horrible no one could stand near us.'

'But after a time you recovered and returned to work in the factory?'

'No, I never recovered. My sister was sent back to the factory, but I was unable to. Maria Viskova pretended to keep me as her assistant so they would not send me to the gas chamber. I stayed with her until I was strong enough to do very light work in a book-binding barrack which repaired old books to send to the German soldiers. It was a place where we were not treated too harshly.'

'Mrs. Halevy, would you tell us the circumstances of your marriage?'

She relayed the story of a sweetheart in Trieste when she was fourteen and he was seventeen. Before her sixteenth birthday she was deported and lost track of him completely. After the war in the staging and relocation centres in Vienna and elsewhere it was customary for the survivors passing through to leave notes on a bulletin board in hopes that a friend or relative might find it. By some sort of miracle her note was found by her sweetheart, who had managed to survive Auschwitz and Dachau. After a two-year search he found her in Palestine and they were married.

'What effect has this operation had on your life till now?'

'I am a vegetable. I spend most of my time in bed.'

Sir Robert Highsmith stood before his rostrum with a page of notes of the discrepancies between the testimony of the two sisters. There was no question that Bannister had made inroads and these victims were making a telling effect. Nonetheless, they had not been able conclusively to pin the operations on Dr. Kelno and he himself believed it was not Kelno. He realized the girls had sympathy. He had to handle them carefully.

'Madame Halevy,' he said in a manner that contrasted the flair of his earlier examinations. 'My learned friend has suggested that it was Dr. Kelno who performed the operations you and your sister described. But you don't know that to be a fact, do you?'

'No.'

'When did you first hear of Dr. Kelno?'

'When we were brought from the factory to Barrack III.'

'And you remained there for some time after your operation?'

'Yes.'

'But you never saw him or at least you could not identify him?'

'No.'

'And you know that the gentleman sitting between us is Dr. Kelno.'

'Yes.'

'And you still cannot identify him.'

'They were wearing masks in the surgery, but I don't know this man.'

'How do you know you were taken to Barrack V for your operation?'

'I don't understand.'

'Did you see a sign that read Barrack V over an entry?'

'No, I don't believe so.'

'Could it have been Barrack I?'

'It's possible.'

'Are you aware that Dr. Flensberg and his assistant were carrying out experiments in Block I and had their own surgeons?'

'I did not know that.'

'I suggest it is all in his indictment as a war criminal. I also suggest that you only recently recalled that you went to Barrack V. Is that not so, Madame Halevy?'

She looked in confusion to Dr. Leiberman.

'Please answer the question,' the judge said.

'I spoke to lawyers here.'

'In fact you are not able to identify anyone at all, Voss, Flensberg, Lotaki, or Kelno.'

'No, I cannot.'

'In fact, it might have been a Dr. Boris Dimshits who performed the operation.'

'I do not know.'

'But you do know that Sir Adam has testified that he visited his patients after the operation. If this testimony were true then you would be able to identify him.'

'I was very sick.'

'Sir Adam also testified that he gave the spinal and anaesthetic himself in the operating room.'

'I am not certain I was in the operating room then.'

'Then it might not have been Dr. Kelno.'

'Yes.'

'Do you see your sister quite often in Jerusalem?'

'Yes.'

'And you've talked about all of this, particularly since you were contacted for testimony in this case.'

'Yes.'

The robes slipped off Sir Robert's shoulders as he was driving with excitement despite his desire to keep restrained.

'Now both you and your sister are vague and contradictory on a number of points and particularly the dates and time lapses. There is questionable testimony on whether you were taken in by stretcher or wagon ... whether Dr. Tesslar sat on your right or your left or at your head ... whether the table was titled ... whether or not you could actually see a reflection in the overhead lamp ... who was in the room ... how many weeks you spent waiting in Block III after your irradiation ... what people were saying in Polish and German ... you have testified you were quite drowsy and your sister testified she was awake ... you are not absolutely certain your injection was given in the waiting room.'

Highsmith dropped the paper to the table and leaned forward holding the rostrum with both hands and cautioning himself not to raise his voice.

'I suggest, Madame Halevy, you were quite young and all of this happened a long time ago.'

She listened closely as Dr. Leiberman told her everything back in Hebrew. She nodded and said something back.

'What is her answer?' the judge asked.

'Mrs. Halevy said that Sir Robert is probably correct about her discrepancies on many points but there is one thing that no woman can forget and that is the day she knows she is unable to bear her own child.'

FOURTEEN

Hemlines were up in Czechoslovakia. Prague openly displayed her Western heart as well as her Western-oriented thighs. It was the most liberal Communist country, seeing its most liberal days. Flocks of tourists moved in and out from the West in buses and by rail and airline.

Even the landing of an El Al Israel jet created little stir. After all, the affection of the Czechs for their Jewish population and the State of Israel was well established. From the days of Jan Masaryk at the end of the war there was a sincere mourning for the seventy-seven thousand Czech Jews murdered at Teresienstadt and the other extermination camps and it was Masaryk himself who defied the British and allowed Czechoslovakia to be a staging and transit point for the survivors of the holocaust attempting to run the blockade to Palestine.

This El Al flight would have drawn scant attention except that one of the passengers was Shimshon Aroni, whose arrival triggered the usual speculations at police headquarters.

'Jalta Hotel,' he said to the driver of an Opel taxi.

They turned into a swarm of vehicles, trolleys, and buses on Wenceslaus Square and checked in at the reception desk. It was four o'clock. Two hours should get things moving, he thought.

A small single room, the smallest. His life had been lived in small single rooms hunting escaped Nazis. Prague had remained the only decent city among the Communist countries but since the murder of Katzenbach it too took on a sick smell.

His battered bag was opened and its contents put away in minutes. Two million air miles. Two million miles of hunting and hounding. Two million miles of vengeance.

He walked over to the square on a now familiar pilgrimage, first to the U Fleku Beer Garden. Israeli beer was not so good. In fact, it was rather bad. When Aroni travelled before retirement he had a chance to taste good beer, but lately he had the scant satisfaction of the local product at home. U Fleku, an enormous drinking hall, had the best beer in the world, Pilsener to Bohemia.

He gloried in three glasses and studied the crowd and the girls and their short skirts. Czech and Hungarian women were the best. In Spain and Mexico bulls were bred for their courage. In Hungary and Czechoslovakia women were bred for love-making. Subtle, frantic, imaginative, irrational tempers, magnificent sweetness. What a bore it all has been, Aroni thought. He had been too busy hunting Nazis for serious love-making and now he was getting too old, almost seventy, but not that old. No use of dreaming. His trip to Prague precluded a romance.

He mentally converted the Czech koruna into Israeli pounds, paid his bill, and continued on to the Charles Bridge that spanned the Vltava River with its great stone railings adorned every few feet by the statue of a grim saint.

Aroni's step slowed as he walked toward Staromestski—the Old Town—for here were the memories, the pitiful remains of a thousand years of Jewish life in Central Europe. The Staronova Synagogue, the oldest in Europe, dating back to 1268, and the Klaus cemetery, with thirteen thousand broken and crooked tombstones going back to before the time of Columbus.

Aroni had seen the old graveyards in Poland, in Russia, in Roumania, largely unkept and vandalized. At least here was a parcel of sacred ground.

Graveyards. The death place of most Jews was the unmarked mountains of nameless bones of the extermination camps.

The Jewish State Museum held a few relics of fifteen hundred villages profaned during the Nazi occupation and the Pinkas Synagogue carried a grisly memorial.

Read the names again, Aroni. Read them again and again ... Terzin, Belzec, Auschwitz, Gliwce, Majdanek, Sobibor, Bergen-Belsen, Izbica, Gross-Rosen, Treblinka, Lodz, Dachau, Babi-Yar, Buchenwald, Stutthof, Rosenburg, Piaski, Ravensbruck, Rassiku, Mauthausen, Dora, Neuengamme, Chelmno, Sachsenhausen, Nonowice, Riga, Trostinic, and all the other places his people were murdered.

Seventy-seven thousand names of the dead on a synagogue wall and the words, PEOPLE BE VIGILANT.

Aroni returned to the hotel at six o'clock. As he calculated, Jiri Linka waited in the lobby. They shook hands and made to the bar. DINERS' CLUB WELCOME, the sign of peace and progress proclaimed.

Jiri Linka was a cop, a Jewish cop. He looked like a cartoon of an iron curtain policeman. Aroni ordered a Pilsener and Linka a shot of slivovitz.

'How long since you've been to Prague, Aroni?'

'Almost four years.'

'Things have changed, eh?'

They conversed in Czech, one of Aroni's ten languages. 'How long will your comrades in Moscow permit you such happiness?'

'Nonsense. We are a progressive Soviet country.'

Aroni grunted through rivulets of wrinkles. 'I stood at the Charles Bridge today and looked into the river ... Katzenbach.'

Linka turned quiet as Aroni made reference to an

325

American member of the Jewish Joint Distribution Committee whose mission it was to liberate Jews. He was found dead, floating in the river.

'First they'll get the Jews,' Aroni said, 'and then the Czechs. You are seeing too many good things from the West. I predict you'll have the Russian Army in Prague within a year.'

Linka giggled. 'I thought you retired. I thought maybe you came this time to go to the spas and take a mud bath.'

'I am working for a private party. I want to see Branik.'

Linka puckered his lips and shrugged at mention of the head of the secret police. Aroni was one of the best men in the business and never sought out things foolishly. In all the years he had come to Czechoslovakia he had been content to work through channels.

'I want to see Branik tonight.'

'I think he is out of the country.'

'Then I leave tomorrow. I have no time for a run around.'

'Maybe you'd like to talk to someone else?'

'Branik. I'll be waiting in my room.' He left.

Linka drummed his fingers on the table, finished his drink, snatched his hat, and hurried out to the square. He hopped in his small Skoda Octavia and raced toward headquarters.

FIFTEEN

The first of the male victims, Moshe Bar Tov, was called over from the consultation room. He entered the court with an air of defiance and appearing somewhat awkward in a good suit. He gave a small wave to Abraham Cady and

David Shawcross, then glared down hostilely at Adam Kelno, who declined to meet his eye. Kelno appeared tired, quite tired for the first time.

Moshe Bar Tov had been the first to respond to Aroni's search and it was he who brought the others in and was their obvious leader.

'Before we swear in this witness,' Anthony Gilray said, turning to the press, 'I must express concern and distress over a report that came in from a Jerusalem newspaper describing one of the witnesses as a woman in her early forties with two adopted children, slightly set and formerly from Trieste. Now people in Jerusalem, and I understand they are following this trial closely, are apt to identify this lady. I reiterate that there should be a refraining from any kind of description of any sort.'

The offending journalist, an Israeli, busied himself with notes and did not look up.

'Dr. Leiberman, you are still under oath and will continue to be for any other witnesses in Hebrew.'

Brendon O'Conner conducted the examination as Tom Bannister studied it all from a marbleized pose.

'Your name, sir.'

'Moshe Bar Tov.'

'And your address?'

'Kibbutz Ein Gev in the Galilee of Israel.'

'That is a collective settlement, a large farm.'

'Yes, many hundred families.'

'Did you change your name at any time, sir?'

'Yes, my former name was Herman Paar.'

'And before the war you were from Holland?'

'Yes, Rotterdam.'

'And you were deported by the Germans?'

'Early in 1943 with my two sisters, my mother and father. We were transported in cattle cars to Poland. I am the only survivor.'

In contrast to Thomas Bannister, Brendon O'Conner examined with the voice of a Shakespearean actor. Bar Tov showed steel over the death of his family.

'You were tattooed?'

'Yes.'

'Will you read your number to the jury.'

'One hundred and fifteen thousand, four hundred and ninety and a denotation as a Jew.'

'And what happened to you at Jadwiga?'

'I was sent to work with other Dutch Jews in an I.G. Farben factory making shell casings.'

'One moment,' Gilray interrupted. 'I am not defending any particular German manufacturer. On the other hand there is no German manufacturer here to defend himself.'

Dr. Leiberman and Bar Tov engaged in a conversation in Hebrew.

'The court would like to know, Dr. Leiberman, exactly what is transpiring.'

Dr. Leiberman turned red. 'Your Lordship, I'd rather not ...'

'I shall place it in the form of a request for the time being.'

'Mr. Bar Tov says he will gladly send you a copy of the Jadwiga War Crimes Trials in English from the Kibbutz library. He insists he worked in an I.G. Farben factory.'

Anthony Gilray was perplexed and at an unusual loss of words. He fiddled with his pencil and grumbled, then turned to the witness box. 'Well, tell Mr. Bar Tov I appreciate his special knowledge of the situation. Also explain to him that he is in an English courtroom, and we do demand complete respect for the rules of this trial. If I interrupt it is certainly not out of any desire to protect the Nazis or the guilty, but to adhere to normal conduct of fair play.'

After this was told, Bar Tov knew he had his victory and nodded to the judge that he would behave.

'Now, Mr. Bar Tov, you worked in this, er, particular munitions factory for how long?'

'Until the middle of 1943.'

'How old were you at the time?'

'Seventeen.'

'And what happened?'

'An SS officer came to the factory one day and began choosing certain people, myself and several other Dutch boys of about my age. We were taken into the main camp of Jadwiga and placed into Barrack III of the medical compound. After several weeks the SS came and took us away to Barrack V. There was myself and five other Dutchmen. We were ordered to undress in a waiting room. Then, after a time I was taken into a room with an examination table and told to get on it on all fours.'

'Did you ask why?'

'I knew and I complained.'

'What were you told?'

'I was told I was a Jewish dog and I had better stop barking.'

'In what language?'

'German.'

'By whom?'

'Voss.'

'Who else was in the room?'

'SS guards, Kapos, two others who were either doctors or orderlies.'

'Can you identify any of them other than Voss?'

'No.'

'Then what happened?'

'I tried to jump off the table and was hit a blow on the side of the head. I was still conscious but too hurt to struggle against three or four of them who held me on the table. One of the orderlies held a piece of glass under my penis and the doctor or someone in white shoved a long wooden stick like a broom handle up my rectum forcing me to eject sperm on the glass.'

'Did it hurt?'

'Are you serious?'

'Quite serious. Did it hurt?'

'I screamed for mercy to every god I knew and all the gods I didn't know.'

'What happened after that?'

'I was dragged bodily into another room and while they held me they put my testicles on a metal plate on a table. Then, an X-ray machine was directed on one of my testicles for from five to ten minutes. Afterward, I was returned to

Barrack III.'

'What was the effect of all this?'

'I was very dizzy and I vomited constantly for three days. Then, some black stains appeared on my testicles.'

'How long did you remain in Barrack III?'

'A number of weeks.'

'Do you know for a fact that your friends got the same treatment?'

'Yes, and many other men in the barrack.'

'You say you were quite ill. Who took care of you?'

'Dr. Tesslar and, because there were so many Dutch in the barrack, a prisoner, a Dutch prisoner assisted. His name I remember as Menno Donker.'

'How long did you remain in Barrack III before you were removed again?'

'It must have been November.'

'Why do you say that?'

'I recall talk of liquidating the ghettos around Poland and hundreds of thousands being shipped to Jadwiga West. It was so many the extermination facilities couldn't handle them. There were executions by a firing squad going on all the time outside our barrack, shooting and screaming all the time.'

'Would you tell my Lord and the jury about your removal from Barrack III?'

'The SS came for the six of us who had been irradiated together. They also took a Pole, an older man, and Menno Donker.'

'Had Donker been irradiated?'

'No, I thought it strange he should be taken. I remember that.'

'Go on, please.'

'We were marched to Barrack V, the eight of us and six women from the ground floor of the barrack. Then, a scene of madness took place. Everyone was naked and being manhandled and held for injections.'

'How many injections did you have?'

'Only one, in the spine.'

'How was this administered and where?'

'In the waiting room. A huge Kapo locked my arms behind me so I was powerless, a second shoved my head between my legs and the third gave me the needle.'

'Was it painless?'

'I never have to worry about pain from that time on because nothing could ever give me so much pain. I passed out.'

'And when you awakened?'

'I opened my eyes and saw a reflection lamp. I tried to move but my lower body was dead and I was held by straps. A number of men stood over me. The only one I knew was Voss. One of the men in white and wearing a mask held my testicle in a pair of forceps and showed it to Voss. He put it in a bowl and I remembered them reading the number off my arm and writing it on a tag attached to the bowl. I began to cry. That is when I noticed Dr. Tesslar at my side trying to comfort me.'

'And you were returned to Barrack III?'

'Yes.'

'What was your condition?'

'All of us were ill from infection. Menno Donker was the most ill because both of his testicles had been removed. I remember one of the boys, Bernard Holst, was taken away that first night. I heard later he died.'

'And after a time, you were released?'

'No. I remained. We were taken back to Barrack V and X-rayed again.'

'Did you have a second operation?'

'No, I was saved by Dr. Tesslar. There was a death in the barrack. He paid off the Kapos to fill in a death certificate in my name. I took the name of the dead man and was able to continue with it until we were liberated.'

'Mr. Bar Tov, do you have any children?'

'I have four. Two boys and two girls.'

'Adopted?'

'No, they are my own.'

'You'll forgive me for this next question, but it is extremely important and is not meant to make any inference on the nature of your relationship with your wife. Were you examined in Israel to ascertain that you were potent?'

Bar Tov smiled. 'Yes, I'm too potent. I have already enough children.'

Even Gilray joined in a short laugh, then silenced the room with a frown.

'So, even though you were subjected to severe radiation in both testicles, you were not sterilized?'

'That is right.'

'And whoever took out your testicle may well have been removing a healthy and not a dead gland?'

'Yes.'

'No further questions.'

Sir Robert Highsmith arose and contemplated quickly. This was the third victim paraded before the court. Obviously, Bannister was saving some firepower for later. The web of innuendo was being woven around Kelno with the coup to come in the form of Mark Tesslar.

He went into a swaying motion. 'Mr. Bar Tov, in fact weren't you sixteen when you arrived at Jadwiga?'

'Sixteen or seventeen. . . .'

'You testified you were seventeen, but you were sixteen. It was a long time ago, two decades ago. Many things are hard to remember exactly, isn't that so?'

'Some things I forget. Some things I never forget.'

'Yes. And those things which you forgot, you were refreshed on.'

'Refreshed?'

'Did you ever testify or give a statement before?'

'At the end of the war I made a statement in Haifa.'

'And no other statements until you were contacted within the last several months in Israel.'

'That is true.'

'By a lawyer who took a statement in Hebrew?'

'Yes.'

'And when you arrived in London, you sat down with another lawyer and Dr. Leiberman and went over what you had said in Israel?'

'Yes.'

'And on many points you refreshed your recollection of

332

what you stated in Haifa.'

'We cleared up some points.'

'I see. Points about morphia ... a pre-injection. Did you talk about that?'

'Yes.'

'I suggest that you passed out in the waiting room, not from the pain of the spinal, but you had been put under by morphia in Barrack III and it took effect in Barrack V.'

'I don't remember any other injection.'

'And being unconscious during the operation you recall no brutality, you remembered nothing.'

'I have testified I was unconscious.'

'And of course you are not identifying Sir Adam Kelno as either the surgeon or the man who induced sperm from yourself.'

'I cannot identify him.'

'You saw photographs of Dr. Lotaki in the newspaper, I suppose. Can you identify him?'

'No.'

'Now then, Mr. Bar Tov, you are quite grateful to Dr. Tesslar, are you not?'

'I owe him my life.'

'In a concentration camp people save people's lives. You know that Dr. Kelno saved lives, don't you?'

'I heard.'

'And since the liberation, you have remained in contact with Dr. Tesslar, have you not?'

'We lost contact.'

'I see. But you have seen him since you've been in London.'

'Yes.'

'When?'

'Four days ago, in Oxford.'

'Yes.'

'To have a reunion as old friends.'

'Dr. Tesslar had quite an influence on you.'

'He was like our father.'

'And you were quite young and your memory quite faulty, you could have forgotten some things.'

'Some things I will never forget. Have you ever had a wooden handle shoved up your rectum, Sir Highsmith?'

'Now, just a moment,' Gilray said. 'You will address yourself to the questions.'

'When did you first hear the name of Dr. Kelno?'

'I heard it in Barrack III where we were held.'

'Who told you the name?'

'Dr. Tesslar.'

'And recently in London you were shown a floor plan of Barrack V.'

'Yes.'

'To get all the rooms straight in your mind.'

'Yes.'

'Because you did not remember exactly what room you were in at what time. I suggest that. And were you shown photographs of Voss?'

'Yes.'

'Now then, what is your job on your kibbutz?'

'I am in charge of marketing and the truck co-operative with other kibbutzium in the area.'

'And before that?'

'I was a tractor driver for many years.'

'It is very hot in your valley. Wasn't it difficult work?'

'It is hot.'

'And you were a soldier in the Army?'

'In two wars.'

'And you still do your military service each year.'

'Yes.'

'So, with four children, your health was not impaired by this operation.'

'God was more fortunate to me than to some others.'

Bannister now launched a massive frontal assault, coming back with three more men, a Dutchman and two Israelis who had been with Bar Tov on that night in November. As the story was hammered home by repetition, there were fewer and fewer differences in the testimony. Each of them insisted that Dr. Tesslar was present in the operating room, thus building toward the climax of the de-

334

fence case. The main difference was that they had no natural children of their own as did the more fortunate Bar Tov.

After the third testified, Bannister called still another man forward, a former Dutchman named Edgar Beets, who was now Professor Shalom of Hebrew University.

In this battle of attrition, Highsmith suddenly wearied. He turned the cross-examination of Shalom over to his junior, Chester Dicks.

Professor Shalom proved extremely articulate as the pace slowed for another recounting of the events. As Dicks ended his questioning, Bannister came to his feet.

'Before this witness is withdrawn, I am going to call your attention to the fact that my learned friend has not challenged this witness on several points of the plaintiff's case, most importantly he did not challenge the witness that Dr. Tesslar was present. And I call to his Lordship's attention that neither of my learned friends suggested that the testimony of any of these witnesses was untrue.'

'Yes, I see what you mean,' the judge said. 'Well, what is the situation, Mr. Dicks?' He leaned forward. 'I think the jury is entitled to know if you think the witnesses have let their imaginations run loose and dreamed all of this, or if they are perfectly honest men and women who cannot be relied on. Now, just what is your case, Mr. Dicks?'

'I do not think they can be relied on,' Dicks answered, 'due to the distressing circumstances.'

'You are not suggesting,' Gilray said, 'they are all telling a pack of lies.'

'No, my Lord.'

'It is usual,' Bannister insisted, 'to challenge a witness if you do not accept the witness's evidence. You have not done that on the major issue.'

'I have asked a number of questions about the presence of Dr. Tesslar.'

'There's no need to put every point to the witness. Oh very well, why don't you put it to the witness,' Gilray said, annoyed somewhat with Bannister.

'I suggest that Dr. Tesslar was not in the operating room,' Dicks said.

'He was there,' Shalom answered softly.

SIXTEEN

A few moments after the Czech national anthem ended the day's telecast at midnight, a phone summons was answered by Aroni.

'You will walk to the top of the square to the National Museum, and you will wait before the statue.'

Although it was now past midnight, there was music and laughter from the cafés of the tree-lined Vaclavske Namesti. How long would the laughter last in Czechoslovakia? Aroni was concerned for his own fate. Certainly in police headquarters they had speculated on his mission and Prague had gotten dangerous since the mysterious death of Katzenbach.

A car slowed before him and the back door opened. He found himself sitting next to a silent guard. Jiri Linka was in front with the driver. Wordlessly they crossed the Charles Bridge to a nondescript large house on Karmelitska bearing the plaque: DEPUTY DIRECTOR OF ANTIQUITIES AND ARCHAEOLOGICAL STUDIES, which everyone knew in Prague to be the headquarters of the secret police.

The office was sordidly plain with a long table covered in green felt. The wall at the end of the room was sanctified with the usual portrait of Lenin, who could hardly be considered a Czech hero, and portraits of the current heroes, Lenart and Alexander Dubcek. Aroni reckoned the latter pictures would be off the wall before too long.

Branik did not look like a cop. He was slender, outgoing,

and debonair.

'Are you still at it, Aroni?'

'Just enough to keep my hand in.'

Branik nodded for everyone except Linka to leave the room and produced a round of drinks.

'First of all,' Aroni said, 'you have my word I am here on a private matter. I am conducting no government business, moving no funds, and contacting no one.'

Branik placed a cigarette in a long holder and lit it with a very non-proletariat gold lighter. He understood that what Aroni was saying was he didn't want to end up in the river like Katzenbach.

'My business concerns the trial in London.'

'What trial?'

'The one on the front page of every Prague newspaper today.'

'Oh, that trial.'

'There is a strong opinion that Kelno may win unless a certain witness is produced.'

'You think this man is in Czechoslovakia?'

'I don't know. It's a last desperation gamble.'

'I promise nothing,' Branik said, 'except that I'll listen.'

'For obvious reasons the Jewish people cannot lose this case. It would be construed as a justification of many of the Hitler atrocities. For the most part you have always been fair with us ...'

'Save the speech, Aroni, and let me hear the facts.'

'There was a man in his mid-twenties from Bratislava by the name of Egon Sobotnik, a half Jew on his father's side from a large family of twenty or thirty people by that name. Most of them perished. Sobotnik was deported to Jadwiga and served as a medical clerk in charge of surgical records. He knew Kelno intimately, perhaps observed him closer than any other single person. I have gone through the entire Czech Association of Israel and only a few days ago discovered a distant relative, a man named Carmel. His name used to be Sobotnik but as you know a great number of immigrants changed to Hebrew names. May I?' Aroni asked, nodding to the packet of cigarettes.

Branik whipped out his gold lighter and the old man puffed.

'Carmel had kept a correspondence with a second cousin, a woman by the name of Lena Konska, who still lives in Bratislava. According to Carmel, she escaped the Germans by crossing into Hungary and lived underground in Budapest as a Christian. For a time she hid Egon Sobotnik, but the Gestapo found him. I may add, he was a member of the underground in Jadwiga who was making it a point to record what Kelno was doing.'

Smoke began to swell in the room as Linka joined in.

'It was known he survived the camp.'

'And you believe he is in Czechoslovakia?'

'It is only theory but it seems certain he would have headed back to Bratislava and made some contact with his cousin, this Konska woman.'

'Why his disappearance?'

'It is only a question that Sobotnik can answer, if he is still alive.'

'And you want to see this Konska woman?'

'Yes, and if she can shed light and we find Sobotnik, we want to get him to London immediately.'

'This brings up complications,' Branik said. 'We have no official position in this trial but things with the Jews are touchy.'

Aroni looked directly at Branik transmitting a message the secret police chief could not help receive. 'We need a favour,' he said. 'In this business favours are reciprocal. Someday, you may need one.'

Some day rather soon, Branik thought.

Just before dawn they raced east from Prague and then south into the Slovakian countryside. Linka nudged Aroni, who had dozed. The first light of day fell on the distant square-turreted Bratislava Castle, which hovered over the Danube River at that place where Austria, Hungary, and Czechoslovakia came together and the landlocked Czechs had their only major port.

It was shortly past noon when the car stopped before Mytna 22. The name of Lena Konska was on the door of

Apartment 4. A woman in her early sixties opened the door curiously. On a single look, Aroni could well imagine her beauty twenty-five years earlier, enough to live on false papers. Yes, the women of Bratislava were a special sort.

Linka introduced himself. She became apprehensive but showed no fear.

'I am Aroni from Israel. We are here to see you on an important matter.'

SEVENTEEN

'My Lord, our next witness will testify in Italian.'

Ida Peretz, a plumpish woman plainly attired, entered the courtroom seemingly as confused as a bull who had suddenly found itself in the bull ring. Sheila Lamb gave a thumbs-up from the solicitors' table, but she did not see. She searched the courtroom as the Italian interpreter was sworn in, then she seemed to relax as she sighted a young man in his late teens in the last row of spectators and she nodded slightly and he nodded back.

She was sworn in on the Old Testament, giving her maiden name as Cardozo from Trieste.

'Would you tell my Lord approximately when you were sent to the Jadwiga Concentration Camp and under what circumstances.'

There was a lengthy and confused conversation between Ida Peretz and her translator.

'Is there a problem?' Anthony Gilray asked.

'My Lord, Madame Peretz's mother tongue is not Italian. Her Italian is mixed with another language so that I don't seem to be able to give a truly accurate translation.'

'Well, is she speaking Yugoslavian?'

'No, my Lord. She is speaking a mixture of things, some kind of Spanish with which I am not familiar.'

A note was passed from the back row of the courtroom to Abraham Cady; he gave it to O'Conner, who discussed it with Bannister, who rose.

'Can you shed some light on this?' Gilray asked.

'It seems, my Lord, that Mrs. Peretz speaks Ladino. It is a medieval Spanish tongue similar to what Yiddish is to German, only more vague. It is spoken by certain Jewish colonies along the Mediterranean.'

'Well, can we find a Ladino translator and return this witness later?'

A flurry of notes passed down.

'My client has, from personal research, run into Ladino and says it is a very rare tongue these days and we may not be able to find anyone in London capable of interpretation. However, Mrs. Peretz's son is in the courtroom and has spoken the language with his mother all his life and has volunteered.'

'Would this gentleman kindly approach the bench?'

The son of Abraham Cady and the ward of Adam Kelno watched a very Italian-looking young man of nineteen or twenty edge his way to the aisle and down into the knot of standing spectators, through them, and to the associate's table beneath the bench. In the balcony above, the son of Pieter Van Damm also watched as the young man bowed to the judge, awkwardly.

'What is your name, young man?'

'Isaac Peretz.'

'How is your English?'

'I am a student at the London School of Economics.'

Gilray turned immediately to the press.

'I am going to request that this conversation is off the record. Obviously this lady could be easily identified. I should like to call a recess to consider the matter. Sir Robert would you and Mr. Bannister come to my chambers along with Mrs. Peretz and her son?'

They walked the solemn polished hallway that separated the courtrooms from the chambers to find Anthony Gilray wigless. He had suddenly taken on a nonjudicial appearance of a rather ordinary Englishman. They were seated about his desk and the usher left the chambers.

'If it will please his Lordship,' Sir Robert said, 'we will concede that a fair translation will be given by Madame Peretz's son here.'

'That is not my main concern. First off, there's this business about identification and secondly, the ordeal it imposes on these two people. Young man, do you know fully of your mother's past unpleasantness?'

'I know I am adopted and that she was experimented on in the concentration camp. When she wrote and told me she planned to testify in London, I felt she should too.'

'How old are you?'

'Nineteen.'

'Are you quite sure you can speak of these things about your mother?'

'I must.'

'And you realize, of course, that everyone at the London School of Economics will soon know about this and everyone in Trieste also.'

'My mother is not ashamed and is not that concerned to remain anonymous.'

'I see. Tell me something for my own curiosity. Was your father a man of means? It is rather unusual to have a student here from Trieste.'

'My father was a simple shopkeeper. My parents hoped I would study in England or America and worked very hard for my education.'

The court was called into order as Isaac Peretz was sworn in and stood behind his mother's chair with his hand on her shoulder.

'We are taking into consideration the relationship of the interpreter and the fact he is not a trained translator, and I do hope that Sir Robert will grant us a reasonable latitude.'

'Of course, my Lord.'

Thomas Bannister arose. 'Would you read your mother's tattoo number?'

The boy did not look at his mother's arm but recited

from memory.

'My Lord, in that a great deal of Mrs. Peretz's testimony is identical to that of Mrs. Shoret and Mrs. Halevy, I wonder if my learned friend would object if I lead the witness?'

'No objection.'

The story was told again.

'And you are certain of Dr. Tesslar's presence?'

'Yes. I remember his hand stroking me as I saw red in the lamp above, like my own blood. Voss spoke in German, "*macht schnell*" he repeated, "quicker, quicker!" He said he wanted the report to Berlin to show how many operations could be performed in a day. I knew some Polish from my grandfather so I understood Dr. Tesslar arguing about the instruments not being sterile.'

'And you were fully conscious?'

'Yes.'

The story of how Dr. Viskova and Tesslar kept them alive seemed bitterly clear in her mind. 'My twin sister, Emma, and Tina Blanc-Imber were the worst. I will never forget Tina's cries for water. She was in the next bed haemorrhaging badly.'

'What happened to Tina Blanc-Imber?'

'I don't know. She was gone in the morning.'

'Now, if Dr. Kelno had made visits to the barrack to examine you, would he have found you cheerful?'

'Cheerful?'

'He testified that he usually found his patients cheerful.'

'My God, we were dying.'

'And you weren't cheerful about that?'

'No, not hardly.'

'When did you and your sister return to work in the arms factory?'

'Several months after the operation.'

'Would you tell us about that?'

'The Kapos and SS in this factory were particularly cruel. Neither Emma nor I had regained our former health. It was all we could do to live to the end of a day. Then, Emma began to pass out at her work bench. I became frantic to

342

save her. I had nothing to bribe the Kapos with, no way I could hide her. I would sit next to her, propping her up and talking to her for hours to keep her head up and her hands moving. It went on for a few weeks and one day she fainted, and I could not get her to regain consciousness. So ... they took her away ... to Jadwiga West and she was gassed.'

Tears fell down Ida Peretz's plump cheeks. The room was hushed, then everything stopped.

'I believe a short recess is in order.'

'My mother would like to continue,' the boy said.

'As you wish.'

'Then, after the war you made your way back to Trieste and married a Yesha Peretz, a shopkeeper?'

'Yes.'

'Madame Peretz, it is extremely painful for me to have to ask the following question but it is most important that we do. Did anything unusual happen to you physically?'

'I found an Italian doctor who took special interest in me and after a year of treatment, my menstrual period began again.'

'And did you become pregnant?'

'Yes.'

'What happened?'

'I had three miscarriages and the doctor thought it best to remove my other ovary.'

'Now, let us get this clear. You were X-rayed in both ovaries, were you not?'

'Yes.'

'At the same time and for the same period of time, five to ten minutes. Is that correct?'

'Yes.'

'Then being able to conceive with an irradiated ovary, one must assume both ovaries were quite alive.'

'My glands were not dead.'

'So, in fact, a healthy ovary was removed from your body.'

'Yes.'

Sir Robert Highsmith smelled the mood of the room. He

343

slipped a note back to Chester Dicks. TAKE THE CROSS-EXAMINATION AND BE EXTREMELY CAREFUL NOT TO INTIMIDATE HER.

Dicks went through the motions ending on the suggestion that Adam Kelno was not the surgeon.

'You and your mother are free to go,' Gilray said. As the woman stood, her son put a strong arm around her waist; everyone in the courtroom arose as they passed.

EIGHTEEN

As Sir Francis Waddy was sworn in there was a sense of relaxation from the tension. He was a calm crisp fellow, who could speak to them in their own language.

Brendon O'Conner was up. 'Sir Francis, you are a Fellow of the Royal College of Physicians, a Fellow of the Royal College of Surgeons, a Fellow of the Faculty of Radiologists, a Professor of Therapeutic Radiology at the University of London and the Director of Wessex Medical Centre, and Director of the Williams Institute of Radiotherapy.'

'I am.'

'And,' peeled off O'Conner vocally, 'you have been knighted for three decades of distinguished work.'

'I have the honour.'

'Now, you have read the testimony in which we have suggested that if a testicle or ovary is subjected to severe radiation by a semi-skilled technician then the partner testicle and ovary would most likely be affected.'

'Beyond question, particularly in the case of the testicle.'

'And a surgeon removing the irradiated testicle or ovary would best be serving the interest of his patient to remove both of them.'

'If those were his grounds, but I should say that his grounds are groundless.'

'Now, sir, if an ovary or testicle is submitted to X-ray, no matter how intense in the year of 1943 or today, is there any reason whatsoever to think it might develop cancer?'

'None whatsoever,' Sir Francis answered crisply.

The jury became extremely attentive. Sir Adam Kelno's face pinched with a wave of anger.

'None whatsoever,' O'Conner repeated. 'But of course there must be two medical opinions on that, Sir Francis.'

'Certainly not in 1943 or in any medical literature with which I am familiar.'

'So that in 1943 or now, so far as irradiation of a testicle or ovary is concerned, this is absolutely no medical reason whatsoever for the removal of that organ.'

'Absolutely none.'

'No further questions.'

Sir Robert Highsmith unscrambled himself quickly from the onslaught and went into a consultation with Chester Dicks. Dicks dived into a stack of papers as Sir Robert swayed before the rostrum with a hurt smile on his face.

'Sir Francis, let us say we are in Central Europe two decades ago and a competent surgeon has been locked away in a concentration camp for several years without any enlightenment as to medical progress. Suddenly he is confronted with a serious problem of radiation damage. Might he be anxious about that?'

'Oh, I would rather doubt it.'

'Well, I suggest he is not a radiologist and would be gravely concerned.'

'There is a great deal of misapprehension about radiation hazards.'

'In 1940, 1941, 1942, a doctor is locked away and suddenly comes face to face with sterilization experiments.'

'I think not if he is a suitably qualified physician and surgeon. They did teach those chaps about X-rays in Poland, you know.'

Highsmith licked his lips and delivered an audible sigh of frustration. The robes slipped off his shoulders as he went

345

into his swaying motion in search of a question.

'Consider again the circumstances if you will, Sir Francis.'

'Oh, it's all pure supposition. There has never been any information to ever suggest that an irradiated organ could ever become malignant.'

'It was all discussed by competent doctors, more than one of them, and they felt there was risk.'

'I read the testimony, Sir Robert. Dr. Kelno seems to be the only one worried about cancer.'

'Are you suggesting, sir, that no other doctor in Jadwiga in 1943 could have also entertained notions of danger?'

'I think I'm quite clear on that.'

'Well now, Sir Francis, exactly what are the limits of irradiation damage when practised by a semi-skilled technician?'

'There would be burning of the skin and if the dosage had been serious enough to damage an ovary, it would have first damaged the more sensitive structure of the intestine.'

'Blisters?'

'Yes, burns that could become infected but certainly not be the cause of cancer.'

Chester Dicks' eyes opened wide with discovery. He tapped Highsmith on the shoulder and handed him a pamphlet. Highsmith was relieved. He held it up then read, 'The Hazards to Man of Nuclear and Allied Radiations. I shall read to you the paragraph entitled, "cancer". This is a publication of the British Government. Will you accept that?'

'I most certainly will accept it,' Sir Francis answered. 'I wrote it.'

'Yes, I know,' Highsmith said. 'That's what I want to question you about. Because you imply there was a concern for cancer.'

'Actually we are discussing the risk of leukemia in patients treated for ancylostomiasis, something the ordinary surgeon would have no special knowledge of.'

'But you mention in the paragraph headed "cancer" a study among persons exposed to irradiation after the

346

atomic bombing of Hiroshima and that there is an increase in the death rate and an excess of certain types of cancer, particularly cancer of the skin and abdominal organs.'

'If you will go on to read, Sir Robert, we refer to latent cancer which did not show up for nine or ten years.'

'I suggest that in the eyes of a prisoner/doctor faced with unskilled irradiation, the effect of such irradiation could be in doubt.'

'Sounds more like an excuse to me.'

Highsmith knew he'd better drop it. 'No further questions.'

O'Conner arose. 'Sir Francis. The statistics you used in your pamphlet. Where did you get them?'

'From the American Bomb Casualty Commission.'

'To what conclusion?'

'The incidence of leukemia in those exposed to irradiation was less than a third of one per cent.'

'And this evidence was not handed down until many years after the war.'

'Yes.'

'Have you read the medical war crimes trials at Nuremberg on the same question?'

'I have.'

'To what conclusion?'

'There was no evidence to prove that irradiation is a possible cause of cancer.'

NINETEEN

Daniel Dubrowski, the withered remains of a once strapping robust man, approached the witness box a portrait of abject tragedy, a thing, a vegetable who had not laughed for twenty years. Time and again Bannister and the judge asked him to speak up as he gave his home as Cleveland in

America and his birthplace in Wolkowysk, then in Poland and now a part of the Soviet Union. At the beginning of the Second World War he was married, had two daughters, and taught Romantic languages in a Jewish gymnasium.

'Did something particular happen to you in 1942?'

'I was transported with my family into the Warsaw Ghetto.'

'And later, you took part in the uprising?'

'Yes, in the spring of 1943 there was a rebellion. Those of us who had survived till then lived deep below the ground in bunkers. The fight against the Germans lasted over a month. In the end, when the ghetto was in flames, I took to the sewers and escaped to the forest and joined a band of Polish underground.'

'What happened?'

'The Poles didn't want any Jews among them. We were betrayed. The Gestapo seized us, and we were transported to Jadwiga.'

'Would you continue and please speak up, sir?'

Daniel Dubrowski lowered his head and sobbed. As the court fell into silence the reporter wrote: THE WITNESS BECAME DISTRESSED. Gilray offered a recess, but Dubrowski listlessly shook his head and gained his composure.

"Would his Lordship and my learned friend object if we spared Mr. Dubrowski recounting the details of the demise of his wife and daughters?'

'No objection.'

'May I lead the witness?'

'No objection.'

'Is this all correct? You were taken from a munitions factory to Barrack III at the end of the summer of 1943 and subsequently irradiated in Barrack V and had a testicle removed in the same group of operations as the previous witnesses.'

'Yes,' he whispered, 'that is correct.'

'And Dr. Tesslar was present at your operation and later during your recovery.'

'Yes.'

'Three months after the removal of your first testicle, you

348

and Moshe Bar Tov, then known as Herman Paar, were irradiated a second time.'

'Yes.'

'We can assume, can we not, from Mr. Bar Tov's testimony that he was not sterilized the first time and that Colonel Voss wanted to have a second go at it and perhaps you had not been sterilized either. Was the second X-ray of longer duration?'

'About the same time, but I heard them speak of heavier dosage.'

'Would you tell my Lord and the jury what transpired?'

'After our second exposure to the X-ray we had no doubt but that it would only be a matter of time until we were operated on again and made into eunuchs. Menno Donker,' he said in reference to Pieter van Damm, 'had already been entirely castrated so we realized we would not be spared. There was a corpse one morning as there often was, and Dr. Tesslar came to me to speak over the matter of buying off the Kapo guards with a false death registration. It meant either Herman Paar or myself. We were the two waiting for second surgery.

'I made the decision that Paar must be spared. He was the youngest and had a chance for life. I already had lived and had a family.'

'And so, Paar assumed the dead man's identity and never was operated on a second time and you were. Did Paar know of this decision?'

Dubrowski shrugged.

'I'm so sorry,' Mr. Justice Gilray said, 'the shorthand writer cannot record a gesture.'

'He was only a boy. I did not discuss this with him. It was the only human thing to do.'

'Would you tell us about your second operation?'

'This time four SS guards came for me. I was beaten, tied and gagged, and dragged to Barrack V. They took the gag from my mouth as I almost choked, then they pulled my pants off and bent me over for a needle in the spine. Although I was bound, I continued to struggle. I screamed and fell to the floor.'

'What happened?'

'The needle broke.'

The courtroom held a mass of queasy stomachs. Eyes were turning to Adam Kelno more often now and he was becoming studied at avoiding contact.

'Go on, sir.'

'I writhed on the floor. Then I heard someone over me speaking in Polish. From the build and voice it was the same doctor who had operated on me the first time. He was in his operating gown and had a mask over his face, and he complained he was waiting for his patient. I cried up to him . . .'

'What did he do?'

'He slammed his heel into my face and cursed me in Polish.'

'What did he say?'

' "*Przestan szezekak jak pies itak itak mrzesz.*" '

'What does that mean?'

'Stop barking like a dog. You will die, anyhow.'

'What happened then?'

'I was given another needle and placed on a stretcher. I begged to be spared another operation. I said, "*dlaczego mnie operujecie jeszcze raz prziciez juzescie mnie ras operowali.* Why operate on me again? I have been operated on once." He continued to be rude and brutal to me.'

'In Jadwiga you were used to being spoken to like that by Germans.'

'Always.'

'But you were Polish and this doctor was Polish.'

'Not exactly. I was a Jew.'

'How long had your family been Polish citizens?'

'Almost a thousand years.'

'Did you expect to be spoken to like this by a Polish doctor?'

'It came as no surprise. I know a Polish anti-Semite when I hear one.'

'I am going to ask the jury,' Gilray interjected, 'to put the last sentence out of their heads. Do you want to leave it at that, Mr. Bannister?'

'Yes, my Lord. Go on, Mr. Dubrowski.'

'Voss entered in SS uniform and I appealed to him. The doctor then spoke to me in German. He said, "*Ruhig.*" '

'Are you fluent in German?'

'In a concentration camp you learn many German words.'

'What did he mean by, "*Ruhig*"?'

'Silence.'

'I am going to rise,' Sir Robert said. 'This testimony is a continuation of unproved innuendo that Dr. Kelno was the person who performed this operation. This time my learned friend is not even suggesting that Tesslar was present but that the witness thinks it was the same man who operated earlier. The implication goes deeper because of a conversation held in the Polish language. I suggest an extraordinary amount of liberty has been taken in some of the translations. For example, the word *ruhig* is used in the Heine poem, *Lorelei* as gently. Gently flows the Rhine. If he had meant shut up he would have more likely said, *halte maul.*'

'I see your point, Sir Robert. I take note that Dr. Leiberman is among the spectators today. Would you kindly approach the bench and bear in mind you are still under oath. German is your mother tongue, is it not, Dr. Leiberman?'

'It is.'

'How would you translate, *ruhig*?'

'In this context it is a command to shut up. Any concentration camp survivor will testify to that.'

'What do you do now, Mr. Dubrowski?'

'I have a used clothing store in a Negro neighbourhood of Cleveland.'

'But you are still qualified as a teacher of Romantic languages, are you not?'

'I have no desires left. Perhaps ... that is why I submitted to the second operation in place of Paar. ... I have been dead since my wife and daughters were taken from me.'

Moshe Bar Tov had been brought into the consultation room and while Dubrowski underwent cross-examination Dr. Leiberman and Abraham Cady left the courtroom and he was told for the first time about the other man's sacrifice.

'Oh my God!' he wailed in anguish. He fell against the wall and pounded his fist on it and wept. In a little while the door opened and Daniel Dubrowski entered. Moshe Bar Tov turned to face him.

'I think we'd better leave them alone,' Abe said.

TWENTY

THEY'RE ALL GONE NOW EXCEPT HELENE PRINZ, THE LADY FROM ANTWERP. DR. SUSANNE PARMENTIER IS WITH HER SO SHE'LL BE ALL RIGHT.

THEY'VE GONE BACK TO ISRAEL AND HOLLAND AND TRIESTE. I AM GOING TO MISS THE GENTLE DR. LEIBERMAN LIKE HELL.

MOSHE BAR TOV LEFT STILL IN SHOCK OF THE REVELATION OF THE TRIAL. HE INDUCED DANIEL DUBROWSKI TO COME TO HIS KIBBUTZ FOR A WHILE, TO SHOWER HIM WITH LOVE, TO WEEP AWAY HIS GUILT TO THE ONE WHO GAVE HIM HIS MANHOOD.

I FELT SO EMPTY WATCHING THEM LEAVE. A FAREWELL DINNER, TOASTS, LITTLE GIFTS, AND LOTS OF TEARS. WHAT THEY DID HERE TOOK A SPECIAL KIND OF COURAGE I STILL DO NOT COMPREHEND, BUT I DO KNOW THAT BECAUSE OF IT THEY WILL ALWAYS OWN A FLEETING MOMENT IN HISTORY.

SHEILA LAMB TOOK THEIR DEPARTURE THE HARDEST. FROM THE INSTANT THEY ARRIVED SHE TOOK THEM IN WITH DETERMINATION NOT TO LET THEM FALTER OR FEEL UNLOVED.

SHE WAS PRESENT WHEN THE WOMEN WERE EXAMINED. WHEN SHE SAW THEIR SCARS SHE DID NOT LET HERSELF GIVE AN OUTWARD INDICATION OF THE REVULSION SHE FELT.

AT THE FAREWELL DINNER AT LADY SARAH'S, SHEILA SUD-

DENLY LEFT THE TABLE AND RAN TO THE BATHROOM AND BROKE INTO TEARS. THE WOMEN WENT AFTER HER. SHE LIED TO THEM THAT SHE WAS UPSET BECAUSE HER PERIOD WAS COMING ON. BECAUSE NONE OF THEM HAD PERIODS, IT TURNED INTO A MOMENT OF EXCITEMENT AND THEN LAUGHTER.

I WASN'T ALLOWED TO GO TO HEATHROW TO SEE THEM OFF. I DON'T KNOW WHY. THE BRITISH MIND THEIR OWN BUSINESS.

BEN AND I WALKED LIKE WHAT SEEMED FOREVER ALONG THE THAMES EMBANKMENT TRYING TO EQUATE ALL OF WHAT WAS HAPPENING. WE CAME UPON THE IMMENSE LAWNS OF THE TEMPLE AND WERE DRAWN UP MIDDLE TEMPLE LANE.

IT WAS ONE IN THE MORNING BUT THE LIGHTS WERE STILL BURNING IN THE CHAMBERS OF THOMAS BANNISTER AND BRENDON O'CONNER. WANT TO KNOW ABOUT THOSE PEOPLE? O'CONNER HASN'T SPENT AN EVENING WITH HIS FAMILY SINCE TWO WEEKS BEFORE THE TRIAL STARTED. HE TOOK A SMALL ROOM AT A NEARBY HOTEL SO HE COULD WORK AROUND THE CLOCK. OFTEN AS NOT HE SLEPT ON THE COUCH IN HIS CHAMBERS.

EVERY DAY AFTER COURT, SHEILA TRANSCRIBED THE TESTIMONY AND DELIVERED IT TO THE TEMPLE. O'CONNER, ALEXANDER, AND BANNISTER STUDIED IT ALONG WITH THE NEXT DAY'S WORK AND EVERY NIGHT AT ELEVEN O'CLOCK THEY MET AND WORKED UNTIL TWO OR THREE IN THE MORNING. WEEKENDS WERE A BLESSING. THEY GOT TO WORK STRAIGHT THROUGH.

AND SHEILA? WELL, HER DAY STARTED AT SEVEN IN THE MORNING IN A HOTEL WITH THE WITNESSES. SHE'D BREAKFAST WITH THEM, GET THEM TO COURT CALM, DO HER DAY'S WORK IN COURT, TRANSCRIBE THE TESTIMONY, EAT DINNER WITH THEM AND TAKE THEM TO THE THEATRE, MUSEUMS, OUR PRIVATE DINNERS, AND ON THE WEEKEND TO THE COUNTRYSIDE. SHE WAS THERE WITH THEM EACH NIGHT COMFORTING THEM, OUT DRINKING WITH THE MEN OR WHATEVER WAS NEEDED OF HER. I WATCHED HER AGE BEFORE MY EYES FROM THE HURT INSIDE HER.

BEN AND I WALKED FROM THE TEMPLE AND STOOD BEFORE THE LAW COURT. I LOVE THE ENGLISH. I COULDN'T BELIEVE

THESE PEOPLE WOULD GO AGAINST ME.

LOOK AT THE QUEUES ON OXFORD STREET. NO PUSHING,
NO CUTTING LINES. FORTY MILLION PEOPLE JAMMED TOGETHER
IN WEATHER SO FOUL IT DRIVES THE SCANDINAVIANS TO
MADNESS. AND FROM IT ALL A SYSTEM OF ORDER BASED ON
RESPECT OF ONE'S NEIGHBOURS AND THE REASONABLE ASPIR-
ATIONS OF LIFE WITH THE ULTIMATE REWARDS OF KNIGHT-
HOOD.

LOOK AT THE CALM WAY THEY HAVE TAKEN THE NEW
GENERATION. IT ALL STARTED HERE IN ENGLAND. MOUS-
TACHED MEN IN PIN STRIPES, BOWLERS, AND UMBRELLAS IN
THE QUEUES BEHIND A CHICK WITH HER SKIRT UP TO HER
ASS AND IN FRONT OF A BOY WHO LOOKS LIKE A GIRL.

A BOBBY PASSES US BY AND PUTS A FINGER TO HIS CAP
TO SALUTE. HE DOESN'T CARRY A GUN. CAN YOU IMAGINE
THAT IN CHICAGO?

EVEN THE PROTESTERS ABIDE BY THE RULES. THEY PRO-
TEST WITH REASONABLE NONVIOLENCE. THEY DON'T SMASH
GLASS OR BURN OR RIOT. THEY PROTEST ANGRILY, BUT FAIRLY,
AND IN TURN THE POLICE DON'T BASH THEM ABOUT.

HELL, NO BRITISH JURY IS GOING TO DO ME IN.

Ben and his father were in the kind of mood to talk the
night out when they returned to the mews.

'What about Vanessa and Yossi? That boy going to be
able to make her happy?'

'He's an officer in the paratroops,' Ben said. 'He's been
confined in Israel all his life with his back to the sea. You
know how tough he is. I think this trip has been good for
him. It's good for him to see gentle, gracious, and sophisticated people. He tries to pass it off, but London has impressed him deeply. Now that he's seen it, more and more
of Vanessa will rub off on him.'

'Hope so. He's a brain all right.' Abe loaded his glass.
Ben held his hand over the rim of his, not wanting any
more. 'You're picking up bad habits in Israel, like not
drinking.'

Ben laughed. It was a wide, uninhibited laugh. He was
full of the devil. Then, he turned serious. 'Vinny and I hate

to see you keep on going through life alone.'

Abe shrugged. 'I'm a writer. I'm alone in the middle of a crowded ballroom. That's my bag.'

'Maybe you wouldn't be so alone if you started looking back at women like Lady Sarah the way she looks at you.'

'I don't know, son. I think maybe your uncle Ben and you and I were all moulded out of the same kind of cast. None of us can stand most women socially for more than fifteen minutes. They're only good for balling and not too many of them pass the grade at that. Our problem is that we like to be around men. Air bases, locker rooms, bars, fight clubs, where we don't have to listen to female dribble. Then, you find a woman like Sarah Wydman who is about as complete as a woman can be and even that's not enough. She can't be a man and a woman at the same time. But even if she understood this need I don't think any woman deserves to take the crap of being a writer's wife. I busted your mother. If a woman's got anything to give, I drain her. I'm happy that I'm a writer, but I sure wouldn't want my daughter to marry one.'

Abe sighed and turned his eyes away from his son, dreading to bring up what had been tormenting him all day. 'I saw you and Yossi with the military attaché from the Israel embassy.'

'The situation is not good, Dad,' Ben said.

'God damned Russian sons of bitches,' Abe said. 'They're putting them up to it. When in the name of God are we going to have a day of peace?'

'On the plains of heaven,' Ben whispered.

'Ben ... now you listen to me. Son ... for Christ sake ... don't be a hot pilot.'

TWENTY-ONE

A bleary-eyed Abraham Cady and his bleary-eyed son entered the court. A man's lavatory stood between the two consultation rooms. Abe made to the urinal. He felt someone next to him and looked over his shoulder. It was Adam Kelno.

'Here's one pair of Jewish balls you're not getting,' he said.

'Silence!'

Helene Prinz was small and pertly dressed and moved into the courtroom with more assurance than any of the other women. Although outwardly she was the leader of them, Sheila felt she was extremely high strung and the most apt to break.

Through a French translator she said that she was from Antwerp, gave her birth date in 1922, and read off her tattoo number. It had been done many times but never failed to affect those who saw it.

'You continued to carry your maiden name of Blanc-Imber even though you and your sister Tina were married after the outbreak of the war.'

'Well, we were not really married. You see, the Germans were sending away married couples so both my sister and I took our vows in a secret ceremony by a rabbi but it was never officially registered. Both our husbands perished at Auschwitz. I married Pierre Prinz after the war.

'Am I given leave to lead the witness?' Bannister asked.

'No objection.'

'You were taken to Barrack III in the spring of 1943 with your sister Tina and subjected to irradiation treatment. Now, so this is quite clear, this was all done some time before the two other sets of twins, the Lovino and Cardozo sisters from Trieste, arrived at the barrack.'

'That is quite correct. We were irradiated and operated

on quite some time before the other twins arrived.'

'At that time a female doctor, a Polish woman, Gabriela Radnicki, was in charge. She is the one who committed suicide and was replaced by Maria Viskova?'

'That is correct.'

'Now then, a month or so after you were irradiated you were taken to Barrack V, and will you tell us what happened?'

'Dr. Boris Dimshits examined us.'

'How did you know it was Dr. Dimshits?'

'He introduced himself.'

'Do you recall his appearance?'

'He seemed very old and somewhat feeble and absent-minded and I remember his hands were covered with eczema.'

'Yes, continue please.'

'He sent Tina and me back to Barrack III. He said our irradiation wound had not healed sufficiently to undergo an operation.'

'Was anyone else present?'

'Voss.'

'Well, did Voss protest and tell him to operate anyhow?'

'He complained, but he did nothing. After two weeks the black spots faded and we were taken back to Barrack V. Dr. Dimshits said he was going to operate on us and promised us he would leave a healthy ovary. I was injected in the arm and it made me very sleepy. Then, I remember being wheeled into an operating room, and I was put to sleep.'

'Do you know what kind of anaesthetic you were given?'

'Chloroform.'

'How long were you bedridden after this operation?'

'Many, many weeks. I had complications. Dr. Dimshits visited us often but could hardly see in the semi-darkness. He was failing fast.'

'And afterward you heard that he had been sent to the gas chamber?'

'Yes.'

'And Dr. Radnicki committed suicide.'

'Yes, in the barrack.'

'And toward the latter part of the year after the Lovino and Cardozo sisters came to Barrack III you were submitted to X-ray again.'

'This time Tina and I became frantic.'

She described the scene of bedlam in the waiting room of Barrack V. 'I struggled. Tina and I fought not to be separated, but they held me and injected my spine. I was injected but my body did not become numb. I could still feel everything.'

'It did not take effect?'

'No.'

'And when you were taken into the operating room you were not given anything to put you under, were you?'

'I was terrified. I could feel everything, and I told them that. I was able to sit up and get off the table. Two of them twisted my arms behind me and dragged me back on the table. The doctor hit me in the face several times and across my breast and shouted at the top of his lungs. "*Verfluchte Judin ... you damned Jewess.*" I begged him to kill me for I could not stand the pain. Only because of Dr. Tesslar was I able to survive.'

'Were you quite ill after the operation?'

'I ran a very high fever and was half out of my mind. I remember through the haze hearing Tina screaming ... and then I heard nothing. I don't know how much time passed until I was able to think clearly. It may have been days. I asked about Tina, then Dr. Viskova told me Tina died of a haemorrhage the first night.'

She swayed and her fists pounded on the witness box rail. Suddenly she sprang to her feet and pointed down to Adam Kelno. 'Murderer! Murderer!' A wail of agony shrieked out from her.

Abe pushed down the aisle knocking people out of his way. 'That's enough!' He shoved past the press box and put his arms around her. 'I'm taking her out of here,' he said.

The usher looked to the judge, who gestured to leave them alone, and as Abe half carried her from the courtroom she cried that she had failed him.

Gilray wanted to start a speech admonishing the scene and serving warning, but he was unable to. 'Are you going to wish to cross-examine the witness, Sir Robert?'

'No. The witness is obviously too distressed to carry on.'

'The jury has seen and heard all this,' the judge answered. 'They aren't apt to forget it. Members of the jury,' Gilray said in a drained and tired voice, 'Sir Robert has made the kind of gesture one would expect of an English barrister. When I am summarizing the evidence for you later I will ask you in all sense of fair play to bear in mind that there was no cross-examination of this witness. Shall we stand adjourned?'

TWENTY-TWO

'I should like to call to the stand Mr. Basil Marwick,' Brendon O'Conner said. Marwick was totally British of the old school in dress and manner. He took the oath on the New Testament. Marwick gave his name and a Wimpole Street address. It was established that he had a long credential as an anaesthetist, teacher, and author of numerous papers covering a period of twenty-five years.

'Would you explain to my Lord and the jury the two major types of anaesthetics?'

'Certainly. There is the general anaesthetic in which the patient is rendered unconscious and the local anaesthetic to deaden that part of the body being operated on.'

'And a surgeon, of course, makes the choice and would make it alone if there were no anaesthetist for consultation.'

'Yes. Sometimes he may give a combination.'

'What general anaesthetics, those to render a patient unconscious, were available in the early forties in Central and

Eastern Europe?'

'Ether, ethyl chloride, choloroform, Evipal, nitrous oxide mixed with oxygen, and others.'

'I must rise,' Highsmith said. 'We have heard testimony from two surgeons at Jadwiga that general anaesthetic was not usually available.'

'And we dispute that,' O'Conner snapped back.

'I see,' Gilray mused. 'You are suggesting general anaesthetic was readily available in Jadwiga.'

'Well, we've heard testimony from Dr. Kelno's own witnesses that they were put under,' O'Conner said. 'You heard the testimony of Mrs. Prinz that in her first operation by Dr. Dimshits she was put under. I suggest that Dr. Kelno found no general anaesthetic available only when it came to his Jewish patients.'

'Mr. O'Conner, I'm going to allow you to continue, but I suggest you are on thin ice. I am advising the members of the jury that until this is entered as evidence, this part of Mr. Marwick's testimony is for the purpose of background.'

O'Conner did not bother to thank his lordship, but plunged ahead restlessly. 'So some of these anaesthetics are given for short operations and others for longer operations.'

'Yes, a surgeon's choice.'

'You have told us what general anaesthetics were available in that area of Europe in the 1940s. Would you tell us what local anaesthetics were available?'

'Procaine, also known as novocaine, most commonly used by dentists. There was, let me see, percaine and pontocaine and decicaine and others.'

'All used as spinals?'

'Yes. By introduction into the spinal cord it would render the adjacent nerve trunks insensitive or deaden them.'

'Just how is this done?'

'Well, it has been my practice to minimize the discomfort. At the site of the injection I would first inject a little local anaesthetic with a very fine needle to deaden the immediate area which will take the larger needle necessary to infiltrate the deeper tissues.'

360

'Speaking again of the 1940s. Was it standard practice in Poland to first inject the patient with a smaller needle before the main injection?'

'Absolutely. In every text I have seen in that time or today.'

'You heard or read the testimony of four female and six male witnesses who were victims of experiments in Jadwiga. Had you been involved at that time, would you have used a preliminary injection of morphia?'

'I may have refused to be involved. I do not know. But in any event the circumstances called for morphia.'

'Much obliged. And would you have used local or general anaesthetic for the operations?'

'My Lord,' Highsmith interrupted. 'We are back to the same thing. My client has testified that when he gave a spinal he used a preliminary injection of morphia.'

'Which a number of witnesses have disputed,' O'Conner said.

'There is still no evidence before this court that Dr. Kelno performed these operations,' Highsmith argued.

'That's our case,' O'Conner answered. 'Each of our ten witnesses has not been challenged in that Dr. Tesslar was in the operating room. You are aware of Dr. Tesslar's statement and what he is going to testify to.'

'I am going to give the same ruling,' Gilray said. 'The jury will consider all of this as hypothetical expert testimony as to general background and not evidence. When I instruct you later I'll define what evidence was brought forth on whether or not Dr. Kelno performed the operations in question.'

'But would you say,' O'Conner insisted, 'that you would use a general anaesthetic?'

'Yes.'

'Not a spinal?'

'No.'

'Well, exactly why would you put them under?'

'For humane reasons.'

'If there were no preliminary injection is a spinal likely to be painful?'

'Acutely painful.'

'How many spinals do you reckon you've given?'

'Between fifteen hundred and two thousand.'

'Is it always easy to find the exact site to inject the larger needle?'

'No, one must take great care about that.'

'Well, would you carry out a spinal if the patient is screaming and struggling?'

'Certainly not.'

'Why?'

'The actual placing of the needle must be done with extreme accuracy. It is inserted between two bones with very little room to manoeuvre. It must be in midline and angulated to the curvature of the patient's back. One simply cannot do it without the total co-operation of the patient. I'd say it was impossible. You see, any violent movement of the patient could run the risk of breaking the needle.'

'You heard testimony that a needle broke. What would happen then?'

'If it breaks beneath the skin it could be a frightful disaster. It could cause permanent injury if not retrieved successfully. The pain would be unbearable. Of course if the needle breaks outside, you'd pull it out of the skin.'

'You've heard or read testimony that several of these people still feel the pain today.'

'Considering how they said they were treated, I'd rather suspect they do feel it.'

'Do you have with you in court the kind of needles used in 1940?'

Marwick produced a kit and showed the fine needle for the preliminary injection and then the larger one. They were marked as an exhibit and passed to the jury. The manoeuvre had its effect by the grimaces as the needles were passed from one to the other.

'Now, in the application of a spinal, we are very concerned, are we not, that the anaesthetic stay in the lower part of the body?'

'Yes. If it rises and, say, reaches the nipple line it could produce a fall in blood pressure resulting in the brain being deprived of blood and the patient would become dizzy and faint.'

'You heard the testimony of Mr. Bar Tov that he passed out. Was it likely because of this?'

'Oh yes.'

'And you heard the other witnesses say they were quite conscious. Does this surprise you?'

'Not from their testimony.'

'Is morphia always given in surgery?'

'Always.'

'Would you expect people premedicated with morphia to stand in a queue and wait for their operation?'

'Of course not.'

'And if they were ill nourished and debilitated by brutal treatment would morphia tend to be more effective?'

'They would be very dazed by it, all right.'

'It would certainly be difficult for them to struggle with morphia.'

'They could, I suppose, but not effectively.'

'No further questions.'

Highsmith arose as the needles left the jury box and were placed on the associate's table. The shorthand writers changed as Adam Kelno seemed fixed on the kit. His hands drew up as though for an instant he had an unstoppable urge to take up the needle. Smiddy tapped his wrist and his attention turned to Marwick.

'Mr. Marwick, did you read or hear testimony of Dr. Boland given in behalf of Sir Adam Kelno?'

'I did.'

'And in your expert opinion, would you qualify Dr. Boland as also distinguished in the field?'

'Yes.'

'You heard him testify that he himself had received two spinals for surgery done on him and both were given without morphia. He also testified that in the question of premedication it made little difference to the comfort of the patient.'

'Yes, that was his testimony.'

'Would you comment?'

'Well, your own client, Sir Adam, would disagree with Dr. Boland, would he not? And I certainly disagree.'

'But you do agree that in England in 1967 there are two different opinions about this from qualified anaesthetists.'

'Well, he has his views.'

'Different from yours.'

'Yes.'

'Dr. Boland goes on to testify that properly given with a sharp needle a spinal causes very little discomfort. What do you say to that?'

'There is a possibility if given under absolutely perfect conditions.'

'In the hands of a skilled surgeon doing it quickly.'

'As a matter of fact, Sir Robert, it must be done slowly. One must feel his way through delicate ground. On occasion it has taken me ten minutes and there are a number of occasions where experts have failed.'

'You were asked a number of hypothetical questions about surgery in Jadwiga. If you were a surgeon at Jadwiga under pressing circumstances and had no anaesthetist or someone trained in giving a general, it would make sense to give a spinal, would it not. What I mean is that a surgeon can't do two things at once, can he? He can't operate at the same time he's giving an anaesthetic.'

'The way you phrase it.'

'And while he is operating he just can't put ether or chloroform in the hands of an unskilled assistant?'

'You're quite right that he needs a skilled assistant to give a general.'

'A spinal produces good operating conditions for a surgeon, does it not?'

'Yes.'

'Particularly if a surgeon is pressed and harassed.'

'Yes.'

'Where did you practise in 1940 to 1941?'

'Royal Air Force.'

'In England?'

'Yes. As a matter of fact I recall administering anaesthetic to one of the defendants after his plane crashed.'

'Conditions weren't like those in Jadwiga, were they?'

'No.'

'But even in England in those years Dr. Boland administered spinal anaesthetic without pre-morphia. Does that surprise you?'

'No, but it makes me wince.'

'So what we have here is expert testimony of two anaesthetists which is diametrically opposed. Two differences of opinion, both of which are right.'

As Highsmith seated himself, O'Conner thumbed through a book he had among his papers. He asked the usher to give a copy to Sir Robert and a copy to Mr. Marwick.

'Before we go into this work written by Dr. Boland,' O'Conner said, 'you heard and read testimony by Dr. Kelno that he was short of trained assistants and for that chief reason he made the choice of a spinal and administered it himself.'

'Yes, I heard that.'

'You also heard or read testimony by Dr. Lotaki that he assisted Dr. Kelno in a number of these operations.'

'Yes.'

'In your opinion, from Dr. Lotaki's background, would he be qualified to administer a general to keep a patient unconscious during an operation?'

'Dr. Lotaki is fully qualified.'

'Then the excuse that he didn't have a skilled assistant isn't a valid reason.'

For the first time in the trail, Sir Robert Highsmith found himself staring at Adam Kelno. Was it a bald lie or an oversight in all the testimony, he wondered.

O'Conner opened the book. 'This work of Dr. Boland was published in the year of 1942 and entitled, *New Advancements in the Field of Anaesthesia*.'

'I find all of this rather strange,' Highsmith said, 'that none of this was put to Dr. Boland when he was in the witness box.'

'With respect to my learned friend,' O'Conner said, 'we

had no intention of reading all the books ever written by anaesthetists in England, and we had no idea Dr. Boland was going to be called for the plaintiff. If you had said so beforehand, then we would have brought this into court at that time.'

'Well, I don't think it proper to put to Mr. Marwick something Dr. Boland wrote and cannot answer for himself.'

'You can recall Dr. Boland to the stand if you wish, Sir Robert,' the judge said. 'We won't deny you that.'

Highsmith sat down.

'I call your attention to page two hundred and fifty-four, paragraph three and I read: "Local anaesthesia such as a spinal should never," I repeat, "never be applied indiscriminately and without preparing the patient psychologically or it could result in psychic shock and actual insanity has been known to occur." He states further down the page, "in the case of an extremely nervous or frightened patient the choice of a general anaesthetic should be given. If, however, the surgeon deems a spinal more suitable then a premedication by morphia of one and a fourth grain would be in order." What I am saying is that in the circumstances we have described you and Dr. Boland are not diametrically opposed at all.'

'We are completely of the same mind,' Mr. Marwick said.

TWENTY-THREE

Angela held the curtain back and peeked outside. They were both there, across the street, a plain clothes man from Scotland Yard and a private detective hired by the Polish Association to guard the house. All phone calls were now screened in the central office.

After the first several days of the trial there were threats and obscenities over the phone, followed by vicious letters and personal visits of people venting their hatred of Adam Kelno.

Scotland Yard assured them it would all die down in due course when the trial was done. Angela, who kept the family spirits up, insisted they leave immediately on a world cruise of a year and then relocate in the anonymity of a small town.

The strain had ground Adam down, and he did not protest the plan. It would be only a matter of a few years when Stephan would have an architect's degree. They could think about retirement. He had to abandon the idea of having Terrence Campbell take over his medical practice. But Sir Adam knew in his heart that Terrence wanted to go back to Sarawak, to his own father, and practise missionary medicine.

Although Adam appeared emotionless in court Angela did her sleeping these nights with one eye open, ready to help him from the terror of the recurring nightmares and to calm his fitful sleep.

They all picked at their dinner, disheartened that it was impossible for Stephan to get back to England.

'How much longer do they think it's going to go on, Doctor?' Terry asked.

'Another week or ten days.'

'It will be over soon enough,' Angela said, 'and we're going to get through it much better if we eat.'

367

'I suppose there's all kinds of talk at Guy's.'

'You know how those things are,' Terry answered.

'What do they say?'

'Quite frankly, I haven't got time to listen if I expect to do my work. Mary and I have split up, and I think it's rather final.'

'Oh, I'm sorry to hear that,' Angela said.

'No you're not. Anyhow, I should like to remain here with you, now that we all know Stephan can't come.'

'Well, you know how happy that makes us,' Angela said.

'What happened between you and Mary?' Adam asked.

'Nothing really,' he lied. 'We just found that being away from each other gave us a lot more freedom.' Terry did not want to add to the burden he had helped create by telling them Mary had some doubts about Sir Adam and Terry had stormed out in anger.

The doorbell rang. They could hear Mrs. Corkory, the housekeeper, speaking to someone in the vestibule. 'Beg pardon,' Mrs. Corkory said, 'but Mr. Lowry and Mrs. Meyrick are here on a matter they feel quite important.'

'Are they ill?'

'No, sir.'

'Very well, show them into the parlour.'

Lowry, a stocky baker, and Mrs. Meyrick, the housewife of a warehouseman, came to their feet awkwardly as the Kelnos entered.

'Evening, Doctor,' Mr. Lowry said. 'I hope you'll excuse the interruption. Dr. Kelno, we've been talking among ourselves.'

'Your patients, that is,' Mrs. Meyrick interrupted.

'Well, anyhow, we want you to know we're with you one million per cent.'

'That pleases me a great deal.'

'We are highly incensed, we are, at the lies they're trying to pin on you,' Mr. Lowry continued, 'and we feel it's all part of a bloody, beg your pardon, all part of a Communist plot.'

'At any rate, Doctor,' Mrs. Meyrick said, 'we've written

you this letter of our loyalty and support and went about to everyone collecting their signatures, even the little ones. Here, sir.'

Adam took the letter and thanked them again. After they left he opened it and read it: WE THE UNDERSIGNED EXPRESS OUR HIGH ESTEEM TO SIR ADAM KELNO WHO HAS BEEN GRAVELY MALIGNED. HE HAS TREATED US WITH GREAT CONSIDERATION AND NEVER TURNED A SICK PERSON AWAY FROM HIS DOOR. THIS DOCUMENT IS AN INADEQUATE TOKEN OF OUR AFFECTION.

There were three pages of signatures, some barely legible, some printed, some obviously of children.

'That was a lovely gesture,' Angela said. 'Aren't you pleased?'

'Yes,' Adam said, but he read the names over again. Many patients had not signed and the signatures of all his Jewish patients were missing.

TWENTY-FOUR

An instantaneous murmur of anticipation swept the court as Professor Oliver Lighthall was called to the stand. Everyone looked attentively as the man whom many considered England's foremost gynaecologist ascended to the witness box. He was tailored but dishevelled in a studious way. He had made his adamant decision to testify against a great deal of pressure from a segment of his colleagues.

'This testimony, of course, shall be in English,' Tom Bannister said. 'Would you give us your name and address?'

'Oliver Leigh Lighthall. I reside and practise at 2 Cavendish Square in London.'

'You are a doctor of medicine, a Fellow of the Royal College of Surgeons, a Fellow of the Royal College of Obstetrics and Gynaecology for the University of London, Cambridge, and Wales, and for two decades Director of Obstetrics at the University College Hospital.'

'That is all correct.'

'How long have you practised in your field?'

'Over forty years.'

'Professor Lighthall. If an ovary is irradiated is there any medical benefit whatsoever to remove it by surgery?'

'Absolutely none.'

'Well, isn't an irradiated ovary or testicle often dead?'

'In so far as its physiological function. For example, the ovary is no longer able to produce eggs nor can the testicle produce sperm.'

'Well doesn't this occur also to a woman when she experiences change of life and often to a man who has undergone certain illnesses?'

'Yes, an ovary ceases to function after menopause, and illness can cause the cessation of male sperm.'

'But you don't go about cutting women's ovaries out just because they've undergone the change of life?'

'No, of course not.'

Arrogant bastard, Adam Kelno thought, arrogant English bastard in his snob clinic on Cavendish Square. O'Conner passed a note back to Shawcross and Cady: WATCH FOR LIGHTNING TO STRIKE.

'Were there two schools of thought about removal of an ovary that had ceased to function in 1943?'

'Only one school.'

'Aren't X-rays, in fact, used to cure cancer?'

'Certain types of cancer will respond to X-ray treatment.'

'Heavy dosages.'

'Yes.'

'And the same goes for a cancerous testicle.'

'Yes, they receive X-ray treatment.'

'Professor Lighthall, it has been suggested that in 1943 it was possible that irradiation of testicles and ovaries could produce cancer. What is your view?'

'That's utter nonsense, poppycock, bordering on the hocus-pocus of a tribal medicine man.'

Adam Kelno flinched. Oliver Lighthall had thrown up at him his own struggle with the fakirs of Sarawak. Behind his English calm, Lighthall was obviously incensed and was not holding back.

'Now, if one was conducting an experiment to see if a testicle is still potent would that testicle be of any use if it were removed by an unqualified operator?'

'If the tissue is to be later examined in a laboratory it is essential that it be removed by a capable surgeon.'

'So that a doctor threatening to use an unskilled SS orderly would more than likely be bluffing for he'd defeat his own purposes.'

'Some things are so logical they need not be argued. I have read the testimony and Voss had no intention of allowing an SS orderly to perform these operations.'

Highsmith started to his feet, stopped midway and seated himself again.

'Have you examined the four women who gave testimony in this case?'

'I have.'

The blood rushed from Adam Kelno's face. Highsmith was once again fixed on his client, trying desperately to glue a passive expression to his face.

'If these women had been exposed to irradiation for a period of five to ten minutes, a surgeon would have been able to see evidence of it, burn marks, blisters perhaps, infection.'

'Some of their burns are visible today,' Lighthall answered.

'Twenty-four years later?'

'In the cases I examined the pigmentation of the skin will remain for the rest of their lives.'

'Well now, if a surgeon sees such burns a short time after the irradiation, would he take the view that an ovary should be removed?'

'I should think quite strongly to the contrary. He would run all sorts of grave risks.'

'Now, Professor Lighthall, in carrying out an ovariec-tomy in England which is done with a spinal, is it usual to strap the patient to the operating table?'

'Most unusual procedure. Well, one might strap the arms only.'

Adam felt as though his chest were going to burst. A severe pain knifed from his chest to his stomach. He fumbled for a pill and took it as anonymously as possible.

'Not common practice?'

'No. The patient is paralysed by the injection.'

'Could you tell us what surgical procedures are used after the removal of an ovary.'

Lighthall asked for a life-sized plastic model, which he placed on the rail facing the jury. He brushed the hair back that had fallen into his eyes and he pointed his educated finger. 'This is the womb here. These yellow structures the size of a walnut on either side and behind the womb are the ovaries. What a surgeon must do is cut deeply to the stump which is known as the pedicle to the place where the ovarian artery enters the main artery. The surgeon then clamps and ties to prevent the raw stump from bleeding from the main artery.'

He nipped at his water. The judge offered him a seat, but he answered that he preferred to lecture standing.

'The next procedure is called peritonizing. There exists a very thin membrane which covers the inside of the abdo-men. We lift this membrane and use it to cover the stump. In other words, use of the membrane called peritoneum to cover this raw stump is done to prevent adhesions and assure that the stump will clot properly.'

Bannister looked to the jury, incredibly attentive. He let Lighthall's words sink in.

'It's extremely important to do this step, then. It is vital that the raw stump be covered by peritoneal flap?'

'Yes, mandatory.'

'What would happen if you didn't?'

'You'd be leaving a raw stump. The clot which forms in the artery is apt to become infected and adhesions are apt to form from the intestine. If the stump is not properly sealed off there would be haemorrhaging and the possibility of a secondary haemorrhage at a later date of seven to ten days.'

He nodded to the associate who removed the model.

'Are you familiar with the testimony of Sir Adam Kelno?'

'I read it with extreme care.'

'When I asked him if it was proper to cover the stump by use of the peritoneal flap as you have just described he said there was no peritoneum.'

'Well, I can't imagine where he learned surgery. I have been practising gynaecology for over forty years and in performing over a thousand ovariectomies I have never failed to find the peritoneum.'

'It's there then?'

'Goodness, yes.'

'Sir Adam further testified that his method of tying off the raw stump was by a single cross-stitch from the so-called infundibulopelvic ligament. What would you say to that?'

'I'd say it's very bizarre, indeed.'

The eyes of everyone were on Adam Kelno, particularly those of Terrence, who sat openmouthed and felt himself becoming numb.

'How long should an ovariectomy take from the incision to the end?'

'The better part of a half an hour.'

'Is there any virtue in doing it in fifteen minutes?'

'Not unless there is a calamity such as an abdominal haemorrhage. Otherwise I would opine that it is bad surgery to operate with such celerity.'

'Would there be any connection between speed and post-operational haemorrhage?'

Lighthall looked to the high ceiling in meditation. 'Well, if one is working to the clock, one cannot do this surgical toilet which I described. One simply cannot tie off the raw stump and control the bleeding when working at such speed.'

Bannister looked at the jury as Oliver Lighthall continued to collect his thoughts. 'Do you have anything further on this, Professor?'

'When I examined those four women I was not in the least surprised to hear that one of them had died the night of the surgery and another failed to recover. It is my opinion,' he said, looking directly down at the solicitors' table at Adam Kelno, 'it was due to improper tying of the stump.'

It was now becoming apparent that Oliver Lighthall's testimony was an answer in fury over what he had seen.

'If in a series of operations the surgeon did not wash his hands or sterilize his instruments between operations, what is apt to occur?'

'I cannot conceive any surgeon not attending to these basic principles. Since the days of Lister it would be tantamount to criminal negligence.'

'Criminal negligence,' Bannister repeated softly, 'and what would be the results of such criminal negligence?'

'Serious infection.'

'And what of the condition of the operating theatre itself?'

'Everyone present should be made as germ free as possible, masks, gowns, antiseptics. For example, in this court now our clothing is filled with bacteria. In a surgery it would spread through the air onto the exposed body of the patient.'

'Is one more or less likely to haemorrhage because of the choice of anaesthetic?'

'Yes. Spinals are absolutely notorious for the risk of haemorrhage because of the drop of blood pressure and doubly so if the raw stump is not properly attended to.'

'How long should it take for the wound to heal after a normal successful ovariectomy?'

'A week or so.'

'Not weeks or months?'

'No.'

'In fact, if it were taking weeks and the wounds secreted pus and gave off a noxious odour, what would that indicate?'

374

'Infection at the time of the operation, an improperly performed operation, not enough care to antiseptic and sterilization.'

'What of the needle?'

'Well, let us see. It has been plunged through the tissues of the back. It has gone into the spinal canal and damage could occur to the membranes covering the spinal cord. This could cause permanent damage.'

'And lifelong pain?'

'Yes.'

'Would you tell us your observations in your examination of the four women?'

'My Lord, may I refer to some notes I took?'

'Certainly.'

He patted through his pockets and slipped on his glasses. 'In the order of their testimony. The first lady, one of the twins from Israel. Yolan Shoret. She had a very marked deficiency of the scar. There was a gap, a hole if you please, that was covered only by the thickness of her skin between the outermost layer and innermost layer which covered the cavity of her abdomen.'

He looked to the judge and held up his hand. 'For the sake of demonstrating measurement, I'd like to use the width of my finger-tips.'

'Does the jury understand that?' the judged asked. They all nodded slightly.

'Mrs. Shoret's scar was three finger-tips wide and she had a hernia indicating improper healing.'

He fumbled through his notes again. 'Now her sister, Mrs. Halevy, had an extremely short incision two finger-tips wide or of about an inch in length. A very small incision, indeed. She also showed a deficiency in the middle of her scar where it had not healed and deep pigmented brown from the radiation.'

'The burn still showed.'

'Yes. Now the worst of them was the third lady, Mrs. Peretz from Trieste. The lady whose son translated for her. Her wound was covered literally by the thickness of a piece of paper. She had the same marked deficiency of the layers of the abdominal wall, the belly wall, and also a very small star of two finger-tips.'

'Could I interrupt,' Bannister said. 'You said her wound was covered by the thickness of a piece of paper. How thick is the normal abdominal wall?'

'It consists of several layers, namely skin, fat, a fibrous layer, a layer of muscle, and the peritoneal layer. In her case there was no fat, muscle, or fibre. In fact you could put your finger almost to her spine by poking the scar.'

'Like a hole straight through to the back of her body covered by a piece of paper.'

'Yes.'

'And the last lady?'

'Mrs. Prinz from Belgium.'

Highsmith was up. 'I believe we have agreed that due to her distress I had no opportunity to cross-examine her.'

'What I ruled, Sir Robert, was that it would be called to the jury's attention. This is not Mrs. Prinz's testimony. It is Professor Lighthall's. You may continue, Professor.'

'Mrs. Prinz had two scars from two operations. One was a vertical scar quite longer than the other scar, which resembled the scars of the other ladies. This would indicate to me that the vertical scar was that of a different surgeon. The horizontal scar was very brown from irradiation, again had a deep depression and was a short two finger-tips. It had obviously not healed properly.'

'Was the long vertical scar the right, or the left?'

'Left.'

'Mrs. Prinz testified that her left ovary was removed by Dr. Dimshits. What would you say was the general condition?'

'I found no evidence of depression, infection, or irradiation burn. It appeared to be a proper operation.'

'But not the other one?'

'No, it was like the other ladies, more or less.'

'Now, Professor, what in your experience is the normal length of such an incision?'

'Oh, three to six inches depending on the surgeon and the case.'

'But never an inch or two inches?' Bannister asked.

'Certainly not.'

'How do you compare these scars with ovariectomies you have observed elsewhere?'

'I have practised surgery here and in Europe, and in Africa, the Middle East, Australia, and India as well. I've never seen such scars in all my years. Even the final stitching was abhorrent. All the wounds reopened.'

As Lighthall shovelled the notes back in his pocket a sickening cloud of disbelief had descended on the courtroom. Sir Robert knew he had been damaged and had better neutralize the testimony.

'From your evidence,' Highsmith said, 'you appreciate the difference between the swank comforts of the posh clinics of Wimpole and Wigmore Streets and that of the Jadwiga Concentration Camp?'

'Very much so, indeed.'

'And you are very aware that Her Majesty's government has knighted this man for his skill as a physician and a surgeon?'

'I am aware.'

'Skills so obvious that despite different surgical procedures they would make it impossible for Sir Adam Kelno to have performed the surgery you have described.'

'I'd rather think that no proper surgeon would have done it, but obviously someone did.'

'But not Sir Adam Kelno. Now then, you are aware of the hundreds of thousands of persons put to death in Jadwiga with a single quick snuff?'

'Yes.'

'And we are in a hell, not in Cavendish Square, but an abnormal hell where all human life has been totally minimized.'

'Yes.'

'And you would agree, would you not, that if you were a prisoner/doctor working without hours and in life and death struggle and an SS officer walked into your surgery without a gown and mask there was very little you could do about that?'

'I must agree.'

'And you know, do you not, Professor Lighthall, that the British medical journals are filled with articles about irradiation hazards in leukaemia and to unborn children and of their genetic effects and that irradiated women have produced monsters or congenitally malformed foetuses?'

'Yes.'

'And you know that doctors and radiologists have died from radiation and that in 1940 it was not the skill it is today?'

'I do.'

'Can you not conceive that a doctor torn away from the world and plunged into a nightmarish hell could not have grave apprehension?'

'I would have to concede that.'

'And will you not concede there were many different opinions about the length of incisions and the time it took to perform certain operations?'

'Just a moment now, Sir Robert, I feel a bit stampeded here. Keyhole surgery and undue speed are bad business and Polish doctors recognized it in those days.'

'Would you tell my Lord and the jury if a British doctor is apt to be far more conservative than a Polish doctor?'

'Well, I must testify with pride that we do stress careful painstaking surgery. But I have testified to the examination of Mrs. Prinz, who had surgery by two Polish doctors, one done properly and one not.'

Sir Robert rocked forward and his robe slipped from his shoulders. 'I suggest that there are so many different theories between British and Continental surgeons that you could have a convention for a year and not agree on certain points.'

Oliver Lighthall waited until the fury of the wind of Sir Robert's blast had dissipated. 'Sir Robert,' he answered softly. 'There cannot be two schools of thought about the examination of those women. It was crude, bad surgery. In non-medical terms I'd describe it as butchery.'

The silence and the glower between the two was like a burning fuse about to lead to explosion.

'I should like to question Professor Lighthall on certain matters of medical ethics,' the judge said quickly, to save the situation. 'Would you mind, Sir Robert?'

'No, my Lord,' he answered, glad to be taken off the spot.

'Mr. Bannister?'

'I certainly think Professor Lighthall is qualified, and I think it proper of your Lordship to do so.'

'Thank you,' the judge said. Anthony Gilray dropped his pencil and leaned his face on his hand and weighed his thoughts. 'What we have here, Professor, is the testimony of two doctors who said they would have been put to death or surgery would have been performed by somebody without proper skill. Mr. Bannister has strongly contested whether or not such surgery would have ever been performed by an unskilled SS orderly. However, in the circumstances of Jadwiga we may assume that the threat was truly made and might have been carried out, if only as an example to the other doctors who may have been called upon later. We are not at a point in this case where it has been proved that Sir Adam did the operations you described. What I am seeking from you is an ethical concept. In your view, is a surgeon justified in carrying out an operation with questionable legitimate medical purpose against the will of the patient?'

Lighthall once more withdrew into the sanctity of meditation. 'My Lord, it is completely contrary to any medical practice I have known.'

'Well, we're talking about medical practices no one ever heard of. Say a man in an Arab country had been sentenced to have a hand cut off for thievery and you are the only skilled physician about. It's either you or someone will hack it off.'

'In such a case I would say to the chap that I am without choice.'

Adam Kelno nodded and smiled a little.

'Nothing,' Lighthall continued, 'would have made me consider it if the patient did not agree and nothing could force me to commit crude surgery. But I believe, my Lord, as I was about to do it, I would have the strength to turn

379

the knife on myself.'

'Fortunately,' Gilray said, 'this case will be settled on law and not philosophy.'

'My Lord,' Oliver Lighthall said, 'I am going to take difference with you on the matter of medical practice under duress. Granted, Jadwiga was at the bottom of the pit, but physicians have practised in all sorts of hells, in all sorts of plagues, famines, battlefields, prisons, and all imaginable evil situations. We are still bound by the Hippocratic oath of twenty-four hundred years standing, which binds us to help our patient but never a view to injury or wrongdoing. You see, my Lord, a prisoner has the right to protection from a physician for the oath also states, "and will abstain from every voluntary act of mischief and corruption and further from the seduction of females or males of freemen and slaves".'

TWENTY-FIVE

The room reverberated from the testimony of Oliver Lighthall, who was smothered in the consultation room by Abe and Shawcross and Ben and Vanessa and Geoffrey and Pam and Cecil Dodd. Lighthall was still angry and felt he had not said enough. The press ran to telephones and down Fleet Street.

FAMED PHYSICIAN RECITES HIPPOCRATIC OATH ON WITNESS STAND the headlines would blare.

'Before we adjourn for the weekend,' Anthony Gilray said, 'I should like to know, and I am certain the members of the jury will be much obliged, if you could tell us how many more witnesses you plan to call and of what duration, Mr. Bannister.'

'Three, your Lordship, and an outside chance of a fourth. Only one, Dr. Tesslar, will be examined at great length.'

'So taking into consideration your closing speeches and my instructions there is a possibility the case can go to the jury by the next weekend.'

'I should think so, my Lord.'

'Thank you. In that event I am going to ask the associate to pass the jury copies of *The Holocaust*. I take it into consideration that this is a book of over seven hundred pages and it is hardly likely that you could read it carefully in two days. However, I do ask you to go through it as thoroughly as you are able so as to have a basic understanding of what the author wrote. I ask you to do that for when I give you my instructions we will bear in mind that the offending portion of the book takes up a single paragraph and this will have to do with the weight or sting of the libel. The court stands in recess until Monday.'

TWENTY-SIX

The LOT plane from Warsaw bearing Dr. Maria Viskova cut its Soviet-built engines. She passed through customs dressed in a severe two-piece suit, flat heels, and without make-up. Even so she could not conceal a certain beauty.

'I'm Abraham Cady. My daughter Vanessa and my son Ben.'

'Ben? I knew your uncle Ben in Spain. He was a fine boy. You resemble him, you know.'

'Thanks. He was a great man. How was your flight?'

'Just fine.'

'We have a surprise for you,' Abe said, taking her arm and leading her into the lobby where Jacob Alexander stood with Dr. Susanne Parmentier. The two women approached each other, separated by twenty years' absence. They took each other's hands and held them and looked into the other's face, then embraced softly and walked arm in arm from the terminal.

The trial entered its third week. The Shawcross–Cady forces showed the wear of a nonstop weekend of preparation for the final push. Even the frigid Thomas Bannister was showing the effects.

As Maria Viskova entered the court, she paused for a moment to stare at Adam Kelno. Kelno turned away and feigned talking to Richard Smiddy. Abe helped Susanne Parmentier to a seat beside him. Jacob Alexander passed up a note. I TALKED TO MARK TESSLAR THIS MORNING. HE SENDS HIS DEEPEST REGRETS THAT HE WAS NOT THERE TO MEET DR. VISKOVA'S PLANE, BUT HE IS A BIT UNDER THE WEATHER AND WANTS TO SAVE HIS STRENGTH FOR HIS TESTIMONY. PLEASE HAVE DR. PARMENTIER RELAY THIS TO DR. VISKOVA.

Maria Viskova's voice and eyes were mellow as she was affirmed through her Polish interpreter. They had decided her English was not quite good enough for direct testimony.

'I am Maria Viskova,' she said in answer to Bannister's question. 'I work and live at the Miners' Sanatorium, Zakopane, Poland. I was born in Krakow in 1910.'

'What happened after you completed your secondary education?'

'I was unable to get into any medical school in Poland. I am a Jewess and the quotas were filled. I studied in France and after I received my degree I moved to Czechoslovakia and practised in a mountain health resort in the Tatra Mountains, a tubercular sanatorium. It was in the year of 1936.'

'And you met and married a Dr. Viskski?'

'Yes, he was also Polish. Our Czech name is Viskova.'

'Dr. Viskova. Are you a member of the Communist Party?'

'I am.'

'Would you tell us the circumstances?'

'I joined the International Brigade with my husband to

fight for Loyalist Spain against Franco. When the civil war was over we fled to France, where we worked in a sanatorium for respiratory diseases in the town of Cambo on the French–Spanish border in the Pyrenees Mountains.'

'And during the second war, what kind of activities did you engage in?'

'My husband and I established an underground station in Cambo to smuggle out French officers and soldiers so they could join French forces in Africa. We also smuggled arms in from Spain to the resistance, the FFI in France.'

'After two and a half years of this underground activity you were caught and turned over to the Gestapo in the occupied portion of France, is that right?'

'Yes.'

'After the war, did the French government recognize your activities?'

'I was decorated with the Croix de Guerre with star by General de Gaulle. My husband was awarded one posthumously. He had been executed by the Gestapo.'

'And in the late spring of 1943 you were sent to the Jadwiga Concentration Camp. Would you tell us what happened on your arrival?'

'It was discovered, at the selection shed, I was a doctor, so I was assigned to the medical compound to Barrack III. I was met by SS Colonel Voss and Dr. Kelno and learned that a Polish woman doctor had just committed suicide, and I was to take her place in charge of the women on the ground floor. I found out shortly what Barrack III was all about. It always held two to three hundred women being experimented on or waiting to be experimented on.'

'Did you come into contact with the other doctors?'

'Yes. A short time after my arrival, Dr. Tesslar came to take care of the men on the upper floor. I was quite sick from exposure in an open wagon on the trip to Poland and contracted pneumonia. Dr. Tesslar nursed me back to health.'

'So you saw him on a daily basis?'

'Yes, we were extremely close.'

'It has been testified to by Sir Adam Kelno that it was

383

common knowledge that Dr. Tesslar not only co-operated with Voss in his experiments but performed abortions on camp prostitutes.'

'It is too ridiculous to comment on. Nothing but a lie.'

'But we do want your comments, Madame Viskova.'

'We worked together day and night for months. He was the greatest humanitarian I have ever known—a man morally incapable of any wrongdoing. Dr. Kelno, who made these accusations, has made them only to cover his own foul deeds.'

'I'm afraid your comments are getting rather editorial,' Judge Gilray said.

'Yes, I know. It is difficult not to editorialize a saint.'

'It has also been testified to that Dr. Tesslar had private quarters in the barrack.'

Maria Viskova smiled and shook her head in disbelief. 'The doctors and Kapos had a space of seven feet by four feet. Enough for a bed, a chair, and a small stand.'

'But no private toilet or showers or dining facilities. Hardly luxurious?'

'It was smaller than any prison cell. They gave it to us so we could write out our reports.'

'Were there any other doctors associated with this particular area of the medical compound?'

'Dr. Parmentier, a French woman. She was the only non-Jew around Barrack III. Actually, she lived in the main compound but had access to come to Barrack III to try to help the victims of Dr. Flensberg's experiments. Flensberg was driving people insane. Dr. Parmentier was a psychiatrist.'

'How would you describe her?'

'She was a saint.'

'Any other doctors?'

'For a short time, Dr. Boris Dimshits. A Russian Jew, a prisoner.'

'What did you discover about him?'

'He was doing ovariectomies for Voss. He told me so. He wept about what he was doing to fellow-Jews, but he did not have the strength to protest.'

384

'How would you describe his physical appearance and his mental state?'

'He seemed ancient. His mind began to wander and his hands were covered with eczema. His patients, whom I cared for, were coming back from surgery in progressively worse condition. It was apparent he had become incompetent.'

'On some of his earlier operations, what did you observe?'

'His operations seemed proper. The scars were of a three-inch length, and he used care and put the girls to sleep with general anaesthetic. Of course there were always complications because of the terrible sanitation and lack of proper medicines and food.'

'So then when Dr. Dimshits was no longer able to do his work, Voss sent him to the gas chamber?'

'That is correct.'

'Are you quite certain he wasn't sent to the gas chamber for other reasons?'

'No, Dr. Kelno told me that is what Voss told him. Voss told me the same thing later.'

'Because Dimshits was useless, unable to perform, I see. Is Adam Kelno in this courtroom?'

She pointed with a steady finger.

'Were any other doctors sent to the gas chamber?'

'Of course not.'

'Of course not? Weren't tens of thousands of people being murdered in Jadwiga?'

'Not doctors. The Germans were desperate for doctors. Dimshits was the only one ever sent to the gas chamber.'

'I see. Did you ever meet a Dr. Lotaki?'

'Very casually.'

'Dr. Kelno testified that when Voss informed him he was going to do those operations, he and Dr. Lotaki talked it over with the rest of the doctors. What did he say to you?'

'Ne never spoke to me about it.'

'He didn't? He didn't discuss the ethical concepts, or ask your blessing, or seek your counsél, or get your decision that it was for the best for the patients?'

385

'No, he ran things in an arrogant manner. He asked advice from no one.'

'Perhaps that was because you weren't free to leave Barrack III. Maybe he made a mistake and forgot about you?'

'I could move freely all around the main medical compound.'

'And you could talk with all the other doctors?'

'Yes.'

'Did any of the other doctors at any time relate to you conversations they had with Dr. Kelno in which he sought their advice and consent?'

'I never heard of any such conversation. We all knew that ...'

'What did you know?'

'We all knew the experiments were a sham, an excuse for Voss to stay off the Eastern Front so he would not have to fight the Russians.'

'How did you know that?'

'Voss joked about it. He said so long as he kept reports going to Berlin he wouldn't have to see action and as long as he wormed his way into Himmler's good graces he would eventually get the reward of a private clinic.'

'So Voss himself realized his experiments had no scientific value?'

'He got pleasure from butchering.'

Bannister let his voice rise on this rare occasion.... 'Did Dr. Kelno know that Voss's experiments were useless?'

'It is impossible he did not know.'

Bannister played with some papers on the rostrum. 'Now then, what did you notice after Dr. Dimshits's death?'

'The quality of the surgery degenerated. We were faced with all sorts of post-operative complications. There were terrible complaints about the pain from the spinals. Dr. Tesslar and I called for Dr. Keino to come many, many times. We were ignored.'

'We come now,' Bannister said with melodious and ominous monotone, 'to a certain night in mid-October of 1943 in which you were summoned to Dr. Voss's office in

Barrack V.'

'I remember,' she whispered, with tears forming in her eyes.

'What took place?'

'I was alone with Voss in his office. He told me that Berlin wanted more information about his experiments and that he was stepping things up. He needed more doctors and he was assigning me to the surgery.'

'What did you answer?'

'I told him I wasn't a surgeon. He told me I would give anaesthetic and assist. Dr. Kelno and Dr. Lotaki were having trouble with unwilling patients.'

'And what was your answer to that?'

'I told him I would not do it.'

'You mean, you refused.'

'Yes.'

'You refused an SS colonel with power to send people to the gas chambers?'

'Yes.'

'What did Voss do about that?'

'He screamed the usual curses and ordered me to report to Barrack V again the next day for operations.'

'What happened then?'

'I returned to my room in Barrack III and thought it over and came to a decision.'

'What was that decision?'

'To commit suicide.'

A dozen gasps pierced an otherwise stunned silence. Adam Kelno wiped the perspiration from his face.

'What was your intention?'

She slowly unbuttoned the top of her blouse, reached in her bosom, and took out a locket. She opened it and withdrew a pill and held it out. 'I had this cyanide tablet. I have kept it till this day to remind me.' She stared at it as she must have a thousand times.

'Are you able to continue, Dr. Viskova?' the judge asked.

'Yes, of course. I placed this on a wooden crate which was used as a nightstand beside my cot and took a pad and wrote a note of farewell to Dr. Tesslar and Dr. Parmentier. My door opened. Dr. Parmentier came in and saw the pill.'

'Did she become alarmed?'

'No. She was quite calm. She sat beside me and took the pencil and paper from my hand ... and she stroked my hair, and she said words to me that I have remembered in all the difficult moments of my life.'

'Would you tell my Lord and the jury what she said?'

Tears fell down the cheeks of Maria Viskova and more than a few who heard her. 'She said ... "Maria ... it is not possible that any of us are going to live and get out of this camp. In the end the Germans must kill us because they cannot allow the outside world to know what they are doing." And she said ... "the only thing that is left for us is to behave for the rest of the short time we have left as human beings ... and as physicians." She said ... "we cannot leave these people to suffer alone."'

Thomas Bannister looked at Adam Kelno as he spoke. 'And you did not report to Barrack V the next day to assist in the operations?'

'I did not.'

'What did Voss do about that?'

'Nothing.'

TWENTY-SEVEN

Lena Konska had undergone four days of intense grilling by Aroni and Jiri Linka but it was impossible to find many flaws in her story. She admitted to seeing her cousin, Egon Sobotnik, briefly at the end of the war and at that time he told her he was going to go somewhere far away, he could not bear the ghosts.

Aroni was not easily discouraged. He knew, after all, that Lena Konska had the wit to live illegally for five years. Each day Aroni brought newspapers of the trial and pleas were interspersed with threats.

As they mounted the steps to her flat, Linka wanted to quit. 'We are wasting our time. Even if she knows something, she's too crafty an old witch.'

'So long as Prague finds no new information on Sobotnik we have to keep going at her.'

'Have it your way.'

'Suppose,' Aroni said to Lena Konska, 'we discovered you have lied to us.'

'Are we going over all that again?'

'We know you are clever, clever enough to keep a secret from everyone but God. You'll answer to God for this.'

'What God?' she answered. 'Where was God in the concentration camps? If you ask me,' she said, 'I think that God has gotten a little old for the job.'

'You lost all your family?'

'Yes, the merciful God took them.'

'Well, they would be proud of you now, Madame Konska. They will be extremely proud of you if Adam Kelno wins this case because of information you withheld. The memory of them will annoy you. You can depend on that, Madame Konska. As you grow older their faces will become more vivid. You can't forget. I tried.'

'Aroni, leave me alone.'

'You've been to the Pinkas Synagogue in Prague. You've seen that, haven't you?'

'Stop it.'

'Your husband's name is on the wall of martyrs. I've seen it, Jan Konska. Is that his picture, there? He was a handsome man.'

'Aroni, you act like a Nazi yourself.'

'We've found some neighbours,' Aroni said. 'They remember Egon Sobotnik returning. They remember him living here with you, in this apartment, for six months then suddenly disappearing. You have lied to us.'

'I told you he stayed for a short while. I didn't count the

389

days. He was restless.'

The phone rang. It was police headquarters for Jiri Linka. He listened for a moment, then handed the phone to Aroni as the words were repeated.

Aroni replaced the phone slowly, his wrinkled face distorted, a sort of madness in his expression. 'We have heard from Prague.'

Lena Konska did not betray what was happening within her, but she saw something horribly different about Aroni, the hunter.

'The police have found statements dating back to 1946, three statements in which Egon Sobotnik was implicated with Kelno's surgery. That's when he fled Bratislava, isn't it? All right, Madame Konska, which way do you want it? Do you tell us where he is or do I find him myself? I'll find him, you know.'

'I don't know where he is,' she repeated firmly.

'Have it your way.'

Aroni picked up his hat and nodded to Linka, and they passed through the draped opening to the small foyer off the parlour.

'Just a moment. What will you do to him?'

'He'll be taken care of if you force me to find him.'

She licked her lips. 'To the best of my knowledge his guilt is very small. If you were to suddenly find him ... what kind of a deal would you make?'

'If he testifies, he will leave the courtroom free.'

She looked desperately to Linka. 'You have my word as a Jew,' he said.

'I swore ... I swore ...' her lips quivered. 'He has changed his name to Tukla, Gustuv Tukla. He is one of the directors of the Lenin Factories in Brno.'

Aroni whispered in Linka's ear, and he nodded. 'We are going to have to detain you to remove the temptation of calling him until we make contact.'

TWENTY-EIGHT

'Dr. Viskova, do you recall any particular incident about twins in Barrack III?'

'When I arrived there were twins from Belgium, Tina and Helene Blanc-Imber, who had been irradiated and had an ovary removed by Dr. Dimshits. Later, two other sets of twins were sent in, the Cordozo and Lovino sisters from Trieste. I remember how terribly I felt because they were so young, the youngest in the barrack. Sometime later they were irradiated again.'

'And they have testified to their sickness afterwards. We now come to a particular night in early November of 1943. Would you tell us what happened?'

'A number of SS guards and Voss himself entered the barrack. Of course there was always alarm. They ordered the Kapos to get the three sets of twins. From upstairs they brought a number of young Dutch boys, an older Polish man, and a medical clerk. His name was Menno Donker. They were taken away quite hysterical. Dr. Tesslar sat with me. We knew what would be coming back to us. We were grief-stricken.'

'How long did you and Dr. Tesslar wait?'

'A half hour.'

'What happened?'

'Egon Sobotnik, a medical clerk and orderly, came with two SS guards and told Dr. Tesslar he must come to Barrack V. There was pandemonium, and he had to keep the people quiet. So he rushed out.'

'How long was Dr. Tesslar gone?'

'It was just after seven o'clock when he left and a little after eleven when he came back with the victims. They were brought back on stretchers.'

'So, fourteen of them were operated on in a little over four hours. Would that not be about fifteen minutes each if done by a single surgeon?'

'Yes.'

'Did Dr. Tesslar say there was more than one surgeon?'

'No, only Adam Kelno.'

'And with one surgeon doing an operation every fifteen minutes there was not time to sterilize instruments or himself between operations. What was it like in Barrack III?'

'A bedlam of screams and blood.'

'You were on the ground floor and Dr. Tesslar on the upper floor, is that right?'

'Yes.'

'Did you see each other?'

'Often. We were running up and down with each new crisis. I first came up to assist with one of the men who was going quickly.'

'What happened to this man?'

'He died of shock.'

'And you returned to your own problems.'

'Yes. Dr. Parmentier arrived, and thank God she was there to help. We were in serious trouble with the haemorrhaging and almost helpless. We didn't even have enough water to give them. Dr. Tesslar tried to get Dr. Kelno to come but got no response. They lay bleeding and screaming on wooden beds with straw mattresses. At the caged end of the barracks, the mental patients of Flensberg became hysterical. I saw I could not stop the haemorrhaging of Tina Blanc-Imber so we moved her into the corridor away from the others. At two in the morning she was dead. All night we struggled to get control of the situation. By some miracle, the three of us managed to keep the others alive. At dawn the Germans came to take away Tina and the man. Egon Sobotnik made out death certificates which we signed. Then I heard him receive orders to change the cause of death to "typhus".'

A sob broke out in the balcony and a woman ran from the courtroom.

Bannister spoke so low he could not be heard, and he had to repeat the question. 'Did Dr. Kelno ever come to visit these patients?'

'A few times he came to the door of the barrack. Once, he glanced at them briefly.'

'On that occasion, did he find them cheerful?'

'Are you joking?'

'I assure you I am not.'

'They were very sick for months. I was forced to send the Cordozo sisters back to their factory even though I knew Emma could not last. Sima Halevy was the most ill, and I kept her as an assistant so she would not go to the gas chamber.'

'Is there any question in your mind of who did these operations?'

'I object, my Lord,' Highsmith said without passion.

'Objection sustained. Instruct the witness not to answer.'

Her silent answer, her eyes on Adam Kelno were answer enough.

TWENTY-NINE

Linka and Aroni raced north along the Austrian border from Slovakia into the rolling fields of Moravia, rich in the barleys and wheats that immortalized Czechoslovakian beer. A detour forced them near the battlefield of Austerlitz, where Napoleon once took on the imperial armies of Russia and Austria in a short blood-soaked encounter costing the lives of thirty-five thousand men. The Battle of the Three Emperors as it was poetically remembered.

Aroni, who slept sitting upright with head nodding and bobbing, suddenly came awake as though an alarm had been set off inside him.

'I don't quite understand how you got such co-operation from Branik,' Linka said.

Aroni yawned, lit a cigarette. 'We speak the same language. Concentration camp language. Branik was almost hanged for his underground activities in Auschwitz.'

Linka shrugged. He still didn't understand it.

They entered Brno, the pride of Czech industry with one of the greatest heavy industrial complexes in the world and an enormous Trade Fair Centre covering hundreds of acres which attracted a million annual buyers and visitors throughout the world.

They checked in at the Hotel International, an ultra-modern glass and concrete affair that belied the chunky, drab Communist hotels throughout Eastern Europe.

There was a message waiting. GUSTUV TUKLA HAD BEEN TELEPHONED FROM PRAGUE BY MUTUAL FRIENDS AND TOLD TO CO-OPERATE. HE IS EXPECTING ARONI AT TEN O'CLOCK. BRANIK.

Aroni found Gustuv Tukla a polished, urbane man in his late fifties, yet with the rugged face and hands of a professional engineer. His office, which looked out over a yard to the mammoth Lenin Factories, also showed Western affluence. Along the window a table held a model of the Blansko exhibit at the coming International Trade Fair. Tukla and Aroni settled opposite each other on a pair of couches separated by a coffee table holding a number of catalogues of the Blansko products. A mini-skirted secretary brought them thick espresso. Aroni smiled as she bent over and set it down.

'Set me straight,' Aroni said, 'exactly who called you from Prague?'

'Comrade Janacek, the party chairman for the Committee on Heavy Industry. He is my direct superior except for the head directors here.'

'Did Comrade Janacek tell you anything about my business here in Czechoslovakia?'

'Only that you were a very important gentleman from Israel and, frankly, to make a good deal with you.'

'Good. Then we can get down to cases.'

'Confidentially,' Tukla said, 'I am glad we are going to do business with Israel. It is not said in public but there is a great deal of admiration for your country.'

'We like the Czechs. Especially their arms when they were available.'

'Masaryk, thank God we can now mention his name, was a friend of the Jews. So, perhaps you are interested in our Kaplan Turbines?'

'Actually I'm interested in one of your personnel.'

'As an adviser?'

'In a manner of speaking.'

'Who?'

'I am interested in Egon Sobotnik.'

'Sobotnik? Who is that?'

'If you will roll up your left sleeve and read me your tattoo number, I think we can stop wasting time.'

Aroni then said who he was and Gustuv Tukla turned from a self-assured executive into a mass of confusion. It had all happened so suddenly. The call from Janacek only this morning. Obviously this Aroni was dealing with the hierarchy.

'Who told you? It must have been Lena.'

'She had no choice. We caught her lying. She did it for your own good.'

Tukla spun off the couch sweating, grunting, pacing. 'What's it about?'

'The trial in London. You know about it. The newspaper on your desk is open to the story. You've got to come to London and give testimony.'

Tukla tried to shake the confusion, tried to think. It was so sudden! So sudden!

'Are these Janacek's orders? Who?'

'Comrade Branik is interested in this case.'

The mention of the head of the secret police had its effect. Aroni watched him coldly as he sat again, wiped his face and bit the back of his hand. Aroni set his cup down and walked to the window. 'Are you ready to listen?'

'I'm listening,' Tukla whimpered.

'You are an important party member and your testimony may prove embarrassing to the Czech government. The Russians have long memories when it comes to assisting

Zionism. However, your people think you ought to come to London. Fortunately, even some Communists know right from wrong.'

'What are you suggesting?'

'You know,' Aroni answered.

'A defection?'

Aroni stood over him. 'It's a short distance to Vienna. You are a member of the Brno Flying Club. There will be an aeroplane at the airport large enough to hold your family. With a defection, no one will be able to blame your government.'

Tukla trembled violently. He managed to gulp down a tranquillizer. He blinked, dazed. 'I know their tricks,' he whispered. 'I will take off from the airport and the plane will develop engine trouble. They can't be trusted.'

'I trust them,' Aroni said, 'and I'll be in the plane with you.'

'But what for?' Tukla wailed. 'I have everything. Everything I've worked for will be gone.'

'Well now, Sobotnik ... you don't mind if I call you Sobotnik? A Czech engineer from the Blansko works isn't going to have much trouble finding a highly suitable posiion in England or America. Frankly, you're lucky to be getting out of the country. You'll have the Russians down your throats inside a year and there will be purges like the Stalin days.'

'And if I refuse to defect?'

'Well, you know how that works. Transfer to a remote power station. Demotion. Your son may suddenly be dropped from the university. Perhaps the Kelno case publicity will entice Comrade Branik to open certain old files ... certain statements made against you at the end of the war.'

Tukla dropped his face in his hands and cried. Aroni hissed close to his ear, 'You remember Menno Donker. He was also a member of the underground. They cut his nuts off for that. Well ... what happened when Kelno found out you were a member of the underground?'

Sobotnik shook his head.

'Kelno made you assist him, didn't he?'

'God!' he cried. 'I only did it a few times. I've paid! I've lived like a frightened rat. I've run. I've lived in fear of every footstep, every knock on the door.'

'Well, we all know your secret now, Sobotnik. Come to London. You will leave the courtroom a free man.'

'Oh my God!'

'What if your son learns this from someone other than his father. He will, you know.'

'Have mercy on me.'

'No. Get your family ready by this evening. I will meet you at your home at six o'clock.'

'I'll kill myself first.'

'No you won't,' Aroni said cruelly. 'You would have done that years ago if you intended to. Don't ask me to feel sorry for you. If you did those things for Kelno, then the very least you can do is do something decent for us. I'll see you at six, ready to go.'

When Aroni had left, Tukla waited until the tranquillizer took effect. He told his secretary to cancel all appointments and phone calls and locked his office. He opened the bottom drawer of his desk and stared long at the pistol, then put it on the top. The drawer had a false bottom so masterfully built the most trained eye could not detect it. His broad fingers tapped on one end and the lid gave way. Tukla slid it out. In the hidden compartment lay a book. A tattered yellowed book. He set it on the desk next to the pistol and stared. The faded lettering on the cover read, MEDICAL REGISTER, JADWIGA CONCENTRATION CAMP—AUGUST 1943—DECEMBER 1943.

THIRTY

'The next witness will testify in French.'

Dr. Susanne Parmentier ascended to the witness box with the aid of a cane but testily refused a chair. Mr. Justice Gilray was in a certain glory being fluent in the French language and having been afforded this opportunity to display his mastery to an audience. He greeted her in her native tongue.

She gave her name and address in a strong, clear voice.

'And when were you born?'

'Must I answer that?'

Gilray stifled a smile. 'No objection to passing on that question,' Highsmith said.

'Your father was a Protestant pastor?'

'Yes.'

'Have you ever belonged to any political party?'

'No.'

'Where did you study medicine?'

'In Paris. I was qualified in 1930 as a psychiatrist.'

'Now, Madame Parmentier. What peculiar position did you find yourself in at the time France was occupied?'

'Nothern France was occupied by the Germans. My parents lived in Paris. I was working in Southern France in a clinic. I learned that my father was gravely ill and applied for a travel permit to visit him. These permits were difficult to get. It took days of investigation and red tape, and I felt a great sense of urgency. I tried to cross the demarcation line illegally and the Germans caught me and put me in prison in Bourges in late spring of 1942.'

'What happened there?'

'Well, there were hundreds of Jewish prisoners, including children, extremely maltreated. As a doctor I received permission to work in the prison clinic. Finally, things got so bad I asked to speak to the commandant.'

'Was he regular army or SS?'

'Waffen SS.'

'What did you tell him?'

'I told him the treatment of the Jews was a disgrace. They were human beings and French citizens, and I demanded they receive the same treatment and rations as the rest of the prisoners.'

'How did he react to that?'

'He was stunned at first. I was returned to my cell. Two days later I was taken to his office again. Two other Waffen SS officers were seated on either side of his desk. I was made to stand before them and told I was standing trial there and then.'

'What happened as a result of this so-called trial?'

'I was given a badge of cloth to sew on my clothing with the words, "Friend of the Jews", and early in 1943 I was sent to Jadwiga Concentration Camp for my crime.'

'Were you tattooed?'

'Yes, number 44406.'

'And after a time you were sent to the medical compound?'

'In the late spring of 1943.'

'You worked as a subordinate to Dr. Kelno?'

'Yes.'

'And did you meet Dr. Lotaki?'

'Yes, on occasions, like anyone working together in a large medical facility.'

'You met Voss?'

'Yes.'

'And you became aware of the fact that Dr. Lotaki and Dr. Kelno were doing surgery in Barrack V for Voss.'

'It was known, certainly. Kelno did not particularly hide the fact.'

'Of course it became known when Dr. Kelno and Dr. Lotaki called all of you together and discussed the ethical problems of the operations.'

'If there was any such meeting, I did not attend.'

'Did the other doctors ever tell you they were consulted about this?'

'Dr. Kelno did not consult with the other doctors. He told them what to do.'

'I see. Do you think you would have known if such a meeting ever took place?'

'Certainly.'

'Sir Adam has testified that he does not remember you.'

'That is very strange. We were in daily contact for over a year. He certainly recognized me this morning in the corridor of the court. He said to me, "Well, here is the friend of the Jews again. What lies are you going to tell?" '

Smiddy slipped a note to Adam: IS THAT TRUE?

I BECAME ANGRY, he wrote back.

YOU TESTIFIED YOU DIDN'T REMEMBER HER.

WHEN I SAW HER, I SUDDENLY RECALLED.

'Do you know a Dr. Mark Tesslar?'

'Intimately.'

'Whom you met in Jadwiga.'

'Yes, after I saw Flensberg's experiments I went almost every day to Barrack III to try to help the victims.'

'Were there prostitutes being kept in Barrack III?'

'No, only people waiting to be experimented on, or those who had been returned from experiments.'

'Were there prostitutes in the medical compound?'

'No, they were locked up in another camp and they had their own medical facility in their own barrack.'

'How do you know that?'

'There were a number of mental disturbances and I was sent for on numerous occasions.'

'Were there doctors in the prostitutes' barrack who performed abortions?'

'No. Any prostitute who became pregnant was sent to the gas chamber automatically.'

'What of the female Kapos?'

'The same. The gas chamber. It was a closed rule in Jadwiga for all females.'

'Certainly not the wives of SS guards or other German personnel?'

'There were extremely few wives. Only the top-ranking SS officers, and their wives were treated in a private German clinic.'

'In other words, Dr. Parmentier, it would have been impossible for Dr. Tesslar to commit abortions because none were being performed in an organized manner.'

'That is correct.'

'Well, if a prisoner/doctor found a pregnant woman and wanted to save her from the gas chamber would a secret abortion be performed?'

'It is an extremely rare situation. The men and women were segregated. Of course they always found ways to get together, but we speak of isolated cases. Any doctor would do it to save a woman's life in much the same way it is done today to save a woman's life.'

'Who were the prostitutes kept for?'

'German personnel and high-ranking Kapos.'

'Is it possible that a favourite prostitute could have been kept alive by an SS guard?'

'Hardly. The prostitutes were very drab and very disturbed. They were only performing in order to stay alive. However, they were dispensable. It was easy to get new women at the selection shed and force them into prostitution.'

'So, in any event, to the best of your knowledge Dr. Tesslar could not have been and was not involved with abortions in Jadwiga?'

'No. He was occupied day and night in the men's portion of Barrack III.'

'But that is Adam Kelno's testimony.'

'He seems quite confused on a number of things,' Susanne Parmentier answered.

'Now would you tell us about your first meetings with SS Colonel Dr. Otto Flensberg?'

'Otto Flensberg was of equal rank to Voss, and he had an assistant, Dr. Sigmund Rudolf. Both of them were in Barrack I and Barrack II in the restricted experimental area. I was taken to Otto Flensberg in the summer of 1943. He had learned I was a psychiatrist and told me he was doing important experiments and needed me. I had heard of the kind of things he was doing, and I told him I would

401

not take part in them.'

'What did he say to that?'

'Well, he tried to convince me. He said that Voss was a pseudo-scientist and what he was doing with X-rays was worthless. And that his own assistant was equally useless.'

'What was Captain Sigmund Rudolf doing?'

'Attempting to introduce cancer into the cervix of the womb, trying sterilization by injections of caustic fluids into the Fallopian tubes, and some other rather bizarre blood and sputum experiments.'

'And his own assistant said they were useless.'

'Yes, he gave his assistant Barrack I to play in and get enough reports back to Berlin to keep him off the Russian front.'

'What did he say about his own work?'

'Flensberg considered himself vital. He said he had worked at Dachau during the mid-thirties when it was a prison for German political prisoners. Later he worked on obedience experiments for the SS. He dreamed up all sorts of tests for SS cadets to prove their loyalty and instant obedience. Some of them were gruesome, such as murdering a puppy they had trained, stabbing prisoners on command, that sort of thing.'

'And Otto Flensberg was proud of that?'

'Yes, he said it proved to Himmler the absolute obedience of the German people.'

'What did he tell you about coming to Jadwiga?'

'Himmler gave him carte blanche. He even had his assistant assigned to come with him. Flensberg became nonplussed when he found that Voss was his superior. There was a definite rivalry and he felt Voss was wasting human material, while his work was important to Germany's being able to occupy Europe for centuries.'

'How?'

'He felt that the obedience of the German people was an accomplished fact. Yet, there were not enough Germans to control an entire continent of hundreds of millions of people. He wanted to find methods to train the conquered peoples to control the general population. In other words

402

immediate obedience to German orders.'

'Like Kapos?'

'I should say, to sterilize people mentally. To turn them into robots.'

A weird fascination gripped the courtroom. The unreality of a mad scientist in a fiction story. But it was not science fiction. It happened. And Otto Flensberg was still alive, escaped to Africa.

'Would you explain to my Lord and the jury what kind of experiments Otto Flensberg was carrying out in Barrack I?'

Highsmith was up. 'I am going to object to this line of questioning. I fail to see to what point all of this is relevant.'

'It is relevant to the point that a German doctor in a concentration camp was carrying out experiments on prisoners and brought in a prisoner/doctor to assist in these experiments.'

'I think it is relevant,' the judge said. 'What was Flensberg doing, Dr. Parmentier?'

'He was running a series of obedience experiments in a number of small rooms. Each room had two chairs. The people were separated from each other by a glass window so they could see each other. In front of their chairs was a panel of switches. Each switch threw an increasingly higher voltage, and was marked, and had words like *slight shock* and up to five hundred volts with the words *possible death*.'

'How ghastly,' Gilray uttered.

'There was an operator's booth where Flensberg was stationed which also had a panel of switches.'

'Just what did you witness, Dr. Parmentier?'

'Two prisoners were brought in from Barrack III. They were males. Both of them were strapped into the chairs but had freedom of their hands. Flensberg from his booth called down and told prisoner *A* he must give prisoner *B* on the other side of the glass a shock of fifty volts or he, Flensberg, would punish him for not obeying.'

'Did prisoner *A* do as he was told?'

'Not at first.'

'And Flensberg shocked him.'

'Yes. *A* screamed. Flensberg then ordered prisoner *A* again to shock prisoner *B*. Prisoner *A* resisted until he was getting almost two hundred volts and at that point he began to obey the commands and shock prisoner *B* so he would not receive any more himself.'

'So the gist of what was happening was forcing people to inflict punishment on other people or get it themselves.'

'Yes. To obey out of fear.'

'Prisoner *A* started giving prisoner *B* shocks on command of Flensberg. Didn't he see and hear what he was doing to the other fellow?'

'Yes.'

'How much voltage did prisoner *A* apply on orders?'

'He eventually killed prisoner *B*.'

'I see.' Bannister drew a long breath. The jury seemed puzzled as though they were not certain of what they were hearing. 'After showing you this experiment, what did Flensberg do?'

'First I had to be calmed down. I was demanding that the experiments stop. I was forcibly removed to his office by a guard. He told me he really wasn't interested in killing the fellow, but it happened sometimes. He showed me graphs and charts and records. What he was looking for was the breaking point in each individual. That point at which they would become robots to German commands. Beyond that point they tended to go insane. He showed me experiments in which he forced blood relatives to shock one another.'

'I am curious, Dr. Parmentier,' the judge said. 'Did any people resist entirely from hurting their fellow man?'

'Yes, resistance increased between husbands and wives, parents and children. Some would resist until their own death.'

The judge continued to question her. 'Were there cases of, say, a father or mother killing his own child?'

'Yes ... that is why ... I am sorry ... no one asked a question of me....'

'Please go on, Madame,' Gilray said.

'That is why Flensberg began searching for twins. He felt he could perform some sort of ultimate test on them. The girls from Belgium and Trieste were brought to Barrack III for his experiments and then Voss irradiated them. This upset Flensberg considerably. He threatened to protest to Berlin and was pacified when Voss told him he would recommend to Himmler to give Flensberg a private clinic and Dr. Lotaki to do his surgery.'

'How utterly appalling,' Mr. Justice Gilray repeated.

'Let us digress for a moment,' Bannister said. 'After you saw this experiment and read the reports, what transpired?'

'Flensberg assured me that once the initial surprise settled, I would become fascinated by the work. It was a rare opportunity for a psychiatrist to have human guinea pigs. Then, I was ordered to work for him.'

'And what did you answer to that?'

'I refused.'

'You refused?'

'Certainly I refused.'

'Well, exactly what was said?'

'Flensberg said that Barrack III was, after all, only filled with Jews. I said I knew it was filled with Jews. Then he said to me, "Don't you realize that some people are different?" '

'What did you answer him?'

'I said, "I have noticed the difference in some people, starting with you." '

'Well, he must have taken you out and had you shot for that.'

'What?'

'Were you executed? Were you shot or sent to the gas chamber?'

'But of course not. I am here in London. How could I have been shot?'

THIRTY-ONE

Sir Robert Highsmith was clearly on the spot. During trial times he abandoned his place in Richmond, Surrey, for his flat in Cadogan Square and its proximity to the West End and the Law Courts. Tonight he studied, hard.

No one could question but that Thomas Bannister had built a powerful case on circumstantial evidence and in catching Kelno on some questionable testimony. Yet, Kelno's mistakes were largely that of a layman up against a mental giant, a master of legal gymnastics. Surely the jury, while recognizing Bannister's genius, would more closely identify themselves with Adam Kelno.

At bedrock it all now hinged on Mark Tesslar, the single alleged eyewitness. Throughout all the years and all the trial, Sir Robert Highsmith refused to believe that Adam Kelno was guilty. Kelno's career had been long and distinguished. Certainly, if he had the qualities of a monster, it would have shown up elsewhere along the line.

He worked over his line of questioning absolutely determined to discredit Mark Tesslar.

Oh, he had moments of doubt, all right, but he was a British barrister, not judge or jury, and Adam Kelno was entitled to the best he had.

'I am going to win this case,' he vowed to himself.

'Where the devil is Terry?' Adam said angrily. He took another sharp drink of vodka. 'I'll bet he went to Mary. Did you phone?'

'There is no phone there.'

'He was in court today,' Adam said. 'Why isn't he here now?'

'Perhaps he's at the college library studying late. He's lost a lot of school time due to the trial.'

'I'm going to Mary's,' Adam said.

'No,' Angela said. 'I went after court. Mary hasn't seen him in days. Adam, I know what is bothering you but these barristers are clever at twisting things. It's their profession. But the jury knows the truth the same as your patients do. They've rallied to you. Please don't drink, Terry will be around soon.'

'For God's sake, woman, for once in my life let me get drunk without whining about it. Do I beat you? Do I do evil things?'

'You'll get that nightmare.'

'Maybe not if I drink enough.'

'Adam, listen to me. You have to be strong in that court-room tomorrow. You have to be strong when Tesslar is on the stand.'

'Hello, Angela. . . . Hello, Doctor.'

Terry wobbled in and flopped on the sofa. 'As you know,' he said, 'I do not drink like the son of my father. I've always figured that Father Campbell could drink for the two of us.'

'Where the hell have you been!'

'Drinking.'

'Leave the room, Angela,' Adam commanded.

'No,' she answered.

'We won't need a referee, Angela,' Terry slurred. 'This is clearly a doctor and doctor situation.'

She backed away apprehensively but left the door ajar.

'What's on your mind, Terry?'

'Things.'

'What things?'

Terry hung his head and his voice cracked and wavered to a point of almost being unrecognizable. 'The shadow of doubt has descended upon me,' he mumbled. 'Doctor . . . I . . . I don't care what the jury decides. I want to hear from your own lips, between you and me . . . did you do it?'

Adam stormed to his feet consumed with rage. He rose over the boy with both fists coming down on Terry's neck. Terry doubled over making no attempt to defend himself.

'Bastard! I should have beaten you years ago!' His fists smashed down and Terry slid off the couch on all fours.

Adam brought his foot up into the boy's ribs. 'I should have beaten you! That's what my father did to me. He beat me like this ... like this!'

'Adam!' Angela screamed, throwing herself over Terry as a shield.

'Oh my God,' he cried in anguish, sinking to his knees. 'Forgive me, Terry ... forgive me.'

The morning was fraught with rising tension as Highsmith and Bannister bandied about on some legal points. The night before Mark Tesslar arrived from Oxford. There was a quiet dinner with Susanne Parmentier and Maria Viskova after which Abe, Shawcross, Ben, and Vanessa joined them for coffee.

'I know,' Mark Tesslar said, 'what Highsmith intends to do. I will never be broken about the night of November tenth.'

'I don't know if I can put into words how I feel about you,' Abe said. 'I think you are the most noble and courageous man I have ever met.'

'Courage? No. It is just that I am beyond all pain,' Mark Tesslar answered.

For the first part of the morning, Chester Dicks took Susanne Parmentier through a relatively mild cross-examination until the afternoon recess.

Shawcross, Cady, his son and daughter, and Lady Sarah Wydman hit their drinks hard at the Three Tuns Tavern and played with their kidney pies as Josephson went to fetch Mark Tesslar from the hotel.

Adam Kelno was the first back into the courtroom. He was glassy-eyed, under sedation. He stared pleadingly at his wife and Terry in the first row of spectators as the room filled and then jammed to overflowing.

'Silence.'

Anthony Gilray seated himself and after the bows of the assemblage nodded to Thomas Bannister. At that moment Josephson rushed into the room to the solicitors' table and whispered excitedly into Jacob Alexander's ear. Alexander turned crimson, scribbled a note and handed it to Thomas

Bannister. Thomas Bannister totally lost his composure, slumping into his chair. Brendon O'Conner leaned down from the juniors' table, snatched up the note, then wobbled to his feet.

'My Lord, our next witness was to have been Dr. Mark Tesslar. We have just been informed that Dr. Tesslar has dropped dead of a heart attack on the street outside his hotel. May we ask your Lordship for a recess for the day?'

'Tesslar . . . dead . . .'

'Yes, my Lord.'

THIRTY-TWO

The flat in Colchester Mews was dimly lit when Vanessa opened the door for Lady Sarah. Abe looked up, half seeing her, half not. All of them were red-eyed from weeping.

'Abe, don't take this on yourself,' Lady Sarah said. 'He's been very sick for a long time.'

'It's not only Dr. Tesslar,' Vanessa said, 'the embassy contacted Ben and Yossi this afternoon and ordered them to return to Israel immediately and report to their commands. It's a mobilization.'

'Oh dear Lord,' she said, standing above Abe and stroking his hair. 'Abe, I know what you must feel but there are decisions that have to be made. Everyone is gathered at my flat.'

He nodded that he understood and arose and put on his jacket.

They were all there at Lady Sarah's sharing communal grief. Thomas Bannister was there, and Brendon O'Conner was there, and Jacob Alexander, Lorraine and David

Shawcross, Josephson, Sheila Lamb, and Geoffrey, Pam Dodd, and Cecil Dodd. Oliver Lighthall was there also.

And there were four others. Pieter Van Damm and his family. The missing Menno Donker.

Abe embraced Van Damm and they held each other and patted each other for a moment.

'I flew in from Paris the moment I heard the news,' Pieter said, 'I must go on the stand tomorrow.'

Abe went to the centre of the room and faced them all. 'Since I have been involved in this case,' he said hoarsely, 'I have found myself the chief barker in a carnival of horrors. I've opened old wounds, brought back nightmares, and taken the lives of people into my hands who should have been left in peace. I told myself that their anonymity would be preserved. But here we have a man who is an international figure and it is impossible for the world not to know. You see, when the light went out in my eye a strange thing happened. Strangers in bars would try to pick fights with me. When people know you are a cripple their blood instincts rise to the surface and you are like a wounded animal on the desert with only a matter of time until the jackals and vultures devour you.'

'May I interrupt you,' Bannister said. 'We all certainly know the problems of Mr. Van Damm's future privacy. Fortunately British law takes these rare occasions into consideration. We have a procedure called In Camera. In Camera is testimony given in secret in unusual circumstances. We will appeal to have the courtroom cleared.'

'Who will be there?'

'The judge, the jury, his Lordship's assistant, and the legal representation of both sides.'

'And you really think this can remain a secret? I don't. Pieter, you know how cruel the jokes will be. Do you honestly think you'll ever be able to perform again before an audience with three thousand people staring between your legs? Well, the one thing I will not be responsible for is taking the music of Pieter Van Damm from the world.'

'The trouble with you, Cady,' Alexander snapped, 'is that you've become enchanted with the idea of martyrdom. I think you are glorying in becoming the new Christ figure and want to immortalize yourself by getting lynched.'

'You're very tired,' Abe answered, 'you've been working too hard.'

'Gentlemen,' Bannister said, 'we simply can't afford the luxury of a quarrel among ourselves.'

'Hear, hear,' Shawcross said.

'Mr. Cady,' Bannister said, 'you have won the universal respect and admiration of us all. You are a logical man and you must be made aware of the consequences of not permitting Mr. Van Damm to testify. Consider for a moment that Adam Kelno has won a large judgement. You would be responsible for the ruination of your closest friend, David Shawcross, and end his distinguished publishing career on a black note. But more important than Shawcross or yourself would be what Kelno's victory would mean in the eyes of the world. It would be an insult to every Jew, those living, those courageous men and women who came forth in this case, and certainly it would be a most abominable affront to those who had been murdered by Hitler. You would be responsible for that too.'

'There is another matter,' Oliver Lighthall said. 'What about future medical ethics? How ghastly it would be for doctors in the future to point back at this case and use it as a justification for the maltreatment of patients.'

'So you see,' Bannister said, 'your stand, no matter how virtuous, is filled with counter-responsibilities even more important.'

Abe studied them all, his worn-out little band of idealists. 'Ladies and Gentlemen of the jury,' he said in a voice that literally moaned with sorrow, 'I should like to make a statement by quoting in effect the words of Thomas Bannister, Q.C., when he said that no one in their wildest imaginations would have believed Hitler's Germany before it actually happened. And he said, if the civilized world knew what Hitler intended to do then they would have stopped him. Well, here we are in 1967, and the Arabs vow daily to finish Hitler's work. Certainly the world will not stand for another chapter of this holocaust. There is a right and a

411

wrong. It is right for people to want to survive. It is wrong to want to destroy them. It's quite simple then. But alas, the kingdom of heaven is concerned with righteousness alone. The kingdoms of the earth run on oil. Well now, certainly the world should be appalled by what is happening in Biafra. The stink of genocide is everywhere. Certainly, after Hitler's Germany, the world should step in and stop genocide in Biafra. However, that becomes impractical when one considers England's investments in Nigeria conflict with France's interests in Biafra. And after all, members of the jury, it is only black people killing other black people.

'We should like to think,' Abe said, 'that Thomas Bannister was right, when he said more people, including the German people, should have risked punishment and death by refusing to obey orders. We should like to believe there would have been a protest and we ask why didn't the Germans protest? Well, today young people march in the streets and protest Biafra and Vietnam and the principle of murdering their fellow man through the medium of war. And we say to them ... why are you protesting so much? Why don't you go out there and kill like your father killed?

'Let us, for the moment, forget we are in jolly, comfortable London. We are in Jadwiga Concentration Camp. SS Colonel Dr. Thomas Bannister has summoned me into his office and says, "See here, you have got to agree to the destruction of Pieter Van Damm. Of course it will all be done IN CAMERA. Barrack V was a secret place just like the courtroom will be. After all, we don't do that sort of thing in public. And I quote to you again from Thomas Bannister, Q.C., when he said, "There comes a moment in the human experience when one's life itself no longer makes sense when it is directed to the mutilation and murder of his fellow man." And I submit, members of the jury, I can bring no greater calamity or no more positive form of destruction upon this man than to allow him to take the witness stand. In closing, I say that I respectfully decline to murder Pieter Van Damm.'

Abe turned and started for the door.

'Daddy!' Vanessa cried and clung to him.

'Let me go alone, Vinny,' he said.

He reached the street and stopped to catch his breath. 'Abe! Abe!' Lady Sarah called, catching up to him. 'I'll get my car,' she said.

'I don't want a goddam Bentley. I want a goddam Austin taxi.'

'Abe, please let me be with you.'

'Madame, I am en route to Soho where my intentions are to get shit-faced drunk and sleep with a whore.'

'I'll be your whore!' she cried, grabbing him. 'I'll scratch and scream and bite and curse and you'll drool on me and hit me and cry ... and then I'll hold you.'

'Oh Jesus, God,' he groaned, clinging to her, 'I'm scared. I'm scared.'

THIRTY-THREE

There was a cruel expression in Adam Kelno's face as he glared from the plaintiff's table to Abraham Cady. Their eyes met. Adam Kelno smiled slightly.

'Silence!'

Mr. Justice Gilray seated himself. 'We are all shocked and distressed over the untimely passing of Dr. Tesslar, but I'm afraid nothing can be done about that. What are your intentions, Mr. Bannister, about placing his statement into evidence?'

'That won't be necessary,' Bannister answered.

Gilray blinked in disbelief. Highsmith, anticipating a long involved hassle, was taken aback.

Shimshon Aroni slipped next to Abe and passed him a note. I AM ARONI, it read; WE HAVE SOBOTNIK.

'Where do things stand now, Mr. Bannister?' the judge asked.

'I have one more witness to call.'

The smile left Adam Kelno's face and his heart raced.

'There are some rather unusual circumstances surrounding this witness, my Lord, and I should like to seek his Lordship's advice on the matter. This witness held an important position in a Communist country and only last night defected with his family. He arrived in London at two in the morning and has asked for and been granted political asylum. We have been searching for over a year for this gentleman but had no idea if he were alive or if he would come forward until he showed up in London.'

'Is his entry into this trial on a completely voluntary basis?'

'I have no idea what induced him to defect, my Lord.'

'What is our problem? If the witness has volunteered there is no question of issuing a subpoena. If he is here against his will, it would be a muddled bit of business because we don't know if he is in the jurisdiction of the British courts even though he has claimed asylum.'

'No, my Lord. The problem is that usually when a defector asks asylum he is taken into seclusion for a long period of time until his rehabilitation. We cannot rule out the possibility of foul play against this witness and therefore he was accompanied to the Law Court by several gentlemen from Scotland Yard.'

'I see. Are they armed?'

'Yes, my Lord. Both the Foreign Office and Scotland Yard share the opinion they should be handy at all times. We are obliged to protect him.'

'It is indeed distressing to think that any foul play could take place in an English courtroom. I don't like closed courts. We practise our law in the open. Are you asking that this witness be heard In Camera?'

'No, my Lord. The fact that we have discussed this matter and everyone knows there are Scotland Yard men present, that in itself should discourage anyone who intended foul play.'

'Well, I don't like armed men in my court, but I'm not going to clear it. I shall yield to the unusual circumstances.

Call your witness, Mr. Bannister.'

'He will testify in Czech, your Lordship.'

Adam Kelno strained for remembrance of the name Gustuv Tukla. The standing crowd in the rear of the room was separated by a pair of detectives. Between them walked a haggard, frightened man. Outside the courtroom, Scotland Yard detectives sealed off every exit. As the veil of time lifted Adam Kelno gasped and scribbled a desperate note to Smiddy. STOP HIM.

'Impossible,' Smiddy whispered. 'Get hold of yourself.' Smiddy passed a note up to Sir Robert, KELNO IS EXTREMELY DISTRESSED.

Gustuv Tukla's hand trembled as he was affirmed and he took a seat. He looked about in animal desperation as the translator was sworn in.

'Before we continue,' Mr. Justice Gilray said, 'it is apparent that this witness is under a great deal of strain. I will tolerate no harrassment of this man. Mr. Interpreter, kindly inform Mr. Tukla he is in England, in Her Majesty's Court, and he will receive no maltreatment. Advise him to be certain he understands every question clearly before he answers.'

Tukla managed a small smile and nodded to the judge. He gave his last address in Brno and his birthplace as Bratislava, where he lived until the war broke out and worked as a civil engineer.

'What was your most recent position?'

'I am one of the directors and production managers of the Lenin Factories, a large factory of many thousand workers in heavy industrial manufacturing.'

Mr. Justice Gilray, in an effort to put the witness at ease, discussed with him a number of articles he had read on the Brno Trade Fair and the Czech reputation in this field.

'Were you, at the time of your defection, an official of the Communist Party?' Bannister began.

'I was District Chairman of the Industrial Committee and a member of the National Committee in the same group.'

'That is a rather important post, is it not?'

'Yes.'

'Were you a member of the Communist Party at the outbreak of the war?'

'No. I officially joined the party in 1948, when I went to work in Brno as an engineer.'

'Have you changed your name, sir?'

'Yes.'

'Would you tell us about the circumstances?'

'At the time of the war my name was Egon Sobotnik. I am half-Jewish on my father's side. After liberation I changed my name because I was afraid to be found out.'

'About what?'

'Some things I was made to do in Jadwiga Concentration Camp.'

'Tell us now, if you will, about being sent to Jadwiga Concentration Camp.'

'I fled to Budapest when the Germans occupied Bratislava and lived with false papers. I was picked up by the Hungarian police and returned to Bratislava and sent by the Gestapo to Jadwiga, where I was assigned to the medical compound. This was late in 1942.'

'Who did you report to?'

'Dr. Adam Kelno.'

'Is he in this courtroom?'

Sobotnik pointed a shaky finger. The judge repeated that the shorthand writer could not transcribe a gesture. 'That is him.'

'What kind of work were you given to do?'

'Clerical. Keeping records, mostly. Finally I kept the clinical and surgical record books.'

'Were you, at some time, contacted by the underground? By the underground, I refer to the international underground. Do you understand my question?'

'May I have leave, your Lordship,' the interpreter said, 'to explain this to Mr. Tukla?'

'Yes, go on.'

They conversed and Tukla nodded and answered. 'Mr. Tukla understands. He says there was a small underground group of Polish officers and a larger one that encompassed

416

everyone. He was contacted in the summer of 1943 and told that there was great concern about the medical experiments. At night he and a Dutch Jew, Menno Donker, copied from the surgical records what operations had taken place in Barrack V and turned it over to a contact.'

'What did your contact do?'

'I don't know but the plan was to smuggle this information to the outside.'

'Risky business.'

'Yes, Menno Donker was discovered.'

'Do you know what happened to Donker?'

'He was castrated.'

'I see. Did it not occur to you as strange that the Germans wanted records kept of this sort of thing?'

'The Germans have a mania for records. At first I am sure they thought they were going to win the war. Later, they felt by taking records and then falsifying them they could justify a great number of deaths.'

'How long did you keep the surgical records?'

'I started in 1942 and kept it until the liberation in 1945. There were six volumes.'

'Now, going back, sir. You said you changed your name and apparently your identity after the war because of things you were forced to do in Jadwiga. Would you tell us about that?'

'At first I only did clerical work. Then, Kelno found out I was a member of the underground. Fortunately, he did not know I was smuggling out records of his operations. I was terrified he would turn me over to the SS. He forced me to do a number of things to help him.'

'Like what?'

'Hold patients still while they were being given spinals. At times I was made to give the spinals.'

'Were you trained at this?'

'I was shown once for a few minutes.'

'What else were you forced to do?'

'Also restrain patients who were having sperm tests.'

'You mean, shoving a wooden handle up their rectums to induce sperm?'

'Yes.'

'Who did that?'

'Dr. Kelno and Dr. Lotaki.'

'How many times did you see Dr. Kelno do that?'

'At least forty or fifty separate occasions. There could be any number of men worked on each time.'

'Were they in pain?'

Tukla lowered his eyes. 'Very much so.'

'And this was done to healthy men prior to being irradiated and then operated on as the beginning of the experiment.'

'My Lord,' Highsmith said. 'Mr. Bannister is leading the witness and asking conclusions of him.'

'I'll put it another way,' Bannister said. 'Was Dr. Adam Kelno collaborating with the Germans in medical experiments?'

'Yes.'

'And how do you know that?'

'I saw him.'

'Did you see him operate in Barrack V?'

'Yes.'

'Many times?'

'I saw him perform two or three hundred operations in Barrack V, anyhow.'

'On Jews?'

'Once in a while a court order case but ninety-nine per cent Jews.'

'Did you observe Dr. Kelno in surgery in his regular clinic, in Barrack XX?'

'Yes, on many occasions. Many dozens of times.'

'And you saw him hold clinic. Perform the minor bits of business such as boils and cuts.'

'Yes.'

'Did you observe any significant difference between Dr. Kelno's behaviour in Barrack V from his behaviour in his regular clinic?'

'Yes, he was brutal to the Jews. He often beat them or cursed them.'

'On the operating table?'

'Yes.'

'Now, Mr. Tukla. I am going to refer to a particular series of operations performed in the early part of November of 1943. There were eight men who had testicles removed and three sets of twins who had ovariectomies.'

'I remember it quite clearly. It was November 10. It was the night Menno Donker was castrated.'

'Tell us about it please.'

He drank some water, spilling it with trembling. His face became devoid of colour. 'I was told to report to Barrack V. There was a small army of Kapos and SS. Around seven o'clock the fourteen victims were brought to the anteroom and we were told to shave them and give them spinals.'

'In the anteroom, not in the operating room?'

'Always in the anteroom. Dr. Kelno didn't want to waste time in the surgery.'

'Had these people been given a previous injection?'

'No. Dr. Viskova and Dr. Tesslar complained on several occasions that it was only humane to give them morphia.'

'What did Dr. Kelno say to that?'

'He said, "We don't waste morphia on pigs." On other occasions it was suggested it would be better to put the people under, put them to sleep as he did in Barrack XX. Dr. Kelno said he didn't have time to waste.'

'So injections were always given in the anteroom without morphia and by unskilled or semi-skilled people?'

'That is correct.'

'Were these people in pain?'

'Severe pain. That is my guilt ... that is my guilt ...' He rocked back and forth biting his lip to stave off the tears.

'Are you quite able to continue, Mr. Tukla?'

'I must continue. I have held this in for over twenty years. I must finish with it so I can have peace.' And he sobbed, 'I was a coward. I should have refused like Donker.' He heaved a number of deep sighs and apologized and nodded that he wished to continue.

'Now, sir, you were present in the anteroom of Barrack V on the night of November 10 and you assisted in the preparation of these fourteen people. Please continue.'

419

'Menno Donker was first. Kelno told me to come into the surgery and keep him quiet.'

'Did you sterilize yourself?'

'No.'

'Who else was present?'

'Dr. Lotaki assisted. There were one or two orderlies and two SS guards. Donker cried that he was healthy, then pleaded for Kelno to leave him one testicle.'

'What did Kelno answer to that?'

'He spat on him. In a moment or two there was such mayhem outside Voss ordered me to go to Barrack V to get Mark Tesslar. I returned with him to a scene so macabre I cannot forget it for a single day or a single night. Those young girls having the clothing torn from them, the screams of pain from the injection, the fighting and beating even on the operating table, the blood. Only Mark Tesslar was sane and human.'

'And you were present in the operating theatre?'

'Yes, I moved all the victims in and out.'

'Who did the operations?'

'Adam Kelno.'

'All of them?'

'Yes.'

'Did he clean himself between operations?'

'No.'

'Did he sterilize his instruments?'

'No.'

'Was he considerate of his patients?'

'He was like a butcher turned loose with an axe in a slaughterhouse. It was a massacre.'

'How long did this go on?'

'He was doing it very fast, every ten or fifteen minutes. Around midnight I was told to take them back to Barrack III. There were stretchers, and they were on them side by side. The anteroom floor was gory with their blood. We carried them back to the barrack. Tesslar pleaded with me to get Kelno ... but I fled in horror.'

Adam Kelno wrote a note. I AM LEAVING THE COURTROOM. SIT STILL! Smiddy wrote back.

'What was your next contact with this situation, Mr. Tukla?'

'I was ordered to Barrack V the next morning and told to fill out death certificates for one of the men and one of the women. At first I put "shock" for the reason of death for the man and "haemorrhage" for the woman, but the Germans made me change the cause of death to "typhus".'

'Now, Mr. Tukla, all of this has been preying on your mind for a long time.'

'I lived in fear of being named a war criminal.'

'Do you know what became of the six volumes of surgical records?'

'There was a great deal of confusion when the Russians liberated the camp. Many of us fled as soon as the SS retreated. I do not know what became of five of the volumes. I kept the sixth one.'

'Hidden all these years?'

'Yes.'

'Out of fear of your own involvement?'

'Yes.'

'What period of time does this volume cover?'

'The second half of 1943.'

'My Lord,' Bannister said. 'I should like to offer in evidence at this time the medical register of Jadwiga Concentration Camp.'

THIRTY-FOUR

A war of words unleased. This was law that was!

'My Lord,' Sir Robert Highsmith said, 'my learned friend has achieved a certain drama in a last-minute attempt to present new evidence. I am going to object most arduously to its introduction as inadmissible.'

'On what grounds?' Mr. Justice Gilray asked.

'Well, in the first place I've never seen this document or had a chance to examine it.'

'My Lord,' Bannister said, 'the register came into our hands at three o'clock this morning. During the night we gathered together a volunteer staff of forty people who have sifted through the pages to find relevant information. I have listed here on two pages of paper that information I feel essential. I will gladly supply this and photocopies of those pages of the register from which we will ask questions for my learned friend to study.'

'Then, you're really asking to amend the Particulars in your claim of justification?' the judge asked.

'Exactly, my Lord.'

'And that's what I object to,' Highsmith said.

Richard Smiddy slipped a note to his secretary to fetch Mr. Bullock, his managing clerk, and have him round up a staff of people in the event that Bannister prevailed. She darted from the court.

'It has been my experience,' Mr. Justice Gilray said, 'that the defence can amend the Particulars during a trial if new evidence is brought forth.'

'I've seen no such application for an amendment,' Highsmith countered.

'I have one here, drawn up on a single page,' Bannister answered.

The usher handed copies to the judge and Chester Dicks and Richard Smiddy, who pored over it as Sir Robert continued the debate.

'Your Lordship and my learned friend will see that our application is on a single page and relates solely to the medical register,' Bannister said.

'Well, what do you say to that?' Gilray asked Highsmith.

'In my practice of law, which covers several decades, I have never seen or known of a case, particularly one which comes close to the length of this trial, where the court has ever allowed an amendment to a Particulars which would change the entire nature of the case.'

Chester Dicks was handing him down law books and Richard Smiddy was handing them up. Highsmith read a half dozen precedents where such applications had been turned down.

'Would you advise the court on this, Mr. Bannister?' Gilray asked.

'I certainly don't agree we are changing the nature of this case.'

'Certainly, we are,' Highsmith cracked back. 'Had this document been placed in evidence at the beginning of this trial, the plaintiff would have presented an entirely different kind of case. Here we are, over a month into the trial in its closing moments. Most of the defence witnesses have returned to Europe, Asia, and America. We have no chance to question them. Our chief witness after Sir Adam Kelno is locked away in Poland. We have inquired if Dr. Lotaki can be recalled, and he is not going to be given another visa. It is completely unfair to the plaintiff.'

'What about that, Mr. Bannister?' the judge asked.

'I intend to confine my questions solely to the register and none of the witnesses for the defence can shed any light so they wouldn't be needed in any event. As for Dr. Lotaki, we would agree to pay for his passage to return to London but it is not our fault if his government will not let him come. Actually, if Sir Robert is going to allow Sir Adam to return to the stand I can cover what I want to know in an hour, and I will be glad to supply my learned friend in advance the gist of my questions to his client.'

Here was the soul of the barrister's training. The extemporaneous and instantaneous ability to think and orate on one's feet flanked with a catalogue-like memory and quick-working assistants.

'Sir Robert, in the event the medical register is admitted into evidence, are you going to allow Sir Adam to be questioned?' asked Mr. Justice Gilray.

'I cannot reveal at this time what my tactic will be.'

'I see. Have you anything further to add, Mr. Bannister?'

'Yes, my Lord. I see nothing unusual or unique about the introduction of the medical register as evidence. It has been in this courtroom in spirit since the outset of this case. I suggest to his Lordship that no single piece of evidence in all of English history has cried out more strongly to be heard. Here, after all, is the heart of the matter. Here are the answers we have searched for in every corner of the world and in this courtroom. Inadmissible, indeed! If we attempt to silence this medical register in a British courtroom it will cast a shadow over our very system of justice, for in any event it will not be ultimately silenced. If we silence it here we are saying that we really don't want to know what happened in Jadwiga or the Nazi era. It was all some people's fantasy. And, are we not to consider the brave men and women who gave their lives to leave behind them such documents for the future to know what really happened?'

'In all fairness,' Highsmith interrupted, 'my learned friend is making a closing speech to the jury. He'll have time to do that later.'

'Yes, Mr. Bannister. What other grounds do you have to guide the court?'

'The strongest possible grounds. The testimony of the plaintiff, Sir Adam Kelno, on direct examination by his own counsel. I quote to you. Sir Robert asked, "Were any records kept of your operations and treatments?" To which Sir Adam answered, "I insisted on accurate records. I felt it important that there could never be doubts of my behaviour later." A moment later, Sir Adam said from that witness box, "I wish to God we had the registers here now because it would prove my innocence." And again later on under direct examination he said: "In every single case I insisted the operation be entered into the surgical register." Your Lordship, nothing can be more clear than that. If Sir Adam made those statements in testimony are we not led to believe that if the register had been found by him he would have entered it as a document?'

'What do you have to say to that, Sir Robert?' the judge asked.

'Sir Adam is, after all, a physician and not a lawyer. Not having seen or studied the document I would have done so and advised my client whether to offer it as evidence or not.'

'I suggest,' Bannister returned quickly, 'that as long as it seemed that there were no chance at all the register could be produced, as long as he felt all these volumes were lost forever, Sir Adam could use it as implied evidence in his behalf. But alas, one of the missing volumes has survived and found its way into this court and now he is singing a different tune.'

'Thank you, gentlemen,' Gilray said.

He studied Bannister's application. Legally the document seemed in good order, the kind an English judge could rule on in a moment.

Yet, for some reason, he continued to stare, his mind not really on it at all. The vast parade was suddenly passing before him.

During the trial, he was to be affected for the rest of his life. He had seen them ... human beings ... mutilated. It was not Kelno's guilt or innocence that seemed the great question. It was what happened at the hands of one's fellow man. For an instant he was able to cross the line and understand this strange loyalty of Jew to Jew. Those Jews who lived free in England were only there due to some quirk of fate instead of Jadwiga and every Jew knew that genocide could have happened to his own family except for that quirk of fate. Gilray was strongly taken by those two handsome young people, Cady's son and daughter. After all, they were half English.

Yet, as time stood suspended, Gilray was all gentiles who never quite understood Jews. He could befriend them, work with them, but never totally understand them. He was all white men who could never quite understand black men and all black men who could never quite understand whites. He was all normal men who could tolerate or even defend homosexuals ... but never fully understand them.

There is in us all that line that prevents us from fully understanding those who are different.

He looked up from the document into the eyes of the expectant courtroom.

'The application of the defence for an amended Particulars is approved. The medical register of Jadwiga Concentration Camp is hereby entered as evidence and will be marked as defendant's exhibit W. In fairness to the plaintiff, I shall call a recess for two hours in order for them to study this document so they can prepare a proper defence.'

And with that, he left the courtroom.

The blow had fallen! Highsmith remained silent. The judge had said, TO PREPARE A PROPER 'DEFENCE'. Sir Adam Kelno, the accuser, had become the accused, even in the mind of the court.

THIRTY-FIVE

Sir Adam Kelno was ushered into the consultation room where Robert Highsmith and Chester Dicks and Richard Smiddy and a half dozen assistants pored over the photocopies of the register and copies of Bannister's proposed questions. He was greeted coldly.

'It was a long time ago,' he whispered. 'Something happened to my mind, there. For years afterwards I was in a state of semi-amnesia. I have forgotten so many things, Sobotnik kept the register. He may have falsified entries against me. I did not always look what I was signing.'

'Sir Adam,' Highsmith said curtly. 'You are going to have to take the stand.'

'I can't.'

'You have to,' Highsmith answered tersely. 'You have no choice.'

Adam Kelno was not fully able to disguise the sedation. He seemed departed as he sat in the witness box and Anthony Gilray advised him he was still under oath.

Photocopies of certain selected pages were handed to him as well as the judge and jury. Bannister asked the associate to hand the medical register to Adam Kelno. He stared at it, still in disbelief.

'Is the volume in evidence before you the medical register of Jadwiga Concentration Camp for the last five months of 1943?'

'I believe so.'

'You'll have to speak up, Sir Adam,' the judge said.

'Yes ... yes ... it is.'

'Will my learned friend agree that photocopies in his possession and supplied to the court and jury are accurate reproductions of various pages of the register?'

'So agreed,' Highsmith said.

'In order to assist the jury, let us open informally to an ordinary sample page to establish the general format of the register. I ask you to open to a double page, fifty and fifty-one. Going from left to right we see eleven different columns. The first column merely lists the number of the operation and on this particular page we see that we are up to thirteen thousand odd cases of surgery. The second column tells the date. Now what is the third column?'

'It is the tattoo number of the patient.'

'Yes, and that is followed by the patient's name, then a diagnosis of the illness. Is that all correct?'

'Yes.'

'We have now completed the first half of the double page and move on to page fifty-one. What is in the left hand column of that page?'

'A brief description of the operation.'

'And the next short column?'

He did not answer. Bannister repeated the question and received only an inaudible mumbling. 'Isn't that column the name of the surgeon and the next one the name of the assistant?'

'It is.'

'And the next column. Tell my Lord and the jury about that.'

'It's ...'

'Well?'

'It's the name of the anaesthetist.'

'The anaesthetist,' Bannister repeated in one of his rare raises of voice. 'Would you glance briefly either through the photocopies, or the register itself, in reference to the column concerning the anaesthetist.'

Sir Adam turned the pages numbly, then looked up watery-eyed.

'Wasn't there always an anaesthetist present? On all occasions?'

'Not fully trained in many cases.'

'But wasn't it your testimony that in most cases you didn't have an anaesthetist and therefore you had to give it yourself and that was one of the reasons you chose spinal?'

'I did ... but.'

'Will you accept that the register bears out that in one hundred per cent of the cases you either had a qualified doctor as your assistant or a doctor acting as the anaesthetist?'

'It appears so.'

'So you were not telling the truth when you testified you did not have a qualified anaesthetist present?'

'My memory may have failed me on that point.'

Oh God, Abe thought, I should not be feeling delight from all this. Thomas Bannister is now performing articulate legal surgery on him, and I should not feel any glory or vengeance.

'Let us move along to the next column. I see the word, "neurocrine". Would that describe the actual drug used in the spinal?'

'Yes.'

'And the final column is headed, "remarks".'

'Yes.'

'Are pages fifty and fifty-one, including the column headings, in your handwriting, and your signature in the column marked "operator"?'

'They are.'

'Now studying the register again, do you see Dr. Tesslar listed anywhere as either the surgeon or the assistant?'

'He probably hid it.'

'How? You were his superior. You had a dialogue with Voss and Flensberg, whom you described as your associates. How could he have hidden it?'

'I can't know. He was very crafty.'

'I suggest he performed no surgery of any kind in Jadwiga.'

'It was rumour,' Adam answered, breaking into a sweat.

'Please turn to page sixty-five. Now that seems to be quite a different handwriting except the signature of the operator. Would you explain that?'

'Sometimes a medical clerk filled out everything except the surgeon's signature. It could be Sobotnik who falsified the operations for the Communist underground.'

'But you aren't suggesting you didn't sign it or the signature is a forgery? If you caught him forging your signature later you'd have done something about that, like what you did to Menno Donker.'

'I am going to object,' Highsmith said.

'The register will bear out what was done to Menno Donker,' Bannister said in an unprecedented show of outright anger. 'Well, Sir Adam?'

'I was very tired at the end of many days and sometimes I did not read carefully what I signed.'

'I see. We have photocopied twenty double pages from the register and each one of these double pages lists some forty operations. In those operations that are marked amputatio testis, sin or dex, we refer, do we not, to the amputation of a right or left testicle.'

'Yes.'

'Now, how does that differ from the operation described as castration?'

'One means the removal of a dead or irradiated gland as I testified. The other means ... well ... it means ...'

'What?'

'Castration.'

'The removal of both testicles?'

'Yes.'

'Thank you. I will now ask the associate to hand you a

document which was your sworn statement to the Home Office during the extradition proceedings of 1947. It was written by you in Brixton Prison.'

Highsmith bounced up. 'This is out of order, most out of order. In having approved the defendant's amended Particulars it was understood by us all that the questioning would be confined to the medical register.'

'In the first instance,' Bannister said, 'Sir Adam entered his Home Office statement as part of his own evidence. It was a document he himself brought forth. There now appear to be enormous discrepancies between what he said in 1947, what he testified to earlier in the trial, and what the medical register is saying. If the register is lying, then all he has to do is say so. I believe the jury has every right to know which is the correct testimony.'

'Your objection is overruled, Sir Robert. You may continue, Mr. Bannister.'

'Thank you. On page three of your statement to the Home Office you state, "I may have removed a few unhealthy testicles or ovaries, but I was performing surgery all the time and in thousands of cases one is always bound to find this part of the body diseased like any other part of the body." That's what you swore to in 1947 to escape extradition to Poland, is it not?'

'It was very long ago.'

'And a month ago in this courtroom you testified that you may have performed a few dozen and assisted Dr. Lotaki on another dozen. Is that what you said here?'

'Yes, I recalled a few more operations after my statement to the Home Office.'

'Well, Sir Adam, I suggest that if you add up the ovariectomies and testicle amputations you performed that are recorded in this volume of the medical register it will add up to two hundred and seventy-five, and that you assisted in another hundred.'

'I am very confused as to the exact number of operations. You can see for yourself there were almost twenty thousand operations. How can I remember the exact number?'

'Sir Adam,' Bannister pressed, now softening his tone

again, 'you heard Tukla's testimony that there were two more volumes of the surgical register completed before you left Jadwiga. Is that a fact?'

'Yes, perhaps.'

'Now, what do you think these two volumes would bear out if they suddenly showed up? Wouldn't the total show us that closer to a thousand of these operations were performed or assisted by you?'

'Unless I see it with my own eyes, I would not say so.'

'But you agree that you operated or assisted in three hundred and fifty operations borne out in this volume.'

'I think it may be right.'

'And do you now agree you had an anaesthetist available and actually you never did give the anaesthetic yourself in the operating theatre as you previously testified?'

'I am confused on that point.'

'I ask you to turn to page three of your statement to the Home Office, and I quote your words, "I categorically deny I ever performed surgery on a healthy man or woman." Did you say that in 1947?'

'I believe that was my recollection at the time.'

'And did you give the same testimony in this court-room?'

'I did.'

'Will you open the medical register to page seventy-two and look at the fourth operation from the bottom performed on an Oleg Solinka and tell the court about this.'

'It says ... gypsy ... court order ...'

'And the operation?'

'Castration.'

'Is that your signature as the surgeon?'

'Yes.'

'Now, kindly turn to page two hundred and sixteen about mid-page. We see a Greek name, Popolus. Would you read for my Lord and the jury the diagnosis, the operation, and the surgeon?'

'It is another court order case.'

'A castration performed by you because this man was a homosexual?'

431

'I . . . I . . .'

'Will you kindly now turn to page two hundred and eighteen. At the very top we see a woman's name, apparently a German woman, a Helga Brockmann. What does it say about her?'

Kelno glared at the page.

'Well?' Gilray prodded.

He took a long sip of water.

'Is it correct,' Thomas Bannister said, 'that this woman, a German criminal sentenced to Jadwiga, had her ovaries removed by a court order because she was not a registered prostitute, and she was practising prostitution?'

'I think . . . it could be.'

'Now kindly turn to page three hundred and ten and let me see, twelfth from the top. A Russian name, Borlatsky, Igor Borlatsky.'

Again Adam Kelno stalled.

'I think you'd better answer the question,' Gilray said.

'It is a court order for castration of a mentally incompetent.'

'Was there anything wrong with these people?'

'Well, the prostitute may have had a venereal disease.'

'Do you hoick out a woman's ovaries for that?'

'In some cases.'

'Well, tell my Lord and the jury what kind of disease mental incompetent is and how that can be cured by a castration.'

'It was the crazy things the Germans did.'

'What kind of disease is gypsy?'

'The Germans sentenced certain people by court order, "inferior to Germans".'

'Now kindly turn to page twelve, bottom third of the page, a castration performed on an Albert Goldbauer. What is the diagnosis?'

'Court order.'

'For what?'

'Smuggling.'

'What kind of illness was smuggling?'

Adam did not answer again.

'Isn't it true that smuggling was a way of life and that you yourself engaged in it? It was universal in Jadwiga, was it not?'

'It was,' he croaked.

'I suggest there are in this volume twenty court order cases, fifteen males and five females in which castrations and double ovariectomies were performed by you on healthy people. I suggest you were not telling the truth in that witness box when you testified that you never performed a court order surgery. You did not do this, Sir Adam, to save their lives or because they had dead organs as you justified before, you did it because the Germans told you to do it.'

'I simply did not recall the court order cases earlier. I did so much surgery.'

'I suggest you would have never recalled it unless this register showed up. Now, Sir Adam, in addition to testicle amputation and ovariectomies, for what other type of operations would you prefer to use a spinal?'

Adam closed his eyes a moment and gasped in air. It was now almost as though he were hearing it all in an echo chamber. 'Well?' Bannister repeated.

'An appendectomy, a hernia, a laparotomy, most anything below the belly.'

'You have testified, have you not, that in addition to your personal preference for a spinal, there was little or no general anaesthetic available?'

'We had many shortages.'

'I suggest that in the month before November 10, 1943, and the month afterwards you performed nearly a hundred operations, ninety-six to be exact, in the lower body. I suggest that in ninety of these cases you personally chose a general anaesthetic and you used a general anaesthetic in dozens of other cases of minor surgery such as boils, and I suggest there was plenty of general anaesthetic available as well as an anaesthetist to administer it.'

'If the register says so.'

'I suggest that you chose spinal injections in only five per cent of the lower body operations in the entire register in

433

your own surgery, and you always wrote under "remarks" that you gave a pre-injection of morphia, except in Barrack V.'

Adam began flipping the pages of the register again and looked up and shrugged.

'I suggest,' Bannister continued to assault, 'that you did not tell the truth to the jury when you testified you preferred spinal but developed a certain penchant for it on the Jews in Barrack V, and you did not give pre-morphia because I think you were getting pleasure out of their pain.'

Highsmith was up but sat without speaking.

'Now then, let us clear up one more point before we get to the night of November 10. You will kindly turn to page three of the register and look at the name Eli Janos, who was castrated for smuggling and black marketeering. Do you recall an identification line-up at the Bow Street Magistrate's Court some eighteen years ago.'

'Yes.'

'And an Eli Janos was unable to identify you although he said he saw the surgeon without a mask. Would you read the name of the surgeon?'

'Dr. Lotaki.'

'And if it had been you, who were also doing the same thing, you would have been returned to Poland to stand trial as a war criminal. You know that, don't you?'

Adam longed for a recess, but Anthony Gilray would not call one.

'You will kindly open the register to page three hundred and two and tell my Lord and the jury the date.'

'November 10, 1943.'

'Beginning with tattoo number 109834 and the name Menno Donker you will kindly read the number and names of the next fifteen people listed.'

Adam began after a long silence. He read in monotone, '115490 Herman Paar, 114360 Jan Perk, 115789 Hans Hesse, 115231 Hendrik Bloomgarten, 115009 Edgar Beets, 115488 Bernard Holst, 13214 Daniel Dubrowski, 70432 Yolan Shoret, 70433 Sima Halevy, 70544 Ida Peretz,

70543 Emma Peretz, 116804 Helene Blanc-Imber and 116805 . . .'

'I did not hear the last name.'

'Tina.'

'Tina Blanc-Imber?'

'Yes.'

'I hand you the names and tattoo numbers of ten of these persons who have testified in this trial. Considering the name changes to Hebrew in some instances, and by marriage, are these not the same people?'

'Yes,' he whispered even before the associate handed him the paper.

'Is there any listing for a pre-injection of morphia?'

'It may have been overlooked.'

'Is there or isn't there?'

'No.'

'Who is listed as the surgeon? Whose signature is on all fourteen operations?'

'Doctor . . .' Terry cried from the balcony.

'I suggest the signature reads Adam Kelno.'

Adam looked up for a brief instant as the young man disappeared from the courtroom.

'And in the remarks column, in your handwriting, what is listed after Tina Blanc-Imber and Bernard Holst?'

Adam shook his head.

'It says, "deceased that night" does it not?'

Adam came to his feet. 'Can't you see all of you it's a new plot against me. When Tesslar died they sent Sobotnik after me! They're out to get me! They'll hound me forever!'

'Sir Adam,' Thomas Bannister said softly, 'may I remind you, it was you who brought this action.'

THIRTY-SIX

Sir Robert Highsmith adjusted his robes and faced the jury, a drawn, hurt man yet unable to go against the core of his being, a British barrister who would fight for his client until the last breath. He went into his familiar swaying motion and thanked the jury for its patience, then reviewed the case hammering away at the enormous discrepancy between what was written in *The Holocaust* and what actually happened in Jadwiga.

'What the defendants have published is that Sir Adam Kelno carried out fifteen thousand operations totally experimental in nature and without the use of any anaesthetic. Your task, members of the jury, is to decide what the ordinary reader, perhaps whiling away a long train journey, is going to think those words mean. And he is going to think, is he not, "My God, that man must be a monster." And some of those ordinary readers of this bestselling novel are going to say, "How appalling. That must be *Sir Adam* Kelno, *my* Dr. Kelno, who did these diabolical things in Jadwiga." And the diabolical things will be these: Sir Adam Kelno, a Nazi, Sir Adam Kelno, a vivisectionist; Sir Adam Kelno carrying out fifteen thousand or more experimental operations without the use of anaesthetic. In English law, we are not allowed to call evidence as to the meaning of the words complained of; this is a matter rightly within your province. Members of the jury, as sensible, reasonable people, I do not think it is an affront to you if I say fifteen thousand means fifteen thousand. It does not mean fifty; it does not mean two hundred and fifty; it means fifteen thousand.

'And in support of these accusations, what have the defence said? "Well, we have to admit it wasn't actually fifteen thousand, it was more like a hundred or two, and we have to admit that Dr. Kelno did not operate without

anaesthetic, but nevertheless what we published was true."
My learned friend, Mr. Bannister, has dragged a few rather
feeble pink herrings across the trail, but the facts are clear.
Dr. Kelno's wrongs, like Caesar's wounds, cry out for
themselves. *Is* it true, members of the jury, that Sir Adam
Kelno carried out fifteen thousand operations without
anaesthetic? This is merely a question of fact, and then a
question of damages.'

Sir Robert Highsmith's persuasive tones occupied the
hours with his assessment of the evidence.

'In Jadwiga in 1943 the defence have shown, and Sir
Adam Kelno has not denied, that he carried out about two
hundred or so operations on sexual organs. These operations were performed in an operating theatre which would
not have existed but for his efforts in the years 1940 to
1943, and in which he had saved the lives of thousands of
unfortunate creatures who had been maltreated by the Nazi
guards and officers. And he carried out these operations in
Jadwiga in 1943, members of the jury, not in a London
Hospital in 1967. Why did he do these operations? Because
in effect he had no choice. Sir Adam Kelno was in the fetid
stench of Jadwiga where "consent" was a meaningless word
both for the poor people who had to undergo these operations and for the doctors forced to carry out the Germans'
orders. What were the alternatives? The gas chambers, certainly for the prisoners and probably for the doctors themselves. Or butchery followed by a slow death if the operations were carried out by unskilled hands. Dr. Lotaki has
testified as to their dilemma. When thousands were sent to
the gas chambers daily, when the selection routine was a
constant horror, what would you have said? Do you really
think any sensible man could or should have said "I don't
believe it. The Nazis wouldn't do that." So the doctors
discussed it. And one thing is beyond argument; it was considered the best thing that could be done in the circumstances. In the circumstances, members of the jury. Not in
Wimpole Street, but in Jadwiga.

'We are not in Jadwiga any longer. We have moved out
of the shadows of Jadwiga. We are not in Nuremberg. We

are in London. You are an English jury hearing an English case, about to be directed by an English judge according to English law. I have according to my rights striven to put my client's case fairly before you. In your hands I confidently leave the reputation of a grossly and wickedly maligned man.'

THIRTY-SEVEN

Thomas Bannister reconstructed his case over a period of several hours with the same melodic underplayed voice with which he conducted the trial.

'This is the story, as history will record it, of what the Christians did to the Jews in the middle of the twentieth century in Europe. And in all of history we have no blacker chapter. Of course Hitler and Germany are to bear the brunt of what happened, but it would not have happened if hundreds of thousands of others did not co-operate.

'I agree with my learned friend that armies are taught to obey, but one sees a growing evidence of people refusing to obey orders to kill other people. And the story of Abraham and God. Well, we all know the ending to that. God was using a little semantics and didn't take his son at all. But somehow I cannot equate SS Colonel Dr. Adolph Voss to playing God any more than I can envision Adam Kelno as Abraham. The fact is Voss didn't have to make an Otto Flensberg experiment on Dr. Kelno. Dr. Kelno took a long look at things and did not resist whatsoever. He did what he did without hesitation, without threats, without terror tactics being used on him.

'Well, you heard him testify that he refused to give a fatal injection of phenol to a prisoner. What happened to him for that? How was he punished. He knew full well doctors weren't shot or sent to the gas chamber. He knew that!

'You'd think a man who has done what Adam Kelno did would shut up and consider himself lucky and try to get along with his conscience, if he has one, and not rake it all up again after almost twenty-five years. He did it because he thought he could get away with it. But alas, the medical register showed up and he had to confess to lie after lie after lie.

'Can anyone in this room with a daughter of his own ever forget Tina? Tina Blanc-Imber had a mother and a father and they survived the holocaust, and they learned that their daughter had been murdered as a human guinea pig. It was not a Nazi doctor who killed her, but a Pole, a fellow ally. And had this happened to any of us and we learned later that an English doctor had destroyed our child in a useless, perverted medical experiment by butchery ... well, we would know what to do with him.

'I agree that Jadwiga Concentration Camp was as awful as things had ever come to. Yet, members of the jury, the inhumanity of man to man is as old as man itself. Just because one is in Jadwiga or anyplace else where people are inhumane, that does not give him leave to discard his morality, his religion, his philosophy, or all of those things that make him a decent member of the human race.

'You heard the testimony of some other doctors in Jadwiga Concentration Camp, two of the most noble and courageous women to ever grace an English court. One a Jewess and a Communist and the other a devout Christian. What happened when Voss threatened to throw the switch on Dr. Viskova. She refused and prepared to take her own life. And Dr. Susanne Parmentier ... she was in the very same hellhole of Jadwiga too. Will you kindly remember what she told Dr. Flensberg.

'And you heard from the bravest of them all. An ordinary man. A teacher of Romantic languages in a little gymnasium in Poland. Daniel Dubrowski, who sacrificed his own manhood so that a younger man might have a chance to know a normal life.

439

'Members of the jury, there is a moment in the human experience when one's life itself no longer makes sense when it is directed to the mutilation and murder of his fellow man. There is a demarcation line of morality beyond which no man can cross and still claim membership in the human race and this goes for London or Jadwiga.

'The line was crossed and for that there can be no redemption. Anti-Semitism is the scourge of the human race. It is the mark of Cain upon us all.

'Nothing he did before or since can redeem him for what he did there. He has forfeited his rights to our compassion. And I suggest he should not be rewarded by a British jury for what he did with anything but our contempt and the lowest coin of the realm.'

THIRTY-EIGHT

'Members of the jury,' Anthony Gilray said, 'we have come to the end of a month's testimony in what has become the longest libel trial in British history. The kind of evidence given here has never been heard by a civil English court and much of it is filled with conflict. Future generations will describe the Jadwiga Concentration Camp as the greatest crime ever committed. But we are not here to act as a war crimes tribunal. We are here trying a civil case according to the common law of England.'

The summing up was an arduous affair, which Gilray dispensed with unusual brilliance, reducing everything into common law and what issues and evidence were relevant and what had to be settled. After a day and a half, he turned the burden over to the jury.

Thomas Bannister arose for a final time. 'My Lord, there

are two issues to be settled. Would you explain them before the jury retires.'

'Yes. First you will determine if you hold for the plaintiff or the defendants. If you hold for Sir Adam Kelno and agree he has been libelled, then you must determine how much damages you will award him.'

'Thank you, my Lord.'

'Members of the jury,' Gilray said, 'I can do no more. The task is upon you now. Take as long as you like. My staff will do their best to see that you are supplied with whatever you wish in the way of food and light refreshments. Now, there is one final matter. The government of Poland, through its ambassador, has laid claim to the medical register as a document of great historical significance and wishes it returned to that country for proper display in one of their national museums. Her Majesty's government has agreed to do so. The Polish ambassador has given us leave to have the register in the jury room during the deliberations. Kindly treat it with utmost care. Do keep cigarette ashes away from it and do be careful not to have any coffee or tea stains damage it. We should not like future generations of Poles to think a British jury took this document lightly. You may retire now.'

It was noon. Those nameless nondescript Englishmen left the courtroom, and the door to the jury room closed behind them.

Adam Kelno and Abraham Cady had come to the end of their battle.

At one-thirty Sheila Lamb rushed into the consultation room and said the jury was returning. The corridor was jammed with newsmen who had to obey the stringent rules of no interviews or photographs inside the court. One of them was unable to resist. 'Mr. Cady,' he said, 'do you think the short time the jury was out is an indication you're going to win?'

'Nobody is going to win this case,' Abe answered, 'we're all losers.'

He and Shawcross shoved their way in and found themselves standing next to Adam Kelno.

Gilray nodded to the associate who approached the jury box.

'Have you agreed upon a verdict?'

'Yes,' the foreman answered.

'And this is the verdict of you all?'

'It is.'

'Do you hold for the plaintiff, Sir Adam Kelno, or the defendants, Abraham Cady and David Shawcross?'

'We hold in favour of the plaintiff, Sir Adam Kelno.'

'And have you all agreed on a sum of damages?'

'We have.'

'What is that sum?'

'We award Sir Adam Kelno one halfpenny.'

THIRTY-NINE

Angela burst into the office where Adam sat motionless. 'It's Terry,' she said. 'He's returned and he's packing his suitcases.'

Adam rushed out, bouncing off the corridor walls and up the steps. He flung the door open. Terry was closing the suitcase.

'Haven't taken much,' Terry said, 'just enough to get along with.'

'Are you going back to Mary?'

'I'm going away with Mary.'

'Where?'

'I don't know really. I'm leaving London, England. Angela will know where I am.'

Adam blocked the door. 'I demand to know where you're going!'

'Out among the lepers,' he screamed. 'If I'm going to be a

doctor, let me be like Dr. Tesslar!'

'You stay right here, do you hear me ...'

'You lied to me, Doctor.'

'Lied! I did all of this because of you and Stephan.'

'And I thank you for that. Now stand aside.'

'No.'

'What are you going to do? Cut my nuts off?'

'You ... you ... you're like the rest of them. You're out to get me too. They paid you to leave me. It's the same plot!'

'You're a bloody paranoid whipping through life cutting the balls off Jews to get even with your own father. Isn't that right, Sir Adam?'

Adam slapped him across the mouth. 'Jew!' he screamed. He slapped Terry again and again. 'Jew! Jew! Jew! Jew!'

FORTY

Abe opened the door of the mews. Thomas Bannister stood on the outside. He was let in wordlessly and followed Cady into the living room.

'You had an appointment with me,' Bannister said. 'I waited.'

'I know, sorry about it. Whisky?'

'Please, make it neat.'

Bannister took off his coat as Abe poured the whisky. 'Look, I've had my fill of good-byes in the last couple of days. Plain ones, fancy ones, tear-filled ones. Anyhow, I saw my daughter off to Israel.'

'So sorry to miss your daughter. She seems like a lovely girl. I should have liked to have known her better. The news from the Middle East is indeed distressing.'

Abe shrugged. 'You learn to live with it. When I was writing *The Holocaust*, Shawcross would get into a dither every time a new crisis came up, and he'd badger me for the manuscript. I told him, don't worry, whenever I finish the book, the Jews will still be in trouble.'

'Must be very taxing.'

'Writing or being a Jew?'

'Actually I meant the writing. Sort of going inside of people and filming their minds for months on end.'

'Something like that. Bannister, I've been avoiding seeing you because you can be damned frightening.'

Bannister smiled. 'Well, I didn't intend to put you in the witness box.'

'Know who I've been thinking about?' Abe said.

'Adam Kelno.'

'How did you know?'

'Because I've been thinking about him too.'

'Highsmith is right, you know,' Abe said. 'There but for the grace of God go all of us. A simple man with his pecker caught in a wringer. What the hell would I have done?'

'I think I know.'

'I'm not so damned sure. The world doesn't have enough Daniel Dubrowskis or Mark Tesslars or Parmentiers or Viskovas or Van Damms. We talk courage and end up acting like piss ants.'

'There are more than you are willing to believe right now.'

'I left somebody out,' Abe said, 'Thomas Bannister. The night you were listing my responsibilities you didn't mention yourself. Wouldn't that have been a pistol, to deny the English people of you as their prime minister.'

'Oh that. Well, one must do what one thinks right.'

'Why? Why did Kelno bring this suit? Sure, I know he has to be a big fish in a little pond. He feels inferior so he has always gotten himself placed into a position where he could be superior to those around him. In Sarawak, in Jadwiga, in a working-man's clinic in London.'

'Kelno? Tragic figure,' Bannister said. 'He's paranoid, of course, and as a paranoid he is incapable of introspection

444

and cannot judge right from wrong.'

'What made him that way?'

'Perhaps the result of some cruelty toward him as a child. Poland handed him anti-Semitism. He had a place to go with his sickness. You know, Cady, surgeons are a strange breed and often as not surgery fulfils their blood lust. So long as Adam Kelno was in civilized places, surgery took care of his needs. But turn a man like this loose in a place where all social order has collapsed and you have a monster on your hands. And then, when he went back to a civilized society again, he became a proper surgeon with absolutely no guilt about what he had done.'

'After what I heard in that courtroom,' Abe said, 'after learning what people can be made to do to people and after the holocaust seeing it still go on and on, I feel that we are wrecking our world beyond our ability to save ourselves. We have polluted our planet, and the creatures who live on it, I swear to God, and we have destroyed each other. I think we've run out of time, and space, and I think it's not a case of *if* it is going to happen, it's only a matter of *when*. And from the way we're behaving, I think God is getting very impatient.'

'Oh, God is patient enough,' Thomas Bannister said. 'You see, we mortals are so pompous that we have deluded ourselves into believing that in all of eternity, and all of the vast universe, that we are the only ones who have undergone the human experience. I've always believed that it's happened before, on this very earth.'

'Here . . . how . . . ?'

'Well, in God's scheme what is a few billion years, here and there. Perhaps there have come and gone a dozen human civilizations in the past billion years that we know nothing about. And after this civilization we are living in destroys itself, it will all start up again in a few hundred million years when the planet has all its messes cleaned up. Then, finally, one of these civilizations, say five billion years from now, will last for eternity because people will treat each other the way they ought to.'

They were interrupted by the phone. Abe's face became

445

very tense. He wrote out an address and said he would come over within the hour. He set the receiver down, puzzled.

'That was Terrence Campbell. He wants to see me.'

'Well, that shouldn't surprise you. You see, if we are going to hang on to this world for a little longer it's going to be up to him and Kelno's son and your son and daughter. Well, I shan't hold you up any longer. How long will you be about?'

'I'm leaving for Israel in a few days. Back where I started, as a journalist.'

They shook hands. 'I can't say you've been my most restrained client, but it's been interesting,' Bannister said, unable to find words in one of the rare instances in his life. 'You know what I mean.'

'I know what you mean, Tom.'

'Good luck, Abe.'

ON THE WAY TO SEE TERRENCE I ASKED THE TAXI TO STOP AT THE LAW COURT. WELL, THAT'S NATURAL. TO SAY GOOD-BYE TO THE ONE DECENT THING I'VE DONE IN MY LIFE, FIGHT THIS CASE.

I CANNOT SHAKE BANNISTER'S NOTION THAT THERE HAVE BEEN CIVILIZATIONS BEFORE US, AND IT WILL HAPPEN AGAIN. WHEN THIS ONE GOES, I'M GOING TO BE VERY SORRY ABOUT LONDON.

DOWN THE STREET FROM THE LAW COURT IS ST. CLEMENT DANES CHURCH. IT'S THE ROYAL AIR FORCE CHURCH, AND I KNEW IT WELL DURING THE WAR. IN FACT, I WROTE SOME COLUMNS ABOUT IT.

ST. CLEMENT DANES IS EXACTLY WHAT BANNISTER WAS TALKING ABOUT. IT WAS BUILT BY THE DANES IN 871 OR THEREABOUTS WHEN KING ALFRED EXPELLED THEM BEYOND THE CITY WALL AND THEN IT WAS DESTROYED. IT WAS REBUILT BY WILLIAM THE CONQUEROR, AND DESTROYED, AND REBUILT IN THE MIDDLE AGES AND DESTROYED IN THE FIRE OF 1666, AND REBUILT, AND DESTROYED IN 1680, AND REBUILT BY CHRISTOPHER WREN, AND STOOD UNTIL THE GERMAN BOMBERS DESTROYED IT IN THE SECOND WORLD WAR. AND IT WAS

REBUILT AGAIN.

WHAT THE HELL'S THAT NURSERY RHYME SAMANTHA USED TO TELL THE CHILDREN?

> ORANGES AND LEMONS,
> SAY THE BELLS OF ST. CLEMENT'S
> YOU OWE ME FIVE FARTHINGS
> SAY THE BELLS OF ST. MARTIN'S
> WHEN WILL YOU PAY ME
> SAY THE BELLS OF OLD BAILEY
> WHEN I GROW RICH
> SAY THE BELLS OF SHOREDITCH
> WHEN WILL THAT BE
> SAY THE BELLS OF STEPNEY
> I DO NOT KNOW
> SAY THE GREAT BELLS OF BOW
> HERE COMES A COPPER TO PUT YOU TO BED
> HERE COMES A CHOPPER TO CHOP OFF YOUR HEAD

Tel Aviv, June 6, 1967 (AP) The Israel Defence Ministry announced that its casualties were light in the strike that destroyed the Arab air forces. Most prominent among those killed was Sergen (Captain) Ben Cady, son of the well-known author.

A SELECTED LIST OF FINE TITLES FROM CORGI

WHILE EVERY EFFORT IS MADE TO KEEP PRICES LOW, IT IS SOME-
TIMES NECESSARY TO INCREASE PRICES AT SHORT NOTICE. CORGI
BOOKS RESERVE THE RIGHT TO SHOW AND CHARGE NEW RETAIL
PRICES ON COVERS WHICH MAY DIFFER FROM THOSE ADVERTISED IN
THE TEXT OR ELSEWHERE.

THE PRICES SHOWN BELOW WERE CORRECT AT THE TIME OF GOING
TO PRESS (AUGUST '85).

□ 12140 1	No Comebacks	*Frederick Forsyth*	£1.95
□ 11500 2	The Devil's Alternative	*Frederick Forsyth*	£2.95
□ 10244 X	The Shepherd	*Frederick Forsyth*	£1.75
□ 10050 1	The Dogs of War	*Frederick Forsyth*	£2.50
□ 09436 6	The Odessa File	*Frederick Forsyth*	£2.50
□ 09121 9	The Day of the Jackal	*Frederick Forsyth*	£2.50
□ 11320 4	Chesapeake	*James A. Michener*	£2.95
□ 11755 2	The Covenant	*James A. Michener*	£2.95
□ 12612 8	Poland	*James A. Michener*	£2.95
□ 08501 4	Tales of the South Pacific	*James A. Michener*	£2.50
□ 08405 0	Rascals in Paradise	*James A. Michener*	£2.50
□ 08502 2	Caravans	*James A. Michener*	£2.50
□ 09945 7	Centennial	*James A. Michener*	£3.95
□ 09240 1	The Drifters	*James A. Michener*	£2.95
□ 07594 9	Hawaii	*James A. Michener*	£3.95
□ 12283 1	Space	*James A. Michener*	£2.95
□ 10565 1	Trinity	*Leon Uris*	£2.95
□ 08384 4	Exodus	*Leon Uris*	£2.95
□ 08091 8	Topaz	*Leon Uris*	£2.50
□ 08385 2	Mila 18	*Leon Uris*	£2.95
□ 07300 8	Armageddon	*Leon Uris*	£2.95
□ 08521 9	The Angry Hills	*Leon Uris*	£1.95
□ 12614 4	The Haj	*Leon Uris*	£2.95

*All these books are available at your bookshop or newsagent, or can be ordered
direct from the publisher. Just tick the titles you want and fill in the form below.*

CORGI BOOKS, Cash Sales Department, P.O Box 11, Falmouth, Cornwall.

Please send cheque or postal order, no currency.

Please allow cost of book(s) plus the following for postage and packing:

U.K. CUSTOMERS – Allow 55p for the first book, 22p for the second book and
14p for each additional book ordered, to a maximum charge of £1.75.

B.F.P.O. & EIRE – Allow 55p for the first book, 22p for the second book plus 14p
per copy for the next seven books, thereafter 8p per book.

OVERSEAS CUSTOMERS – Allow £1.00 for the first book and 25p per copy for
each additional book.

NAME (Block letters) ....

ADDRESS ....

....